A SUMMER OF DROWNING

By the same author

A SUMMER OF DROWNING

John Burnside

JONATHAN CAPE
LONDON

Published by Jonathan Cape 2011

2 4 6 8 10 9 7 5 3 1

Copyright © John Burnside 2011

John Burnside has asserted his right under the Copyright, Designs
and Patents Act 1988 to be identified as the author of this work

First published in Great Britain in 2011 by
Jonathan Cape
Random House, 20 Vauxhall Bridge Road,
London SW1V 2SA

www.rbooks.co.uk

Addresses for companies within The Random House Group Limited can be found at:
www.randomhouse.co.uk/offices.htm

The Random House Group Limited Reg. No. 954009

A CIP catalogue record for this book
is available from the British Library

ISBN 9780224061780

The Random House Group Limited supports The Forest Stewardship
Council (FSC), the leading international forest certification organisation. All our titles
that are printed on Greenpeace approved FSC certified paper carry the FSC logo.
Our paper procurement policy can be found at www.rbooks.co.uk/environment

Mixed Sources

Product group from well-managed
forests and other controlled sources
www.fsc.org Cert no. TT-COC-2139
© 1996 Forest Stewardship Council

Typeset in AGaramond by Palimpsest Book Production Limited,
Falkirk, Stirlingshire

Among friends I argue that the true inventor of painting was Narcissus, that youth who, according to the poets, was transformed into a flower. And, since painting is the flower of all the arts, this story of Narcissus is most apt. For what is painting, if not an attempt, through the discipline of art, to embrace the surface of the pool in which we are reflected?

Leon Battista Alberti, *De Pictura*

The study of the visible universe may be said to start with a determination to use our eyes. At the very beginning there is something which might be described as an act of faith – a belief that what our eyes have to show us is significant.

Arthur Stanley Eddington,
Science and the Unseen World

Late in May 2001, about ten days after I saw him for the last time, Mats Sigfridsson was hauled out of Malangen Sound, a few miles down the coast from here. They say he must have gone into the water at Skognes, then drifted back down to the pier near Straumsbukta, not far from where he lived – and I like to think that the sea took pity on the puny child it had killed, and was in the process of carrying him home, when a fisherman caught sight of that distinctive, almost white shock of hair through the summer gloaming and, with due care and sadness and habitual skill, fetched him to shore. Later, they found a boat drifting in the Sound, halfway between Kvaløya and the shipping channel where the great cruise and cargo vessels from Tromsø glide out into the open sea. The boat, it turned out, had been securely moored half a mile from Mats's house, which seemed to confirm that he must have stolen it – but that really was beyond explanation, for there was no less likely thief than Mats Sigfridsson, and nobody could think of a reason why this quiet, well-behaved boy would even be out on the water in the middle of the night. The whole thing was a mystery and everyone had his own theory about why Mats was in that boat, or what his intentions might have been. There were those who spoke of suicide: it was the end of the school year and, like me, Mats had just completed the exams that would decide his future – a stressful time for any eighteen-year-old – but he hadn't left a note and there was nothing to indicate that he had been depressed in the weeks leading up to the incident. If anything, he had seemed happier than usual. Some of the adults said it was just a prank that had gone wrong, one of those acts of adolescent folly that boys get up to from time to time, for reasons of their own – but nobody who knew Mats put any credence in that theory. Some of the kids in town hinted at foul play, though none of them had even the ghost of a reason for why anyone would want to hurt a boy like Mats Sigfridsson.

As for me, I didn't have any theories – not at the time. Mats was a classmate of mine and I had always liked him, if only from a distance. Mostly, I liked his blanched, Struwwlepeter hair and the odd half-smile he would put on when one of the teachers asked him a question he couldn't answer. He and his brother Harald went around together all the time, like twins. People would say that they were insepa-rable, almost indistinguishable, in fact, though Harald was a year younger and it wasn't that hard to tell them apart. It was an illusion, that twin-ness: an illusion that they had created, by force of will, because they *wanted* to be the same. For reasons only they understood, they needed to be identical. Naturally, they were together that last time I saw them: it was Grunnlovsdag and they were watching the parades on Sjøgata, two white boys in a river of Norwegian flags on the other side of the street from me, their eyes following the parade in exactly the same way, their heads turning and craning to see in unison, so it made them look mechanical, almost, like automata at an old-fashioned fairground. They always stood out and it always seemed, even in a crowd, that they were alone in their own world, a world that nobody else could enter. Only they weren't alone that day, and they weren't really together any more, for, where there had once been two, and only two, there were now three: Mats, Harald, and that other one. *Maia*. I knew who she was, of course; she had been in Harald's class for a while, coming to school pretty much when she felt like it, before she dropped out altogether, and I could see right away that, as unlikely as it seemed, she actually was *with* them. That came as a surprise, but evidently it was no accident that they happened to be standing there, three where there should have been two, vanishing and reappearing in all that red and blue and white, and I remember wondering about it at the time.

I had no reason, then, to suspect her of any ill will towards those boys, however. That was over a week before Mats died, and a month or more before Kyrre Opdahl started telling his crazy *huldra* story – so I really had no reason at all to think badly of the girl. It was just odd, her being there with those beautiful, white boys, and I remember wondering what had brought the three of them together. I didn't suspect Maia of actual mischief, though – not then. Not on that day, and not later, when Mats died. I didn't think she was actively malicious, I just thought that something wasn't right about her. She was too dark, too attentive, too *solid*. Those boys moved through the world in their own homespun dream, and they didn't care about anything else: they weren't bright, they weren't sporty, they weren't *into* anything. Maybe they were a little wild, but wild like animals – horses, say – not wild like some of their classmates, kids doing crazy things to get noticed, or trying to prove that they didn't give a shit about all those people who didn't give a shit about them. There were a few like that at our school, makeshift rebels with no obvious cause,

over-the-counter vampires and goths, but Mats and Harald
didn't belong with that crowd, and they didn't belong with
this dark, intense girl, either. So, obviously, I noticed how odd
they looked as a threesome – but I didn't think any more
about it, and they soon moved on, walking off into the crowds
that had gathered for the coldest and snowiest Independence
Day parade in years, definitely together, three instead of two.
Naturally, I had no idea that, by the time of the midsummer
bonfires, both of those boys would be dead, first Mats and
then, ten days later, his little brother, inexplicably drowned
in water that was too still, too calm and far too indifferent to
have wanted them in the first place.

I didn't see Harald during the days that followed Mats's
death. By then, classes already seemed long done with, and
we were all dispersed across the islands, waiting for results and
thinking about what would come next. I didn't go into Tromsø
much, and I didn't keep up with anybody from school. I was
glad to be away from the world of classroom politics and
teenage gossip, and I'd never been much for sleepovers or
going out with the girls on a Saturday afternoon to look at
make-up and shoes. I could imagine how painful it must have
been for Harald, losing his brother like that, but I couldn't
imagine him *wanting* to die and, to this day, I still don't think
it was a suicide. He drowned in calm water, just as Mats had
done, and that was strange, but it doesn't mean he did it on
purpose. Afterwards, Kyrre Opdahl would say – to me, and
probably to anyone else who would listen – that it was because
of *her*, because of the *huldra*; but that was ridiculous. There
was no *huldra*. Something out of the ordinary had happened,
but it was something that could be explained. Something
psychological. There's no proof that Harald even *saw* Maia
during that week or so before he sneaked out of his house in

the middle of the night and walked out to the shore in the gloaming, and there's no reason to believe that she had anything to do with his going.

Still, it has to be said that something strange happened. The meadows were quiet, the sky was clear – and the water was still, just as it had been when his brother was lost, so there was no reason for Harald to die. There was no reason for any of them to die, in fact. Not Mats, not Harald; certainly not Martin Crosbie, who shouldn't even have been here in the first place. Everybody knows this and, even though most people have explained away everything they could explain and dismissed everything they couldn't, I know we still think about it, all of us when we are alone, going over the sequence of events in our minds and trying to explain the impossible – and I know it haunts us still; it haunts, not just me, but all of us, because none of those drownings made any sense. Nobody should have died out there, in those conditions, at that time of year. Like Mats before him, Harald vanished on a still, moonlit night when the water was utterly calm and the boat – they found the boat at Kvitberg, sitting upright not far from the shore, as if waiting for him to return – the same boat Mats had used, stolen from the same neighbour, was in perfect condition. Besides which, there was no more reason for him to have been there than there was for Mats, no reason for him to row out till he was alone on the open water and no explanation for why he ended up dead. There was no reason for any of it, in fact. Not Mats, not Harald, not Martin Crosbie. Most of all, there was no reason for Kyrre Opdahl to disappear, along with the girl he hated so much, the two of them vanishing into thin air on the path from our house to the shore, leaving nothing more than a trail of spots in the grass that might have been ash or dust. A trail that was

5

washed away by the rain before anyone could see it – though *I* saw it, and I see it now in my mind's eye, a thin trail at the edge of the meadows, melting into the quick, dark rain before I could really make out what it was. So, yes, we are all of us haunted by what happened that year, even if we don't talk about it any more – but I am haunted more than most, because of what I saw and couldn't tell.

That was ten summers ago. The summer of my eighteenth year; the summer my dead father appeared and then disappeared into the silence from which he'd come; the summer of spirits and secrets; the last summer when I thought of myself as one of God's spies. A long, white summer of stories that no one could possibly believe, and stories that we all accepted, though we knew they were lies from beginning to end. The summer when the *huldra* came out from wherever she had been hiding and drowned three men, one by one, in the still, cold waters of Malangen. Now that everybody else has stopped talking about what happened that summer, only one story remains, and I can't say it out loud, because it belongs to another world. I didn't catch more than a glimpse of that world, but if I tried to talk about what I *did* see, the people in the town would think I was crazy, just like Kyrre Opdahl – and maybe I am because, even if I don't believe what Kyrre said about the drownings, I know that *something* terrible happened, and I know that I saw what I saw, on that last day, when Kyrre and Maia vanished. People in the town would say that it was all just a series of unfortunate coincidences, because they want more than anything to explain this story away – but then, Kyrre always said that people in the town were stupid. All his life, he was surprised, and disappointed, that everyone around him took things so literally: they thought trolls were squat, crab-faced monsters that lived under bridges

6

and ate stray goats; they thought the *huldra* was a pretty woman in a red dress dancing around in the meadows, waiting for a young man to beguile and destroy. People from the town didn't believe in such things, of course they didn't, so they made fun of the old stories, not realising that, for a true believer like Kyrre, nothing was ever that crude. But *I* realise; *I* know. In Kyrre's house, there were shadows in the folds of every blanket, imperceptible tremors in every glass of water or bowl of cream set out on a table, infinitesimal loopholes of havoc in the fabric of reality that could spill loose and find you, as the first hint of a storm finds a rower out on the open sea. In Kyrre's house, there were memories of real events, of long-dead farm lads and schoolgirls who went out at first light fifty years ago and came home touched – touched, for the rest of their lives – by something unnameable, a wing-beat or a gust of wind in their heads, where thought should have been. Kyrre believed in all that stuff, but it had nothing to do with monsters or fairies – and now, because of what I have seen and can't explain, I find that I believe in it too. If I don't want to speak about that in the town, or when I sit down to dinner with Mother and she looks at me, knowing that something has changed – something she is surprised to find she cannot put her finger on – if I don't want to repeat Kyrre's stories, ever, to anyone, it's not because I am ashamed of them. It's not even that I'm afraid that the people in town will say I am just as crazy as that old man who lost his mind and wandered off, all those years ago. As it happens, I don't think the people in the town are stupid – at least, I don't imagine they are any more stupid than people elsewhere. I just know that they belong to one world, and the stories belong to another. Somewhere in between, four souls were lost, and the *huldra* disappeared, but I couldn't say for sure that any of them are really gone, and I keep going back to the places where I last saw them, looking for clues that must have been there, once upon a time, but which are now long gone.

SEEING THINGS

The moment I woke, I could tell something was wrong. I had the feeling that sometimes comes with waking, the feeling of dread that begins in a dream and then, as that night logic fails, solidifies for a moment into some dark, looming shape before it collapses into nothing but daylight and fairy-tale cliché. A phantom state, a will-o'-the-wisp, one of those tricks the mind plays on itself when it has heard too many stories. A stray thread of superstition, more real than anything else, more real and more persuasive, until you are finally awake and it becomes absurd. For a moment, I think, I really was scared and I didn't quite know where I was. Then I heard voices downstairs and I realised that it was a Saturday morning in our grey, sunlit house above the meadows, a house that has become a metaphor over the years – a metaphor, or perhaps a talisman – for a certain way of living, a grey-painted timber house seen far and wide on gallery walls in Oslo and London and New York, in scarce and highly prized landscapes by the famously reclusive painter, Angelika Rossdal – a woman who happens to be, yet bears no actual resemblance to, my mother.

Because the voices were there, in the dining room directly below my bed, it had to be some time after eleven o'clock, when Mother's friends – Mother's *suitors* – came to the house, as they did every week, no matter what the weather, driving over from Mjelde or Kvaløysletta on fair days, or skiing cross-country when it snowed, always punctual and always bearing gifts. Packets of seeds or new plants from Harstad, who had an alpine nursery further up the shore; books and newspaper cuttings from Ryvold, our tame scholar who, like Kyrre Opdahl, spent his time collecting stories – though for what seemed, at the time, quite different reasons. Rott, who was, in some ways, Mother's favourite among that happy band of unrequited lovers, brought confectionery and sweetmeats, or fine teas from his shop in Tromsø. They never arrived empty-handed, and they never came without a story to tell, some titbit of gossip or local news gathered during the week just passed, the details carefully memorised so they would have something to talk about over the tea and pastries. They were all good men, and I didn't actively dislike any of them, but I avoided their company whenever I could. Individually, they were decent, or even admirable; collectively, however, they made me sad, not because their lives were worse than anyone else's, but because they were all so *in love* with Mother, each in his own way, and they all so clearly expected nothing in return.

I sat up and looked at the clock on my bedside table: it was eleven fifty-five precisely, which meant that they had been there for almost an hour, and I was still in the house, when I should have been long gone. Usually, I spent Saturday mornings with Kyrre Opdahl, dreaming over a mug of coffee in his ramshackle kitchen while he worked on some ancient clock or outboard motor that nobody else could fix, sitting out by the boathouse watching the ferries and cargo ships go by on their way to Nordkapp or Russia, or maybe tidying his little summer cottage, his *hytte,* for the next batch of tenants – it didn't really matter where it was, as long as it wasn't *here.* I

12

would stay out until the suitors were gone and, then, when I got home, I would pretend that the dining room had been empty all along. There would be no sign of the intruders, by then: Mother would have cleared the plates and wiped the crumbs off the table before going up to her studio to continue work on whatever she was painting and I would have the place to myself again. The hallway, the dining room, the staircase would be utterly still, preternaturally quiet. Quiet, and empty, and apparently uncontaminated.

The suitors. That was my name for them, not hers: *suitors*, like those men in the Greek myth, come to beguile, or charm, or just outwait Penelope while her lost husband wandered the wine-dark sea trying to find his way home. Mother had read that story to me when I was a child, along with all the other classic tales of heroes and Vikings and seventh sons of seventh sons that she loved so much – and I think she was a little bemused when life began to imitate art and these men started turning up with their stories and gifts, patient men who had waited years in this subarctic settlement for someone like her to arrive. Angelika Rossdal. The renowned artist who had turned her back on the big wide world and come north to live as a recluse on this remote island, but also just happened to be the impossible beauty they had been waiting all their lives to fall hopelessly in love with. Some of the men who frequented our house over the years were married, some came to Mother's Saturday-morning tea parties for a month or two, then drifted away, dismayed by her beauty and remoteness, but the core group – Harstad, Ryvold, Rott – came every week, no matter what, and sat hopeless and spellbound at her table, romantics of the old school, whose only real fear was that their prayers might be answered. The core group were all bachelors of one sort or another, and they were all from elsewhere, men who had chosen to live in the far north for their own reasons, whether from shyness, or some exaggerated need for quiet, or because they were escaping from some answered prayer further south. Mother did nothing to encourage them, though I have to say that she did nothing to put them off either. On the contrary, she never betrayed the least sign to anyone of what she might or might not have been feeling. She merely served her visitors tea and cakes, listening as they competed to bring stories that might win her approval, sidestepping their occasional attempts to engage her on some more intimate level and, when they left, returning to her work as if there had been no interruption. By that summer, the ritual had been going on for years – so long, in fact, that it had become a formal arrangement – and I think Mother was not only surprised by that, but also bewildered by their attentions, just as Penelope must have been when her admirers continued to wait, day after day, year after year, while she wove and then unwove her great tapestry in the light and in the dark.

And yet, considering how fascinated they were by this mysterious woman, considering how curious they were about her ideas on painting and literature and life in general, it was interesting – interesting to me, at least – that none of them ever enquired as to where *I* figured in the great scheme of things. She was a single woman with a teenage daughter, but nobody ever asked who my father was, or where he might be now – and that struck me as odd, even though I knew that, *had* they enquired, she wouldn't have told them a thing. After all, she hadn't even told me any more than the bare minimum. She had said, in response to repeated questioning when I was younger, that she'd met a man – whose name, she told me, was irrelevant – at a party in Oslo and they had been together for a short time; then he had moved unexpectedly to Argentina and they had fallen out of touch. According to this version of events, the man had left to pursue his own interests and she had decided, for the good of all concerned, to bring me up on her own – and though it may seem odd, I accepted her story at face value. Naturally, it bothered me for a while that she wouldn't even tell me his name, but she was adamant about that, and once Mother decides something, nobody in the world can shift her. 'That's all in the past,' she would say. 'And besides, we're fine as we are, aren't we?' And I had to admit that we were, indeed, fine as we were. Once, I over-heard the suitors talking about me, saying how difficult it must be to grow up in the shadow of such a remarkable woman, and I spent a whole afternoon wondering about that, before deciding that what they had said was ridiculous. I didn't see myself as growing up in my mother's shadow. I was living in a world of my own making, a space that Mother had marked out and then left for me to define as I wished. She lived exactly as she chose, and I always knew that her work came first, but that only gave me the freedom to live as I chose, and to choose what came first for me – and I never once doubted that she was right. We *were* fine. We had the house, we had the whole island, in fact. We had enough quiet and space to live our own lives as we wanted, not somebody else's version of how life should be, and we were more or less self-sufficient. We were perfectly able to look after ourselves and we didn't need a thing from anyone.

It wasn't just that Mother didn't *need* other people, though; it could also be said that, because she was so involved with her work, they were more or less irrelevant to her. She didn't ask for company, she tolerated it – and, over the years, a fixed and, to her mind, satisfactory routine had been established, allowing for a minimum of human contact with a band of men that she could quite easily control. On Saturdays, from eleven o'clock till two in the afternoon, the suitors would arrive and they would all sit in the dining room, drinking tea, eating the cakes that Mother ordered in from the store at Straumsbukta, carefully studying one another across the table – and, all the while, they would *talk*. Endlessly, tirelessly, almost never falling silent, taking turns or talking across one another to lay out their tales and theories and items of human interest, while Mother listened, sifting out details and fragments and shreds of random information and quietly storing it all away for later. I couldn't stand it. Usually, I made myself scarce before they even arrived, and Mother knew why, though she didn't mind, as long as I wasn't too obvious. That morning, however, because I had stayed up half the night, sitting at the window and staring out for hours at the first summer gloaming, I had slept in and, now, just before noon, the suitors were nicely settled in, the tea things spread out before them, the Danish china, the sandwiches and petits fours, the wafers and chocolate biscuits and, in pride of place, the big willow-pattern plate laden with those napoleon cakes that Rott liked so much. I could picture him in my mind's eye: Rott – horse-faced, lank-haired, always half smiling, an ageing schoolboy in a fisherman's sweater, watching with undisguised pleasure as Mother set out her store of treats. Looking back, I realise that Mother really did love Rott, after a fashion – though not as a suitor. She kept her love a secret, of course, because she kept *everything* secret; that was her nature. Nevertheless, though the cakes she carefully laid out on Saturday mornings were for everyone, in reality they were intended for Rott and I am sure the others knew that. I am sure, in fact, that she intended them to know. She wanted her kindness to him to be infectious;

she wanted them to love him too – because if ever a man needed to be loved, it was Rott.

Now it was noon. That morning, Kyrre Opdahl would be at the *hytte*, just below our domain of garden and birch woods, making things ready for his first guest of the year and wondering where I was. I had promised to help. I always helped, not just because I was fond of that foolish old man, but also for reasons of my own, and I didn't like the idea of being late. I got out of bed and went to the window to see if his van was in the usual place, parked at the end of the track by the *hytte*, which is clearly visible from the upper level of our house – and at that moment, as I looked out across the meadows towards the shore, I realised that it was summer. True summer, not just white nights, the months of snow, then thaw, then snow again, finally over. Sugar snow, drift snow, dirty snow that lingers underfoot, even into the first weeks of midnight sun. Spring snow. There are people who cannot take living this far north, because of the long winter darkness, and there are others who cannot bear the endless, mind-stopping white nights of insomnia and wild imaginings, but for me, the worst time is the season of dirty snow, when the sky is bright, but the earth is still frozen underfoot, a false summer of white skies and cold earth when nothing seems to fit. We have a name for the dark time and a name for the white gloaming of high summer, but there is no name for this season, even though it happens every year, a slight, yet significant unseemliness on the land that, at its worst, amounts to a barefaced mockery, like a red dress at a funeral. That year, our unnamed season of snow and sullen light had lingered too long, but now, in what felt like an instant, it was over – and even if the change was subtle, there was no mistaking it. I opened the window. The freshness was almost overwhelming.

17

The night before had been hard and silent; now there was a softness to the air, a new sweetness of grasses and wildflowers, and mountain water gathering in the meadows. I could hear bird calls and wind-sifted murmurs from Mother's garden, far-sounding cries from the meadows by the old ferry dock, and a low drone from the shipping channel beyond. Common birds, meadow birds, shore birds; the faraway putter of a motor-boat; an engine buzzing further up the coast, towards Mjelde. It's always a surprise, in the first days of summer: all this noise and activity begins and yet, when you go to a window and look out, it seems there's nothing there but space and light. This is the time when visitors start coming to Kyrre Opdahl's summer cottage, the only other dwelling place that's visible from our house and, that morning, the first of those visitors was about to arrive. I could see, by the van parked outside the *hytte*, that the old man was already at work, clearing and tidying and setting out his welcome box of coffee and tea bags and fresh bread, putting milk and some *gjetost* in the little fridge, checking there was gas for the stove and a stockpile of logs and kindling in the woodshed. And by now, he would be worried about me, because I wasn't there and that old man could always find a reason to worry.

I pulled on some jeans and a sweater, then I walked out onto the landing and paused at the top of the stairs to listen. From inside my room, I hadn't been able to make the voices out, but here, directly above the open door to the dining room, I could hear everything. I wasn't usually much interested in their conversation, of course – but that morning was different and I lingered a minute or two, trying to figure out why. Down below, Harstad was talking, in response to something Rott had just said.

18

'There's nothing suspicious about it,' he was saying. His voice sounded unusually sharp. Normally, he was quite soft-spoken, but then his usual topics of conversation had to do with his garden, or with some new plant he'd acquired from a friend who worked at the university. 'Even on a fine day, the currents are treacherous. Everybody knows that.'

'But what on earth was he doing out there in the middle of the night?' Mother put in softly, to keep the peace. 'In a stolen boat? All by himself?' I could see her in my mind's eye, looking around at the assembled company, the perfect hostess from eleven till two, when they would all leave, almost exactly to the minute. 'You have to admit, Amund, that does seem odd.'

'Word is, he was always a little strange,' Harstad said. 'A bit of a loner –'

Mother laughed at that cliché, but she didn't pursue it. 'Well,' she said, 'we'll have to wait and see. But I wouldn't be surprised if there was more to this than meets the eye.'

There was a longish silence, though not an uncomfortable one. Silence did sometimes fall upon those Saturday gatherings, and Mother always lingered over it a while, observing the moment as if it were some unexpected blessing. She liked silence and she mistrusted those who were uncomfortable with it, which made such occasions dangerous for the likes of Rott, who seemed incapable of sitting quietly. After a few seconds, though, the quiet was broken – tactfully, and with all due ceremony – by one of the others in the room, someone who had not spoken till now. 'Where did they find him?' he asked, his voice only just audible. It was Ryvold. He didn't say much, but when he did, there was always a suggestion in the words he spoke, or in the way he spoke them, that he had been lagging behind. Going at his own pace. Thinking.

19

There was another silence, then Harstad answered. 'At Straumsbukta,' he said. 'Not far from where he lived. But they think he drifted down from somewhere up this way.'

That unaccustomed quiet descended again, then someone – I suppose it would have been Mother – got up and started moving about. There was a rattle of crockery and the sound of a kettle boiling and, though the conversation only stopped for a moment, I couldn't make sense of what they were saying through the background noise. Still, I was a little intrigued by what I had heard – obviously, someone had drowned, and in a stolen boat, which was surprising in a place like Kvaløya – but I didn't know, then, who they were talking about and, by itself, the story wasn't enough to make me linger. Besides, I didn't want to be any later than I was to see Kyrre. I could have gone down to the kitchen to fix some coffee and toast, just to listen in for a while before I made my escape – because I *was* curious, and the rising scent of something warm and buttery was making me hungry – but I knew Kyrre would at least have coffee on the go down at the *hytte* and, whatever the story was, I could be sure that he would know as much as anyone about what had happened. So I sneaked down quietly, hoping that no one would hear, and I slipped out through the front door, crossing the garden and closing the gate behind me. Then I hurried down through the stand of birch trees that Mother had planted there, between the gate and the road, and out into the sunshine, to the cool, lush meadows that led to the shore.

I have very few memories that I would be prepared to call my own. I have snapshots, sketches, fragments of stories and unfinished anecdotes, but none of them fit together and, when I try to retell them, they seem false, like something invented, or borrowed. For the first three years of my life, we lived in

Oslo, but I don't remember anything at all from that time. All I know is this island – Kvaløya, latitude seventy degrees north, far in the Arctic Circle, the place Mother chose when she decided to change everything and start her life over again. Back in Oslo, she was pretty successful and, though she wasn't as well known as she is now, she was heading that way. At that time, she had a reputation mainly as a painter of portraits. She had a large apartment, interesting friends, professional standing – all the things she'd thought she wanted when she was growing up. Then, one day, she decided to move to the Arctic Circle. She didn't really have a reason: she had never even been to the Arctic, and she didn't know a soul north of Trondheim. But then maybe that was why, once she had made up her mind, she chose to come here, to a place she had never even heard of before she spread the map out on her drawing board and scanned what, at the time, must have looked like remote, empty places: long archipelagos of bird-haunted islands, the white yawn of the Finnmarksvidda, the fjords and coastal towns she knew from old paintings and children's books. For a time, she had considered moving to Røros, where Harald Sohlberg spent much of his life. Sohlberg was then, as he is now, her favourite painter, an influence on her work that she talks about whenever she gives interviews (which she does far more often than might be considered normal for a supposed recluse). In the end, however, that probably seemed too obvious. So, instead, she chose Kvaløya, because it was far enough away from everything she knew and, if you really believe what she says in interviews, because she liked the name. There are other Kvaløyas, but this is the one she chose and, once she got here and saw this stretch of coast, and this high grey house looking out over Malangen, she knew she would never leave. I must have been with her on that first journey to our new home, but I don't remember anything about it. I don't remember living in Oslo either, and I don't remember leaving. For me, it is as if I have never been anywhere else and, on the handful of trips we have made to Bergen and Oslo and, once, when I was twelve, to London, those other places didn't seem real.

No: Kvaløya. Tromsø. Sommarøy. Hillesøy – for me, these are the real places, the home places. I picture my mother on the day she decided to come north, studying the map in her studio at the heart of the city, and I imagine her reading the names aloud to herself, like the promise of some parallel country where everything is as it has always been. There's something different about time here, the old stories persist in the wood of the boathouses and the ferry docks, time drifts and founders in the pools of summer grass and willowherb that grow along the roadsides. All you have to do is choose the right day, the right weather, and you come upon a hidden place in the morning light where time stopped long before you were born. Or you turn off on some narrow path through the meadows and arrive at the secret country those names describe, somewhere in the sunlight of the 1960s. Of course, time still exists – it's out there in the world where other people live, but it's only an idea. It's purely theoretical. Out there, in the busy world, the clocks are ticking, but we are mostly alone on our Whale Island and, whether it's white night or winter dark, there's not much here to betray the passing of clock-time. That was why Mother chose this particular grey house on this particular stretch of road between Mjelde and Brensholmen – she wanted not to be away from other people so much as to be unburdened of time, and the only way to do that is to live apart. The one neighbour we have on this stretch of shore, other than Kyrre Opdahl's house, is the tiny *hytte*, one of those little summer dwellings people used to keep for hunting or fishing, let out now, to summer guests, but it's not really a house, it's just a cabin hunkered down on its own patch of grass and weeds by the shore. It's closer to the sea than we are, almost as close as the little hut where Kyrre keeps his old boat and various leftover pieces of machinery and netting, and it seems to belong, half to the water and half to the land, just as that boathouse does.

I love the boathouse. It's like a tabernacle: Kyrre puts as much work into it as he does into the *hytte*; he gives his narrow, well-weathered boat a fresh coat of red and blue paint every year, he takes the engine apart and cleans every single component and he keeps the interior of the thing spotless, but you never see him out on the water. He's too old for that, he says – though he doesn't look much more than fifty, and he's as fit as a fiddle. I suppose the truth is, he's lost the habit of doing things for pleasure. He only has time for work. He could have retired a long time ago, and nobody knows what he does with the money he earns from his various enterprises, but then, as he always says, he wouldn't know what to do with himself if he didn't keep busy. Sometimes he gets depressed in the winter, when it's too cold for real work, but in the summertime he lets out this *hytte* and a couple of other properties further up the coast, near Brensholmen. His own house is a short walk from here, just out of sight through the birch woods, but even that is little more than a storehouse-cum-workshop, a sprawl of boxes and tools and half-constructed machines that runs from the kitchen, where he spends most of his time, along the hall and into the large spare room that looks more like a chandler's workshop than a bedroom, threading through the ordinary details of his domestic life till it's impossible to tell one from the other. He's old now, so he says; but he's as active as he ever was and, except for the few occasions when he sits down with me to drink coffee and tell me his stories, he never rests.

As busy as he is, however, he's never too busy for Mother, and she relies on him for all manner of practical support. He supplies the logs for our stove; he helps in the garden; he mends things when they go wrong; he picks up our groceries and the art materials Mother has shipped up from Oslo or Bergen. He was the one who drove me into Tromsø every weekday, all through my school years, and I can still picture him as he was on that first morning, an immense, steady man with birdlike features and very close-cropped hair, climbing out of the driver's seat and coming round to the back of the car to open the door with great ceremony and let me in, a shy schoolchild suddenly transformed into the Princess Royal. He was absurd, of course – he reminded me of the cockerel in a picture book I had – but I could see that he was also proud and dignified, a man with an inner life, whose sense of importance wasn't confined to his own corner of existence, but spread out to touch the lives of everyone he met, even if they didn't quite see the significance of the occasion. He was also my own personal storyteller, someone who charmed and frightened me, in more or less equal measure, all the time I was growing up.

Kyrre's *hytte* is down by the beach, across the road and the meadow beyond, but it's clearly visible from my bedroom window and from the landing where I would sit back then, keeping watch on the Sound and on the comings and goings of Kyrre's tenants. It's just a few feet from the waterline, when the tide is high and a summer guest can stand on the lawn to watch the terns as they hover above the shallow water, waiting for the glint of silver that will send them diving into

24

the wash, like tiny lightning bolts, flashing in and out of the lit waves and returning with a sliver of a fish clasped tightly in their beaks. I call the *hytte* a dwelling place, not a house, because it's so simple: a living room with a stove and a picture window looking out across the Sound, a tiny kitchen, two plain bedrooms furnished with bunks and narrow wardrobes at the back, where the shadows and the rain-scent of the meadows are always present, even on the finest days. According to Kyrre's brochure, this *hytte* can sleep two adults and up to three children but, quite often, the summer guests are solitaries, men, for the most part, who have come north looking for quiet. Mostly, they are Norwegians, but occasionally there will be an Englishman or a German and, three years ago, through a long wet July, a Canadian philosopher sat at the window facing the Sound, listening to the rain bouncing off the roof and thinking about Kierkegaard. Or so Mother said. She had encountered him in a downpour one afternoon, while she was out on one of her solitary rambles, and she had invited him to tea but, to her great amusement, he had politely explained that he was too busy.

Mother doesn't make a habit of inviting Kyrre's guests round for tea, though, and she was probably glad when he declined her offer. It would have been a novel experience for her, of course: to be refused. Usually she was the one who did the refusing. Declined, refused, denied, withdrawn – these are the words that best describe her relations with the outside world, not just in her work, but in her personal life as well. She refuses to become an art celebrity, just as surely as she refuses the suitors, and yet, no matter how final these refusals are, it only brings her more critical success, and higher prices for her paintings. That surprised her at first, I think, because I know that her withdrawal wasn't calculated, but it wasn't long before she saw that she could use it to her advantage. And the truth is, nobody would ever deny that her remoteness – the mythic seclusion, the supreme integrity – is central to her artistic success. I know, now, that the suitors who came to our house back then were aware that it was precisely the impossibility of winning her heart that drew them back, week in, week out, year after year. They admired her painting, just as they admired her beauty – but what they admired most was her gift for refusal. A gift that would be mistaken for a pose, perhaps, were it not for the fact that, more than anything else, it is *herself* that she refuses – and *that*, above all, has always been her secret. *That* is her power. To turn away from the busy world is interesting, up to a point – and she didn't become the artist she is today until she left Oslo and committed what many people considered professional suicide – but to refuse oneself is exemplary. To become nothing, to remove yourself from the frame – that is the highest form of art. Mother was always aware of this and the discipline of it extended into everything in her life – even into her dealings with Kyrre's summer guests. She has always played a part, but the part she plays is her true self. You only have to know her work to understand that.

Throughout my teenage years, however, I made a hobby of Kyrre's guests. Some I befriended, and I spent an occasional long afternoon in the room that faces the Sound, or on the tiny lawn that sits between the *hytte* and the beach, listening to their stories over coffee or bottles of Solo, but the majority I chose to observe in silence, watching from afar as they enjoyed the Arctic landscape, or the solitude they had come here to find. Watching – or, as Kyrre would have it, *spying* – which was probably fair. For several years back then, I was a spy of sorts, one of life's observers. I would watch the summer guests from my bedroom window, tracking their movements through the binoculars Mother gave me for my thirteenth birthday and trying to work out what they were thinking. Occasionally, I'd even take photographs, using the zoom lens on my fancy camera – another birthday gift – but it never seemed prurient or intrusive and, when all's said and done, mere watching struck me as a harmless activity, so long as the subjects had no idea that they were being observed. Every year, the guests would come and, every year, I decided which of them were interesting enough to be the subject of my observations and which would be ignored. I never bothered with the families who came from time to time and they weren't about the place that much anyway, they just used the *hytte* as a base, driving back and forth to Tromsø and points north, or setting out mid-morning with picnic baskets and fishing nets for excursions to Sommarøy. I never bothered with them, or with the couples who came, thinking they'd found some empty landscape where they could be romantically alone together. No: it was the solitaries who interested me, the ones who were looking for the only miracle they could ever believe in – that miracle where time stops, or at least slows for a season, and the living, usually so haunted by clockwork, are permitted a fleeting glimpse of perceptible happiness. I liked those people as much as I liked anyone in those days and I wished them well. That was the main reason why I spied on them, I think. It was because I wanted them to be happy.

I found Kyrre Opdahl in the little shed next to the *hytte*, wiping cobwebs and birdshit off the deckchairs he supplied for his guests, so they could sit out at 3 a.m. and read by the midnight sun. *That* cliché. He knew I was there, of course, but he didn't look up. He never did. That was a game he liked

27

to play, pretending he hadn't noticed that you were back, so you could both pretend you'd never gone away. A very subtle form of courtesy that was probably quite bewildering to people who didn't know him. 'Hey hey,' I said. I scanned the room for something to do, but he was almost finished.

He looked up then. 'Good afternoon,' he murmured. His face was streaked with dust and gossamer. 'That was good timing.'

'Really?'

He smiled. 'I was just about to take a break,' he said. 'So *you're* just in time to put the kettle on.'

Nobody knew how old Kyrre Opdahl was. He seemed to have been there for centuries, so much a part and parcel of the island that he could disappear into it at will – or that's how I saw it, at least, when I was a little girl and he was my steady companion, driving me to school in the mornings and returning to fetch me in the afternoons, a rock-like, impassive, yet hopelessly courteous throwback to another time, old even then, his hair clipped short, his eyes a surprising, almost charcoal grey. And all my life, he had been the keeper of stories. Some people thought of him as an absurd, superstitious old man, a sad leftover from an age when, in all seriousness, people here would gather around a fire and recite tales of the *huldra*, who came out of the earth or the sea tides in the form of an unbearably beautiful woman in a red dress to claim any unwary man she chanced upon. Or they would frighten the children with stories that seemed almost true, stories about the fisherman far at sea who finds a baby in his nets and brings it aboard, still living, its eyes a dark mica glitter, its voice so beguiling that, even though he knows the creature means him harm, he cannot help but take it home. After a while, people didn't tell those stories any more, but they couldn't quite

28

suppress them either and, occasionally, through a gap in the usual conversation, or when a couple lay sleepless in their bed, the talk would drift dangerously into strange territory – a hint here, a half-joking suggestion there, and, before they knew it, mischief had got so far in that everything would change. A man's eye would stray, a wife would turn cold, and a word, or a look, would lead to terrible violence or abandonment. There would always be an explanation, of course – a *rational* explanation – but under it all, in the nerves and in the blood, that other knowledge haunted them – and people like Kyrre were the keepers of that knowledge. They were the ones who unlocked the doors to the spirits nobody believed in; they were the ones who passed through the house in the small hours, like the sleepwalker in some old vampire film, opening the windows just wide enough for the terror by night to slip through.

Not all of Kyrre's stories were old ones, though. For people like him, there was no old time – it was all present, all continuous. What happened now, in the plain light of day, was part of an eternal mystery, a story in which the living and the dead, the mad and the sane, the substantial and the ghostly, were interchangeable – and that afternoon, as we sat drinking coffee, the story he told was both matter-of-fact and magical. The story of a boy I knew and a local tragedy as old as the earth itself, in which the names of the participants barely mattered. At the time, he didn't know where this story would go – but as he talked, I remembered the feeling I'd had on waking, that feeling of dread that I had dismissed too readily. Something really *was* wrong, only I hadn't known what. Nobody had.

He didn't begin until we had gone through to the *hytte* and, even then, he must have thought he was just passing the time. 'I suppose you heard about Mats Sigfridsson?' he said, as he washed his hands.

I have to admit, my heart skipped a beat then. I didn't know what had happened to Mats, but I knew someone had drowned and it wasn't much of a leap to put the two things together. I put down the coffee pot. 'What about him?' I said.

Kyrre turned. 'You haven't heard?' His face was calm, but I could see he was thinking, wondering how to proceed.

I shook my head. 'No,' I said, trying to sound as neutral as possible. 'What happened?' I picked up the coffee pot and started to pour. After all, Mats Sigfridsson was nothing to me. He was just a boy in my class at school. He wasn't a friend, or a boyfriend; if anything, I had always thought of him as a little odd. It alarmed me to see how, whenever he was parted from his brother, he fell into a strange, apathetic state, troubled in his soul, remote from the rest of the world, and almost frighteningly alone. It bothered me when I turned round in class and caught him staring at me, or perhaps through me, as if I were thin air. I wouldn't want to make too much of it, but there had been times when I'd caught sight of him sitting in the back corner of a classroom, gazing out at the world with a remote, slightly puzzled air and I'd found myself thinking of him as a kindred spirit, because at least he liked the quiet, and he preferred his own company. I rarely had anything to do with him, it was true, yet there were occasions when we passed each other by with care and an odd, slightly troubled curiosity – like woodland animals, say, who meet by chance in a clearing and navigate passage, watchful, curious and, at the same time, slightly awed. I don't know what interested me about him, and I had no good reason to believe he took the same more or less friendly interest in me. I just suspected that he was a boy who could have understood how I saw the world, if I'd ever been able to get close enough to explain.

I'm not talking about a romance here, of course. He wasn't

30

attracted to me, and I certainly wasn't *attracted* to him. The fact is, I was never very big on attraction back then, or on any of the usual stuff people my age were supposed to obsess about. I had a couple of close calls in my mid-teens, but by that summer there was no question about it, just as there is no question of it now: no romance, no little secrets and late-night confidences over the phone, and no sex either. In truth, the whole idea of romantic love just leaves me cold. I'm not repelled by it, or anything like that. I'm not *repressed* or *lonely* or *frigid*, I'm just not interested. At that time, I couldn't help thinking that it was all a trick – that *love* was one of the things I was *supposed* to want, like clean, volumised hair or a new stereo. Attraction just felt like another product they were trying to sell me – and it still does. *I've not met him yet*, is what I always say when people ask me if I have *anyone special*, or if I'm *seeing anybody*, though what I'm tempted to answer is that, surely, it's none of their business. At such times, I wonder: how did it come about, that people feel so free to enquire into the deepest secrets of another person's life? *Have you got a special friend? Do you have a boyfriend right now?* What am I supposed to say? What does anybody say? *Yes, but I'm not sure if I love him, and even if I did, I'm pretty certain it won't last.* Or, *No, it's just sexual, we get together twice a week to do things to each other's bodies, in that curious way people have, of not being able to let one another alone.* As it happens, I've been a somewhat sceptical party to something like both those scenarios, but I was never very convinced. So it's safe to say that I wasn't *attracted* to Mats, and I couldn't say I even knew him – but I was sad to hear that he was dead and, for an odd, slightly confused moment, I felt as if *something* had been taken away from me.

Of course, Kyrre Opdahl was no fool, and he must have

seen that I was affected by the news, but he was also a life-long storyteller, and he had to finish what he'd started. It was a good story, after all, a proper mystery in some ways – and I am glad, looking back, that it was Kyrre who told me what had happened. He didn't know much more than Rott or Harstad, of course – and at that stage, he hadn't begun to formulate his sinister explanation of events. Mats Sigfridsson had gone out in a boat by himself, the boat wasn't his, it was a calm night, so there had been no obvious reason for his falling overboard, or whatever he'd done. Kyrre knew that much; but that was nothing, really. All this was just *the facts*. Yet even then – perhaps because it was Kyrre who was telling it – the story somehow promised more than the mere facts suggested. It was like one of those tales people in the old days made into legends, stories about wraiths and seal people and mermaids, all of them dark warnings about what the woods or the sea or the mountains can do, if you don't show them enough respect. Neither of us acknowledged it that day, but I think it was in both our heads: the drowned boy, the sugges-tion of something still to be told, the little, local puzzle that contained within it a kernel of the wider mystery – we didn't say so, but we both knew there was more to come.

Though it has to be admitted that it was me, not Kyrre, who thought of Maia first – thought of her, in fact, that after-noon, drawing her out of the Grunnlovsdag crowd and into the light, a dark-eyed, mocking girl with a loose tomboy walk who had always been the outsider, the one who came and went as she pleased and didn't give a damn about anybody, the one, among all those basically decent, but deeply worried kids at school, who so very obviously wasn't worried about anything, an imp of a girl who had somehow slipped into the Sigfridsson brothers' private world and settled there, where

32

nobody else had ever been permitted to go. It was me who thought of her first and, even if I did have second thoughts about her, even if I tried to put my suspicions aside, it was me who introduced her into the story, when I told Kyrre what I had seen on Grunnlovsdag – and, though it didn't detain us for long, he lingered on that one detail for a moment, the germ of a new story already beginning to form at the back of his mind, where all the stories begin, shadowy and undefined, the first step in a logic that had nothing to do with reason.

'So what was so odd about it?' he said. 'Two boys and a girl – it's not the first time a pair of brothers fell for the same girl –'

I shook my head. 'No, no,' I said. 'I don't think it's like that.'

'Then what is it like?'

'I don't know.' I looked around, as if I could find an answer in that little wooden room by the shore, the windows wide open to the first of the summer air and the cries of the terns and the oystercatchers further along the beach. 'I was surprised to see her with them, but then, there's probably a perfectly simple explanation, and I'm sure it has nothing to do with . . .' I thought for a moment. What did I want to say? Sex? Romance? One of those love triangles they have in the movies?

Kyrre smiled and patted my hand. 'Well,' he said, 'whatever it's like, the boy is at peace now.' He stood up. 'Besides,' he said, 'it's not the dead who should be pitied.'

I nodded. 'Poor Harald,' I said. 'I don't know what he'll do without Mats.'

Kyrre didn't say anything. He picked up our cups and carried them to the sink, then he came back for the coffee pot. 'At least he has a friend,' he said – which confused me. Did he mean Maia? Or was he talking about me? He looked at the clock on the kitchen wall. 'Now,' he said, 'I wonder where my guest is? He's staying for the entire summer, you know.'

'Really?' That was a surprise. Usually, they came for a couple of weeks, a month at most. 'Till when?'

'Till the end of September,' he said. 'He's paid the whole thing in advance. He says he needs somewhere to come and work, to get some peace and quiet.'

'What work?'

'He didn't say.'

'Oh,' I said. I was curious. To the best of my knowledge, nobody had taken the *hytte* for that long before. 'Anyway. That's good, isn't it?'

Kyrre nodded. 'I hope so,' he said. He didn't want to tempt providence, I suppose. I had known him long enough to understand that. He wasn't a man to be caught out taking anything for granted. He worried to keep trouble at bay and, when trouble came, it was just the confirmation he'd needed that he hadn't worried enough. He gave me one of his baleful looks. 'It all depends what he's like,' he said. I laughed, and he pretended to be offended. 'Well,' he said, 'you never know. He could be a *monster*.'

When I got home, at around four, the suitors were long gone. Mother was in the studio and the house had that air it sometimes took on, an air of being, if not quite deserted, then at least inhabited only by phantoms. It's an air Mother has deliberately contrived, I think; from the moment a visitor arrives at our gate, there's a sense of things being not what they seem, a sense that everything here is based on illusion. Which is fair, because that's what it mostly is: an illusion, an improbable house and garden that somebody has conjured up out of nothing, in this northern wilderness. Everything Mother creates

34

is a work of art, so everything is, by definition, an illusion. The garden, for example. Every year, after six months of cold and darkness, she raises it from the dead, filling the gaps where things have rotted off with shrubs and poppies and bright annuals, forcing them to quicken and root in the cold ground, thousands of miles from the alluvial plains and sunlit terraces where they belong, red and orange and golden against the fence posts and carved stones that divide the inner, cultivated sector of our land from the zone of calculated wildness just outside. That is how it is, still, even though we rarely have visitors these days, and that was how it was then. It was always a miracle, always an illusion, what she did there: Harstad would bring pots of Arctic poppy and saxifrage seedlings, telling her they were far better suited to the climate than the exotics she favoured, but she would laugh him off and go on with what she was doing. It didn't matter what it cost, in money or effort. She wanted big colours, she wanted immense, blowsy flower heads and delicate, sweet-scented things that nobody else round here would even consider trying – and, by application and sheer force of will, she made it work. Some years, all her plans would be destroyed overnight, in one big wind or heavy rain, but she simply cleared the plot and started again. Harstad would tell her that our native poppy was just as delicate and just as beautiful as her exotics, but he didn't understand what she was after, pinching out seedlings and striking cuttings in the garden room year on year, never content, always searching for the blossom that would bring to life one of those deep, wet hues she saw in her mind's eye, colours out of a Sohlberg painting, or an Italian altarpiece. She didn't want flowers that were naturally adapted to the climate – had she lived in the Mediterranean, she would have worked just as hard to grow saxifrages and gentians – she wanted what was

35

most unlikely. She wanted the miraculous. Yet, as Harstad once had the temerity to point out, there was something about that garden, as beautiful as it was, that didn't seem altogether true. It was, he said, an elaborate and terrifying illusion. I'm quite sure Mother was pleased when she heard him say this, even though she knew, without question, that Harstad wasn't paying her a compliment.

The house was an illusion too; or rather, it was a series of illusions. Mother always laughs off the idea that she is a recluse, and she pretends to be surprised when interviewers ask about her solitary life. Most journalists don't observe their subject, she says, they just repeat what they've read in the files, but the fact is that this house is designed to hide all those objects and possessions that really matter to her. On the ground floor, the furniture is comfortable, and the kitchen is well appointed, the pictures on the walls are carefully chosen – exhibition posters in the hallway and on the lower staircase, prints and drawings by people she used to know in Oslo and Bergen – and the books on the shelves are exactly the kind of books you would expect in a house like ours, but it's all hopelessly predictable. Nothing on this lower level reveals the slightest clue about the woman who lives there. Even if a visitor were permitted to climb to the upper floor, there is almost nothing of specific interest there, either, and certainly nothing that might not be found in a professional or academic household in Tromsø, or Trondheim. More books, neatly shelved on a long corridor leading to a locked door at the back of the house; more prints from exhibitions in Bergen and Oslo; a couple of antique sea chests full of art catalogues and guidebooks; a dark elmwood chair on the landing, opposite my bedroom, with a view over the garden and the Sound. The one clue that an artist lives here is the painting that hangs above this chair, and that one painting is unfinished.

It's not a particularly impressive work, at first sight. Competent, but not at all typical. I suppose, if it were in a catalogue, it would be described as 'a study of a young girl', or some such thing, but it is, I would say, somewhat more significant in the artist's oeuvre than that would suggest. To a casual viewer, it is nothing more than a portrait of a thirteen-year-old girl in a yellow dress, her face tilted to the summer sky, her long hair almost silvery and her eyes far bluer than they could have been in real life – but, even though it remains unfinished, and even though the figure it portrays could be seen as an abstract personification of girlhood innocence rather than a specific individual, a careful observer would quickly realise that the chosen model is, in fact, the artist's daughter. Of course, even the most knowledgeable viewer couldn't tell by looking at it that this was Mother's last attempt to render a human likeness, begun and abandoned three or four years after she had supposedly given up portraiture for good. A connoisseur of the artist's work might be interested to see how clearly it foreshadows the ghostly, almost indecipherable figures who sometimes appear in much later paintings, shadows in a landscape, perhaps, yet as much part of that landscape as the trees and the meadow grasses and the stones on the beach, and no more or less significant than any of these things. And it's true; this unfinished painting is a transitional work, not so much a last attempt at a portrait as a first rendering of the human figure as idea, something non-specific, almost emblematic. As far as I know, Mother has never been troubled by the fact that this first phantom in her work is modelled on me, just as it never seems to have occurred to her that *I* might be troubled by it – and the fact is, I'm not. Not really. Once upon a time, I had mixed feelings about that picture; now, I barely give it a second glance as I enter or leave my room or when I settle into the old elmwood chair that Mother bought especially for this spot on the landing. Here, on certain days, I can look out over the meadows to the waters of Malangen beyond and think I am quite alone in the world. When I'm there, by myself, I barely give the painting a second glance, and I don't see the girl it depicts as *me* any more, even though the likeness is unmistakable. For Mother, everything is a form, everything is a possible subject, to be observed and transformed by her imagination, and there's no reason why I should think of it any differently.

Still, I don't know why she keeps this half-finished painting there. None of her other works hang in the main part of the house: they are confined to the studio at the far end of the landing, behind closed doors, and nobody ever sees them until they are packed up and driven away by a man who – according to Mother – looks like a murderer and never speaks to anyone but her. That man, whose name I have never learned, works for Dag Fløgstad, the dealer who handles all of Mother's work, and he's been coming to the house, driving all the way from Oslo, with an overnight stop at his sister's in Mo I Rana, for as long as I can remember. He is nothing more than a delivery man, but he is the only one who is permitted to enter Mother's true house, the house that sits, like a kernel, inside the dream house she has created and, though he is completely unaware of the privilege he enjoys, he is more real to her, in some ways, than the suitors, who come every week and are never allowed past the foot of the stairs, much less through the door to the studio. It's Mother's lair, her secret place, an empty, whitewashed space, with a single, north-facing window and no furniture other than a chaise longue and a couple of rickety wooden chairs – this is where her real life happens.

Nobody else but me. And I am only admitted on special occasions. Once, when I wasn't just her daughter, but a subject she found interesting, I was admitted every day, and I had to stand still for hours at a time, with my eyes fixed on that wide, north-facing window, while she worked to transform me into an idea, something that would become definitive, and so last forever – or that, at least, was how I saw it, when she caught the ghost of me and set it down on the canvas. I have no idea why she never finished that painting: one day, she simply told me that she didn't need me to pose any more and, when I asked if it was finished, she said it wasn't. Not quite. 'Something isn't working,' she said. 'I'll have to leave off for a while, and come back to it.'

Even though she seemed calm, and I had no cause to doubt her, I sensed that this wasn't the whole story. 'Why?' I said. 'What's wrong with it?'

She smiled. 'It's fine,' she said. 'I just need to take a break.'

I hadn't been particularly eager to sit for the portrait to begin with but, now that she was setting it aside, I couldn't conceal my disappointment. Or the sense, right at the back of my mind, of somehow failing to live up to some image she had been looking for. 'Well,' I said, 'can I see it?'

She shook her head. 'Not yet,' she said. 'When I work it out, you can. But only when it's finished.'

But it was never finished and, as far I knew, she did no more work on it. It was the last portrait she did – or rather, the last she did before that summer, when she painted the *huldra* in a few hurried sittings – and it remained in her studio for months, locked away in a cupboard to which she had the only key. For a while, I wondered what had gone wrong, assuming I was to blame somehow, but she didn't seem to give it a second thought and, by the end of that long-ago summer, I had pretty much forgotten about it. Mother hadn't, though. I'm fairly sure she didn't touch it again, and even a cursory glance reveals that it is nothing like finished – the background is more complete than the figure itself, yet even there, among the summer grasses and wildflowers, there is a sense of something missing which is both obvious at first glance and, at the same time, rather subtle. You can see that something is wrong, but it's impossible to say what – and the painting is all the more unsettling for that. The girl – not me, myself, but the girl that Mother imagined for the purposes of this particular painting – has a more or less finished face, and you can see that she is wearing a grey dress over a rust-coloured blouse or shirt, but she has no hands and she doesn't quite fit into her surroundings, while all around her, in the air and in the meadow plants at her feet, there are dozens of gaps and unfinished scribbles that make it seem, not that this is an unfinished painting that could have been completed, given enough time, but that it is an attempt at rendering the unfin-ished and frighteningly perishable fabric of things, an attempt, whether deliberate or unconscious, to make the viewer see that *nothing* is permanent. A fairly commonplace, even rather banal philosophical notion – and one that Mother would never think of expressing in so many words – but rather disturbing when it's made visible, in what seems, at first glance, to be nothing more than a portrait of a young girl. More disturbing still, I suppose, if you are the subject, and the painter is your mother, and I have to think, not only that Mother chose to leave the thing unfinished for a reason – a reason she did not care to explain – but also that later, in the dark hours of the following winter, when I was away at school and she took it out and hung it on the landing, directly opposite my door, she did that, too, for a reason that she at least partly understood, and whose logic she could not resist. I noticed it immediately that same evening, when I came home from Tromsø, and my first impulse was to run downstairs and ask her about it. But I didn't. I lingered just long enough to see, in this strange, unfinished work, that what Mother was offering me, by hanging it in that carefully chosen spot, was a gift she couldn't explain, any more than she could resist giving it. A dark gift, perhaps, but a gift nonetheless. An hour later, when she called me down to dinner, neither of us said a word about it, because it wasn't a gift you discussed, or even gave thanks for. Some gifts are like that. They are given and received in silence, almost in secret and, no matter how inexplicable or strange they may seem, they are never mentioned again.

I spent the rest of that day looking at picture books. I knew Mother was busy, and I didn't want to disturb her. I had a quick snack to tide me over till dinner, which might happen at seven, and might not come till nine, then I gathered an armful of books from the shelves in the hall – Harriet Becker, Christian Krohg, Robert Robinson's *Captured by the Norwegians* – and I shut myself away in my room. It was a habit I developed that summer, looking at pictures. It didn't matter what – photographs, illustrations, reproductions of the old masters. I would have liked to read, but I couldn't. Whenever I tried, I started thinking about what I was supposed to do with my life. Which university, which field of study, which career. All the usual questions for someone my age – questions that didn't interest me in the least, but seemed suddenly urgent. I had worked hard at school and I had always been a good student, but now, after years of books and grammar and revising for exams, I couldn't read at all, because I had forgotten how to read without taking notes. All I could do was look at pictures – and there were thousands of pictures to look at. Mother had a huge collection of illustrated books: monographs on her favourite painters, lavish histories of printmaking and photography, several shelves of old children's stories with beautiful illustrations, art books in Norwegian and English and French, books in languages I didn't even recognise. She kept the novels and poetry and the leather-bound copies of Ibsen's plays downstairs, and I would often find her curled up in a chair on some grey winter's afternoon, immersed in *David Copperfield*, or *Vildanden*, but the shelves that lined both walls of the landing, from my room to the door of the studio on either side, contained nothing but picture books. I suppose she wanted them close by, so she could refer to them when she was working, but that summer I almost worked my way through the entire collection, taking them from the shelves five or six at a time and turning the pages slowly, scanning the images of Victorian Christmases and Dutch courtyards, the still lifes with oyster shells and half-peeled lemons, the luminous self-portraits, the landscapes and anatomical studies. I didn't know what I was looking for, but there were times when I felt that I was on the verge of finding *something* – not the answer to a specific question, of course, or a clue as to what I should do with my life, but something I couldn't have identified in so many words, some change in my internal weather, some new atmosphere or mood that would have allowed me to begin thinking about those things on my own terms. For after all, as reluctant as I was to contemplate it seriously, I knew that there *would* be a future, and I would have to take part in it. Only, I didn't want to consider it until I was ready, and I didn't want to do what was expected of me. I wanted to make a free decision – and there are moments, now, when I can look back with something like admiration for the girl I was then, if only because she knew, in any number of surprising ways, that a free decision is far more difficult than everyone pretends.

The time passed quickly and it was eight o'clock before Mother emerged to cook us a meal and ask me about my day. We hadn't seen each other since the previous night and while there was nothing unusual about that, I could tell that she was preoccupied. As soon as we had eaten, she vanished back into the studio for what I suspected might turn out to be another night-long session: she was working on something big and, though she hadn't said very much about it, I knew her well enough to read the signs, and so anticipate, first the obsessive, insomniac, abstracted state that would carry her to the end of that work and, then, when she knew for sure that it was done, the day or two of anticlimax and restlessness that would follow, a mood that she would always try, and never quite manage, to conceal.

That didn't bother me, though. It had done, when I was younger, but now I enjoyed seeing her busy, and I told her that I would clear the table and wash up, so she could go straight back to work. She smiled. 'Thank you,' she said. I loved it when she smiled like that. It wasn't the beautiful smile she kept for the suitors, or the two or three journalists who had come to the house. There was no effort to it, no reserve. It was just a smile.

'That's all right,' I said. 'I know you're busy.'

She nodded. 'And you?' she said. 'What are you going to do?'

I wanted to smile too, but I didn't do it so easily, or so well. She used to laugh at me when I was little and pretend to be shocked by how serious I was – though I imagine she always thought I would grow out of it. She didn't think I'd stay like that forever. 'I'm going to wash the dishes,' I said.

'And after that?'

I shook my head – and I did smile then, just a little, because it made me happy, thinking how I would spend what was left of the day. 'Nothing,' I said – and then I said it again, because I wasn't just talking about that day, I wasn't just talking about the next few hours, I was talking about something that I hadn't really figured out yet, but knew was there, at the back of my mind, as some new possibility. Some new promise. 'I'm going to sit in a chair and do absolutely nothing at all.'

An hour later, when the kitchen was tidy, I went back upstairs to my picture books, with that wisp of a promise in my head – and that was when I saw Martin Crosbie for the first time. It must have been around ten o'clock and, because we were in *midnattsol*, I saw him quite clearly; yet for a moment, perhaps because of the light and perhaps because he looked so obviously out of place, I thought I was imagining things. He was standing by the gate that divides the inner, cultivated garden from the meadowlands beyond and he was gazing up at the house as if he thought it was something he ought to know, but couldn't quite remember. Of course, he would have been unfamiliar with real *midnattsol* and he wouldn't have been prepared for the effect it had on him. No doubt he had heard about the midnight sun before he came – everybody knows about that – but no amount of reading could have prepared him for the real thing and, besides, that term is hopelessly misleading. *Midnight sun* suggests a golden, perennial sunset quality, and it's almost never like that. *White nights* is closer, though even that is too narrow a description: these midsummer nights can be blue, or red gold, or silver grey, depending on the weather and also, as Mother

44

always says, on the mood of the observer. On that particular night, the air was cool and fresh after the first day of real summer, and the light was that still, silvery-white gloaming that makes everything spectral: ghost tracks winding past our house and out along the shore as if returning for one night from the distant past, ghost birds hanging on the air above the glassy water of the Sound, ghost meadows for miles in every direction, every blade of grass and flower stem touched with a mercuric light, like the foliage in those ancient photographs I had been poring over earlier. It would have been easy to suppose that Martin Crosbie was a ghost too, that first time I saw him, for there was nothing factual about him, other than his unexpected presence there, in a place where he should not have been, and even that was provisional, a figment of the summer night that might crumble and fade before I could make out what it was. The sensation only lasted a moment, of course; still, at first glance, it seemed to me that he was a man without substance, not a ghost so much as an illusion, a phantasm in which he himself scarcely believed. It was as if he had stumbled upon presence by chance, just moments before, and now he was somewhere between a trick of the light that had, by some accident, become a human being, and a man who was on the point of vanishing, his features forming and, at the same time, on the point of melting away.

He wasn't an illusion, however. He wasn't even a ghost. I had never seen him before, but I knew who he was; just as I knew, from what Kyrre had said about him in passing, where he had come from and where, for the time being, he belonged. What I didn't know was what he was doing *there*, staring up at our house with an expression that looked like dismay, or disbelief, and I was almost concerned enough to go out to him. I didn't, though. I could tell that, even though he was

45

staring at the house, he had not seen me and, half concealed and motionless on the landing, I took the opportunity to size him up. He was tall and thin; around thirty, I thought, with pale, sandy hair and gold-rimmed glasses. If Mother had been there, she would have said he was sensitive, or delicate, but to my mind there was more to it than that, something that had to do with my first impression of his being hurt or lost, like some animal that has strayed from its own habitat and finds itself exposed, out on a road among backyards and wire fences and cars, a creature from the woods flushed from its cover, with nowhere to hide. Yes, his face *was* delicately made, but it really was the delicacy of feature you see in some animals, in deer, say, or foxes. It was a delicacy that came as the natural complement of a worried spirit, the delicacy of someone who was always waiting for something more: waiting, or dreading, or hoping – which, for him at least, was probably much the same thing. In ancient times, there were men who belonged to the horizon – Kyrre told me this once, during one of his stories – and because those men could see further than anyone else, the people made them their lookouts, quiet, abstracted sentinels who knew what was about to come, but never really grasped its importance, watchers of the skies who could report, but never interpret, the patterns in the stars. Martin Crosbie was one of those men.

I had never seen him before, but I knew he was Kyrre's summer guest. He had that bemused, abstracted look of the recent arrival and it was quickly evident that he was searching for something to anchor him in this new landscape of water and light, trying to convince himself, not that he belonged so much, as that belonging was at least possible. He needed a way into all this and it must have seemed to him that our house – a house he must have convinced himself he had seen before, in a tourist brochure, or some line drawing in an old guidebook – would supply the focal point to what was, otherwise, nothing more than a dream. What he wanted, in fact, was something he could recognise. I suppose he didn't know, then, how strong a feeling déjà vu can be in this part of the world, even for people who have lived here all their lives.

I'd seen that look before, though, more than once. When people come here they can't quite take it all in: the light, the sky, the deep quiet. When you read about it in a geography book, it doesn't sound like much: a small island, or rather a string of islands running from Tromsø in the east to Hillesøy in the west, with Kvaløya right in the middle, three islands in one, like a clover leaf. Our southernmost leaf is the most populous. On the map, it looks like an angel in flight, but it is only another island in the Arctic Circle, an unexciting fringe of coastal settlements – Straumsbukta, Skognes, Mjelde, Bakkejord, Sandvik – around a silent, almost deserted heartland of woods and low mountains, populated by herds of elusive, non-native elk, but haunted by something older and less amenable to language. There is one good road that rings the island, running through the straggling, sea-facing settlements and out to the ferry at Brensholmen, or the white beaches at Sommarøy, before it stalls on the mystery of Hillesøy. On Hillesøy you can see reindeer, and our delicate northern orchids, subtler and, to my mind, more beautiful than the exotica you find in florists' shops. As the summer ends, you can gather cloudberries out on the point; Mother says nothing tastes as fine as those particular cloudberries, just as there is no sight so fine as the northern lights seen from the far side of Hillesøy, where the island turns its back on its dozen or so houses and faces out into the dark.

For a stranger, though, this place can be overwhelming. It's

47

not dramatic, or picture-postcard beautiful, like the western fjords, it's just stark, and empty-seeming and, at night, so still and wide that it can make even the most pragmatic of souls think about spirits. Here, seventy degrees north, it's not rare for new visitors to spend their first several days wondering why they ever came. They had chosen to make the journey, they'd bought tickets for the various ferries or driven two thousand kilometres to rent a primitive *hytte* from Kyrre Opdahl but, all of a sudden, they don't know why. While they were planning the journey, while they were on the boat, or coming in to land at Tromsø airport, they had found reasons for coming, reasons they had dreamed up and repeated in casual conversation to make it all seem plausible, but in the white night, in the lull of *midnattsol*, those reasons have evaporated.

Which is how it must have been for Martin Crosbie. Everything was unfamiliar and, after the first faint glimmer of recognition, our house turned out to be just as strange as everything else. Nothing was as he'd expected it to be – and, like so many visitors before him, he was beginning to suspect that there was nothing here at all. Kvaløya was a mirage, nothing more; the whole string of islands was an illusion. Standing at our gate that first night, he must have thought he'd made a long, wishful journey for nothing, that he'd travelled all that way just to end up being nowhere. For what seemed a long time, though it was probably no more than two, or maybe three minutes, he stood staring at our house, willing it to be real – and though I should have been clearly visible, right there on the landing in his direct line of vision, it was obvious that he couldn't see me. For as long as he stood there, he was staring straight at me, yet he saw nothing. Nothing and nobody. Then he turned and walked back along the path, without once looking round – and I couldn't help thinking that, by the time he got back to Kyrre's *hytte*, he would already have begun to suspect that nothing he had seen in his entire life, whether here or anywhere else, was real.

It's a summer's morning. I've just been for a long walk, down across the meadows and along the shore and, all the way, I could feel how alone I was, now that everyone else is gone. Of course, Mother is still here, working in the studio as always – perfect, silent, wishing for nothing. She has worked long and hard to achieve that state and, though it might have seemed to the rest of the world that she achieved it long ago, I know that she's only just arrived there. I know because, even before I knew what I was doing, I have been watching her all my life, and now that I see her clearly, I'm beginning to understand what that achievement cost her. The odd thing, though, is that I am there too, now. I'm in exactly the same place, exactly the same state, and I can seriously say that it has cost me nothing at all. All that happened ten years ago, during our summer of drowning, and almost everything that has happened since, happened to someone else, not to me. The only thing that happened to me was that I chose, one day, to become invisible. Not to go away, like Mats and Harald, or like Martin Crosbie, who travelled so far from home to stage his own, rather theatrical disappearance. No: I have remained in these meadows, on the shores of Malangen Sound, where I have always been, and I have done nothing at all; or nothing other than to choose the life I am living now, a life someone else would think of as close to non-existent. No career, no husband, no lover, no friends, no children. I am not an artist, like Mother, or not in the usual way. I make things perhaps, but they are just *things* for their own sake, and I wouldn't ever pretend that I have something to say. I simply look out, over the meadows, over the water, and I pay attention. I can't remember where I first heard it – I think it might be from Shakespeare – but I do recall being struck by a phrase, a phrase that now has no worldly context for me at all, a fragment drawn from a play or a novel, in which the phrase *God's spies* occurs. It's preposterous, I'm quite ready to admit it, but I cannot help feeling that that phrase describes me perfectly. I am one of God's spies. I do not believe in God, or not in the usual way, but I do find that I am here for a reason, and that is to keep watch. To pay attention. There was some ancient Mexican tribe whose members took turns each night to watch the sun go down and then waited in vigil through the dark till it returned – and they never assumed that it would, they never took that light for granted. They took turns to stand watch, and they believed that the real reason why the sun reappeared each day wasn't to do with gravity, or how the earth turned on its axis. They thought it was their attention that drew it back – and I live in that same state of attention, day and night. It is an easy, comfortable attention, and it has no purpose. I'm sure it mystifies Mother, who cannot help but make something new of everything she sees or hears. For my part, though, I have no wish to do anything, no wish to create. I am a witness, pure and simple, an unaffiliated, lifelong spy.

Back then, though, I was a different kind of spy. In those days, it was people I watched, mostly because they puzzled me. Their desires, their fears, what they wished for and what they hoped to get away with, the stories they told and the stories they chose not to tell – it all puzzled me, and I watched them from a distance, through the binoculars, or my camera lens, because I wanted to understand them. Or, maybe what I wanted to understand was why I wasn't *like* them. They were so attached to things that I didn't see any use for. They took the world so literally, and they seemed to want the things they wanted, not because they really *wanted* them, but because these things were the prescribed objects of desire. At the time, I suppose, I thought *that* was what interested me, but it wasn't the reason for my spying – not really. The reason I watched, the reason I became a spy, was that I thought something was wrong with me, and I wanted to know what it was. I wanted to understand why I didn't want anything at all.

That summer, I still thought that spying was a game and I played it because I found people both sad and amusing, especially Kyrre's guests. Naturally – I was eighteen, after all – I enjoyed the sadness as much, if not even more, than the amusement. I didn't want to spy on Martin Crosbie, however, not after that first vision of him at our garden gate. I wasn't sure why, but there was something in his face that made me want to leave him be, some concealed thing that I didn't understand, but saw quite clearly, even on that first night, when he stood looking up at the window, staring right at me, and seeing nobody. I had no desire to watch from the landing, the next morning, as he walked back and forth between his car and the *hytte*, bringing in boxes of bottles and groceries. I didn't want to know what was in the bags he retrieved from the boot of the car, or what books he read. I didn't want to know anything about him. But I'd been up half the night and I was bored, and it didn't really feel like spying, when I picked up the binoculars and trained them, first, on the meadows and then, gradually, one yard at a time, moving across the bright tide of summer grass, on Martin Crosbie's car, standing in the place Kyrre's van had occupied the day before, its rear door open, the boot and all but the driver's seat piled high with luggage of various kinds. With the binoculars I could

51

make out some of the contents of the boxes and bags: there was a huge quantity of books, almost as many bottles of various shapes and sizes, a camera bag, a quantity of CDs, and their owner – I knew his name, because Kyrre had said it the day before, when he'd told me about the strange arrangement the man had made, to stay the whole summer – their owner, this Martin Crosbie, was different in the daylight, more alert, and significantly more substantial, than he had seemed in the night-time. He worked quickly and, even though some of the boxes looked fairly heavy, he carried them easily – and all the time, it seemed, he was talking or singing to himself, the way a child does when it's occupied and doesn't think it's being watched. For as long as it took him to unload the boot, he only stopped once, setting a box down on the roof of the car and pulling out a squat, dark bottle, from which he took a long swig, before moving on. That was the one time he stopped singing, that time when he took a drink, and I could see, through the binoculars, that his face altered for a moment, assuming a serious, even slightly troubled look, as if he were thinking of something that he would have preferred not to remember. A moment later, he was working again, and singing to himself as he went – and I have to confess that, as senti-mental as it seems, I felt sorry for him. He was so like a child – so blithe and, at the same time, so determined not to think again about whatever it was that had troubled him. Finally, when the last box was inside, he closed the car up and locked it – which was absurd, of course, in a place like this – and I didn't see him again until he emerged about an hour later, got into the car and drove away.

Three hours passed. I sat on the landing with a pile of books, only glancing up now and then when my attention was drawn to some change in the light, or the slow, stealthy apparition of one of the big cruisers that slide in and out of Tromsø, keeping to the far shore of the Sound and moving silently past the dark, mountainous backdrop of Malangseidet. I wasn't waiting for Martin Crosbie, I wasn't spying on him, but I happened to look up as he came back along the track and I didn't think there was any harm in taking a peek through the binoculars, as he got out and started unloading a new set of bags and boxes from the store at Eidkjosen. It took him several trips to get it all inside: obviously, he'd decided to stock up. Later, when he wasn't around, and I was interested enough to want to know more about him, I saw what he had bought that day and stacked away in the *hytte*'s cupboards: dried goods, jars of sild and pickled beets, bottled sauces for cooking, economy packs of rice and pasta, tinned soups and vegetables, film-wrapped packs of Ringnes beer. Practical choices, for someone who wanted a simple life, the kind of thing people have stocked up on for decades, out here, but he had bought other things too – odd, non-essential items that, at that time, struck me as quite touching. A local newspaper and a pile of children's comics. A box of imported chocolates. A red geranium in a pot – one solitary flourish of colour to brighten the place up a little. And I think he really did believe that would be enough. A sufficiency of tinned food, some treats, a pile of books and CDs, a nice pot plant. That, and a whole summer of peace and quiet. It wouldn't be long, though, before he admitted to himself that he had no idea what real quiet was, that he wasn't prepared for the plaintive sounds that seeped in, day and night, through the constant light. No doubt, he'd thought of quiet as something pleasant, a tonic for the soul, a refuge from whatever he had left behind; he hadn't expected the endless field of murmurs and far-off cries that he had so casually drifted into, like a man wandering haplessly into a house of ghosts, seeing nothing out of the ordinary but troubled, from time to time, by random changes in the atmosphere, fine but significant shifts in the quality of the light and the background noise. It was as if someone had altered the dials by the merest fraction on a radio he had been listening to all his life and, over the next few days, while he hid himself away from the world and I tried to stick to my resolution that I wouldn't spy on him, he gradually became aware of other voices, other sounds, from some station that, up till then, had never even existed.

I really did *try* not to spy on him, over those next couple of days – and I don't know why I changed my mind and went down there, thinking I would just put my head around the door and say hello. That would have been the Thursday, a warm, still day as I remember, with only the faintest hint of a breeze off the Sound and the terns flickering over the water just a few yards out, fixed on what, for them, was a complex puzzle of light and movement, an endlessly shifting maze of grey and silver and salt-blue that they had to read, moment by moment, through the long white days and into the midnight gloaming. I'd read how they spent their whole lives like that, following the solstice from southern Argentina, in mid-December, to this scatter of islands in June and July, creatures of the white nights who needed perpetual sun to see their prey in the lit water. I loved them. They were the most beautiful birds on that stretch of coast, but that wasn't what drew me. What I loved was that they were so perfectly focused, so far beyond distraction, seemingly tireless as they watched for the least thread of live silver in the shifting glitter of the tide. Then, when they saw what they were after, they plunged in recklessly, vanishing into the water so completely that it seemed they would never return, only to surface again and flicker away with the glittering, miraculous catch.

I stopped for a moment to look out. The air was perfectly clear, the sky was a soft, hazy blue, and the birds were there, in their usual places, spaced out, each in its lit territory, up and down the beach. I looked around. I could never think of this place as belonging to someone else, even when the summer guests were here; it was too integral a part of my territory, too much a part of the inward map that I carried in my head. Someone had placed a deckchair in the middle of the lawn, and there was a plate of half-eaten croissants on the grass next to it, but the little garden seemed deserted and, at first, no doubt because my attention was drawn to the empty chair, I didn't notice Martin Crosbie, sitting off to the side in a second deckchair by Kyrre's old boathouse, watching me as I took it all in. I had been deceived by the odd, *Marie Celeste* feel that the place had taken on, an absurd and faintly sentimental sense of someone having been and gone, possibly never to return and, for some reason, the idea of that disappearance prompted an odd, yet not unfamiliar sensation in my throat and chest, a sensation that I cannot quite name, though it has something to do with justness, or perhaps a fulfilment, of sorts, like knowing a promise has been kept, against all the odds.

That sensation lasted for no more than a second or two – and then I turned and saw him sitting by the boathouse, a few yards off to my right. He was sitting with his back to the boathouse door and, from the look of things, he had been reading a book when I appeared. It came as a surprise that I hadn't noticed him there, but it was obvious that he had seen *me* right away, and I could tell that he had been watching me with interest – and, perhaps, some amusement – wondering how long it would be before I realised I wasn't alone. And, now that I had, he appeared a little shamefaced, suddenly, as if I'd caught *him* spying on *me*. Only, it was a mock shamefacedness and, to demonstrate as much, he did a little theatrical turn that involved sitting back and taking a moment to consider something he already knew he was going to say, then speaking as if he were inviting me into a conversation he'd already begun in his own head. 'It says here,' he said, 'that April is the cruellest month.'

I glanced at the book in his hand. The cover wasn't visible, but I knew the reference. I shook my head. 'I don't think so,' I said.

'It says here –'

'January,' I said, joining in the game without knowing why. I paused for a moment, pretending to think. 'Yes,' I said. 'Definitely January.'

He smiled. 'Why's that?' he said.

'Dark. Cold. Snowdrifts up to the windowsill,' I said. I didn't mind this game, if that was what it was. I thought it was innocent enough at the time – and maybe I wasn't altogether wrong. But then, it's surprising how innocent anyone can look, if you find them on the seashore, reading poetry.

'Sounds beautiful,' he said.

'It is,' I said. 'Until you have to go somewhere.'

He thought for a moment. 'Fair enough,' he said. 'But does it breed lilacs out of the dead land?'

I pretended to consider this, then I shook my head. 'No lilacs,' I said. 'Not in January.'

He laughed, rather sadly I thought. Though it was always hard to know, with Martin Crosbie, how real any of his supposed emotions were. He had worked long and hard on seeming innocent, I think, and sadness had probably served him even better than poetry. 'And what about April?' he said.

'What about it?'

'Is April *cruel*?'

'No,' I said. 'April is frozen. Like the five months that precede it. It doesn't really thaw out till May.'

'And then it's – like this . . .' He looked up at the sky. 'Which is cruel in its own way, I suppose.'

I frowned in spite of myself. 'Cruel?' I said.

He studied my face, as if he thought I was holding back some secret knowledge that he needed in order to survive in his new abode. It was an odd look, soft, yet slightly accusing, or at least suspicious, and I was almost offended by it. Almost, but not quite. Though I didn't know him at all, I had already guessed that Martin Crosbie wasn't someone who ever gave offence; in fact, he had evolved quite a complicated system of gestures and tones of voice to avoid doing so and I could see that too, though it was a long time before I realised why. Finally he spoke. 'It's so white,' he said, simply, as if that were sufficient explanation.

I nodded. 'Yes,' I said. 'It's summer.'

'Summer?' It sounded like a new concept to him. 'I suppose it is. But it's more than that. I feel different. I feel – strange . . .' He pondered this for a long moment, then he looked at me, as if he were explaining some scientific observation he had made, one that was potentially significant in some way. 'I feel strange to myself,' he said. 'My hands feel different. I sound *different*.' He gave an embarrassed laugh, which appeared to surprise him as much as it did me. 'I sound different when I talk. When I move about. Everything is strange here. I can't quite get my bearings.'

Now it was my turn to study him – and for the first time,

I noticed the black around his eyes. 'Ah, yes.' I felt a sudden, utterly involuntary pang of sympathy for him – sympathy I immediately suspected this whole charade had been calculated to win. 'And I imagine you can't sleep either.'

He nodded, squinting slightly, but he didn't say anything. He did seem tired, but it wasn't just insomnia that was bothering him and, for a moment, I thought I could detect a faint whiff of alcohol. I remembered the bottles he had carried in from his car, and I reminded myself that he wouldn't be the first of our summer guests to hit the booze, hoping for a few hours of sleep – and who could blame him? Everyone who lives on these islands has suffered from insomnia at one time or another. Everyone knows the tricks a sleepless mind can play on itself. All of us here have tasted panic at the back of our throats, whether we admit it or not. In all honesty, I wouldn't trust someone who hadn't.

And yet, even though he was acting a little strangely, Martin Crosbie didn't seem drunk. It was just that he was *elsewhere*, in another world, or another time – and I can see, looking back, that he was managing to put a brave face on it that day, because he probably *was* quite close to panic when I turned up. He'd been trying to distract himself with the book, and maybe he had taken a drink or two, but the panic was forming, somewhere at the back of his head – panic about space, panic about time. Panic about time most of all. The way it starts to move differently when you sit a while, and everything slows, till it feels like it could stop at any moment. The way it pools and stalls in the middle of a summer's morning, or in the white gloaming, so you want to go and stare at a clock, just to watch the second hand turning. The way that ancient panic builds behind your eyes – and then, when somebody comes along, just as everything is about to come to a standstill, the absurd gratitude you feel, a gratitude that you try desperately to hide, so you don't look foolish, or needy. Well, that day, *I* was the interruption, and for a moment I knew it, just as I knew that Martin Crosbie had forgotten for a matter of seconds that I was even there. It wasn't till he put aside the book, face down to keep his place, that he seemed to notice me again – and he smiled then, a soft, damp-seeming smile, like the smiles we reserve for babies and eccentric pets. The book, I noticed, wasn't by T. S. Eliot at all. It was an English translation of Ibsen: *An Enemy of the People and Other Plays*. Pulling himself up in the chair, he said something, as much to himself as to me, and I couldn't make it out. I don't know why. He had a slight accent, maybe Yorkshire, or Scottish – Mother would have known – but that wasn't the problem, and it wasn't that I ever had any difficulty understanding English, under normal circumstances. No. It wasn't what he said that made him difficult to understand so much as how he said it. It was as if he was unconvinced by his own words, as if he wanted to delete what he was saying even as he spoke, that he wished there was some other way of expressing the thoughts that were in his mind. His voice was quiet and, at the same time, strangely inexact, like someone speaking on a badly tuned radio, the words seeming to come from far away, or through some dense, staticky medium, through water, say, or a dividing wall.

'Well,' I said. I didn't really mean to say it – I didn't mean to say anything at all, and I was a little irritated by the cheap trick with the book. It was just a reflex, to gloss over the fact that I hadn't heard what he'd said. 'You're not alone. Everyone feels it, from time to time. Ryvold says this first summer light claims something from us –'

'Ryvold?' Because of the book, he had probably imagined

that I was referring to a famous Norwegian writer and not our local philosopher.

'Siegfried Ryvold,' I said. I smiled politely to cover my annoyance. Why had he pretended he was reading *The Waste Land*? What had *that* been about? Just another symptom of the panic, a silly attempt to play, and so trick himself into thinking he was fine? 'He's a neighbour of ours.'

'Ah.' He studied me for a moment, but not so long, this time, that it seemed impolite. 'A neighbour,' he said, when the moment had passed. He looked up across the meadows towards our house, then he looked right and left, almost theatrically searching for other signs of habitation. From the *hytte*, though, ours is the only house that can be seen. 'And you?' he said, looking back to me with a smile. 'Are you a neighbour too?'

'I'm sorry?' I said.

'Where did you come from?' he said. 'Are you –' He searched for a word, then found it, though when he spoke he didn't seem wholly convinced. 'Are you – local?'

I shook my head, which was odd, because I was as local as it was possible to be. Though, of course, I didn't think of myself as *a local* at all. Nobody does. It's other people who are locals. 'I'm from the grey house,' I said. 'Just above –' I almost turned and pointed, but I didn't. I remembered him standing at our gate, looking up at the landing window and something about that image made me uncomfortable, as if I were the one playing foolish games, now.

'Ah,' he said. 'Of course you are.' He laughed softly, to himself mostly, and I thought again that he was drunk, or drugged. 'For a moment I imagined you'd risen from the waves, like Botticelli's Venus.'

I smiled – though I wasn't entirely sure he was joking. He'd surprised me, and I was a little embarrassed, too. And, of course, I should have known, then, that he was – what? Flirting with me? Making the first moves in a game whose only outcome, with me or with any other player, had long since been decided? If I had known what he was like, I wouldn't have said anything else, but I was still playing the game, a game that struck me as both rather squalid and perversely interesting, because I didn't quite know how to stop. I was, in other words, exactly the innocent I was pretending so hard not to be. I shook my head. 'No,' I said. 'I've been here all along.'

He sat watching me then – regarding me, again, for just a moment too long, as if I really was a picture in a museum. Then he gave a slight, mock-apologetic smile, to show that he knew he was being odd, even rude, but he wanted me to know that he meant no harm by it and that, whatever impression he might be making, he was, at the very least, sincere. 'I can see that,' he said. 'It was just . . .' He studied me for a moment, then he stood up. 'Would you like some tea?' he said.

I shook my head. 'I can't stay,' I said – though I had nowhere else to be, and we both knew it. 'I have to get back.'

He nodded. He didn't believe me, but he'd picked up on my discomfort, and it was obvious that he didn't want to seem pushy. 'Well,' he said. 'It's been a pleasure making your acquaintance.' He gave me an odd, questioning look, then he stood up suddenly and held out his hand. 'I'm Martin,' he said. 'Martin Crosbie.'

I didn't want to shake hands – it felt ridiculous – but I did. His fingers were cold and dry, like frozen paper. I didn't introduce myself, though. I didn't know how.

He smiled at my silence. He didn't think me rude, and the

smile was to let me know that he wasn't offended, though he knew that this fleeting physical contact had made me uncomfortable and, for just one moment, I suspected that there was some part of him that enjoyed that discomfort. 'Well,' he said. 'I'd better get busy.' He made a face. 'Lots to do.'

I nodded. 'It was nice to meet you,' I said. I didn't mean it, but it was something to say.

Martin Crosbie smiled and his hand went up, as if he were about to wave. 'You too,' he said. He watched carefully as I started to leave and then, just as I turned, I caught a fleeting look of concern in his face, as if he thought something might suddenly go wrong at the last minute, some everyday accident or inconvenience that could be averted if he were sufficiently attentive. I was five or six yards away when he spoke again. 'Come to tea, though,' he said. 'Some day when you have a moment.'

I looked round. He was still watching me with that odd, concerned look on his face. 'Thank you,' I said.

His hand moved again and, for a second, I really did think he would wave. 'Any time,' he said. 'I'm here all summer. You know where to find me.'

I nodded. I had no intention of popping by, but I didn't want to be impolite. I remember him, as he was then, through the haze of what came after, and I have to remind myself that I didn't dislike him that day. That didn't come until later. Still, while I didn't want to spend my afternoons taking tea with Martin Crosbie, I think I guessed, even at that first encounter, that our lives would run parallel over the weeks that followed – parallel, but never touching; never touching, but cruelly intertwined.

I don't like intertwined. I like intact. There is too much contact in the world. Too much *intertwined*. Maybe it *is* true that we all depend on one another, that everything in the world depends on everything else – but we also depend on the spaces in between. We need the spaces, because the spaces are where the order lies. That's why I like maps, because they recognise the gaps between one thing and another. They stand in mute opposition to those who think that the connections are all that matter. People who reach out to others, just to touch them, even when they don't want to be touched. People who write unexpected letters to complete strangers, because they think that's what they're supposed to do.

I can't remember exactly when the first of those letters came, but I do know that it was around the time Martin Crosbie arrived. The two events happened so close together, in fact, that now they are linked in my mind, as if one had caused the other, though of course, there was no connection at all. I know I didn't see Martin again for several days – I learned afterwards that he had gone to bed that evening and slept solidly for thirty-six hours, and that was probably the last time he had a good night's sleep, ever – and, looking back, I can imagine that what happened to him later had a good deal to do with the insomnia that set in during that first week of his visit. He became suggestible. We all did. That's what happens here, from time to time. As for the letter, what I *am* sure of is that it arrived at about the same time, or maybe just after our first proper conversation, which must have been towards the end of that first week of true summer, and it was enough of a shock – enough of a shock and enough of a distraction – to keep me occupied for several days. All of a sudden, I didn't want to spy any more, because it felt like someone was spying on me – and though I have to admit that it was some-thing of an overreaction, at the time I couldn't shake the creeping fear that she intended to spy on me for the rest of my life. To spy – and, perhaps, to interfere. People like to interfere. They always think they should be *doing* something.

I don't get that much mail, nowadays, but back then any letter would have been an event – though not usually a happy one. I didn't like mail, and I disliked the telephone even more – who wants to talk to someone they can't see? It's hard enough talking to someone who's right in front of you. A boy in my class sent me a note, once, when I was fourteen, and Mother has been known to send me things through the post – surprise gifts and postcards – but I can't recall ever writing a letter myself. I didn't reply to the boy – I suspect he only wrote the note for a joke – and, though I sometimes leave drawings and cartoons on the kitchen table along with brief notes to let Mother know I've gone out, I've never had to address an envelope. The truth is, I've always regarded communications from the outside world with a degree of suspicion. Most mail is for Mother, of course, and, unless it's from Fløgstad, she quite often leaves it unread for days, or even weeks, at a time. Maybe that's where I get it from. Anyhow, whatever the reason, my first impulse was to throw the letter in the bin and forget about it. It had nothing to do with the life I was living. It had nothing to do with the life I wanted and, at the very least, it felt like an imposition. Yet I couldn't throw it away and though I read it with increasing distaste and no little anger, I read it through to the end and then, when I was done, I read it again – hoping, I think, that I had misread something, and the whole thing would turn out to be a mistake. Because it *was* a mistake, as far as I was concerned.

The letter – a single white sheet of unlined paper in a smooth, cream-coloured envelope – was from a woman in England who said she lived with my father. I was out when it arrived and, because it was addressed to me, Mother left it

64

on the kitchen table – and I knew, as I read it that, even though it was completely unexpected, she wouldn't ask me about it, or intrude in any way upon what she would have seen as a private matter. She has always been fastidious that way. She is a person of infinite and careful scruple, governed first and foremost by the rule that, in order to have the space she requires to work and to be herself, she must grant those around her just as much, or even more, of that same space. It's not just a matter of live and let live, it's much subtler and more negotiated than that. The space she needs, and the space she grants, is constantly shifting, and she is never indifferent to anything, but she takes pleasure in concealment for no obvious reason, and she enjoys those moments when things slip by unremarked, or even unseen. She must have been curious about a letter from England, coming out of the blue like that, but she didn't say a word, and I am quite certain that, as soon as she saw that it was addressed to me – a rare occurrence, as I have said – she set it down on the table and chose to think no more about it.

What *is* surprising, looking back, was that the letter didn't say very much and, on this first occasion, it didn't ask for anything from me either – or not in so many words – yet it was a shock nevertheless, because, after eighteen years I was now learning about the existence and present circumstances of my father from someone who wrote in the matter-of-fact, disengaged tone of a new penfriend who doesn't quite know how to break the ice. The address on the envelope was hand-written, but the letter itself was typed, which struck me as odd, under the circumstances. It told me the name of my supposed father – Arild Frederiksen, a name that, oddly enough sounded vaguely familiar – and it went on to say that he had spent the last eighteen years travelling the world, first as a foreign

65

correspondent and then as a travel writer, but that he was now ill and the writer of the letter – who signed herself Kate Thompson – wanted to let me know this, adding, in conclusion, that she hoped that her writing to me at this time would not seem intrusive and that, even though she herself was a stranger, I should think of her as a well-intentioned one.

A well-intentioned stranger. That struck me as funny. How could this woman think it was well intentioned, to write such a letter and send it, out of the blue, to someone she didn't know? And what was it she wanted? I assumed, of course, that she wanted something, or she wouldn't have written, and she must have been banking on my curiosity about a father I had never met, hoping I would respond in some way that would allow her to say what that something was. And it was true, I had wondered about my father for years, and I had told myself, when I was little, that I would find him some day and bring him home to Mother, so they could be together again, even though Mother had always told me that he'd gone to live in South America, and that she didn't want him to come back, because she was happy with me, happy with how the two of us lived, doing what we liked and not needing anybody else. Whenever I asked about him – where he was now, what his name was, why he had gone away – she had told me the same story, a story pared down to the most basic essentials and free of ornament: he had been in Oslo for a summer, they had known each other for a while, but he had left around the time she got pregnant, which was fine, because she was happy and she hoped I was happy too, just as we were. She'd never told me anything substantial, never given me anything to go on, and I hadn't pressed her. For a while, when I was younger, I really did want answers – and I asked my few questions again and again, getting the same vague story over and over, but I

66

didn't push, I didn't *insist* because, to begin with, I didn't know how, when she was so determined, and, later, I realised that I didn't really *care* any more. Or rather: I taught myself to stop asking, because I wasn't inclined to know something that she was so intent on not telling me. I trusted her, and if she felt that strongly about not telling me the whole story, then she must have had her reasons. Besides, I had everything I wanted and, at the back of my mind, there was a nagging, superstitious part of me that suspected having just one thing more might ruin everything. Even at seven, I knew who I was and what I needed – and maybe that was the point. Maybe the one lesson Mother wanted me to learn was exactly this gift for self-reliance we only acquire when we are deprived of something that had once seemed essential. I think that's fair. I learned to live without a father quite happily, because I didn't *need* a father – or rather, I didn't need the father that chance had provided. And no, this is not the story of some poor soul starved of a proper childhood and the usual rich tapestry of family and emotional support. I really was happy, growing up, and I can't think of an alternative history that I would prefer. I am happy now, too, in much the same way and for much the same reasons – a woman living more or less alone, daughter of a mother whose first love was, and continues to be, her work, and of a father who never really existed. I was happy as I was, without this father – and if I could make one change in my life as I have lived it so far, it would be to go back and throw this letter, and everything that came after, into a midsummer night's bonfire, and watch the whole pile go up in smoke.

I didn't throw that letter in the fire, however – and though I didn't look at it again, I spent the next three days thinking about it. I considered sending back a brief and courteous reply, saying I wasn't interested in the blithe correspondence that Kate Thompson had in mind, and I considered writing to say that, as far as I was concerned, I didn't have a father, but I didn't do either. I thought about taking the letter to Mother, and I wonder, now, that I didn't – but then, just as I hadn't wanted to be caught up in whatever this well-intentioned stranger's plan might be – happy reunion, forgiveness, remission of sins – I didn't want to distract Mother with it either. She had seen the letter, after all, and in the days that followed, she didn't ask me who it was from, or what it said, which I could only interpret as an indication that the best thing to do about such letters was to ignore them. Which is exactly what I did. I didn't want that letter and, because I didn't know what to do about it, I put it aside and tried to pretend that it had never arrived. I'm not sure what I expected to happen, but I hid the letter away safely, in a place where Mother would not find it, and I waited. I had no wish to be cruel, but I had no desire to get involved either, so I decided to believe that this Kate Thompson would accept my silence as the least inelegant response I could offer to a message I had never wished to receive.

It's Midsummer Night. All over the country, people are lighting bonfires, gathering on the shore of some southern fjord, or walking to a patch of open ground in Narvik or Mosjoen, for the yearly celebration of life and light – and that is what I will be doing too, on this island in the white north that most of them have never even heard of, driving thirty kilometres along the coast to observe the ritual with whatever handful of almost-neighbours and near-strangers happens by. That's what I have always done, and that is what I shall do for as long as I am here, which may well be the rest of my life. I know, of course, that this notion would strike my former self as more than a little odd, but it's what I've settled on and, for the most part, I am happy enough with the idea of remaining here forever – though *happy* isn't quite the word I am looking for. Certainly, I am happy enough on nights like this, though it isn't the same without Kyrre Opdahl, and I don't suppose it ever will be. It was Kyrre who first brought me to the midsummer fires, and it was Kyrre who told me the stories that, more than anything else, bind me so closely to this place. So I suppose it's his fault that, in spite of all that happened, I will always belong here, and nowhere else. Back then, Mats and Harald Sigfridsson would be there too, eerie and white in the firelight, standing apart from the rest of the crowd, in a world inhabited only by themselves – and every midsummer I remember that, had they only stayed in that world, that summer's events might never have happened. Maia would never have become the *huldra*, and Kyrre wouldn't have lost his mind; Martin Crosbie would have gone home with a few pictures and stories, to make his summer in the Arctic Circle into some kind of romance that, with time and effort, he would have managed to believe. And me? Sometimes, in these last ten years, when chance has taken me that way, or when I've had nothing better to do, I've gone back the next morning to the scene of the fire and stood watching the ashes lift and fritter away in the wind, blowing out over the meadows or along the shore to wherever it is things disappear to, after they are done with this world. I don't know why I do this, unless it's because I am looking for something. A sign, maybe, or some memory of a word or a gesture that I missed back then – or maybe it's just that my eye wants to follow the trail of spent ashes, in the hope of discovering that gap in the fabric of the world where those whom the old stories condemn cannot help but disappear, whether they believe in the stories or not.

That year, in the run-up to Midsummer Day, Mother was busier than usual. She had no fixed schedule, but then she never had; she would vanish for hours, or even days, at a time, only emerging to cook a meal or fix some coffee and carry it back to the studio, and though she did her best to make those mealtimes coincide with mine, it didn't always happen. When I was younger, she was scrupulous about that: she would be there when I was there, only working when I was asleep or in school. Later, though, when I was in my teens, she started observing her own timetables, and she would often be blithely unaware of what was happening in the outside world. The studio was at the back of the house, overlooking the garden and the carved stones just beyond; there was no traffic there, and nothing to see besides a stand of birch trees and the low pine-covered hills, so she was utterly cut-off, completely alone and completely silent. I didn't mind that, though. I liked my own company. I liked sitting in the kitchen by myself, over a sandwich and a glass of milk, quietly revelling in the sensation I sometimes had of being the last person on earth. Saturday mornings excepted, nobody came to our house unless they were summoned or had an appointment and, if anybody had turned up unannounced, they would have had to park on the road below, next to the little garage where Mother kept her own car, which she very rarely used. That summer was no different. In fact, to me, it felt even quieter, even more remote from the world, because school was over and I had no sense, really no sense at all, of anything that might resemble a plan for the future. Time – the time measured out by clocks and calendars and daily routines – had more or less disappeared, to be replaced by a long, slow, pleasurable drift, where nothing was required of me, and I could do exactly what I wanted. I was living in the present, and the present was a sweet, apparently endless limbo.

I spent days wondering what Kate Thompson would do next. It wasn't clear whether she had written to me at Arild Frederiksen's instigation, or even with his consent, and I wondered how sick he actually was, and whether he even knew what she had done. To me, the letter had come as an unwelcome intrusion, to say the least, and I didn't really know what to do about it. Should I write back or would that only encourage her to pursue the matter? Should I tell Mother? She hadn't said anything about the letter: but what would she say if I mentioned it first? My first impulse was to write and tell this well-intentioned stranger to go away, but I was pretty sure that was a waste of time. I could have discussed my options with Mother, I suppose, and she would have supported me in any decision I made – but that was precisely the point: I didn't want to make a decision. It wasn't fair that I had to consider making a decision, because I hadn't done anything to invite this woman into my world. All I wanted was to be left alone and the simple fact, the fact that I kept returning to, was that *this wasn't fair*. I had no interest, now, in Arild Frederiksen, none of the curiosity that, presumably, Kate Thompson was counting on, and I didn't want to think about what the next letter might ask of me – because I knew, of course, that something would be asked, eventually. I thought about the letter all that night, and all through the next morning – all the while waiting to see if Mother would mention it – and then, over a solitary lunch in the kitchen, I decided that I would banish this sudden father and his lady friend to the world of bogeymen and phantoms, the world, in other words, to which they rightfully belonged, and forget that they even existed.

I was being naive, of course. I think I even knew that, but I couldn't see any other option. Or none that I could accept. If I responded to the letter, if I talked about it to Mother, if I did anything at all, I would be acknowledging this man's existence in my life, and I refused to do that. So I sat in the kitchen and ate a chicken-and-tomato sandwich on white bread, followed by an apple and a few slices of *gjetost*, and I determined to put the letter out of my mind. I listened to the radio for a while, then I fetched my camera bag and sat at the dining-room table, cleaning all the lenses slowly and carefully with a soft, blue anti-static cloth. It must have been about two o'clock when Mother appeared in the doorway. 'Busy?' she said, her expression neutral to mildly curious. It might have been intended as sarcasm, but I didn't think so. She wasn't one of those people who thought everybody else should work all the time, just because she did. On the contrary. If anything, I probably could have done with a bit more push from her – school was done, and I ought to have been doing something about my future, but I hadn't lifted a finger. It might have been good for me, if she'd had a good old-fashioned mother-to-daughter heart-to-heart about what I was going to do with my life, but that just wasn't her style. In most people's eyes, she was a successful person – maybe in her own eyes, too, though success would have meant something different to her, something that had more to do with freedom than money or fame – but I didn't think she had ever done anything very calculated in her entire life, other than coming north. That, and having me, of course. She was always careful to let me know that I wasn't something that had just happened to her: she had chosen me, and everything she did, everything she had ever done since the day I was born, was intended to make my life as good as possible. She worked so I wouldn't have to

72

make false choices; she worked so that I wouldn't have to rush into something and then have to pretend that *that* was the bed I had chosen to lie on.

I set the camera down on the table. 'Not especially,' I said. 'Are you?'

She smiled at the hint of sarcasm in my voice, though it hadn't come out quite as I'd intended. 'I should be,' she said. 'But I've got this journalist coming at two thirty.' She looked out of the window. 'That's if he doesn't get lost.'

'What journalist?' I said.

She looked back at me, and her face betrayed something like surprise, with perhaps a hint of irritation. 'The American,' she said. 'I told you he was coming –'

'I don't think so –'

'Yes, I did,' she said. She started through to the kitchen and I could hear her moving about, fetching the kettle, filling it. Her voice sang out above the tap. 'He's coming all the way from New York, or some place,' she said. 'God knows why.' She reappeared in the kitchen doorway and gave me a searching look. 'I told you about him,' she said, but I could see now that she wasn't so sure.

'I don't remember,' I said. I was quite certain that she hadn't mentioned anything about a journalist.

She sighed. 'Well,' she said, letting her head fall in a picture of theatrical resignation before returning to the kitchen. 'I'll have to talk to him. And I don't want to take him up to the studio . . .' Her voice trailed off and I could hear crockery being brought down and set out.

'That's all right,' I said. 'I was planning to go for a walk, anyway.'

She came to the door. 'You don't have to go *out*,' she said. 'I just thought –'

73

'No,' I said. 'I need some air.' I picked up the camera. 'Maybe I'll take some pictures.'

She smiled. 'Well, if it's all right,' she said. 'He *has* come a long way.'

I almost laughed at that. She wasn't usually like this before an interview. Was she flattered that the man had come all the way from New York, just to see her? Or was it something else? It was so easy to slip back into the myth that had built up around her, how she chose to live alone, not saying a word for days on end, lost in her art and entirely self-sufficient – but I think she enjoyed those conversations, when they came, even though she pretended they were a chore. Interviewers always noticed how generous she was; they always made a point of saying how this notorious recluse made time for them and responded freely to their questions – and, because of the myth, they never guessed that those conversations meant much more to her than she pretended. When the interviewers left, with their tape recorders and notebooks, they always thanked her for the time she had so graciously given up; they never seemed to realise that she hadn't given anything at all. She had taken. It hadn't been much – what she took was carefully measured out, and the limit was never exceeded – but it fed her in some obscure way so that, quite often, when the visitor had been safely waved off, she would hurry up to her studio and not emerge until the next morning. That was how it worked, for her, on occasion – but it wasn't what the interviewers said that mattered, it wasn't the questions they asked, or the challenges they posed, that made the difference. No: it was what *she* said, or thought and didn't say, during those long conversations that sent her away in some new direction. Those conversations allowed her to surprise herself from time to time, and that was why she had them. There was no other reason – though I sometimes wished there was.

It was a soft, sweet day, with a light breeze off Malangen blowing in over the land. I crossed the meadow directly below the house, but I took the meagre trail that led off to the west of Kyrre's *hytte* and down, along the bank of a narrow stream, to the beach. It was one of my favourite places, this stretch of sand and drifted stone, a place where I went whenever I was bored or unhappy, or when I needed to think. I liked this place more than anything, maybe because I felt most alone there, as far from the world of school and town and other people with concerns and problems like mine as it was possible to be. Because I didn't like being with other people, especially people my own age. I didn't want to be reminded of the mundane things that mattered to them. I didn't have friends over, like normal girls my age, because I didn't *have* friends, and I didn't go shopping for clothes and make-up in Tromsø because those things didn't interest me. Occasionally, I would drift down to Kyrre Opdahl's house and sit with him while he worked on a clock or some piece of machinery, and he would talk about the old days, or tell histories from a time before either of us was born, traditional stories of trolls and wights and water spirits, along with the gossip and hearsay that he had picked up during a lifetime of watching and listening – wisps and snatches of unreliable history from the whaling days on Andøya, memories of the Nazi occupation, supposedly true accounts of children born with fish scales, or cloven feet. I'd heard much of it before, of course, but I never tired of those stories – and they were always different, always subject to change. Most people thought of them as entertainment, they didn't take them seriously, but Kyrre did – and I suppose Ryvold did too, in his own way. The only difference was, Ryvold thought they were keys to some hidden meaning. The old stories are real, he'd say, but they're not factual. It was philosophical, for him. Theoretical. Kyrre was more of a fundamentalist. In his stories, the devils were just as factual as everything else; in his stories, something hideous or startling was always present, concealed behind the facade people created and running through the customs and prayers that made mortal men comfortable, and I always enjoyed the moment when they came to the surface, and nobody knew how to continue with the illusion of order.

That would have been what I liked about the *huldra* story, at least to begin with. I don't know when Kyrre first told it to me, but I do know that it was long before that summer, before the boys drowned and he became obsessed with Maia. He'd told it for years by then, coming back to it from time to time, as he did with all his stories, and varying it a little with each telling, adding new details here, shifting the emphasis there, but the basic plot was always the same: a young man goes out walking in the forest, or along the seashore, and there he meets an unbearably beautiful girl and falls in love with her – or maybe he just desires her, and tells himself that this is love. He is so smitten that he will follow her anywhere, he is completely at her command and, at first, he is happy, because he thinks she loves him too. She smiles, she beckons to him, she leads him away through the trees or along the beach – and all the time, if he would only look, he would see that she is an illusion, that there is no substance to her. Seen from the front, she is perfectly beautiful, perfectly desirable, but if he could only look past this beautiful mask, he would see that, at her back, there is a startling vacancy, a tiny rip in the fabric of the world where everything falls away into emptiness. But he doesn't see – just as he doesn't see, until it is too late, that this girl, this lover, is actually a hideous troll, with a hideously ugly face and the tail of a cow under her bright red dress. He doesn't see this, of course, until she has drawn him out to some far, lonely place where chaos lurks: dark rocks, wild beasts, a cold, quick undertow.

It's a perfect story, even if it is a cliché and, because it has chaos at its heart, it was always Kyrre's favourite, the darkest and the best, the one he told most often and with the greatest relish. It was also the most typical. For if Kyrre's stories had one thing in common, it was this: no matter what form we give it, or how elaborately it is contrived, order is an illusion and, eventually, something will emerge from the background noise and the shadows and upset everything we are so determined to believe in. Or that's how it is in stories – in real life, that something is always there, hidden in plain view, waiting to flower. A turn of phrase, a blemish, an unspoken wish – it doesn't take much to open the floodgates and let the chaos in. That wasn't my philosophy then – it was Kyrre Opdahl's – but it is now. I don't know if the *huldra* is real, but I know that she exists and, sooner or later, she comes stepping out into the light of day and takes possession of whoever it is she has come for.

I was only away from the house for a couple of hours, but in that time, something had happened. I could hear Mother and the journalist the moment I came in and, to begin with, I assumed Angelika Rossdal was going through the usual interview routine, the one where she talked about Sohlberg and quoted Diderot on Chardin, first in French – I'd heard her say it so often, I could quote it myself from memory – and then in Norwegian, or English, or whatever language was being spoken. *Ne recherche pas la virtuosité de trompe-l'oeil, mais rend perceptible la vie silencieuse des objets* – that was it. She would explain why it was important to her that Chardin refused to settle for mere virtuosity, but pushed himself to find that silent life of things, that painter's revelation of the essential. She really had no idea how to go about giving an interview, and she revelled in the fact – and the feature writer or critic opposite her would sit listening politely for as long as it took, then go back to the office and write the story about the beautiful, other-worldly recluse from the frozen north that they had been planning to write all along. That day, it seemed, she was doing the same routine, sitting at the dining-room table over tea and cakes, talking to keep the questions at bay – and since I always found that entertaining, I stopped for a moment in the hallway to listen.

'I came here for the light,' Mother was saying. 'No other reason. I wanted to work in this light, that was all.'

'Really? That was your only reason?' The man's voice was lighter and, I suppose, more youthful than I had expected and I pictured someone slight and boyish, with fair hair that was just a little too long and a beard or heavy black glasses to make him look older. What caught my attention, though – what troubled me – was the tone. There was an intimacy to it, a warmth that I had never heard before. He sounded like a man who was talking to someone he liked, a friend, maybe even a lover. He didn't sound like a journalist. There was a moment's silence, and I could feel them looking at each other, smiling perhaps, like two people who have decided to share a joke.

'That's it,' Mother said. 'It was the light that brought me here, the light, and the colour.' That silence again, then she continued, in all seriousness. 'There are nuances of colour we only see for sure in the north. Cherry red, leaf green, ash blue – they're all different here. In the summertime, the light at midnight, or in the early morning, reveals depths that you never see in the south. I didn't fully appreciate Sohlberg till I came north. I always liked him, but I also thought he was exaggerating a little. I thought he was being deliberately fanciful.' She laughed. 'Of course, he is, in a way,' she said – and, in that moment, the thought passed through my mind that she was flirting. She never spoke to the suitors like this. Not even to Ryvold. Especially not to Ryvold. She was flirting – they both were – and though I couldn't see his face, I knew that the man was smiling. She liked him, and he liked her too and, after just a couple of hours, the interview that had brought them together here was still an interview, but it was also a game they were playing, a game whose consequences they had no wish to consider. 'Perhaps all genius is fanciful –'

'Is that what you think?'

'Hm?'

'That Sohlberg is a *genius*?'

'Oh, yes.'

'Well, he has his moments. But really –'

Mother was loving this. It was all a game, even this fairly orthodox scepticism – Sohlberg was interesting, yes, perhaps even significant, but he could hardly be called a genius – and she was enjoying herself in a way that she hadn't done in years. Not for as long as I'd known her, in fact. 'He's not consistent,' Mother said. 'Only the mediocre are *consistent*. But look at the *Vinteraften* of 1909. Look at *Fra Sagene*. You remember? That blue-grey house in the snow?'

'Yes. It's exactly the same colour as this house –'

'Exactly.'

'So that's why you came here?' He was playing, but it also felt like a discovery he was making.

Mother laughed. 'Exactly,' she said.

'So you didn't come here to be alone?'

'Not at all,' Mother said. 'It's quieter here, I'll give you that. And I work better when it's quiet, but that's not so surprising, is it?' She paused for a moment and I could feel her listening. I had been standing quite still, barely breathing, but I felt sure it was me she was listening to. Or if not to, then for. She listened for a few seconds, confirmed something to her own satisfaction, then spoke again. When she did her voice was different. 'Anyway,' she said, 'I'm not alone. My daughter is right here. Aren't you, Liv?'

I walked through to the dining room. They were at the table, but the usual paraphernalia was missing. The teapot, the cakes, the Danish biscuits set out neatly on our finest china, the bowl of sugar cubes – all of that had been cleared away and now, to my surprise, they were drinking wine. I looked at Mother; her eyes were bright and she looked more relaxed than I had seen her in weeks, but I knew she wasn't drunk. Mother rarely drank, though she would bring out a bottle of wine for Christmas lunch and set it in the middle of the table, more for effect than anything else. We'd have a glass each, then leave the rest and Mother would use it the next day for cooking. 'Is it a special occasion?' I said.

Mother laughed. 'Have some wine,' she said. 'Mr Verne brought it –'

The American journalist stood up. He was very tall, with short, prematurely grey hair and a long, thin face that belied the youthfulness of his voice. 'Call me Frank,' he said, offering me his hand. He smiled. 'You must be Liv.' I shook hands, and he sat down. 'Your mother has told me so much about you.'

It was a white lie, of course, and I had no idea why he felt the need to tell it. 'I doubt that,' I said.

Mother laughed. 'I'm afraid Liv knows me better than that,' she said. 'All I ever talk about is my work. Isn't it, Liv?'

I fetched a glass from the cupboard and poured myself some wine, but I didn't sit down. 'Pretty much,' I said. I turned to Frank Verne. He wasn't a handsome man, but he was attractive for reasons that I couldn't quite fathom. It had something to do with his eyes; there was a quiet, trusting quality to them that wasn't in any way soft or naive. He trusted others because he trusted himself. The underlying expression in his face, behind all the smiles and polite interest, was that of a man who hadn't come up against anything that he couldn't deal with. 'But then,' I said, 'that's what you're here to talk about, isn't it, Mr Verne?'

'Pretty much,' he echoed back – and though he was smiling, I could see that he was studying me, trying to work out what I was hiding. Because I *was* hiding something. I had to be. Everybody had something they kept hidden and the only difference between one person and another was how long it took to figure them out. That was what he was thinking. I could see that he was sure of this simple fact and the thought passed through my mind that I would either puzzle or disappoint him, because I wasn't hiding anything at all. Or nothing that mattered to me, at least. 'Though I aim to get to *know* my subject, too.' He glanced at Mother. 'As a person, not just for what they do.'

Mother smiled. 'Oh, I wouldn't bother about that,' she said. 'Work is pretty well what I am about.'

Frank Verne nodded. 'We'll see,' he said.

Frank Verne stayed until late that evening. He and Mother sat in the dining room, talking and drinking wine, long after I excused myself and went upstairs. There was no reason to go; if anything, they seemed happy to have me around, listening to their exchanges and occasionally joining in, but I didn't feel happy staying. They were too close, too suddenly familiar, and I felt awkward with that, but I felt even more awkward, knowing that the pleasure they took in being together seemed, if not to require, then at least to enjoy, a witness. They were two people who hadn't been happy in the usual, slightly foolish way for the longest time and, now that they were, they wanted to draw the whole world in. Only, as far as the whole world went, I was all they had. They drank more wine, then Mother made coffee and put out some more cake, but I didn't stay for that. I didn't enjoy standing proxy for the whole world, so I fetched a pile of books from the shelves on the landing and locked myself away in my room. I could still hear them down below, talking and laughing, and I have to admit that I liked the sound of Frank Verne's voice – from a distance. I didn't want to be close to it, though. I didn't want to *see* him when he laughed, or watch his hands move when he explained something and, finally, when Mother saw him to the door, I was glad of his going away. I wasn't so glad, though, when I heard him accept Mother's invitation to dinner the following night, because I knew I would have to be there, all evening, while they talked about art, and books, all the while pretending that they weren't flirting, or whatever it was they were doing – which meant, of course, that I would have to pretend, all evening, that this was nothing out of the ordinary. Only it was. Something was happening and, even if I didn't know what it was, it occurred to me that life might not continue forever as it had done. Frank Verne, Kate Thompson's letter, the end of school – anything at all, no matter how insignificant in my eyes, might set a whole train of events in motion, and everything could change. Only I didn't want things to change. I wanted everything to stay the same. No letters, no journalists, no drowned boys, no *future*. No future, only the present and whatever past I chose to remember. Because remembering is a choice, if it's done well, and nobody can make you remember what you choose to put out of your mind.

Kyrre Opdahl turned up at noon the next day with his bag of tools. He came to the back door and called out, as he always did before he crossed the threshold. 'Here is the repair man,' he said. 'Come at last.'

I'd been on my way through to the kitchen and I hurried to meet him in the hallway and let him know that Mother was busy in the studio. I didn't mention that Frank Verne was there too, much less that he would be staying for dinner, but Kyrre said that it was all right, he didn't need to see her. He'd only come to fix the dryer. He had taken me by surprise, though, because I hadn't been expecting him. Mother hadn't told me that anything was broken, and I didn't know how to handle things. When I was little, he would come to the house all the time, just dropping in for a coffee, or to bring by a bowl of berries or gulls' eggs – but then something happened between him and Mother and he stopped visiting so often. I didn't know what had passed between them – it hadn't been an argument, or any unpleasantness – but they seemed to come to a perfectly amicable, yet oddly formal agreement when I was around twelve or thirteen that defined, under terms of engagement known only to themselves, a new and far less casual regime. It had bothered me a little, when he stopped dropping by, but I soon adjusted, and I was perfectly free to go to his house whenever I felt like a chat or a coffee. Nevertheless, a certain awkwardness remained, and I was always afraid that, somehow, and quite unintentionally, Kyrre was being slighted. 'I'm making coffee,' I said. 'Would you like some?'

'Don't go to any trouble,' he said.

'I was just about to put the kettle on.' I felt awkward, all of a sudden. Frank Verne was upstairs, in Mother's inner sanctum, and though he'd only come to continue the interview, it was a breach of the usual etiquette, an etiquette that applied to everyone who came to the house – an unspoken rule that visitors were not permitted upstairs. Once or twice, Harstad had needed to wash his hands after helping Mother out in the garden, and it would have been easier for him to use the bathroom upstairs, or the kitchen sink, but he'd taken it upon himself to use the tiny sink in the downstairs toilet, next to the little storeroom out back where Mother kept her rakes and plant pots. In all the years we had lived in that house, the only exception to this rule that I could recall was the removal man from Fløgstad's, who came once a year at most, and worked like a determined, muscular ghost, never accepting coffee or lunch, never engaging in anything that could be called conversation, just walking slowly and steadily back and forth all day between his van and the studio, carrying the wrapped paintings down one by one and expertly stacking them away in the back of his specially fitted van, where they would not be damaged on the long drive south.

So it felt awkward, knowing that Frank Verne was sitting on the chaise longue in the studio, right above our heads, asking questions in that soft, too intimate voice of his – and as I set about making the coffee, I was torn between trying to hide that fact and the urge to warn Kyrre that this stranger might suddenly appear at any moment. I was torn, and I felt guilty, because I knew how hurt the old man would be if I kept something from him. Finally, when I had set out cups and a plate of Danish biscuits, I turned to Kyrre, who was standing by the window, with his tool bag at his feet, and because I didn't know what to say, I said the one thing I ought not to have said. 'Did Mother know you were coming?'

Kyrre smiled wryly. 'Yes,' he said. 'I've been meaning to come for days –'

'Oh. She didn't say –'

'Ah. Well. We didn't set a time. Not exactly.'

'I see. Well, I could go and get her, if you like. She's in the studio.' I considered for a moment, then I decided. 'She has a visitor right now, but that won't take long.'

This surprised him, of course, but he barely showed it, and he didn't give in to the temptation to ask who the visitor was. Which was quite a feat, under the circumstances. 'Oh, don't do that,' he said quickly. 'Don't disturb her. I'll just get on with this –'

'It's only a journalist,' I said – which was true, after all, though I already knew it wasn't quite. Or, if it was, it wasn't what *only a journalist* usually meant. Journalists were not unknown in the house, but they were always confined to the dining room, or the day room at the front where they could enjoy the best views of the garden. Now, Mother was prepared, not only to allow Frank Verne into the studio, but also to extend him subtler, unprecedented privileges, and I didn't want Kyrre to have to see that.

He shook his head. 'I'll just get on with this,' he said. 'Then I'll be off. I have some errands to run, anyhow, down the coast.'

He finished his coffee and set to work – and I followed him through to the room at the back, that untidy, loam-scented garden room where the washing machine sat in the furthest corner, surrounded by clay pots and bags of compost.

85

This was another room that outsiders rarely saw and it showed a side of Mother that the journalists never remarked upon. It was a mess, a chaos worthy of Kyrre's own house, and it was the room he felt most at home in, I think, when he came up to help out around the place. This was where the machines that kept us running were stored, this was where we stacked logs for the stove on days that were so cold we didn't want to go out to the woodpile, and this was where Mother did her potting and sowing, on an old table covered with crocks and empty seed packets and piles of dry peat, set off to one side by the door. Kyrre made his way through the maze and set to work. He didn't say anything for a while, other than to himself, muttering away under his breath and giving out odd, almost soundless little whistles. I listened. Upstairs it was quiet. Eventually, with a great air of coming round to it, Kyrre spoke. He liked to add gravitas to any occasion, but this time he had a real tragedy to work with. 'What a terrible thing that was, with Harald Sigfridsson,' he said. He was on his knees by the dryer now, peering into the drum.

'What thing?' I said – but even before he answered, I knew what he was going to say.

'You haven't heard?' He seemed surprised by that, though it wasn't surprising at all. In the summertime, when school was out, Mother and I would go for days without seeing anyone, so our only source of information was the Saturday-morning tea parties, when Ryvold or Harstad would bring us up to date on whatever local news and gossip they thought might interest Mother. He looked up. 'Harald drowned,' he said. 'Just like his brother.'

I had known what he was going to say, somehow, I swear I had, but I was still shocked when he said it. Because it was impossible, of course: two brothers drowning, within days of

86

one another. How could that happen? What could that mean? 'No,' I said. 'That's not . . .' Suddenly, I felt as if I would burst into tears – which shocked me even more, because those boys were nobody to me. I hadn't really known them. It should have been a story to me, a local tragedy, cause for curiosity and the casual pity we feel for those left behind. It shouldn't have been personal. 'When was this?'

Kyrre shook his head, though whether in sorrow or because he was surprised at how far from the world we lived up here, I couldn't tell. 'Two days ago,' he said.

And, yes, I have to confess that I was shocked, not just because this had happened – though it was horrible enough, two brothers dying within days of one another – but because I had gone so long without knowing. Now, for all I knew, the undertaker's men might be preparing Harald for the funeral, washing the body, dressing him in his best clothes, applying make-up to his face so the mourners would remember him as he had been. Or would he be interred in a closed casket? Maybe that was what they did – I had no idea how people were buried. I had never known anyone who died. Would he be set down next to his brother? I didn't know if Mats's funeral had taken place yet; maybe he was still in the mortuary, awaiting further investigations. I didn't know what happened in these matters, either, or not what happened in real life anyhow. All I knew was what I had seen on television. I could imagine Mrs Sigfridsson wandering about her house, going from one room to another, looking in at the boys' treasured possessions – not touching them, just looking, as if, by some effort of magic or will, she could cancel out their deaths by leaving everything exactly as it had been the last time they were there. She would go about, taking note of what she saw – things they had made at school when they were little, books they had read, the CDs and shirts and old diaries that had accumulated over the years, the stamp albums or collectors' cards they had set in pride of place on a shelf or a desktop, and had never got around to putting away. The pile of shoes and worn trainers in the bottom of a cupboard. The old comic books under a bed. I could picture her standing in the light from a bedroom window, like a character in an old Dutch painting, and I could imagine how unbearable it was for her, that lost tenderness and the banality of those ordinary possessions, but it wasn't real, it was a scene from a film, one of those stock moments when the detective, having informed the victim's mother that her child has been found dead in a shallow grave out in the woods, is obliged to watch and wait, while the news sinks in. 'I don't understand,' I said. 'It doesn't make any sense. They can't both . . .'

Kyrre shook his head. 'It was exactly the same,' he said. 'The same boat even. You'd have thought . . .' His voice trailed off and he looked out towards Malangen through the side window. The water was silvery, with just the odd streak of grey where a light wind gusted over the surface. 'Something is wrong here,' he said. 'It's not right.' He looked at me, as if he expected me to guess what he wanted to say next. I couldn't, though; or, if I could, I didn't want to let it form as a thought in my head, because it was too ridiculous and, anyway, it seemed obscene, somehow, to make a fairy story out of this. 'Something happened to those boys,' he said after a moment. 'There's more to this than meets the eye –'

I shook my head. 'No,' I said – because, now, I knew exactly what he was doing. That was one of his favourite expressions and it always preceded some leap of the imagination that, more often than not by the most dubious means, connected the world we inhabited with the old world that had supposedly disappeared, the world of magic and spirits, where nothing ever was what it seemed and an unknown force was concealed in every discarded biscuit tin or empty bottle washed up on the strand. Usually I didn't mind – I liked those old stories most of the time and, even as a child, I knew they had a function, something to do with how we thought about time and what we took for granted – but on that particular afternoon, I couldn't take it. I closed my eyes, as if to block out his voice and, at that, he stopped talking. I waited a moment, then looked at him. 'This is horrible,' I said.

He didn't say anything, but I could see that he was surprised – and I knew he had misunderstood. How, I wasn't sure – maybe he thought I was attached to Harald in some way, maybe he thought I was just being proper – but I had no desire to find out or to set him right. I just wanted to stop the conversation out of respect for the dead or, maybe – and I'm sure he suspected this – out of some sudden, misplaced fear. Some superstition. I thought about Mrs Sigfridsson again, and I wondered what she would do, now that her boys were dead. They hadn't stood out much, they hadn't been clever or talented, they were just a couple of shy kids who went around together all the time, and tried not to be noticed. And to that extent, they weren't so very different from me. They didn't have any distinguishing characteristics, they weren't any trouble, they would be remembered for a short while then quietly forgotten. Nobody really knew them well enough to mourn them – and in that they weren't so unlike me either. The only difference between us was that I didn't have a brother. I imagined Mrs Sigfridsson wouldn't forget them, but then, she didn't have anyone else to distract her from her grief. Her husband wasn't on the scene and she had no other children – and that, too, was disconcertingly familiar. I wondered how

Mother would have felt, if it had been me. How would she take it? Would she be able to stay on in our grey house above the Sound, surrounded by her exotic garden? Would the Saturday-morning tea parties continue? Would she be able to go on painting the world that had taken me from her?

Kyrre was watching me, his eyes fixed on my face. 'I can't believe you haven't heard about this before now,' he said. 'Everybody's talking about it.' He snorted, and went back to his work. 'Though they don't understand, of course,' he said.

'Understand what?'

He didn't look up. He'd found something interesting inside the dryer. 'They think it's just a coincidence,' he said. His voice sounded echoey and hollow. 'They think it's just bad luck.' He lifted his head and his voice sounded normal again. Like an old man, talking. 'They can't see that those boys were *chosen*,' he said.

'No they weren't,' I said. I was annoyed that he'd got back to his favourite subject. 'That's just silly.'

He gave me an odd, hurt look, then – and he was about to answer, when a laugh rang out from somewhere above. Not the studio, I realised immediately. The landing. Kyrre's head dropped again and he started rummaging around in his tool bag.

'I'll go tell her you're here,' I said, but I didn't move and, a few seconds later, I heard the front door open and close. At the same time, Mother said something, and Frank Verne laughed again – a surprisingly loud, deep laugh that wasn't just polite, or even amused. It was the laughter of someone who was happy, and didn't mind that it showed. Happy in a way that, had he known anyone was listening, he might have wanted them not to hear, though I couldn't be sure of that. Not with this man. He wasn't a suitor, he was something else.

Something *dangerous*. Kyrre must have heard it too, because he kept his head down and pretended to be absorbed in what he was doing. He didn't want me to see his face – though whether it was jealousy he was hiding, or disappointment, or embarrassment for the man who had just walked out the door and away, as if it were the most natural thing in the world, with the woman Kyrre had silently adored for over a decade, I couldn't say.

That night, we had dinner together in the dining room: Mother, Frank Verne and me. They had spent the day walking about the meadows and Mother had shown off her garden, talking about the weather and the light, the colours, her early career, the quiet she had found in the north. I'd watched them walking up and down the beach from my vantage point on the landing, trying to work out, from their gestures and their body language, what it was that had passed between them the day before. Because something had passed between them. I had no idea what it was, but it worried me that, in the space of a single day, Mother had become subtly different. Happier, more relaxed, less preoccupied. It was as if this Frank Verne wasn't a stranger at all, but an old friend she had just redis-covered, after decades of silence and isolation. When anyone came to interview her, she always talked quite freely about her work and her ideas, but it was talk for talking's sake, more of a smokescreen than anything else. She couldn't find it in herself to deceive, I think, so she overwhelmed her visitors with anecdotes and theories, till they had no other choice than to fall back on the stories they had meant to write all along. None of that talk was ever very revealing. But for some reason, Frank Verne had presented her with a challenge. She wanted to tell him something he could use in his story, she wanted to open up to him. The problem was, there was nothing to open up. She really was what she had pretended to be, the day before: a painter obsessed with her work, with no other real interests than her garden and her books. There was nothing else – or if there was, I didn't know about it.

They walked for a long time – it was a warm, clear day, and utterly still, though the forecast promised rain – then they made their way back up through the meadows towards the house. I saw them coming and I could see how close – how intimate – they had become, just from the way they walked together, from the way Mother looked at him and the way their bodies drifted back and forth, almost touching then moving apart again, the whole thing a game they were playing, enjoying themselves, drawing it out, seeing what might come of things. I saw it all from the window – and I didn't want to get drawn into it. I wasn't quite sure what I was afraid of getting drawn *into* – I didn't think it was romance, or sex, which may have been naive of me – but I wasn't so foolish as to think I could really be a part of it. Besides, I felt guilty about Kyrre Opdahl. I didn't know why he had been upset when he heard Mother go out with Frank Verne, but I knew he had been hurt, and it had taken considerable effort for him to leave the house without letting me see how hurt he was. But *why*? I knew how fond he was of Mother, but I couldn't imagine he was jealous in the usual way, because I didn't think his fondness for her went *that* far. He had always contrived to appear so remote from such things and, in spite of his appearance, he had seemed old to me from the very beginning. Not old like an old man, but old like the carved rocks in Mother's garden, old like the weather, or the tides – old, and at the same time, perpetual and unchanging, part of the scenery, part of nature. He was too old, in that way, to stoop to such things as love, or infatuation, and too old to be jealous, too – but I could see why he might be concerned, or suspicious, and I knew how far he lived from the world, and how little he thought of the men Mother made tea for every Saturday morning. I didn't credit him with anything but noble intentions, in other words – and because of that, I felt guilty. Guilty towards him, and then guilty towards myself, because I hadn't *chosen* to be part of the secret that Mother and Frank Verne had forced me to keep, the secret that, somehow, his being there involved something more than a mere interview.

They had been for their walk, then; but some time during the afternoon, they had gone shopping too and now, as they came bustling into the kitchen, worryingly familiar and at ease with one another, *like a couple*, I thought – and that was how it seemed: a couple who had known each other for years – they brought out smoked trout and fish from the market, more wine, a chocolate cake and, last but not least, the ubiquitous *gjetost*, that sweet rich cheese that foreigners always have forced upon them, along with stories about how newborns are weaned on it, because it's the best thing in the world after mother's milk, or how it's traditional for the first and last meal you have in a house to consist of bread and *gjetost*, and maybe a glass of *akevit*. Though I'm not sure how traditional that really is. Maybe it's something Mother made up. That's something she does, not just for guests, but for herself. She's only lived in the north for fifteen years, but she likes to pretend she's been here all along, that the island is in her blood, that she's been eating the food and observing the traditions since she was a girl. I wouldn't have been surprised, that evening, if we'd had reindeer stew, or maybe whale meat, just to give our guest a traditional Arctic experience – and it turned out that I wasn't far wrong. In fact, thinking about it later, when the house was quiet, I realised that she had chosen the hardest dish for a foreigner to pronounce, so they could play with the word, passing it back and forth like a token of something – their new friendship, I supposed, or possibly an unexpected romance. They weren't interested in food that evening, they wanted to talk. Or rather, to play. *Sjørøye* allowed them to do just that.

'So what's this fish again?' Frank Verne asked, as Mother served up.

'*Sjørøye.*'

He tried to say the word, and failed so badly that it had to be deliberate.

Mother said it again. '*Sjørøye.*' She looked at me and smiled. She was keen to include me in all this – which, for some reason, left me feeling sorry for her. Frank Verne tried again, then they both laughed. Mother turned to me. 'What do you think?' she said. 'Is it hopeless?'

I smiled, but what I really wanted was to leave them to it. 'Practice makes perfect,' I said.

Frank Verne turned to me. 'You say it,' he said.

'*Sjørøye.*'

He tried again, and almost got it right.

'*Sjørøye,*' I said.

'And what's that in English?'

I turned to Mother. I had no idea.

'Sea char,' Mother said. I was surprised by this, and suspected her of having looked it up in advance.

Frank Verne laughed. 'Ah!' he said. 'That really helps a lot.' He turned back to me, aware that the game had gone as far as it could go, and a little further. 'So, Liv,' he said. 'What's it like living out here?'

'It's fine,' I said. I knew what was coming. Not much for

young people to do. Did I ever get lonely? What did I do to pass the time? Did I have a boyfriend? I didn't mind. I was resigned to it, and the answers came pretty much automatically.

'Really?' he said. 'I can't imagine much happens –'

'You'd be surprised,' I said, coming in a little too quickly. I shot a sideways glance at Mother. 'All kinds of odd things happen,' I continued. 'There's a long history of things happening here. You should talk to our neighbour –'

Mother laughed. 'I wouldn't recommend it,' she said. 'Not unless you can stay for another month.'

Frank Verne looked at her, as if he wanted to speak, but he didn't say anything. He turned back to me. 'Odd things?' he said.

I nodded.

'Like what?'

'Well,' I said. 'Two brothers just vanished . . .' I was about to go on, but I'd felt Mother tense at the mention of the Sigfridssons. She must have heard something about Harald, though I hadn't spoken about it, and I didn't think she had seen Kyrre. Maybe she'd spoken to someone at the shops in Kvaløysletta. Whatever she knew, I could tell she didn't feel happy with this topic of conversation.

Frank Verne was aware of the change in her manner too, but he continued. How could he not? He didn't want to seem dismissive and risk hurting my feelings. 'How do you mean, *vanished?*' he said.

Mother stood up. 'People vanish all the time,' she said, as she went to the cupboard to fetch more wine. 'It's one of their saving graces.'

Frank Verne was surprised by this. Maybe, for a moment at least, he thought she was being callous. Not to the drowned boys – he knew nothing of them I supposed – but to me. Callous in a fun way, of course, but with a warning about it as well, and it was clear that he didn't quite know what to say for a moment – and, for that moment, we both sat watching as Mother took out a bottle, opened it and set it on the table. Then she sat.

'Have you ever noticed that the old stories are all about disappearances,' she said, not changing the subject, but changing the subject. 'Somebody goes out in the moonlight, and suddenly they're gone –'

'But this isn't one of those stories,' I said.

Mother looked at me. The warning was clear now, though it was only in her eyes and I don't think Frank Verne really saw that. When she spoke her voice was light, pleasant, just a touch mysterious, but in a mocking way. 'Are you sure?' she said.

I didn't say anything. I looked at Frank Verne. He seemed surprised, and *interested* in all this, as if he thought he might have stumbled into some revelation, some secret that Mother was on the point of giving away, in spite of herself. Though whether he was interested as a journalist or in some other capacity, I couldn't have said. I suppose Mother sensed that, then, and perhaps she had the same thought – which for her, would have come under the heading of *doubt* – for she gave a low, sad laugh, a laugh that betokened sympathy for Kyrre Opdahl, with his folk tales and superstition, and for anyone else who might share his crazy ideas. 'It's *always* one of those stories,' she said. Her eyes lingered on me, then she turned to Frank Verne. 'The winters are long,' she said, as she refilled his glass. 'And the summers are sleepless. Everybody goes a little crazy from time to time.'

*　　*　　*

96

I went to bed as soon as I could decently leave them, and I lay for a while, listening to the sound of their voices mingling with the thin, oddly sweet drone of the wind in the eaves overhead. It was a cool, white night, and there was no other sound, and I think I drifted off for a while, but I was awake again when Mother showed Frank Verne to the spare room, and I listened, with a mixed feeling of awe and dismay, as she told him what, as a guest, he needed to know. Her voice was only just above a whisper, I couldn't hear the actual words, but I knew what she was saying and I heard the occasional soft murmur of assent or understanding as Frank Verne took it all in. Where the bathroom was, help himself to stuff if he got up early, where my room was so he knew not to disturb me. I knew all this, though in all the time we had lived here, we hadn't had a guest to stay, and I could picture them in the doorway, hesitant and a little awkward, possibly tempted to act in a different way, and constrained only by the fact of *me* – awake, listening, possibly sensed, just a few feet away. Then, when everything that needed to be said had been said, I heard her wish him goodnight, and the door to the spare room closed. A moment later, the door to Mother's room, which she usually left open, swung shut too, and the house was silent, except for the occasional creak as Frank Verne went back and forth next door, wondering what might have been.

Some time later, I woke suddenly. I couldn't hear anything, but I sensed them there – Mother and her journalist lying asleep in their separate beds, divided from me by a wall, yet strangely intimate and magnetic in their closed rooms. I got up quickly, and put my clothes on; then, without even stopping for coffee, I hurried out into the cool air. It was a still, clear end to the night, not a breath of wind and an odd white overhead, the kind of white night they show in the old story-books Kyrre used to give me every Christmas when I was little. It was the world I had grown up thinking of as *the super-natural* – not the dark forests or rocky backlands where trolls lived form of the supernatural, but the romantic, silvery, boy meets ghost-girl on the seashore variety, where everything is beautiful and doomed and, at the same time, strangely reas-suring. I didn't know why it should be so, but I always looked back on those stories with a certain fondness and I remember finding an odd comfort in them, even as a child. In those stories, everyone had a double or a phantom lover on the far side of some unnamed and indefinable borderline, a line that nobody could see on maps or ships' charts, and there was constant traffic between one side and the other. Constant traffic and endless transformation – and I suppose that was what beguiled me about it. The way one thing became another, the way a hand reaching to skim the surface of a lake would feel, if only for a moment, the chill, or the eerie calm, of a proximate world. It wasn't that I believed in spirits and trolls, and I wasn't that interested in handsome princes or seventh sons. No: what I liked about that pictured world was what it said about the world I already knew – that it wasn't as fixed as I'd been led to believe, that it was shifting around me, endlessly reshaping itself. That's an appealing notion to a child; or it was to me, at least. Through all those years when I was growing up there was always the possibility that the world would surprise me – that I would wake up one day and find it exactly as it had been the day before and, at the same time, utterly different.

I headed down to the shore. It felt good, being alone. Being unseen. Usually, on such a night, Mother would have been in the studio and if, by chance, she had looked out from the big window at the back of the house, she would have seen the greenish inland light over the carved rocks and the birch wood, not this silvery shore light. That was what she should have been doing, of course. She should have been in the studio, working on the next painting for the new show, and she should have been completely immersed in the work. Frank Verne should have been back in Tromsø, and Mother should have forgotten him the moment he left, just as she forgot the rest of us, as soon as she closed the door to her studio and found herself alone in what I had come to think of as her natural habitat. She shouldn't have let this stranger stay in the house; she shouldn't have stood in the doorway with him, considering a possibility that wasn't possible. She shouldn't be falling in love, or infatuation, or whatever it was. That wasn't who she was. Not really. *Who she was* would be standing in front of the new painting, listening to it, not thinking about some man. Listening, paying attention, not putting anything between her and the work. That was how she had described it, once, to a woman who had driven over from Tromsø to interview her for the local paper. She had gone to considerable trouble to explain it all, how it was more like listening than looking, how everything was in the waiting, in a state of extreme preparedness for the picture to arrive, and how hard it had been for her, to learn *not* to think, *not* to choose, *not* to make decisions about what she was doing. She had explained it all so carefully, which meant she must have liked that journalist, she must really have wanted her to understand – and I remember how amused she was when Ryvold brought the article to the house the following Saturday, that the woman had either forgotten or chosen not to include that explanation. Instead, she talked about the northern landscape, and influences, and how courageous Mother had been, to leave the city and come to live here on her own. They always talked about what a recluse she was, after they had sat all afternoon with her, drinking her tea and eating her special cakes, and she never seemed to mind. At the time I thought this new journalist, this American, would be no different and that, sooner or later, on some Saturday morning over tea and napoleon cakes with Rott and Ryvold and the others, Mother would have a good laugh over what he had written.

I followed the path down through the stand of birch trees between Mother's garden and the meadows, then I crossed the coast road. It was a still night, but no matter how still it was, there would always be a faint drift of wind along that road, a local current touched with the scent of sea fog and *kråke-bolle*, flowing from one end of the island to the other like a river. I remember that thread of wind flickering across my face as I turned to look for traffic. Then I was crossing the first meadow, veering away from the narrow track that led down to Kyrre's *hytte*, because I didn't want Martin Crosbie to think I was spying on him. The grass was dry, but it was so thick, and so lush, laced with wildflowers and shadows, that I slowed on the first few steps, the way a bather slows as she walks into a quick tide – and that was when I saw the girl, at the far end of the meadow, making her way up from the shore. I didn't see who it was at first and, for a moment, I thought my imagination was playing tricks on me – because, on these white summer nights, I am just as susceptible as anyone else to the fanciful notions that I used to find in Kyrre's old storybooks. After a moment, though, I realised that it was Maia. I hadn't seen her since Grunnlovsdag, when she had stood with the Sigfridsson boys, watching the parade of ball-room dancers and American classic cars sliding by in the May snow, and I hadn't seen her for months before that, but I knew who she was right away. If I'd bumped into her in a shop on Storgata, I would have had to think, to cast my mind back and pick out a name from the class roll of girls I'd ignored for years, but out there, in that sea of grass and shadows, I knew her immediately. She was just as she had always been, it seemed, and I remembered seeing her in the corridor one day, just before she dropped out of school, a girl with cropped hair and a loose, tomboy walk, with a slight bounce to her that said she was ready to take on the whole world – and I remembered that I'd been sad for her that day, because, for me at least, that boyish, fake-tough bounce of hers had precisely the opposite effect to what she intended. It made her fear visible, because anybody who paid any attention at all could have seen that the bounce was an act. She had been smiling that day, but I noticed that her fists were clenched, and her thin, bird-muscled body was not so much lean as under-nourished. Which made sense, considering the stories people told about her home life. It was all bravado – and that night, as she came bouncing up out of nowhere, in a place where she so obviously did not belong, I thought it was the same act, an act all the more pathetic for being, as far as she knew, unwitnessed, and I felt sorry for her again because, even though I didn't think she had belonged with Mats and Harald at Grunnlovsdag, even though she had looked like an intruder in their private, flaxen-haired world, I assumed that she must have felt something for them, some fondness, say, or perhaps some confused romantic attachment, which could only mean that this act she was putting on, for herself, for no one, was a cover for some variety of pain or grief that I was unable to imagine.

I couldn't have imagined it, of course – and maybe that was the reason why I stopped and turned aside, so that our paths wouldn't cross. Had I continued, I would have met her in the middle of that sea of grass and shadows, and I didn't want that, all of a sudden. I didn't want to intrude on her act. I didn't want her to know that it had been witnessed and seen through – so I stopped and, if I didn't exactly duck, I did bend into a crouch, my head level with the top of the surrounding grass. At the same time, I changed course and began walking, still crouched, towards the west edge of the meadow, where the land dipped down to a chill, black stream bordered on both sides by thick veils of a dusty-flowered, water-loving plant that Mother had painted often in the little botanical studies and still lifes she did from time to time for her own amusement. *Enghumleblomst* – an elaborate name for such a common plant. Its botanical name was *Geum rivale*, which made it a relative of those gorgeous red and golden flowers she grew in her sun garden, but where those plants belonged to warmth and dry limestone, the native variety was always a sign of water and thick, sweet mud.

For a moment, it felt like a game. Like hide-and-seek, say – one of those games children play, in fun and in earnest, with other children that they do not especially care for, but are obliged to acknowledge. I was sure she hadn't seen me but, as I veered away, in my half-crouching stance, I was watching her all the while – or at least, I thought I was. For thirty seconds, maybe longer, I watched as she came bouncing up the slope from the shore, her face turned away slightly, her arms raised just a little, as if she were feeling her way through a force field – and then, in a matter of milliseconds, she wasn't there any more. I didn't see how it happened. I didn't see her trip and fall, there wasn't a point at which she noticed me and ducked down, as I had, to avoid being seen, but one moment she was there, and the next she had disappeared. It was ridiculous. I stopped dead and stood up straight, peering out over the thick mass of grass and wildflowers to see where she had gone, no longer concerned whether she saw me or not, but she wasn't there. It was as if the ground had opened up and swallowed her, or like one of those tricks they do in movies, when they can't think of anything better to beguile or mystify the audience: one moment, she was there, the next, she was gone, but there was no event, no transition from there to not-there, no disappearance. I looked off to the left, towards the *hytte*, half expecting her to reappear by Martin's car, or on the track just beyond, but there was nothing. I waited for a movement, or maybe a sudden peal of laughter, in the thick grass between me and the last place I'd seen her, because it wouldn't have surprised me if she had known I was there all along, and had only pretended not to see me. But nothing happened. It really was just as if she had never been there at all – and, after a moment, I decided that she hadn't. It had all been an illusion, a trick of the light that had allowed me to summon up the one person who held the key to the mystery and, obviously, I had allowed myself to be taken in, not by a girl, or a phantom, but by my own susceptibility and a confused fondness for those sad white boys that, until that moment, I hadn't known I possessed.

Mother wasn't alone in not wanting to talk about the Sigfridsson boys. Oh, it's true, people discussed the events of that summer, asking aloud how such a tragedy could have happened, but they didn't *dwell*. They made a space in their lives for these inexplicable events, but it was just enough to set the mystery down and then, with a modicum of care and of giving the boys their due, to forget about it. It wasn't the usual sort of forgetting, of course: there was always something there, at the outer limit of their awareness, the way the cemetery sits at the edge of the town, the headstones set out in ordered rows, the names and dates in gold letters, and so banished into the untellable space of recent history. The only one who didn't want to let it go was Kyrre Opdahl – the boys had been *taken*, he said; we hadn't seen the last of this; this was the *huldra*'s doing – though as far as I know, he didn't choose to air his theory to anyone else but me. He didn't say who the *huldra* was, though I think by then he had put two and two together. As for me, I thought he was just being Kyrre. Nothing he said made any sense as an explanation of what had happened, and I was still looking for answers of my own. I had seen Maia with the boys, but that could have been nothing more than a coincidence and, even if it wasn't, I was probably more concerned for her, at that point, than I was afraid of her. I had heard that, after Harald died, she had run away from home, and was out on her own somewhere, and the questions that troubled me were about the ordinary facts of her day-to-day existence. Where was she? Where did she sleep? What did she eat? What did she do for money? I had an inkling of why she had left her mother's house, but where she had actually *gone* was a mystery. I couldn't imagine anybody else offering her a bed or a meal. I couldn't imagine anyone taking her in. What I could imagine was another drowning. Hers. What I could imagine was some stupid teenage death pact, made between two impressionable boys and a lost, unloved girl, and now that two were dead, I pictured Maia floating in the Sound somewhere downshore, and a stolen boat drifting on the tide, miles away, empty, barely moving, on water that, to all appearances, was as still and unbroken as the surface of an empty mirror.

* * *

There were summers when Kyrre Opdahl's guests would be surprised by how warm it could get, up here in the frozen north. They would come with sweaters and thermal socks, expecting a cold, austere land – and they were disappointed when they found themselves walking on the shore in T-shirts and sandals, or rummaging in the freezer at the Straumsbukta store for Raspberry Ripple ice cream. For us, though, it was different. Our winters were long and dark, and we would start to feel like people under house arrest long before spring came – so when the thermometer rose to twenty or thirty degrees and the land between the shore and the meadows was spotted with gentian and *jåblom*, it became almost impossible for us to stay indoors, even at night. Sometimes, the outdoors seemed so vast and illumined, and the memory of the winter darkness was so strong, that we had to go out and walk on the shore, or wander about the meadows, filling our heads with light. To stay at home, reading a book or watching television, was like sitting in the foyer of a theatre reading the programme, while the play unfolded on a brightly lit stage, just a few yards away.

Sometimes – and sometimes it would rain for days, non-stop. Sometimes it rained so hard, I could hear the raindrops bouncing off the roof, a monotonous, yet strangely pleasant sound that lulled me, not so much to sleep as to a waking torpor not entirely dissimilar to the state meditators achieve, a state of physical suspension combined with a heightened attention to the subtlest details of colour, or sound. On those days, I would sit in my room, or on the chair on the landing for hours, doing nothing, thinking about nothing, free of intentions and unconcerned about what I was supposed to do with my life, plugged into some abstract current of attentiveness that seemed to include, not just me, but everything

105

around me. I wouldn't be listening to the rain, I wouldn't be listening or paying deliberate attention to anything, but I would find myself *included* in that sound, inseparable from it, and from everything it touched and shaped – and then, suddenly, after three or four hours of this, when nothing had altered in any noticeable way, I had to get up and go out, no matter how wet it was. It wasn't restlessness that drew me out, it wasn't impatience with the weather, it was more a feeling of being filled to overflowing, of needing to go out and dissipate some of the charge that had gathered in my hands and behind my eyes. One moment I would be sitting in a chair, with an unread book in my lap, the next I would be downstairs in my coat and boots, with no sense of having decided anything, the wind blowing in through the open door, the sweet, cold scent of the rain in my face.

That was how it was a few days after Kyrre told me about Harald: I'd sat all morning through a rain that sounded like it would never end, then I'd not been able to stand it any more and I'd pulled on a coat and headed out into the downpour and across the meadows towards the shore. I was preoccupied, I suppose, with Mother and Frank Verne, or maybe with what had happened to the Sigfridsson boys, so I didn't see Martin Crosbie on the path until the very last moment. I'd observed him going about the meadows now and then since we'd talked, but I hadn't taken much of an interest and, that day, trailing down to the shore in the thick, sweet rain, I have to confess I'd almost forgotten he even existed. So when I looked up and saw him standing there, rain dripping from his hair and running down his face, I was surprised – and I could see that it amused him, once again, to have caught me off guard. He let that amusement show, for a moment, but then he realised – or *thought* he realised – that something was wrong, and his manner changed. 'Hello,' he said – and, though I didn't really want company, I said hello back. He smiled – and I saw, in that smile, too much sympathy, too much of an assumption of fellow feeling. 'So what are you doing out in all this rain?' he said.

'I could ask you the same thing,' I said.

He smiled at that. I thought he would have liked me to be more girlish. More of a child. He wanted someone younger than him to behave accordingly, so he would know that he was the grown-up. Well, that was what I thought, then. 'Oh, I don't mind it,' he said. 'I'm almost grateful,' he said.

'Really?'

'It reminds me of home.' He smiled. 'Besides,' he said, 'I'm still not used to all this light. I thought I wouldn't notice so much, but it's completely thrown me.'

'Ah,' I said, back on familiar ground. 'I guessed you hadn't been sleeping, the last time I saw you.' I thought about the last time I had seen him. Had he been drunk, or was it just sleeplessness? Or was it a little of both? 'It's not an uncommon problem,' I said.

He seemed puzzled. 'What isn't?'

'Insomnia.'

'Oh, no,' he said. He seemed genuinely surprised by the suggestion, though it was obvious that he hadn't been sleeping well. I could see it in his eyes. 'No. It's not that. I've been sleeping, off and on, and I don't sleep that well at the best of times. But I get enough rest. It's just that –' He broke off and looked up at the sky. 'I don't know. It's so odd. This light. It wasn't that I didn't know. I was even expecting it. Only I was expecting something different.' He smiled and shook his head. 'Strange, isn't it, how you can read a description in a book, or see a film, and still be surprised by everything?'

'Everything?' I was wondering what else surprised him.

'But it's not really the light, or the place that surprises me,' he said, as if he were reading my thoughts. 'It's me. It's how I am here. Though, to be honest, I'm not really sure that I'm here at all. Maybe I'm just dreaming the whole thing . . .'

'Well, don't worry about that,' I said. 'If you were just dreaming all this, then I'd just be someone in your dream, and I can assure you, I'm quite real.'

He laughed softly. There was a hint of sadness to that laugh, a concealed memory of happier times come back to haunt him. 'That's what Alice says to Tweedledum,' he said. 'In *Alice in Wonderland*. Or is it *Through the Looking-Glass*? I always get them mixed up.'

He gave me an enquiring look and I shook my head. I knew what he meant – though it wasn't Wonderland, it was the Looking-Glass World where Alice meets Tweedledum and Tweedledee, and they show her the Red King, asleep under a Tree, and Alice cries when they tell her that she's only a sort of a thing in his dream. Which always amused me, because I knew I wouldn't have cried. Not at all. I knew I was real, just as Alice should have known that, if anything, she was the one who was dreaming it all: the Red King, the crow, those silly overgrown boys, the wood where things have no names. They were in *her* dream – and *that* was what should have troubled her. I liked those books, but I knew Wonderland best, and I liked it better than all that stuff with chessmen and things reflected. Reading those books, having Mother explain things to me, listening to the words over and over again, was how I learned English. Mother had read *Alice in Wonderland* to me when I was quite little, from a book she'd bought in England, an old illustrated edition published by Ward, Lock & Co. in 1916, and I'd made her repeat it again and again, learning whole sections by heart and repeating them back to her, much to her delight. It's been years since I even looked at those books. All those books from childhood, stories from all around the world, fairy tales from France and Spain, the battle of the Kauravas and the Pandavas from a beautifully illustrated copy of the Mahabharata that Mother had picked up in a second-hand bookshop in Lincoln, the old Norwegian legends of trolls and ghostly women – it's been years, but I still remember the pictures in that old *Alice* book, all those manic animals in fancy dress. Father William in his blue jersey and fishing boots, balancing a surprised-looking eel on the end of his nose, the frog footmen in their pink frock coats and three-cornered hats. I remembered it all, and I wanted to say so, but I wasn't sure I really did understand what Martin Crosbie meant, because those *Alice* stories never made me feel dreamlike or insubstantial. Quite the opposite, in fact.

'Well,' I said, looking up in to the rain. 'I don't think *this* is a dream.' I realised how lame that sounded, but I didn't know what else to say: at one level, it seemed that it ought to be a game, all this talk of dreams and disappearances, but at that moment, it was hard to tell.

He nodded, but he didn't say anything. Instead, he turned and looked out towards the Sound, with an odd quizzical smile. The thought struck me, then, that he was right, and his problem wasn't insomnia. His problem, whatever it was, had nothing to do with the light, or this place, or how far he was from home. He'd had it before he came here, and I suddenly realised that he knew more about its true nature than he pretended. 'I'm sure you're right,' he said. 'But I can't help thinking it would take just the barest exertion to melt away. To simply walk out into this meadow and vanish into thin air.'

109

'Yes,' I said. The word 'exertion' bothered me. 'But why would you want to?'

He turned back to me – and at the same time, he switched into another mode, a kind of patient normality. 'I'm sorry,' he said. 'I'm talking nonsense. That's something I do quite often.'

I shook my head. He was putting a brave face on it, but I could see that he was spooked. He was embarrassed, of course he was, but there was something at his back and, because he could feel it, he wanted to talk it into submission. I knew that feeling, though for me it was probably friendlier than it was for him. Mostly it had to do with listening – in a hard wind, you can hear all kinds of things out on the meadows, or along the shore. Voices calling from somewhere close by; odd, fleeting animal sounds in the grass; a baby crying just a stone's throw away, in some drift of sand or shadow that you would never find, no matter how long or how hard you looked. I would hear those noises for days on end; sometimes they would seep into the house and wake me suddenly from the half-sleep of these white nights – but they were strongest down on the shore, where the *hytte* sits out on its spit of land jutting into the Sound, a place better suited to terns and oyster-catchers than to human habitation. I could imagine that he'd been hearing all kinds of things down there, in the wind, and in the stillness, when he couldn't sleep and, at three o'clock, in the summer light, he'd managed to convince himself that he would never sleep again. There would have been times when he really believed that what he was hearing was some terrible creature with a life and intentions of its own; even on those bright, clear nights, nights that were always so idyllic in the tourist brochures, there would be odd rustlings, a far whistle, an elusive singing out across the water. I've lived here all my life and I'm sure, now, that I will never leave, but they still catch me out from time to time. I still have nights when I believe, in my bones, that I will never sleep again, and I still hear phantoms at the window, singing me out to perdition. I don't know what I would do without them. 'You have to take care,' I said. 'Really. These white nights take some getting used to.'

He let out a short, hard laugh, then he shook his head. 'Oh, I'm fine,' he said. 'Really. I've always been a little –' He thought for a moment, then gave up on whatever he was about to say. He smiled. 'Don't you ever get bored, here?' he said. 'There can't be that much to do –'

'I'm not bored,' I said.

'So what *is* there to do?' He brightened – a forced, wholly artificial brightness. 'I suppose you've got a boyfriend tucked away somewhere?'

I shook my head. 'No,' I said. 'Have you?'

He laughed – and now the brightness seemed almost real. 'Well,' he said. 'We can't just stand here getting all wet. Why don't you come back to the house and have some tea?'

'I can't,' I said. 'Maybe another time.'

'Oh, please do,' he said. 'I've got cake.' He was still smiling, but there was a seriousness in his eyes that made me think twice about refusing him again. I didn't want to have tea with him, of course. At that moment, though, I wasn't sure what I thought about him: there was some dislike, I know, but I can't deny that I was beginning to wonder if he might not be a worthwhile subject for observation after all. I think, even then, that I sensed something in his character – an absurd flaw, or some extreme of desire or sentimentality that he was only able to conceal because it was so unlikely – and that interested me. Interested me enough, in fact, that I was beginning to soften,

111

not to him, but to a possible story. 'Well,' I said, 'I couldn't stay long . . .'

'That's fine,' he said – and it was obvious that he was genuinely pleased that I had accepted his invitation. He even allowed himself a soft, happy laugh, but I could see that, behind the laugh, he felt something else. Loneliness, perhaps, or fear – and though I can't explain it, what struck me then, as he turned away and started back towards his little house in the shore, what struck me like a premonition, was that something bad was going to happen to him and that, in some dark part of his mind, he already knew it was coming.

True to his word, Martin Crosbie had cake. He had short-bread, too, which he had brought from England, and a box of petits fours, all set out on the table, as if he had been expecting someone all along – and maybe he had. Maybe we hadn't met by accident, after all. Maybe he had seen me coming down the track and hurried out into the rain to meet me. But why? Why go to such lengths to get me to come and have tea with him? As we stood in the doorway of the *hytte*, shaking off our wet coats, I could see through to the tea things all set out on the table by the window, and I remember thinking that, if Martin Crosbie was the kind of person who didn't enjoy his own company, he had made a big mistake coming to Kvaløya – which only goes to show what an innocent I was. Because I felt sorry for him, then, a little. He was so keen to be a good host, so thoughtful and attentive, as we had our tea and sat, he presumably feeling as damp and uncomfortable as I did. The trouble was that, once we were inside, he didn't seem to have much to say for himself and, for a long moment, we just sat there in silence, trying not to feel awkward. Then, casting around for something to talk about, I noticed a book on the table. It was the same play by Ibsen that he had been reading before, when he had pretended to be reading T. S. Eliot, but it wasn't the same edition. This one was in Norwegian. *En folkefiende.*

I looked at him in surprise. 'So you speak Norwegian?'

He seemed puzzled for a moment, then he noticed that I was looking at the book. 'Oh,' he said. 'That.' He smiled – apologetically, I thought. 'I'm trying to learn,' he said.

'Trying to learn?' It was my turn to smile. 'From Ibsen?'

'Why not? He's the master, isn't he?'

'Yes,' I said. 'But *En folkefiende* is not the best place to start.' We had studied the play in school and, though the language was clear enough, it was too difficult for a beginner. 'Haven't you got something easier?'

He shook his head slowly. 'I've got *Rosmersholm* and this,' he said. 'I bought them in a shop near a glacier, somewhere in the western fjords.' He reached over and picked up the book. 'I've read it in English,' he said. 'Now I'm trying to follow it in the original. I read it, then I write out the words, and then . . .' He opened the book to the final pages and held it up, like an actor in a run-through. '*Sagen er den,*' he said, '*ser I, at den staerkeste mand i verden, det er han, som står mest alene.*' He looked at me, not trying to hide the fact that he was rather pleased with himself. His accent was atrocious. 'Now: that means – "So you see, the strongest man in the world" – which is him, Stockmann – "is the one who stands most alone."' He smiled. 'Right?'

I nodded to show that I was impressed – and I was, in a way. It was the strangest approach to learning a language that I had ever come across, but I don't think he was very inter-ested in actually learning to speak Norwegian. He was playing a game, filling the time – and what better way to fill the time

113

than this clumsy and painstaking process? 'So,' I said, 'you liked *En folkefiende*. I suppose you must have done, since you got all the way to the end. What about *Rosmersholm*?'

He didn't answer for a moment, then he snapped the book shut and sat back in his chair. 'I haven't started that yet,' he said. 'Is it good?'

'I like it,' I said. 'But my favourite is *Vildanden*.'

His face lit up. '*The Wild Duck*,' he said.

'*Akkurat!*' I said. 'Do you know it?'

'I've read it,' he said. 'But only in English.'

I laughed. He seemed to think that reading something in English didn't quite count, whereas working word by word through the original and cobbling together a version of it in his head did – bad pronunciations, misunderstandings and all.

'I'll get that one next,' he said. 'I'm sure it's the best, if it's your favourite.' He was happy now, it seemed, though there was an odd quality to his pleasure, a faint, but discernible feverishness. He looked around. 'Would you like some more tea?' he said.

I shook my head.

'Another cake?'

'I'm fine, really.'

He stood up and walked over to the fridge in the little kitchen area near the door. 'I have Solo,' he said. 'If you'd prefer.'

I didn't say anything, or not right away. For a while there, while we were talking, I had forgotten the premonition I'd had earlier, but now it came back to me and I felt even more strongly that something bad was going to happen. Only I didn't know what and, for a moment, I wasn't sure if this bad thing would happen to Martin Crosbie, or if he would do something bad to someone else – someone as innocent or as desperate as he was. He opened the fridge and took out a bottle. 'Would you like some Solo?' he said.

I didn't like Solo much – it was too sweet – but for reasons that I suspect had something to do with pity, and maybe something to do with fear, I didn't want to refuse him. Though it wasn't him I was afraid of: I was afraid *for* him because, at that moment, I saw in his face a desperation that was utterly unexpected. A desperation – and a fear, too. He was afraid of something – only I didn't know what and maybe he didn't know either. I nodded. 'Thanks,' I said. 'That would be nice.'

The second letter came the next morning, while I was out of the house. Frank Verne was gone by then. He'd stayed that one night, then he and Mother had met one more time in Tromsø before he went back to wherever he belonged, to write his piece. I wondered how Mother would take that, but I needn't have bothered. Within hours, she was in the studio, totally absorbed in her work, for all the world as if nothing had ever happened. Of course, I came to understand later that I was mistaken when I concluded that she was unaffected by Frank Verne's departure, but I didn't know that then. I always took Mother at face value – and I think, at the time, I felt that I had a right to do so, because I was her daughter. It was an absurd position to take, but it didn't seem so to me, because I wasn't aware of taking it. Nevertheless, I have to admit that I was more concerned about Kyrre Opdahl than I was about Mother and, that morning, I had gone down to his house further along the shore, to return an old children's book he had lent me. I'd hung on to it for months, not actually reading it but looking at the pictures, which showed someone's idea of a perfect old-fashioned Christmas, complete with candles

115

and holly wreaths and bowler-hatted lamplighters on cold, grey streets, just before the snow. It was a Danish book, *Peters Jul*, from the middle of the nineteenth century; Kyrre had seen me leafing through it one day at his house and insisted I take it home.

'Don't bother with the rhymes,' he'd said. 'They're nothing. But the pictures are worth a look.' He liked to lend me picture books, because he knew how much I loved those old illustrations, but also because he wanted me to take an interest in art for its own sake, and not just because I was a painter's daughter. 'You have a good eye for these things,' he would say, when he handed over some old book or print he'd found rummaging through one of the big blanket boxes he kept in his spare room. 'Have a look and let me know what you think.'

That spare room had been special to me ever since I was a little girl. It was dim and large and full of strange treasures, like the secret cave in an old enchanter's tale. Kyrre Opdahl had lived alone for a long time and, over the years, he had collected a vast array of strange and sometimes beautiful junk – old engine parts and the inner workings of clocks, naturally, but that was just the beginning. In that spare room, where I was free to rummage whenever I felt like it, I would find boxes full of ancient Christmas decorations, hand-painted or stubbled with fat tinsel; there were timetables for long-forgotten ferries, jars of nails and odd nuts and bolts that he couldn't bring himself to throw away, tangles of copper wire and old fishing line, shoeboxes crammed full of doll and puppet heads from when he used to make and repair toys. There were glass floats and tin boxes full of fishhooks and lures; in one battered old blanket box there was a pile of sun-bleached albums and faded envelopes crammed with old newspaper clippings and grainy black-and-white snapshots of people I had never seen before, people who probably corresponded to the names in the old graveyard in Tromsø, ancient faces so deeply lined and weathered that it was hard to know if they were women or men, stiff boys looking out to the camera in their Sunday best, trying to look blasé, pretty girls about to grow into older sisters or aunts. Best of all, there was the long shelf of children's books, some of them rare and probably valuable, others foxed and tattered. It didn't matter what state they were in: they sat side by side, and Kyrre cared for them equally, though not so much that he had ever minded my taking one away for weeks or months at a time, even when I was too young to know how important to him they were. *Peters Jul* wasn't the best book he had lent me, by any means, but it did contain a beautiful grey-and-white street scene of snow-covered roofs and church spires in which tiny figures went about their daily business in a field of perfect whiteness, untroubled, isolate and immune to the passing of time. That was what I liked about those books, I think: there was no time in them.

'Ah,' he said, when he saw the book in my hand, making a show of being surprised that I'd remembered to return it. I knew he never thought of these books as loans, but I made a point of bringing them back in perfect condition. '*Peters Jul.*' He took it from me and held it at arm's length, studying the cover with an affectionate smile. 'Did you like this one?' He perched his glasses on the end of his nose, like some comedy grandfather in an old film, then opened the book and started to read.

'Det er den danske moder,
hvem bagen bliver sendt;
og, hvorom vi vil bede,
det ved hun vist omtrent –'

He broke off. 'Do you remember this?' he said.

> *'Nar hun blot den vil vise*
> *sin datter og sin pog,*
> *da bliver rigt og proegtigt –'*

I shook my head. 'But you told me not to read the rhymes,'
I said.

'Did I?'

'Yes.'

He peered over the top of the book solemnly. 'And, of
course, you did exactly what you were told to do,' he said.
'As always.'

I smiled. 'Of course,' I said. 'You know I always take your
advice.'

He pursed his lips, then he continued reading.

> *'Hvert billed I vor bog,*
> *og, dersom hun vil laese*
> *den simple, ringe sang,*
> *ja, sa far verset vinger*
> *ved hendes stemmes klang;*
> *thi end bestadnig gaelder*
> *de gamle, gyldne ord –*

'I remember your mother reading this to you,' he said.
'When you were very little.'

'No you don't,' I said.

It came out a little too sharply, but he didn't seem to mind.
Instead, he just smiled. 'Oh yes,' he said. 'When you first
came here. She always had a beautiful voice, your mother.'

I really didn't believe him. I had no memory of Mother

reading children's books to me, other than English classics like Lewis Carroll and Dickens's Christmas novels. When she read in Norwegian, she had always chosen grown-up stories of Vikings and Greek myths and legends from her own library. She had never babied me and she had never read homely old verses about mothers and their babies. 'Why would she be reading to me from a Danish book?' I said. 'This is far too sentimental for her –'

He closed the book suddenly with a snap. '*Akkurat*,' he said. 'But she read them, just the same.'

I was tempted to ask him, then, about what had happened between them when he stopped coming to the house so often, but he'd suddenly become wrapped up in some thought that had passed through his mind. Some thought, or some memory. 'What is it?' I said.

He looked at me. 'Hm?'

'You were remembering something . . .'

'Ah.' He smiled and shook his head. Not sadly. Not at all sadly, I thought. 'No, I wasn't remembering anything specific,' he said. 'It's just that . . . I always think of her, when I read these verses.' His eyes were bright, and he looked happier than I had seen him in a long time. Happy, like some old believer, coming from church of a Sunday morning. 'Those old, golden words carry on still, even now.'

I shook my head. 'You told me not to read the words,' I said – and I immediately felt ashamed, for some reason, as if I had uttered some kind of obscure blasphemy.

He wasn't listening though. 'I remember it like it was yesterday,' he said – and I saw that he was far away, thinking of Mother, in another time and place, but I had missed my chance and now I wasn't even sure I wanted to know anyhow.

* * *

When I got home, there was a small, very neat parcel on the kitchen table. It was wrapped in the old-fashioned way, with thick, textured brown paper and white string. It contained a book: *Walking to Patagonia*, by Arild Frederiksen. It wasn't inscribed, but an envelope had been tucked inside, between the cover and the plain dark endpapers. Inside was a single typed sheet from Kate Thompson, exactly like the letter that had gone before, the one difference being that this one contained a request – a request so carefully expressed that it seemed not to be asking for anything at all – that I would consider visiting this same Arild Frederiksen, who was still in hospital. *I know this can't be easy*, Kate Thompson wrote, *and I can't expect you to just drop everything and come right away, but it would make all the difference to him if you could come soon. I am happy to arrange somewhere for you to stay and I'll pay the airfare, of course, but if you could find the time to come, it would mean so, so much to him.*

I put the letter back in its envelope and slid it back into the book. I wasn't really surprised, I suppose. I had known, from the first, that this was all leading to something, and what else would that be, if not a meeting? What did surprise me was that the request had come so soon, especially considering the fact that I hadn't replied to Kate Thompson's earlier letter. What surprised me even more was her assumption that I would *want* to see my father, that I would be curious, at the very least, to know what he was like. Yet I wasn't curious. Not in the least. I didn't want to know anything about him. I turned the book over in my hands. It was a heavy, cloth-bound hardback, with a wrap-around colour illustration on the dust jacket showing a flock of birds – I couldn't make out what they were – over a wide, empty landscape and, on the inside back cover, there was a photograph of the author in black and white. Arild

Frederiksen was, or had once been, a boyish, overconfident man of around thirty, his dirty-blond hair rather long and brushed back from his face in a style that reminded me of pictures I had seen of French intellectuals in the 1960s. He wasn't smiling, but he wasn't serious either. He looked like someone who was trying not to laugh at the idea of posing for an author's photograph. But none of that mattered, compared to the very obvious family resemblance I saw in his face to the face I saw every day in the mirror, and I knew, with a little rush of horror, that there could be no doubting that he was my father. No doubting it at all, and that was what made me take the letter to Mother.

Mother was in the garden. She had been painting continuously since Frank Verne's departure; now, she was taking a break in the long rock garden to the south side of the house, picking out weeds, enjoying the sun, a woman utterly at ease in her world. The rock garden was her favourite place, perhaps because it had taken so much time and effort to build. This was where the most beautiful flowers grew, in a planting scheme that ran from warm, sulphur yellows and golds through the orange of Turkish poppies and rock roses to fire-red and purple morning glories. Some years, the wind would ruin the effect, and there would be nothing but wisps and ghosts of colour in the deeper recesses between the limestone slabs, but that year it was almost perfect, in spite of Mother having been so busy in the studio. These days, now that her tastes have changed and she has come round to Harstad's way of thinking, there are more alpines here, tiny saxifrages from high scree country and Arctic poppies perched in cool niches among the rocks, but the odd, self-seeded exotic still reappears from time to time, clinging on for a few weeks before it melts back into the stones, never to be seen again. Seed can sit dormant for years in this soil, waiting for the right conditions to prosper, and it's something Mother and I do together, nowadays, watching for surprise blossoms and pointing them out to one another over breakfast or morning coffee. That's a big change from how things were before, and I couldn't say exactly when it began but, looking back, I can't help thinking that it has something to do with the events of that summer. We came together that year, even when it seemed like we were losing everything. Frank Verne. Kyrre Opdahl. The suitors. What others saw, in me, as innocence, and what they saw, in her, as beauty. To my mind, of course, she still is as beautiful as ever, but now that she's a real recluse, it's beauty in a different form. A private beauty, not unlike what I choose to think of as my private form of achieved innocence.

I found a large, wide boulder at one end of a series of rocks that ran east to west through the garden and down to the carved stones by the birch wood, like a mountain range in miniature. That was the warmest spot in the garden and I often sat out there, especially on days like this, when it was warm after rain and that sweet water and loam scent was in the air. Mother was moving back and forth among the rocks, digging weeds from the gravel and pausing every now and then to nip out a dead flower head. She was wearing a big floppy sun hat that looked like it had been handed down for generations from mother to daughter – which was another illusion, I know, because I'd been with her when she bought it, in a fancy shop in London, on a trip she had arranged for my twelfth birthday. But then, that was what always happened with anything Mother possessed. Things aged when she used them: clothes, books, jewellery, even her brushes and tubes of paint developed a shadowy, straw-coloured patina, like objects left out in the sun. It was one of the minor miracles that happened around her, miracles that nobody ever saw but me. She would borrow one of my shirts for a day, and it would come back in altered form, that film of gold and time ingrained in the fabric. A glossy art book would arrive in the mail smelling of new paper and gum and a week later I would find it on the kitchen table, subtly tempered and looking as if it had been there for decades.

I didn't know how to lead into the conversation I needed to have, so I did what I usually did back then: I sat a moment, wrapped in meaningful silence, then plunged straight in. Mother was used to it, of course. Mostly, she found it amusing, which was something I also knew, but even that made no difference. I do it still, on occasion. I'm just no good at beating around the bush. 'Do you remember, years ago,' I said, 'when I asked you if you loved my father?'

She looked up from her work and gave me a wary smile. 'I do,' she said. She seemed about to say more, so I waited a moment, but she didn't speak. She did, however, straighten up and then, with too deliberate, almost exaggerated, care, set her trowel down on the nearest large rock. Then, still smiling, she gave me her full attention. It was an encouraging smile now, though perhaps not inviting. She was ready to hear what I wanted to say, and she wanted me to see that, though I could also see that she would have preferred to let the matter go.

'You said it wasn't something you thought about,' I said. She nodded. 'It wasn't.'

'I didn't understand what that meant,' I said, as if I were asking her to re-explain a maths problem I hadn't quite grasped.

'Well . . . I hadn't thought about it, until you asked. Though if I had, the answer would have been no.'

'You didn't love him?'

'No,' she said. 'I didn't love him. But I really hadn't thought about it before you asked.'

'Then, did you ever love anyone? I mean . . .'

She laughed. 'I know what you mean,' she said. 'And the answer is yes, once upon a time, a very, very long time ago, I did.' She leaned in closer and I thought she was about to tell me the whole story, in all its sad, or beautiful, detail – and once again, I waited, but she didn't say another word.

'So what happened?' I said, after a moment.

'Nothing, really,' she said. 'It didn't last very long, and I didn't get the chance to find out if it was what I thought . . .' She smiled again, then she stood up. 'I was just about to stop for a coffee,' she said. 'Would you like some?'

I nodded. I knew she wasn't being evasive – on the contrary, she wanted me to see that she was taking this conversation seriously and giving it its proper due, rather than rushing into it, as I had done. This was to be a serious discussion, and though she didn't want to have it, she knew that I did. Maybe she needed a moment to think, or to consider her own feelings a little; I didn't know because I had no idea what she thought or felt, or even if she thought or felt anything at all when she wasn't working. She took off her hat and looked up at the sky. 'It's going to stay fair all day,' she said; then she led me into the kitchen and put the kettle on.

The word most often used when people talked about Mother in those days was *beautiful*. And it's true: even though I saw her every day, I could still be surprised by how beautiful she was, even when she hadn't slept for days. She looked tired that day, but it didn't matter. She wasn't beautiful the way women in magazines are beautiful, she had the kind of beauty that fatigue only exaggerates, and it was obvious then, even

124

to me, that she would only get more beautiful as she got older. Yet, even though she knew how others saw her, even though every magazine article about her mentioned how beautiful she was, she never thought about it. She never had the air of being looked at that some beautiful people have; she never stopped to see herself in a mirror, or in the regard of those who admired her so openly. There was no self-portrait among her works; as far as I knew, she had never attempted one. She had shelf after shelf of books about portraiture, and many of her favourite painters – Titian, Rembrandt, even Sohlberg – had painted themselves over and over again, but I don't think the idea had even once occurred to her.

She didn't say anything until the coffee was safely brewing. Then she set two cups down on the table, put the coffee pot exactly halfway between them and sat down. She looked out of the window, smiled at something she saw there, in the garden, or perhaps out across the Sound, then she turned to look at me. 'This is about the mail, I suppose,' she said. There was no emotion in her voice; she was perfectly matter-of-fact; but I didn't read this as indifference. Rather, I knew she wanted to keep everything calm and put me at ease. She wanted me to know that she didn't *mind* – about my keeping the first letter secret, and about anything that might happen because of what I had read there – not that she didn't *care*. She picked up the coffee pot and began to pour, serving me first, then herself. 'What does he want?' she said, rather too quietly.

'It's not from *him*,' I said. 'It came from a woman called Kate Thompson. I think she lives with him.'

'Ah.'

'She sent me a gift –'

'What kind of gift?'

I shook my head. 'A book,' I said. I didn't say it was one

125

of Arild Frederiksen's books, but I'm sure she guessed as much. She leaned forward, placed her elbows on the table and, cradling her coffee cup in both hands, brought it to her lips. 'Now she wants me to go and visit him,' I said, all of a sudden, though I hadn't intended to. I hadn't wanted to rush things – though I could see, immediately, that she had guessed this was coming. 'He's sick, apparently. He's in a hospital. She thinks it will help . . . if I visit.'

'I see,' she said. 'And what did you say?'

'I didn't say anything,' I said. I was a little shocked that she thought I had replied to Kate Thompson's letter without discussing it with her – because it seemed all right, or almost all right, to keep the arrival of the letters a secret, but, for me at least, to have responded in secret *would* have been a betrayal. 'I haven't written back,' I said. 'I didn't want to –'

She inclined her head slightly. 'Yes,' she said, breaking in to show she understood, then she gave me a fond, and surprisingly tender, look. There was something like pity in that look, though it wasn't quite pity – yet it wasn't *just* fondness, either. 'But you know you have to say *something*,' she said. 'It would be rude not to.'

I laughed. 'Rude?' I said.

'Yes,' she said. 'Whatever you decide, you can't just ignore this –'

'I don't see why not,' I said. 'He ignored me for eighteen years, didn't he?'

She didn't say anything to that. She looked away, as if giving me time to collect myself – though I wasn't annoyed, and I didn't think I'd sounded upset when I spoke. I might have done, but I hadn't intended to because, as far as I could see, I had only stated an obvious fact. She put the cup down and sat back in her chair again. 'He's not the one who asked, from the sound of it,' she said, after a moment's pause. 'It was this woman, this Kate Thompson, who asked.'

'Yes,' I said. 'But he's the one who's sick —'

'Where is this hospital?'

'In England.'

'Is that where he lives now?'

'Yes,' I said. 'But —'

'That surprises me,' she said. 'I didn't think he'd end up living *there*.' She gave the matter a moment's consideration, then she looked up. 'It's up to you,' she said. 'If you want to go to England, that's fine —'

'I don't want to go —'

'But it might be a good thing,' she continued, not ignoring me, but talking around me, a little too gently, I thought — and I could see that she had already made up her mind, not that I should go, necessarily, but that she should do nothing to discourage me. It seemed not to have entered into her calculations that I wouldn't want to have anything to do with this sick father. Having concealed everything about him, other than the merest facts of his existence and their brief time together, now she was almost telling me to fly off to have some supposedly meaningful encounter with a complete stranger, because she assumed that my lack of interest in such a proposition was feigned to protect her feelings.

'How could it be a good thing?' I said. I was upset now, and I couldn't hide the fact. 'I don't even know him — and I don't want to know him —'

'He's sick,' she said.

'I don't care,' I said. 'He's *nothing* to me. Nothing at all.'

Mother put her hand on my arm. 'It's all right,' she said. 'Don't be upset —'

'I'm not. It's just —'

'Shh.' She patted my wrist gently. 'It's all right. I was just . . .' She thought for a moment, then she took her hand away. 'If you don't want to go, that's fine,' she said. 'But I think you had better write to his friend and say so.' She leaned back and away from me. 'For your own sake,' she said. 'If not for hers.'

We drifted for the rest of that afternoon, avoiding our unfinished business – then Mother came and stood in my doorway, obviously intending just to make a single and quite passing point of order before moving on. I was looking through a book on the history of the Russian Revolution when she appeared, which struck her, no doubt, as incongruous – the book was open at a large, grainy photograph of ten or so dead Bolsheviks lying stiff and half upright in the snow – and she hovered a moment, possibly waiting for me to close the book and give her my full attention, before she spoke. 'I wasn't trying to say –' She broke off and considered for a moment. 'You don't have to go, of course you don't. It's your business, after all. All I wanted to say was that, if you do want to, that would be fine with me.'

'It's not just *my* business,' I said. 'It concerns both of us, I'd have said.'

'Well, yes. It concerns me that he wants to see you,' she said quietly.

'We don't know that he does want to see me,' I said. 'It might be all her idea. After all, he wasn't the one who wrote.'

'Well,' she said, 'it doesn't matter whose idea it was. What I don't want is for anybody to come *here*.'

I sighed. I was beginning to find it difficult to hide my exasperation with her. 'She doesn't want to bring him here,' I said. 'He's in hospital. From the sound of it, he isn't well enough to travel.'

'Are you sure about that? Did she say so?'

I wasn't sure, not completely, because Kate Thompson hadn't given any details about this illness. But I didn't want to tell Mother that, so I didn't say anything. I just shrugged and turned back to my book of Russian photographs. Behind the row of dead, a group of eight or ten men, in similar clothes – leather coats, peaked caps, carbines slung over their shoulders – stood posing for the camera and I wondered whether these were the ones who did the killing, or if they were other Bolsheviks, who had come across their dead comrades after some massacre.

'Are you really surprised that he wants to meet his daughter, after all this time?'

'He didn't want to see me before,' I said. 'So what's different now?'

Mother shook her head, though whether she was disagreeing with what I had said about my father or not, I couldn't tell. 'He's ill,' she said. She glanced around the room as if searching for something. I could see it was nothing in particular, no single item of furniture, no single picture on the wall or book on the shelves, but an overall effect, an atmosphere. A sensation of home, of belonging. Mother loved our house – the house she had made – more than anything else in the world. It was as important to her as her work, it was an extension of her work, that part of her art which included everything her art excluded, her daughter, her friends, her possessions. In her studio she became a homeless solitary, she had said so often enough, and I knew it was true. All other concerns had to be set aside when she went to work, every connection with the outside world had to be broken. In a real sense, she became nobody when she was alone in that inner world. She turned towards the window and, as she did, the light from the Sound

129

fell across her face and she seemed to have found what she was looking for. Then she turned back to me and gave me a look of quiet, immovable affection – and that look calmed me immediately. For a moment I didn't care if I went to see my father or not. 'You should go,' Mother said, finally. 'Get to know something about him. Not for his sake, but for yours.'

'You said that already.'

'Yes,' she said. 'And it's true.'

'It doesn't matter to me,' I said – but I could see that she thought I was lying.

Mother shook her head. 'You shouldn't imagine that your father ran off and left us,' she said.

I was offended by that – though it was exactly what I was imagining. 'I don't,' I said.

'Because he didn't.'

'Oh?' I looked at her. 'Then what *did* he do?'

She studied my face and I could see that she was trying to make out, once and for all, if I was as upset or confused by all this as she had first thought. I wasn't, though. I couldn't have cared less and I needed her to know that. I needed her to know that I didn't *require* anybody else in my life, because I really was happy with us just as we were. I was happy on my own, and the last thing I wanted was a new-found father, least of all a bedridden one in a faraway hospital. She allowed herself a slight smile – not exactly wistful, but not quite matter-of-fact either. 'At the time,' she said, 'I am quite sure, he was trying to avoid doing something much worse.'

'Oh yes? And what was that?'

She only stayed long enough to say the words. 'Staying put,' she said. She lingered for just another moment, her face serious, so I would know that this wasn't entirely a joke, then

130

she turned away and I heard her steps retreating down the landing, towards the studio.

People used to believe that someone, or something, was watching them. Some thought it was the gods or angels, others pictured their dead ancestors, watching from beyond the grave and, in every case, they felt safer in the knowledge that they were seen. Perhaps they were being judged, but they were also being forgiven. It was a childish sensation, and some of the time they knew that, but they believed it anyway, because they wanted it to be true. They wanted to think of themselves as witnessed from some unknown vantage point: it made them feel more real. That divine gaze was meant to stand in opposition to the looks they were subjected to every day, looks that made them feel less real. They knew that they were diminished by the way other people saw them, but that didn't matter because, every day and moment by moment, they were magnified by heaven. They were wrong, of course. Nobody watches us. We are not witnessed – or not, at least, by anyone who might be inclined to forgiveness.

I don't think Martin Crosbie believed he was being watched – but then, maybe that was his problem. He was too far from what he knew, in weather and light that made him strange to himself, and I think he was beginning to feel insubstantial. That can be a blessing too, as it happens, but it wasn't for him – and I think that being so far from home made him careless with his secrets. Though, when I first started to suspect that he had a secret, I was expecting something that would allow me to understand him – and, after our strange encounter, I felt that I *wanted* to understand him. And maybe that was why I had started spying on him in the first place. I had wanted to understand him from the first, or at least to know

131

the secret he concealed, for reasons that I couldn't have explained, but must have had something to do with the fact that he seemed so lost.

On the other hand, it may be that I was only looking for a distraction. I didn't want to have to think about the letters, and I was still putting off making a decision about what to *do* with my life, now that my schooling was over. I needed something to occupy me – and spying was what I was used to. I don't think it was *just* that, though. Looking back, it strikes me that something had happened during our tea and Solo party. Something about that encounter made Martin Crosbie interesting in a way I hadn't been able to imagine before. To begin with, I had avoided him because he seemed so lost, and so very open; now I was intrigued because, *now*, I thought he had a secret. It wasn't the secret he turned out to have, as it happened, but I didn't know that then. I'm not sure I even know it for sure now. After all, he could have been anything. A sad case, a sexual pervert, a hopeless romantic. Any one, or any combination of these, would have explained what I found, two days later, at the *hytte*.

I was on my way down our path to the lower meadows when I saw him go out in his car, turning at the top of the track and heading off in the direction of Straumsbukta. He didn't see me, I was sure of that. If he had, he would have smiled, or waved, maybe even stopped the car and invited me to come along – because, no doubt, he thought we were friends now. We weren't, though. I hadn't gone out that day to find him, I hadn't even been intending to go down to the *hytte*. I was just out for a walk to pass the time. But then, seeing him raised a possibility in my mind that I hadn't considered before and, a few minutes later, feeling slightly guilty, I was standing at the door of the little summer house. I say only *slightly* guilty, because I'd assumed the door would be locked, and then that would have been that. Only, when I tried it, the door wasn't locked – and *that* was unusual. Most of the summer visitors took the same security precautions they observed in the outside world, out of habit, I suppose, or an inability to imagine a place where security wasn't necessary, so I hadn't expected to be able to get in, but once the chance was there, and feeling quite certain that Martin Crosbie wouldn't be back for a while, I opened the door and slipped inside. And though I had felt slightly guilty before I tried the lock, I wasn't feeling guilty at all now, just curious to see what I would find. Which meant, I realise now, that I was expecting to find *something* interesting. A clue, a sign; not the whole story perhaps, but some hint as to Martin Crosbie's secret.

Inside, the place was clean and tidy, just as it had been two days earlier. That had surprised me, then, and it surprised me again now, because I would have expected Martin Crosbie to be messy, even chaotic, in his domestic life. I couldn't have said why I thought that, though, other than that he'd struck me as disorderly in some vague way, a man who didn't quite know what he was doing, or even thinking – and that was odd, because all the evidence pointed in the other direction. He'd come well prepared on the first day, his car packed with everything he might need for a long stay in a place like this and, looking around now, what struck me immediately was that this *hytte* was inhabited by someone with a neat, simple, almost monastic approach to life. No dirty dishes in the sink, or spilled food around the cooker, no empty bottles and glasses rimmed with foam on the table, no piles of papers or unread newspapers on the floor. The only evidence of occupancy, in fact, was the pot plant on the table and – something I hadn't noticed on my last visit – a computer.

A computer. For no good reason that surprised me too, and I realised that I knew almost nothing about this man. What he did, where he came from, whether he was married or attached in some other way – I knew none of the basic facts that even the most casual conversationalist would pick up in the first five minutes at a party. There I was, a spy in his home from home, and I didn't know the first thing about him, other than his taste in books and his bizarre approach to language learning. I walked over to the computer and switched it on. I supposed that it would be locked, that I wouldn't be able to see anything without a password, but it was worth a try – and though it did come up with a password prompt, it simply let me in when I hit the return key. The wallpaper was an image of a woodland scene in autumn, leafy, red and gold, reassuring. The usual icons came up, along with a couple of work folders labelled 'temp' and 'pics'. I sat down and clicked on temp, but it was empty; then I clicked on pics and a long list of filenames came up. When I double-clicked on the first of them, it went to full-screen.

It was a photograph of a girl in a white shirt or blouse and a pleated skirt, maybe my age, maybe a little younger. She wasn't posing for the camera, it wasn't a family snapshot or anything like that, and I knew, immediately, that it had been taken without her knowledge. It was a good-quality image – very sharp, with nothing to suggest it had been taken through a zoom lens from some great distance, but there was something about it that made me feel quite certain that she didn't know what was going on. She just looked too natural, too preoccupied with something off to the right, just out of frame. She was very pretty, with dark brown hair cut in a bob to emphasise her slender, rather elegant neck. From the background, I would have guessed that she was in a park, or a public garden, and I was immediately convinced, not only that she didn't know she was being photographed, but also that she was a complete stranger to Martin Crosbie, someone he'd seen and captured in passing. Which made *him* a spy, just like me.

Or did it? I closed the file and went to the next one, and there she was again, in a different place, in different clothes, and the shot after that was different again – and all of a sudden, I knew that he wasn't like me at all. He wasn't like me because this girl wasn't an object of observation to him, she was an object of desire. I opened one file after another and found her in various places, various poses – and then, about a dozen files further down the list, a new girl appeared, someone a little younger, with light, almost blonde hair and a very pale, rather haunted-looking face. I looked at her for a while, then I stopped – there were over two hundred pictures in the folder and I was quite sure they were all of girls like the ones I had seen, girls between the ages of fourteen and twenty who had been caught unawares by Martin Crosbie's camera while they were walking in the park, or going home from school, girls in sports clothes and uniforms, blondes, brunettes, redheads, girls who were thinking of someone or something else when Martin Crosbie captured a single moment of their existence and added it to his library of secret pictures. They weren't indecent, they weren't criminal, but they were a form of theft nonetheless. This was *theft*, not spying, because these innocent-looking photographs were intended to steal something from those girls and, even if they didn't succeed – and to Martin Crosbie, success must have been out of the question, because to succeed would have meant bringing this pursuit to an end – their intent was clear.

And then it came to me how foolish I was being. How

innocent. For, though I had never seen Martin Crosbie with a camera, I had felt watched, sometimes, and I had seen the way he looked at me. The way he joked, the way he tried to charm. The way he insinuated. This computer contained hundreds of images, labelled only with strings of digits and letters, but I assumed the most recent would be at the end of the list and I scrolled down to there, to the very last image, and opened it. Then I opened the next-to-last file, and the one before that, and then onwards, backtracking through until I saw a face other than my own. There were eight images of me, most of them apparently taken on the same, slightly over-cast day. In each of them I was wearing my grey sweater, and I had my hair up in a ponytail. The pictures had been taken with obvious care and attention and – there was no mistaking it – with that same longing, that same desire to capture some intimate detail that would make me *his*, just as he had made those other girls his, for a second or two, or maybe longer, when he looked at them again, later, in private. *In private.* That thought was unbearable – and almost before I knew what I was doing, for my own sake and for all those other girls in Martin Crosbie's secret folder, I deleted, first one file, then the next, and then the one before that until the folder was empty. I deleted them one by one, slowly and calmly, like someone doing a routine job that they didn't mind but didn't much like either, then I emptied the Trash, so he wouldn't be able to recover anything. Or not easily, anyhow. I knew, even then, that nothing can ever be completely erased from a computer hard disk, and I had to assume that he'd created backups, but I wasn't deleting the files for deletion's sake, I was sending their owner a message. All the time, I felt quite calm, quite in control of myself, and it wasn't until I was finished that I realised that I was crying, big, unseemly tears rolling down my face and dripping on to the keyboard, where they rested a moment, glistening, before bleeding away between the letters. I stood up, then I mopped my eyes and stood a moment, gazing out over Malangen. There was no sound, no movement out upon the water – not at first. Then I saw the terns, first one, then another, hovering over the tide, watching for signs of life. I closed my eyes. I tried to tell myself that nothing I had seen was criminal, or even sexual, and that it really wasn't personal to me. He hadn't touched me physically, it was just pictures. He hadn't betrayed me, because I barely knew him, and his sad little secret didn't matter to me one way or the other. That was what I told myself and what I tried to make myself believe before I turned round and ran out of the *hytte*, leaving the door wide open, so Martin Crosbie would know someone had been there while he was out, and that his secret wasn't a secret any more.

The days that followed were dull and overcast. The land was very still and the sky was a cool, washed grey, so it felt as if summer might end at any moment. Still, it wasn't cold, and the rain went over pretty fast, which made for ideal wandering conditions. On days like that, people usually didn't opt for strolls on the beach or through the meadows; instead, they visited friends and sat around their kitchen tables, drinking coffee and talking. Now that Frank Verne was gone and the weather had changed, Mother barely showed her face. When she did come out, for meals or coffee, she didn't talk about my father, or the letters, she just did what she had to do, in near silence, and went back to work. Not that I minded. I had finally given up worrying about what I was going to do with myself – all of a sudden, my supposed future felt like a not very good trick that I had been taken in by for far too long – and I was settling into a long, solitary summer of watching the terns come and go, or sitting on the landing with a book or a pair of binoculars, while the world slipped by around me. I did all I could not to think about Martin Crosbie – though, looking back, I can see that this change was linked in some way to what I had discovered about him. Of course, I kept reminding myself that it had nothing to do with me that he took photographs of young girls and stored them on his computer. I kept reminding myself that it wasn't a crime. He wasn't a *real* sex pervert, like the ones in the newspapers; he wasn't some child molester from the old cautionary tales; he was just a fantasist. Besides, the girls in his picture files all seemed to be in their late teens, which meant that, legally at least, he was doing nothing wrong. I resented his having photographs of me in his possession, photographs I hadn't agreed to, but then, I could hardly criticise him, when I'd done the same thing to so many of Kyrre's tenants. That I considered his pictures different – mine were purely observational, after all – didn't mean that I could find it in myself to confront him about them. I wasn't even sure I wanted to. It had nothing to do with me, what he did – and yet, looking back, I can see that finding the pictures changed something for me. I felt that I had misplaced something, I suppose, and I was troubled by that – but I also felt that I had been freed from an invisible influence that had been working on me for weeks, ever since the run-up to exams.

Frank Verne was gone, away back around the world to his deadline in New York, or wherever he came from, and the house was peaceful again, but I couldn't stay indoors. I didn't go far, and I avoided the *hytte* – there were so many tracks and deer runs leading down to the shore, and the meadows were so open and empty, I'd never had any trouble avoiding

138

people, and there were so few people, anyhow. They say that, when you move north, you start to appreciate your fellow humans more, because this far north, you don't know when you might have to depend on a neighbour, or even a passer-by – and I think that's true, but it's also true that one of the best ways to appreciate other people is to see them only occasionally. Most of us, on the island certainly, enjoy our own company. We have a knack for being alone and we appreciate a certain tact in others, the tact that two solitary walkers observe, say, when they meet by chance, and have to negotiate the situation without giving offence and, at the same time, without getting bogged down in feeling that they have to keep one another company. Often, when I see another wanderer in the distance, I find a way of changing course without seeming to avoid him and, often enough, the stranger observes the same strategies, so we skirt around one another in the most natural and, at the same time, the most carefully calculated of games. But later that following week, when I came across Ryvold on the strand about two miles west of our little stretch of beach, I was too preoccupied, too lost in my own thoughts – or, maybe, in my own freedom from the usual thoughts that had plagued me for so long – that, just like the time I'd met Martin Crosbie in the rain, I almost bumped into him. Which would have been annoying, I think, had it been anyone else. I didn't really know Ryvold, and he seemed to view me with a distant, rather casual affection – I think the best word here would be *avuncular* – but that day he seemed genuinely pleased by our encounter. I didn't know if I was just as pleased to see him, but I wasn't annoyed and, for one reason or another – mine or his, I couldn't have said – we missed the chance to part after the first polite exchange, and we ended up walking on together, talking and falling silent, then talking again, like two old friends who meet by chance and find that they still feel comfortable with one another. I think, in fact, that we did feel comfortable together that day, and I wasn't unhappy to have met him – but at the same time, there was no common ground between us, no mutual friends or interests, no shared memories. Nothing, after a while, but Mother – and Ryvold was too careful a soul, and too considerate a human being, to follow that path very far.

So we talked about art – which was, of course, a way of talking about the one person we had in common without actually talking about her. Ryvold, it turned out, knew a good deal about art – perhaps he was a failed artist himself, which might have explained his fascination with Mother – and, once he got started, he was quite interesting on the subject. As always, though, there was something a little too theoretical about him, something too abstract. When he liked a painting, he didn't just *like* it, he wanted to understand everything about it. He wanted to see it from every possible angle, and he wanted to connect it up with everything else that was in his head, with the entire, Byzantine system of what he knew and thought about. Which meant that he made everything far too complicated for his own good. Still, he provided a distraction that day, and I was in need of a distraction. It seemed that, before I met him, he had been thinking about where painting had originated – about how art had come to be – and for him, that was a serious question, one he pursued with me, in the absence of any other topic of conversation.

'Leon Battista Alberti says that it was Narcissus who invented painting,' he said. 'He says, "*What is painting, if not an attempt to embrace, through art, .the very surface of the pool in which we are reflected?*"' We had stopped at the water's edge, and stood looking out over the Sound, for all the world like two Sunday painters who have come out without their easels. Ryvold picked up a stone and tried skipping it across the water. It failed with a loud, slightly vulgar plop. He laughed at himself.

I laughed too, to be polite. I wanted to find my own stone and skip it halfway across the channel, but I was afraid that, if I did, and it worked, he would think I was showing him up on purpose. 'I'm not sure I follow . . .'

'Well,' he said, 'it's odd. There are plenty of theories about the origin of painting. The Greeks thought it came from drawing a line around a shadow, drawing a line around a shadow on the wall when somebody you loved was about to go away, so you would have something to remember them by. But Alberti is the only one who credits Narcissus with the discovery.' He bent down and scooped up another stone. 'So,' he said, 'why Narcissus?' He asked the question, then he bent slightly, to get a good angle – and I could tell, from the way he spoke, that this mattered to him. He took this stuff seriously – which was ridiculous, maybe, but I also enjoyed it, in a way. It felt old-fashioned, like observing some half-remembered tradition. He swung back his arm and cast the stone – and this time it skipped, five, maybe six times before it disappeared, silently, some way out over the water. He straightened up to watch it go, with unashamed satisfaction. Then he turned to me. 'What do you think?' he said.

I didn't think anything; yet all of a sudden, it seemed important to be taking the question just as seriously as he did. 'Well,' I said, 'Narcissus fell in love with a reflection . . .'

Ryvold nodded, then he contradicted me. 'Yes, but he didn't *know* it was a reflection,' he said. 'Not at first. Ovid goes to some lengths to explain that he didn't know it was *himself* he was seeing – not to begin with. He loved what he saw – and

141

then, later, he saw that what he loved was actually himself. He was the one he could see in the pool, along with all the other things – the sky, the trees, the world all about him. And maybe that was what made him so happy – he had thought he was alone, looking at a world that was separate from him, a world of other things, and then, all of a sudden, he sees that he is *in* that world. He is real. Before, he didn't know if he was real –'

I shook my head. 'I don't know about that,' I said. 'It seems a bit far-fetched to me.'

He nodded. 'Of course it does,' he said. 'That's because we've always seen the story of Narcissus as a story of youthful vanity and self-love. But you have to remember that Narcissus was the one who rejected Echo because she did nothing but repeat back to him what he had only just that moment said. She agreed with him all the time – which you'd think would make her the perfect woman for someone who is in love with himself – but he'd have none of that.' He grabbed another stone – a large, flat, almost black one – and skipped it out over the water – and now that he had succeeded, I felt free to join in. And that was how we continued our absurd conversation, skipping stones and talking about Narcissus.

'Well,' I said, 'maybe he just doesn't want Echo because he's too self-obsessed.' I remembered the story, Mother had read it to me years before, and we'd discussed it in school once, taking the usual, psychoanalytical line. 'Maybe he rejects her because he is waiting for someone better –'

'And who would that be?'

'Himself,' I said.

He laughed. 'But that came later,' he said. 'When he sees the beautiful young man, when he first falls in love, he doesn't

142

know it's himself. He doesn't know who it is. It's only later that he discovers the truth – which might have embarrassed anyone else. Anyone less alone. And it's only when he discovers the truth, and sees that his *self* is an object in a world, like all the other objects, that he becomes a painter. Because, for the first time, he is part of the world, and art is his way of confirming that. A way of saying that he is in the world, in the world and of it. Echo mouthing back to him his own speech – that was a sad joke, a parody. Now, though, he's surrounded by the unexpected and the unpredictable. Now, everything is surprising – and now, of course, he is mortal. If he had stayed apart, he could have lived forever. That was what the gods had promised at his birth. But now, when he sees himself and knows he is part of the world, he has to die –'

I suddenly thought of Mats and Harald. 'And he falls into the water,' I said. I looked at Ryvold. Was he thinking of the boys, too?

He heard the question in my voice, then, and he dropped the stone he was holding and looked at me – but I could see that he didn't know what the question was. All he heard was a tone. He had forgotten the boys altogether – or rather, he had left them behind, in the factual world. Here, everything was theory, and he was surprised by the look on my face. He was surprised – and then he thought he understood and tried to explain. 'He doesn't fall into the water,' he said. 'He falls into his own reflection. Because he leans in to see himself and leaning in means you fall. He could have leaned back, to see the wider picture – and that's what painters do, when they're good painters. Wouldn't you say?'

I nodded. I didn't want him to see the thought of those drowned boys in my face. I wanted to keep him there, in his theoretical world, thinking too much. 'And then,' I said, 'he turns into a flower.'

Ryvold laughed again. He had a good laugh and I realised, now, that I hadn't heard it often enough in our house. 'A flower,' he said. 'Yes. He's transformed into a flower, and that's another kind of immortality. But it could have been anything – a flower, a swan, a deer – it doesn't matter. It doesn't matter what you become, what matters is the transformation. You can't live forever, nobody can. Even the gods die. But you can change, and that's how the world continues.'

'So what does this have to do with painting?' I said – and now it was a genuine question. Suddenly, I really did want to understand what was going on in his head, because I knew that, in some odd, tangential way, it had something to do with Mother.

Ryvold looked at me, then he turned and gazed out over the water. In anyone else, it would have seemed a romantic gesture, a piece of theatre, but in him it was just – him. He seemed not to have any sense of himself at all. It was as if he didn't really exist, or not as a man. He was theoretical, a series of questions and propositions, like a book about colour, or perspective. 'I don't know,' he said. 'All I know is that, for a short while, Narcissus sees himself in what he loves.' He turned back and gave me a shy, slightly embarrassed smile. 'Sorry,' he said. 'I slip into professor mode sometimes. I can't seem to help myself.'

I shook my head. 'I don't mind,' I said. 'It's interesting.'

He smiled. What we were talking about had to do with Mother, and we could both see that now, and each of us knew that the other knew as much. We had been talking about her all along. We always did. Ryvold's smile stayed in place, but it softened, and there was a sadness in it from one moment

144

to the next. 'It doesn't last long,' he said. 'Narcissus falls into his reflection, just as we always knew he would. And then he becomes a flower, and we weren't expecting that at all.' He thought for a moment. 'But then, that's how the stories work,' he said. 'They remind us that anything can happen. Everything changes, anything can become anything else – and there's nothing supernatural about it.'

I thought about Kyrre Opdahl, then. He wouldn't have gone along with all this thinking, but he would have agreed, in his own way, with that last remark. Or rather, he would have agreed and, at the same time, begged to differ. He would need a qualification, an acknowledgement that, whatever else, the world was stranger than we gave it credit for. Stranger – and more dangerous. I picked up a last stone and skipped it out across the water. 'That depends on what you mean by supernatural,' I said.

Some time passed. I can't recall, now, how long it was, but then, you never remember, looking back, how much time passed during a period when nothing much happened. Of course, there were events, of a kind, but they weren't enough to break the sense I had of waiting for something. I didn't know what it was, though. It could have been a purely personal matter – more news from Kate Thompson, another talk with Mother about whether I would go to England – but I didn't think that was it. Not at the time. Perhaps I was waiting for another boy to drown. Or maybe it had to do with Martin Crosbie, I don't know. I just knew that the story that had begun with Mats's drowning wasn't finished yet – that there was more to come. I wasn't thinking about Maia, particularly, though I did catch sight of her, once more, down on the shore, and I wondered how she was getting by. I think I still felt sorry for her, then – some of the time, at least. But I also think that, during that strange summer, I felt sorry for everyone. For the boys. For Mrs Sigfridsson. For Kyrre Opdahl. For Ryvold. I felt sorry for them all – and all the time I was waiting for something to happen. Something that would bring the story to a close. Something that would provide an explanation to the mystery – though what the mystery actually was, I couldn't have said.

At some point during that slow, grey time, Frank Verne's article arrived. I think Mother was surprised to see it so soon and something in it must have troubled her. I was there when the post was delivered and I watched as she opened the package, took out the large, very glossy magazine and sat down at the kitchen table to read it. I don't know what she was expecting, but it soon became obvious that something wasn't quite right. Of course, Mother has always been able to conceal her true feelings – so much so that, for years, I suspected her of having almost no feelings at all, other than a passion for her work and a vague fondness for her only child – but there was one moment, one tiny glimmer of something in her face when she closed the thick, beautifully produced art journal and looked up at me with a smile.

'God, what am I doing?' she said. 'I haven't got time for this now.'

I looked at her. 'What is it?' I said. 'What does it say?'

She stood up – and I noticed that she kept hold of the magazine, rather than leaving it on the table, which was what she would normally have done. 'Oh, the usual,' she said. She did it very well, she was almost convincing, but I could see there was something there, behind the facade. Naturally, I was mistaken about what it actually was: I thought, at the time, that she was missing him, that reading his words had upset her, because she had been half in love with the man and now he was gone. She had been doing so well at forgetting Frank: in the days after he left, she hadn't mentioned him once and, as far as I knew, there had been no communication between them. So I assumed that this piece – which he appeared to have sent himself, by express mail – was the first reminder she'd had of his visit. She had been doing so well, and now she had suffered a temporary setback. She had almost forgotten him, and she was annoyed with herself, now, for feeling again what she felt when he was there, or maybe with him, for having sent this reminder. Though that didn't sound like Mother, when I thought about it. It sounded more like some romantic heroine out of a novel.

I was mistaken in these assumptions, as it turned out, but I didn't discover this until much later. That morning, she left the kitchen with the magazine tucked under her arm, casually, as if absent-mindedly, taking it upstairs with a cup of coffee to read later, when she had finished the work that she ought to be doing. I didn't believe that act for a moment – but my curiosity wasn't sufficiently aroused to pursue the matter. My assumption worked for me and I suppose I thought, if I left the subject alone, Frank Verne would soon be put back into some dim room in her memory, along with all the other things she didn't feel the need to recall. It didn't even occur to me to try and find out what the article said, because I assumed that it was just another piece about the beautiful reclusive painter from the far north. I couldn't imagine Mother revealing anything of herself to anyone, but I was mistaken in that, too, because it seems she told Frank Verne things she had kept secret all her life.

She had told him those secrets, for reasons only she understood, on those long walks they took, or over the dinner table after I had gone to bed, and Frank Verne had written it all down. He had won her trust, and let her tell the story she kept from everyone else, then he had published it all in a magazine, for anyone to read. It wasn't an exposé, though. It wasn't about betrayal, or deceit. He had written that story because he felt it *needed* to be written; more: he had written it because he believed she wanted that particular story to be told, and anyone could see, reading the piece – which ran to several pages – that it wasn't so much a work of journalism as a love letter in disguise. I didn't read it until much later, and I saw that immediately. It was a secret, possibly perverse, declaration of love, and I couldn't understand why he had done it that way, because by then I had realised that there was no need for secrecy. No need for perverse declarations from a remote distance, followed by silence and self-refusal, because they loved each other. So why didn't they just say so and act accordingly? I knew it had nothing to do with me. I think, if I had been able to believe that their being together would make Mother happy, I would have accepted the situation, more or less gracefully. But it didn't have anything to do with me and I didn't understand why they would play this particular game, other than from sheer perversity. Refusal. Denial. Mother's game, I had always thought – but now she had met her match.

It was a very tender match, however. Frank Verne's profile was well written and never unsympathetic to its subject, and nothing very surprising, certainly nothing at all shocking to a casual reader, was revealed. It was shocking to me, of course, all those months later, when I finally got to read it, because it told me things about Mother that, at first, I didn't believe. It talked about a childhood that she had never mentioned, a world that I had never glimpsed, people and places and a self – my mother's self – that I had never suspected. The picture it painted was of a shy, withdrawn child who spent her days alone, walking in the woods or reading fairy tales, a child who never talked and never wanted to make friends, a child who was never happy unless she was off by herself. The memories of this childhood that Frank Verne chose to dramatise were minor, ordinary events, yet they were all strangely sinister: Mother at eight, standing in a pool of wildflowers with an old honey jar, catching bee after bee till the jar was full, then sealing it up and carrying it home to set down on the windowsill in her bedroom, so she could listen to the angry buzzing as she sat late into the evening, reading, or sketching; Mother at ten, finding an injured bird and nursing it to health, or what she thought was health, then carrying it to a nearby cliff and throwing it out into the wind, where it hung for barely a moment before plunging to the rocks below; Mother at fifteen, going into a pharmacy and asking for all kinds of embarrassing medicaments – foot powder and wart-removal cream and pills for diarrhoea, in an effort to set aside her shyness, not because she wanted to be more at ease with people, not because she wanted to be able to make people like her, but to teach herself that it doesn't matter how other people see us. All that matters is the private self, the thing you are before you are the person that others make you out to be. Later, she realises that she is beautiful, and she hates it. She doesn't want to be looked at, she wants to be the one who looks – which is why she becomes a painter of faces, because she can look at people with complete detachment and see both what they would like to reveal and what they are desperate to keep hidden. Then, not long after I am born, she moves north in search of something larger and wider, something she refuses to think of as landscape, or abstraction, though it seems to sit perfectly between the two.

Later, when I read that passage, I thought about the unfinished painting on the landing and I wondered what she had seen in *me* that made her give it up. What had *I* wanted to reveal? What had I been desperate to hide? And which of them had forced her to set her brushes aside and take the canvas down from the easel? That was what occurred to me at first – and then I wondered why she had taken the painting and hung it on the landing, so I would see it every morning when I went down to breakfast. What was the nature of that gift? I thought about all these things later, but during that summer, after Mother had tucked the magazine away in one of her hiding places up in the studio, and we had continued with the usual business of our day, I assumed that she was missing Frank a little, and was maybe annoyed with herself for being distracted from her work, and that it would all blow over soon enough. Which, at the time, it gave every appearance of doing – and now, when I look back, it seems to me that, for a while at least, there was nobody in the whole world but us, two women in a silent house, navigating the usual, but now slightly altered, paths between things that could be spoken aloud and things that we were both more or less aware of, but had decided were better left unsaid.

Of course, we weren't alone. We had neighbours. We had the suitors. Martin Crosbie was still in residence down below, though I rarely saw him. After I discovered his collection of photographs, I avoided the *hytte* on my walks in the birch woods around our house, or heading down along the Brensholmen road and following the track that ran past Kyrre Opdahl's house to where it met the Sound, further up the shore. I saw Kyrre from time to time, and some days I would go and sit with him in his kitchen, while he worked on an old engine or a broken clock, just as I had always done. Only it wasn't quite the same as before – and I knew it wasn't, though I couldn't have said why. I couldn't have asked *him* to tell me, either. He still told me stories, and he talked sometimes about the *huldra*, but he didn't talk about the Sigfridsson boys and Maia any more. For he was done with that. Now, the story was fully formed in his head, and he was beginning to put together his plan to rid the land of its curse, even if it meant losing himself altogether.

So we weren't alone – but, in the house at least, we were *apart*. Then, one day – not a Saturday – somebody came to the front door and knocked. I was alone in the kitchen – Mother had been working till the small hours and was sleeping, now, in her room at the back of the house – and for a moment I was startled. I don't know who I thought it was – maybe Martin Crosbie come up from the *hytte* to explain away his deleted photographs, maybe Frank Verne come from New York to whisk Mother off to a new life – but I really was spooked, all of a sudden, and I was relieved when Ryvold appeared in the hallway, peering in tentatively to see if anyone was home. I was relieved – and maybe I was glad to see him, though it was a Wednesday, and he shouldn't have been there.

I had been up for hours, which wasn't unusual. It was normal, in summer, for me to stay awake half the night, lying in bed with a picture book, or sitting by the window staring out over the lit meadows. I would try to sleep, and then I would get hungry, or restless, and I'd need to be up and about. That morning I'd got up, put the kettle on, made breakfast – I'd even listened to the radio. I hadn't made any particular effort to be quiet, even though I knew Mother was in bed. I never did, partly because I didn't like that feeling of creeping around the house like a thief, or a guest who has outstayed her welcome, but mostly because there was almost no risk of my waking Mother. Her room was away at the back of the house, beyond the studio, and besides, after a long night's work she always slept so deeply that the thought of disturbing her never even entered my head. And I really disliked the idea, I disliked and was actually rather repelled by the idea of sneaking around. There is something so theatrical about it, when someone tiptoes downstairs and out the front door, clutching her shoes in her hand – it's just play-acting. It's an excuse for that person to look at herself and see the girl with her secret in some film or a novel. The subject. The heroine. That was what I thought then, anyhow. I much preferred to go about my business in the normal way, as people do when they are not watching themselves, when they are not self-conscious.

So that morning, I had been doing what I did on any other summer morning: I woke and dressed, put on my shoes, walked to the end of the landing and looked in through the half-open door on Mother, who lay stretched out on the bed in a deep slumber, her head turned into the pillow, her left arm outstretched in that odd way she has, as if reaching out for something that is definitely present – in her dream, at least – but just beyond her grasp. I am fairly sure that I lingered a moment at her door that day, as I sometimes did, struck with a sudden, almost sisterly affection for this woman, who was, at that moment, elsewhere, in another world, as another self, someone I could never see or touch or even imagine. Looking back, I understand that I found this a comforting notion, no doubt because the remoter self of her dreams made her waking self seem, by contrast, less faraway and, so, more knowable. Yet, as I watched her sleep, I also felt guilty, because I had to admit that I felt happier about my mother when she was asleep than when she was up and about. Awake, she seemed – what? I'm not sure if this is exactly the right word, but – too perfect, too self-contained, too still. She was a mother, of course, always practical and supportive and concerned for my well-being, but she was, first and foremost, an artist, and there was something too careful, something almost textbook about her motherliness. And the fact was that, no matter how hard she tried to be a good parent to me, she was by nature a solitary, a woman who lived in a space of her own, just a few degrees to the left of the world that other people inhabited. I loved her, of course, just the way she was; I certainly wouldn't have changed her. And I was a solitary too, in my own way. Still, it was difficult at times, like when you are a child and you take apart a mechanical toy, some car or train or wind-up bird that, in the natural course of events, breaks down, or starts to develop eccentricities, odd mannerisms that you feel – with the certainty of a bright child – can easily be fixed with a little logic and application. So you take the thing to pieces, expecting its inner machinery to be differentiated and complex, a tiny piece of precision engineering whose workings will be clear and defined, but what you discover is a crude, flimsy mechanism, not obviously sufficient to the movements for which it was designed and beyond all hope of restoration. What you find, in fact, is next to nothing. The thing is, this toy, this machine, works by some kind of miracle, it has nothing to do with cogs and wheels and springs at all, it's just some mysterious and nebulous tension enclosed within a tin shell, a tension that, once disturbed, can never be regained. And that was how it was with Mother, except that the obvious simplicity, the obvious lack of machinery was on the outside, and the miracle – the movement, the music, the dancing figures – was concealed within. On the outside, there was nothing, or only the perfect, final version of the human being that she had decided long ago it would be right to become. On the inside, however, something was going on, tiny cogs and wheels were turning, something was happening that those who knew her, myself included, could only guess at. That was why I liked to watch her sleep: because once or twice, without her knowing, she gave something away, a hint, a smile, a few murmured words that suggested, if not indecision, then at least some process that was still happening, some wish or fear or trace of longing that had not yet been dispensed with.

I was glad to see Ryvold, and I got up to invite him in, when I turned and noticed him shyly peering round the door, but it was a moment before I noticed his expression. Once he saw I was there, he came in and through the hall to the kitchen doorway – on Saturdays, when the suitors came, the door was never locked and they would walk in and call, to announce that they had arrived – but he had an odd, lost look on his face, a lost look, or perhaps the look of someone who was worried about something – something that, if asked for an explanation, he wouldn't be able to spell out, either because he didn't have a precise answer, or because the reason for his anxiety was too private, or too indelicate, to give away. I waved vaguely at a chair, and asked if he wanted coffee. He didn't answer, but stood in the middle of the room, looking around as if searching for something – and I realised that he was wondering where Mother was. He had come to see *her*, of course, and whatever was troubling him had something to do with her.

'Mother's asleep,' I said. 'She was working all night again.'

'Ah.'

'But sit down anyhow. There's fresh coffee in the pot.'

'Well,' he said, hovering a moment before finally sitting down on the chair nearest the door. 'I don't want to disturb you . . .'

I laughed. 'No danger of that,' I said. 'I'm just idling.' I poured him a cup of coffee and set it down on the table. 'And no danger of disturbing Mother, either. When she's been up all night, like this, she sleeps like a log.' I shot him what I hoped was a reassuring glance. 'So you needn't look so worried,' I said.

He seemed flustered by this. 'Worried?' he said. 'Oh no. No – I'm not . . . worried . . .'

I laughed again. 'Well, you *look* worried,' I said.

'Worried?' He seemed uncertain now, not so much about whether *he* was worried, as about what the word itself actually *meant*. He considered a moment. 'No,' he said, 'I'm not – *worried*. It's just . . .' He took a sip of his coffee, but, really, he was taking a moment to gather himself, because there was something he wanted to say and, though it was Mother he wanted to talk to, he was considering saying it, whatever it was, to me. Considering, but still unable to decide. Then he smiled. It was a smile I had seen before on the occasional Saturday morning when I'd been drawn into Mother's tea party, a smile that signalled withdrawal – withdrawal, though not retreat, a considered choice not to impose himself on the company by saying too much. Saying – or revealing. It wasn't that he was secretive, or protective of his privacy, or not primarily, at least. It was just that he didn't want to be a burden to others, in even the most insignificant way. And, all of a sudden, I understood his obsession with the Narcissus story, how it wasn't just theoretical to him, but exemplary.

155

It was something to live by. He could take pleasure in finding himself in a world, but he wanted to be sure – it was critical for him to be sure – that nobody else had to feel they were party to that discovery. Which is different, yes, from self-effacement, because self-effacement is a disguised attempt to be seen, and what he was after was a subtle form of absence. Which, in turn, was why I had always liked him, and why I had always been suspicious of him, because, for a completely different set of reasons, he was quietly doing the one thing I thought was worth any effort. And now, here he was, putting the whole enterprise in danger. Or almost putting it in danger. He had been right at the brink and now he was pulling away, a soft, almost penitent smile on his face. 'There's a possibility that I'll have to go away for a time,' he said. 'So I thought . . .' He stood up. 'But it's not that urgent,' he said. 'It can wait.' He laughed. 'It's not that urgent at all,' he said – to himself, mostly.

I stood up too, then, but he was already turning towards the hall, with that same strange look on his face. 'Why don't you wait a moment?' I said. 'She's been asleep for hours, so she'd be wanting to get up soon anyway –'

He shook his head. 'No, really,' he said. 'Let her sleep for as long as she needs. I'll come back later.' His face dimmed again and he stood looking at me. He seemed oddly penitent but, at the same time, he was eager to go. 'Thanks for the coffee.'

I waved my hand. His fastidiousness was beginning to bother me now and – though it was a question that had never occurred to me even to ask before that moment – I suddenly understood why he had never married. He was someone who *had* to live alone, someone who found it difficult to be with others for any length of time, because he only had one mode

– that discreet art of withdrawal which had, no doubt, taken him years to perfect. He had no other strategies for getting along with people and, though his colleagues probably saw this as the mark of a gentle, erudite, considerate soul, I was suddenly able to see right through it. Not because I was so very perceptive, but because I was so like him. He had been living in that one mode for so long, he had almost forgotten about it, but I was a near-beginner, and for me it was painfully obvious. 'So,' I said, 'when are you leaving?'

'Oh, it's a while still,' he said. 'I'm just . . . It's not all decided yet.'

That was an evasion, of course, and I knew it. I also knew, as soon as he said it, that there was a chance he wouldn't come back – but, for his sake, more than mine, I kept up the pretence. 'And how long will you be gone?'

He smiled. It was an apologetic smile, but the apology was only an attempt to conceal his sadness, and it didn't altogether work. The sadness didn't show, of course, but I could see that it was what was being concealed. 'That's not certain either,' he said. 'It might not be very long at all . . .'

He didn't say any more – but I knew what the other half of the unfinished sentence was, and I nodded, to show that I understood. 'Well,' I said, finding – to my own mind – just the right level of formality, 'I'll tell Mother you were here.' I fought the urge to offer my hand, in token of the farewell that this exchange was in danger of becoming. And, oddly enough, I thought he was doing the same thing.

'I should have called,' he said, sotto voce now, as he made his way down the hall – and I followed him, thinking he was upset, or disappointed. But then, when he turned round, I saw that, for no reason that I could understand, his face was illumined, suddenly, lit from within in a way I would never have expected, his eyes bright, something far away in his mind emerging into the plain light of day and brightening everything. It was like when you're walking past a lonely house out on the point, some rainy evening, and somebody indoors switches on a lamp, turning the windows to a pale, thin gold. Everything is touched with warmth, then; the darkness feels smaller and more local, all at once, softened and warmed and *hjemlig*. 'I don't know what's going to happen,' he said. 'It's all a little up in the air.' He smiled. 'It will be a while before things are settled.' I wanted to ask what he meant by things being settled, but before I could, he turned away, with that same bright look on his face, and, walking quickly back through the garden, made his way down through the birch wood to the road below.

I can't remember, now, exactly how it was decided – but it *was* decided, two days after Ryvold's strange visit, that I should go to England. I also accept that I was party to that decision, though I only agreed because I had no other choice. Somehow, Kate Thompson had got hold of our number and had telephoned – and it was only by chance that neither Mother nor I were there to pick up. She left a message, of course – why wouldn't she? – and it was this message that set things in motion. It took a whole evening for me to get to the place that Mother had arrived at the moment she heard Kate Thompson's voice, talking about Arild Frederiksen as if it were the most natural thing in the world to do, on *her* answering machine, but it was inevitable, the moment she played the message back to me, that I would choose, once and for all, to lay the matter to rest – and the only way to do this was to go to England. Not to make friends with my new father, or to fit in with some fantasy Kate Thompson had of a happy reunion, but to make them both understand that I had no desire to be reunited with anyone. I would satisfy their curiosity about me – was it theirs? or just hers? – and they would see that I had no curiosity about them, and that would be that. I felt sure that that would be enough, as soon as the decision was made, just as I felt sure that the letters and the calls would continue if nothing was done. And I couldn't allow that, for Mother's sake. She was perfectly calm about it, of course, but I knew she felt intruded upon, and she wanted to put a stop to things, now that they were escalating to the level of phone calls. I also knew that she was only pretending to be calm about it all, in order not to put any kind of pressure on me. Which meant, of course, that I was the one who had to make the choice to go, even though I knew there *was* no choice because, for everyone's sake, my going was inevitable. So I made the choice. I made it that very night and, by the next morning, flights and a hotel were booked for the following weekend. Kate Thompson had offered to pay for the trip, on Arild Frederiksen's behalf, but Mother wouldn't hear of it. Instead, she found the name of a small hotel, booked my flights and worked out a schedule of train journeys to take me to my destination – which, according to Mother's old guidebooks, was a provincial market town in the English Midlands – with the minimum of inconvenience.

Two days later, the man from Fløgstad's arrived to take delivery of the pictures for Mother's forthcoming exhibition – and, that very same morning, I had my last conversation, if it could be called a conversation, with Martin Crosbie. He had been out walking, I suppose, and he must have seen the van – and maybe it had occurred to him, then, that this was a perfect excuse to find out what, if anything, I had told Mother about the pictures on his laptop. Or maybe he had

159

come to the house with a plausible story already prepared, ready to make out that I had misunderstood what I'd seen, that those pictures were part of a project he was working on; maybe he would just point out that such photographs were neither pornographic nor in any way criminal – and I had to admit that, taken singly, they wouldn't have raised any eyebrows. The girls in the pictures had ranged in age from around fourteen to as old as twenty; they had all been fully dressed, and there was nothing overtly sexual about any of them – no lewd poses, no fetishes or scanty clothing. Had he been challenged, he could have argued, with complete conviction, that he had done nothing wrong. He could have said that, for him, those images represented some abstract quality – beauty, say, or innocence – and his only crime was a certain old-fashioned love of the pure and the unsullied. Like his hero Lewis Carroll, he was a shy, reserved man, sufficiently repelled by the vulgarity of modern life to seek refuge in a dream-world that he knew no longer existed, but which gave him solace, nonetheless. Perhaps he would even admit to being a sad case, someone not quite as worldly as the next man, but he would still maintain that he had done nothing wrong. Except, of course, he must have guessed by then that I knew otherwise – and it was a shock to see him by our gate, talking to Mother as if they were old neighbours meeting on the road for a casual chat. That made me angry – but what made me angrier still was his expression, a look of relief that suggested he had, at that very moment, confirmed in his own mind that nothing had been said, and I hurried to where they were standing, wanting to do or say something that would wipe that look off his face – only Mother stopped talking the moment I appeared and turned to me with a smile I didn't recognise. 'Good morning, Liv,' she said, her voice bright and airy. 'You know Mr Crosbie, I think?'

I nodded at Martin. 'Good morning,' I said. I wasn't bright, and I certainly wasn't airy, but my resolve had suddenly vanished and I came over as nothing more threatening than a grumpy teenager, interrupting the grown-ups' small talk.

Nevertheless, Martin permitted himself a brief, questioning look – a look he probably imagined Mother was unaware of, as if Mother was ever unaware of anything – before he decided that I wasn't going to make things difficult. He smiled. 'Your mother was just telling me about your removals man,' he said.

I frowned. 'What about him?'

Martin's face darkened again, momentarily, and he looked unsure of himself, though I couldn't tell whether he was wondering if he'd taken too much for granted, in thinking I wouldn't make a scene, or if he thought he might have spoken out of turn in mentioning the man from Fløgstad's. He looked at Mother.

Mother smiled sweetly. 'Oh, don't worry, Mr Crosbie,' she said. 'Liv knows all about it –'

'All about what?' I said. I couldn't believe she had told our ridiculous story to Martin Crosbie, within minutes of their meeting – a story that I had always considered a private matter, a piece of dark fun that she had concocted to amuse me, when the house was invaded for a day by this tall, sullen man – and I couldn't keep the annoyance out of my voice, that she had betrayed our privacy so easily. 'I wouldn't believe everything you hear, Mr Crosbie,' I said. 'You of all people should know how deceptive appearances can be.'

At that, Mother turned slowly to look at me – and I realised that she had already worked everything out. Not the detail of the pictures, of course, but everything else – because, of course, it was obvious that something was going on. She knew how long Martin had been at the *hytte*, and his sudden appearance on that particular morning was something of a giveaway to someone like her. No doubt she had guessed right away that something was wrong from the way he was acting, and the immediate tension that had developed when we saw each other. Yet her knowing was no comfort to me; on the contrary, I could see that she was doing what she always did in such situations – she was playing a game. She was toying with us – or at least, she was toying with him, and, as if the game had been devised purely for my entertainment, she was making me an accomplice in that game, in what I could only take for a perverted show of familial loyalty. 'I was telling Mr Crosbie about the murder,' she said. 'How he killed his wife with an axe –'

'That's not what happened,' I said. I was angry now, angry that Martin had crossed the line that divided my world from his, angry that Mother was playing one of her games, making light of things and expecting me to join in, when she didn't really know the circumstances. 'That's just a story you made up.' I looked at her and she looked back, interested by the vehemence of my response, though not, I think, terribly concerned.

Martin, on the other hand, was totally confused now – and more concerned than he had any right to be. Obviously, he was beginning to regret having come; but then, how could he not have done? He'd needed to find out what I would do, after all. After so many anxious days, alone in the *hytte* and wondering what stories I might tell about him, he had watched the van turn into our drive and he had used it as an excuse for a fishing expedition. And Mother had sensed all this, or something like it, the moment he introduced himself. Now, apparently chastened, she thought for a moment before resuming the conversation with a half-smile playing about her mouth – though this time the smile was genuine. 'You're right,' she said. 'It's just a story.' She turned to Martin. 'I'm sorry, Mr Crosbie,' she said. 'We don't get many visitors out here, and we have to find ways of entertaining ourselves on the long winter nights.' She craned her neck a little and peered into the interior of the van. 'Anyway,' she said. 'It's very nice to have met you, but there's still a good deal of packing to do, so if you don't mind, I'll go and see how it's coming along.' She held out her hand. 'I'm sure Mr Opdahl is looking after you,' she said. 'But if you ever need anything, do let us know.'

Martin Crosbie forced a smile, but he was far from happy. For a moment, he stared at her, unsure of what to say – and it was obvious that he felt he ought to say something – then he shook hands and, with a shy, sideways glance at me, turned and started off down the path. Mother stood a little longer, to watch him go; then, after he had passed the gate and was out of earshot, she turned to me. 'Poor man,' she said. 'I rather wonder what you see in him.'

I shook my head. 'What's that supposed to mean?' I said.

'Isn't he the one you're always popping out to visit?' she said. She gave me an amused look, as if she had caught me out in a lie.

'I don't know what you mean,' I said. 'I've only spoken to him twice in all the time he's been here.'

'Well, good,' she said, before I could say any more – and I could see that she was only playing to cover up something else, something that was serious for her. 'Maybe you had better keep it that way.' Then she turned and walked back to the house, where the supposed axe murderer had just appeared in the doorway, presumably because he needed instructions or clarification on what to do next – though I couldn't help thinking, given the curious expression on his face, that he knew we had been talking about him, and he wanted us to understand that he didn't care in the least, and that, while he was here, away from his own world, anything other than his work was utterly irrelevant to him.

I was shocked, that day, by the assumption Mother had made about me and Martin Crosbie – even if it was part of a game she was playing. When I think about what happened later, and the effect it apparently had on me, it surprises me even more to realise how little I really did know about the man. I'd had those two encounters with him, when we'd spoken for a while about nothing; I'd watched him go about his business in a desultory way, but I hadn't learned anything at all about his life. I had no facts, no background story, no information about where he had come from or what his usual life was. After my discovery at the *hytte*, I'd gone out of my way to avoid him, but that hadn't been enough to prevent my wondering what he might be up to and I'd started to have ugly fantasies in which he would be watching me, camera at the ready, whenever I went out into the garden or walked down to the shore. I didn't know why he took the pictures I'd seen on his computer; I didn't know if he was nothing more than a sad fantasist who liked to creep about taking pictures of young girls or whether he was an out-and-out preda- tor, for whom the photographs were only a first step in some larger plan. That never seemed very likely but, looking back, I can't be sure of anything. He could have been a hopeless romantic whose imagination had gone slightly astray, a latter- day Dodgson with a database of stolen images and a wry, self-deprecating manner that couldn't quite conceal his keen sense, not only of his own absurdity, but also of the grotesque and puzzling existence of others. Whatever his conscious intentions, whatever reasons he thought he had for taking them, I like to think now that his secret cache of photographs had no more than a ritual significance for him – but, again, I can't be sure. We want to think well of the dead, for reasons that I've never fully understood, and I want to think better of him, now, than I did at the time, because whatever his vice, whatever his weakness, it was that, and that alone, that led the *huldra* to him. First, she brought him a little happiness, and then she killed him. Maybe that was the only way his story could end, and maybe it was the best he could have hoped for. A moment of happiness that must have taken him completely by surprise, then nothing. What was it like for him, to receive as a gift the one thing he'd always imagined he could only ever obtain by theft and deceit? It must have been hard to believe at first, but I think he did manage to believe it, before the gift was taken away, and the *huldra* showed her true form, waving to him from the lit shore, while he stepped willingly into the dark.

Mother drove me to the airport. I had hoped to go without a fuss, to keep the whole thing a secret, but as we made our way into Tromsø that morning, we met Kyrre Opdahl coming the other way and, as usual, he stopped for a chat. He liked that – I think Mother liked it too – it was one of his favourite things to do, to stop in the road and roll down his window to talk to somebody he'd met on the road, whether it was another driver, or someone out walking. It made him think of the old times, I suppose, when things were less hurried. That day, he was on his way back from the store at Straumsbukta with another week's worth of supplies, but he'd also dropped by a friend's house – a friend who lived just half a mile from Mrs Sigfridsson's – to pick up a clock that needed mending. Naturally, he spotted the suitcase on the back seat immediately. 'Off somewhere?' he asked, giving Mother a quizzical look. He seemed disappointed, betrayed even, that she hadn't told him about the trip.

Mother laughed and shook her head. 'Not me,' she said. 'Liv.'

'Ah.' Kyrre allowed himself that soft little gasp of his, as he nodded and looked at me, but he didn't say anything else.

'She's going to England,' Mother continued, still obviously amused. 'To visit her father.'

That shocked me. I had assumed she wouldn't want to talk about *him*. After all, she had been pretending he didn't exist for years. As far as I knew, she had never once mentioned his existence to Kyrre, who was too polite to enquire – and whenever anyone else had asked who my father was, she had always changed the subject, or clammed up. 'She won't be gone long,' she added, turning to me. 'Just a couple of days.'

Kyrre looked at me too, trying hard to conceal his own surprise. 'England, eh?' he said, then he shook his head. 'Well, I'm sure it's very nice, though I can't say I've ever been.' He smiled sympathetically, as if a trip to England was more or less the same as a visit to the dentist's. 'I'm not much of a one for travelling,' he said and, then, after a moment's recollection, he shook his head. 'Well,' he said, 'I did go to Narvik once.' He checked his rear-view mirror to be sure the road was empty behind him. He had started to enjoy the moment – his young friend was going off to a foreign country, and he was there to explain that it was no big deal, leaving the island – so he didn't want any interruptions, and he knew Mother well enough to know that, had he picked up on her remark

166

about my father, she would have politely closed down the conversation and driven away.

I shot Mother a meaningful look, but she ignored me. 'Narvik?' she said.

Kyrre nodded. 'Just for a weekend,' he said.

Mother kept a straight face. 'Well,' she said, 'I'm sure it's a very interesting place.'

Kyrre set his mouth and thought for a moment. 'Maybe it is,' he said. 'But I can't say I enjoyed it.'

Mother laughed, but she didn't say anything – and though they lingered another minute or two, the conversation was already over. No further mention was made of my father, or of my going away on my own for the first time, though Kyrre gave me a long look, just as he and Mother prepared to drive their separate ways, and he made me promise to send him a postcard.

THE FISHERMAN'S HOUSE

As the plane rose and tilted away, I dipped my head and peered out of the window, thinking I should have been able to see Mother walking back to the car, but all I could make out was the green light off the land below and then, off to one side, a yellow windsock, swelling with the breath of the old Sámi wind god, Bieggaålmaj – an ordinary thing, but also a small item of local theatre, filling with light and ozone and summer wind. For a moment, it seemed as if time might stop; then the plane turned south and everything below began to dwindle: houses and supermarkets and roadside cafes set out in mapped impermanence over the earth, an impermanence that nobody ever thought about, though they lived it every day – and some of them were glad, I think, that nothing they did or made was ever really finished, or theirs for certain. Nothing they did would last; nothing was there for good. People like Kyrre Opdahl, and maybe Ryvold too, in his own way, stayed or chose to live here because they knew that, here, only the stories lasted. The stories, and the land from which the stories came. As different as they thought they were from one another, those two solitaries would not only have agreed that the stories are all there is, and that everything else is illusion, they would also have said, as Ryvold said once to the assembled company one Saturday morning, that the individual stories, the separate

171

lives that we think we are living and the accounts we give of them, are continually assumed into one larger narrative that belongs to nobody in particular, but includes, not just everything that happens, but everything that might have been.

The plane circled for a moment above the island, then it turned southwards and in that instant everything I knew disappeared. Outside, Bieggaålmaj was blowing in from the Finnmarksvidda, a cold current that held the plane in the air like a bauble – but, before that, he had gusted across Mongolia, touched with the smoke from horse herders' yurts and the blue of the steppe, because this wind, this spirit, had a memory that lasted forever, beyond locality and time and season, and he remembered other places, other seasons, other peoples sleeping and dreaming in their own settlements, all the way from here to Kamchatka. To him, all our stories were the same – even the story I was enacting, going to visit a man I had not only never seen, but had never really thought of as a creature of flesh and blood. Now, I couldn't tell whether I was glad to be learning the truth at last, or annoyed to discover that he was real after all. For several minutes, Bieggaålmaj shook the plane as if he would pluck it out of the air and toss it into the sea; then, having followed a line of faraway islands down the western coast, the plane turned inward and started across the mountains – and in the white gleam off the snow-capped peaks, I forgot about Arild Frederiksen altogether, forgot everything, in fact, except that clear unearthly light. By the time I woke up, the plane was touching down in a steady grey rain and the voice on the public address system was politely requesting people to remain seated, for their own safety and the safety of others, until the seat-belt signs were switched off.

*   *   *

I changed planes in Oslo. There was a delay before we took off on the next leg of the journey, but I didn't care. I had been to London once before, but I didn't remember it very well. It had been hot and I had been dismayed by the crowds of people in the streets, the way they bumped past each other with distant looks on their faces, as if they were trying desperately to pretend they were alone. Mother had taken me to the National Gallery and the Tate, and we had spent a day in Kew Gardens, walking around the Palm House and the alpine beds – and, though I could see what Mother meant when she said it was beautiful, I didn't really like it. The Palm House was hot and airless and the alpine garden seemed to me nothing more than a sad imitation of the place we had just left. The place where I belonged.

I emerged an hour later than scheduled into the mass of travellers at Heathrow Airport – there had been some kind of security scare just before my plane touched down, and now there were people everywhere: business travellers in crumpled suits trying to push through the crowds, a party of French children roiling and surging back and forth in the passport queue, a half-dozen Chinese women arguing with an unhappy-looking official in a blue-and-red uniform. I didn't try to hurry. There was no point. It was more than an hour before I emerged into the main concourse and caught the Express into the city, the first of the three trains that would eventually take me to where I would be staying for the next three days. Mother had suggested I give myself longer, maybe make a holiday out of the trip, but I had rejected that idea. I didn't know why but, as soon as we had agreed the arrangements and Mother had got on the phone to make my reservations, I had started feeling anxious about going, and I was glad that I wouldn't be away for long. It rained all the way to Birmingham, but every now and then there was a sudden cascade of sunlight through the clouds, and the fields and backyards were transformed, the way a stage is, when the lights go up. It reminded me of home, that light – and then it was gone, and the rain set in again, gradually getting harder and greyer till, by the time I changed trains for the second time, it seemed that there was no light at all. No light, and no darkness; just a wash of dull, cold grey on the roofs and shopfronts and a low, rain-grey sky over the warehouse lots and wrecking yards that slipped by between stations.

There was another delay on the third leg of the journey, when the train pulled up short and sat motionless for fifteen minutes without moving. When it finally did arrive, I got wet carrying my overnight bag from the train to the taxi; nevertheless, by five that evening I was standing in a warm, cosy-looking foyer, checking in to my hotel. I don't know how Mother chose it, but it was perfect. The receptionist was a very thin girl with big, dark eyes and inky black hair pulled back into a tight ponytail, making her look like a character from one of the Gorey cartoons that Mother loved so. She had an accent of some sort, maybe Irish, but the gold name tag on her jacket said FRANÇOISE, which didn't strike me as a very Irish name. She was extremely polite, but she didn't smile when she gave me the key and wished me a pleasant stay, and I was glad of that. I didn't want people to be friendly; I wanted them to do their jobs and then, when I had what I needed, to leave me alone.

The hotel was an old stone building set in its own gardens on what the brochure described as a quiet, leafy street, just a few minutes from the town centre. I assumed that Mother had chosen it because it was family-run, which usually meant *small* – and, at first sight, it looked more like a large suburban house than a hotel. The lobby was dim and slightly cluttered in a friendly way, brass sculptures of horses and dogs stood in pools of gold lamplight on battered side tables, the wall facing reception was lined with shelves and filled with books that nobody had read for years – Kyrre Opdahl would have loved it – and it seemed welcoming, a house from some earlier and better age, when time passed more slowly and you could almost watch the patina forming on the tables and vases. When I got to my room, however, everything was plain and simple: a bed, a wardrobe, a table, a lamp that had been turned on in anticipation of my arrival, but no ornaments, no sculptures, no rows of faded books. There was a picture on the wall above the bed – a hunting scene, as I recall – and that was it. Outside, on the far side of the lawn, a street lamp was already lit, a soft orange light at the window that made me feel insulated and immune from time. I set my bag down on the bed, unpacked it and put my things away quickly, then I went to the window. The view across the gravel driveway and the slightly unkempt front lawn was of the brochure's leafy street and, beyond that, what appeared to be a small children's park surrounded by a barred fence. The road was busy with home-going traffic, but the park was empty and still in the pale orange street light. Someone had done all they could to make the play area seem welcoming: the uprights and bars of the swings were freshly painted in cherry red, the roundabout was gold and white and blue – but, now, in this daylong rain, nobody was there. It wasn't a day for playing, it was a day for sitting on the stairs, listening to the rain, or reading a book about pirates or Cheshire cats.

I sat down on the bed. There was probably still enough time to make it to the hospital, but I was tired and I felt damp and slightly grimy, and I didn't think it would matter if I waited one more night. I was worn out after the journey, I told myself, and it would feel less of an intrusion if I visited in the morning. I would be better company for a sick person when I'd had some rest and, besides, the woman who had written the letters, this Kate Thompson, would surely be there now, and she would be a familiar face, a comforting presence for Arild Frederiksen – and surely that was what he needed, as the night closed in on his hospital room. I didn't want to arrive in the evening, in the rain, just as he was taking his medicine and settling for the night – and I didn't want to turn up unannounced either. Of course, I didn't know, that evening, how serious his illness was, or I'm sure I would have gone to the hospital right away. That goes without saying. I had come to visit a man who was sick and had, presumably, asked to see me – or had it been Kate Thompson's decision to summon me? Had she taken it upon herself to write, suspecting that Arild Frederiksen wouldn't have done so himself? Or, if he had written, he wouldn't have said he was ill. But Kate Thompson had said he was ill and, no doubt, she had known that this would make me feel obligated to come. And I had come, of course, because there really was no choice. But *had* she written to me with his consent, or had she made this summons a proof of how much she cared about him? She had called herself his *friend* but I had immediately assumed there was more between them – and, if that was a fair assumption, then she really did have certain rights, as evening fell and the night drew in. At the very least, she had the right to be alone with him. I did take her number out of my purse, I even set it down on the bedside table and started to dial but, after a moment, I hung up and decided it would be best to wait till the next morning. That was only fair. Besides, I was tired after the journey and I needed to rest –

so I dialled the number for home instead and waited while it rang. But there was no answer and, after a dozen or so rings, the answering machine kicked in. 'This is Angelika Rossdal. I am busy right now. Please leave a message.' It was a plain and simple recording, no frills, no sly touches of irony or humour – and it was the first time I'd ever heard it from a distance. I stood listening to the voice, then hung up when the tone sounded, because I couldn't think of anything to say. Mother's voice sounded so remote, so abstract, and it suddenly seemed to me that the voice I was hearing wasn't her at all, but an impostor – and, though I knew that this was an absurd notion, I began to feel something close to panic, suddenly overwhelmed by the idea that I had travelled too far and for too long and, now that I was here, in this alien place, I wasn't just hearing Mother's voice from far away, I was hearing the entire house – the entire space that I usually occupied – falling silent and closing around my absence. I was far away from everything that I knew or cared about, far away in the rain and the English countryside, and, for a moment, I felt sick with dismay at the thought of somebody else going about my house, using my things, taking my books down from the shelves, listening as the phone rang, but not coming to answer it. That feeling only lasted for a minute or so, but when it left me, I felt utterly exhausted and I lay back on the bed, not even bothering to undress. It was still early evening, but I immediately fell into a troubled sleep, plagued by a dream that, I am sure, recurred several times over the next few hours, a dream in which the Sigfridsson boys were still alive, but they were trapped somewhere – in an underground room, or maybe the space beneath an upturned boat – and I could hear them calling out for someone to come and rescue them. In the dream, that someone was me, but I didn't know what to do and, as I listened helplessly, the cries grew louder and more numerous till, finally, it was a choir of voices, crying out to be saved while the water or the darkness pulled them in, and I couldn't do anything to help.

I woke early the next morning and began preparing for my visit. I took the letter Kate Thompson had sent me, with the name of the hospital and her address, and I tucked it into my pocket, then I checked to see that I still had enough money in my purse and went downstairs. Even though I had fallen asleep early, I hadn't got much rest – the dreams had gone on all night, it seemed, and it had felt odd, sleeping, then waking again, or half waking, in a dark room, hearing strange noises from the rooms below. At one point, I thought I could hear a boy calling – I thought the sound came from out in the park across the street – and, because the cry sounded so desperate, I got out of bed to go and look. I stood for a long time, gazing out over the gardens towards the empty little park under the orange street lamp, but I couldn't see anyone. Now, I was tired and, at the same time, my annoyance at having to be here – my annoyance at having to go to the hospital, to see a sick man that I had never even met – was returning. I didn't want to go to the hospital. I had an image of one of Munch's famous sick rooms: the gaunt figure laid out on the bed, under a pile of blankets, the shadows closing in, the world outside – the sunlight, the flowers – impossibly distant, and I could almost taste the stale air and the faded, sweat-soiled linen. For a long moment, I even considered packing my things and going straight back home – then I thought of Mother, and then I put on my coat and went downstairs.

The girl at reception looked identical to the one I had met

the night before, only her name tag said RENATE and she had a different accent, maybe Polish, or Eastern European. I asked her to call me a taxi and she picked up the phone. 'Where to?' she said.

'The hospital.'

'Which one?'

I took Kate's letter from my pocket and read out the name of the hospital. The girl nodded and repeated what I had said into the phone. There was a short silence; then, without saying anything more, she hung up and made a note in a spiral-ringed notebook. She didn't say anything; she didn't even look at me. It was as if she had forgotten I was there. 'How long will it be?' I said.

She looked up. For just one second, it seemed as if she hadn't understood, and I was about to repeat the question when she finally spoke. 'The taxi will be here in five minutes,' she said carefully.

I thanked her and sat down in the far corner of the lobby, next to a bronze sculpture of a horse. Twenty minutes later, I found myself at another desk, talking to another recep-tionist about the patient I had come to visit – a patient she appeared not to be able to find in her records. 'How do you spell that?' she said, her eyes fixed on the ledger in front of her.

I spelled the name. 'He's Norwegian,' I said. I realised, as I said it, that I had no idea how long Arild Frederiksen had lived in England – and it struck me, as soon as the words were out of my mouth, that his nationality was irrelevant.

The woman didn't look up. She didn't say anything either – or not for a long time. Then, as if something had dawned on her, she raised her head and gave a wary, almost forced smile. 'Let me just call through,' she said. 'Are you a relative?'

I shook my head, wondering why she needed this information; then I nodded, because I thought she might turn me away if I wasn't related to the patient. Wasn't that something they did? I was certain I had the right hospital but, for a fleeting moment, it occurred to me that I might have made a mistake. 'I have a letter,' I said.

The woman shook her head slightly then put her hand on a white telephone on her desk. 'Why don't you have a seat?' she said – and I could see that she didn't want to make the call while I was there, though I didn't know why. She gestured at a large waiting area off to the left by a row of high windows. 'I'll call through to find out what ward your friend is on.'

I shook my head and she gave me a startled look. Stupidly, I had wanted to protest, to say that Arild Frederiksen wasn't my *friend*, but she had obviously misunderstood. She set her face, forcing herself to remain sympathetic, though something else – a trace of hostility, I thought – flitted across her face. 'Please take a seat,' she said. 'Someone will come for you in a little while.' Then, without waiting for a reply, she picked up the receiver and began to dial.

As soon as Kate Thompson appeared, walking slowly through the crowd of random people who were coming and going along the corridor next to the waiting area, I knew who she was. I also knew that something had happened; though, to begin with, I didn't realise that Arild Frederiksen was dead. I imagined complications of some kind, or emergency surgery, perhaps, but not death. Life is such a given, after all. Besides, it would have been ridiculous, my travelling all that way, only to find that the reason for my journey had disappeared a few hours before I arrived. I hadn't wanted to come, I had no desire to meet this supposed father of mine but, now that I was here, it seemed only right that he would be present for the ceremony that Kate Thompson had worked so hard to set up. But he wasn't. True to form, he remained an absence in my life, even now, when I couldn't give a damn, one way or the other. If the receptionist had told me right away that he was dead, if she hadn't been obliged to make that phone call, I would probably have left right away; but she hadn't said anything, presumably because she had been told to contact someone when I finally turned up. I'd thought she was calling a charge nurse, or a doctor – and maybe she did – but the person who came to break the news of Arild Frederiksen's death wasn't a member of staff at all. It was Kate Thompson.

It was a surprise to me that she was a rather *large* woman. Not fat, not even that tall, but *large*. Solid. Prepossessing. I hadn't expected that. The letter had suggested a wispy, almost diffident creature, somebody slender in every sense of the word, but Kate Thompson wasn't like that at all. Even in the waiting area of a hospital, in circumstances that must have been very difficult for her, she filled the space she occupied fully and quite deliberately. It was as if she wanted to say that she was *here* and that she had no intention of being dismissed or contradicted – which I took as a sign that she had been obliged to work hard, at some point in her life, to gain that sense of herself and, though she was humble enough to under-stand this self-possession as a privilege – as much luck as it was judgement or effort – she was determined to *be herself*, no matter what. In that sense, I suppose, she was the exact opposite of Mother, who took it for granted that she was in complete control of everything that happened around her, even though she appeared to occupy no space at all. Or rather, there *was* a space, a space *existed*, but you always knew that it was elsewhere, you always felt that it was distinct from your own clearly defined – and limited – territory. The first impression Kate Thompson gave off, however, was one of stolid presence, an air of deliberate and hard-won self-possession – and it occurred to me, later, that this was odd, considering that she had just lost the man she loved.

She recognised me right away, just as I had recognised her. The waiting area was quite busy, and I could have been anyone, but she walked straight to me and held out her hand. 'Liv,' she said. It wasn't a question. 'You're here.'

I nodded and shook hands, but I didn't say anything. Kate Thompson was around forty-five, I thought, not at all pretty, though possibly the kind of woman that men of a certain type and age would find attractive. Her hair was a deep, coppery colour which I assumed came out of a bottle, her lips were very full, and though it was obvious that she hadn't slept for some time, there was something oddly appealing, something almost glamorous, about her fatigue. She let go of my hand and looked around – and I could tell, right away, that she had something to tell me that she would have preferred to say in less awkward surroundings. At the same time, she needed to tell me immediately and, because she couldn't think of anywhere better to go, she resigned herself to the circumstances and said what she had to say. By then, however, I knew what it was that she needed to tell me. It had been there in her voice, when she'd said *you're here* like that, as if she was saddened by the fact of my presence, and it was there in her face – a look, not of grief, or not just grief, but an odd apprehension. 'I decided you weren't coming,' she said.

'I'm sorry,' I said. 'It took longer than I expected.'

She nodded slightly. We were still standing, and there were people nearby, people sitting or standing all around us, and it was awkward for her, but it was obvious that she couldn't delay telling me any longer. 'He died last night,' she said. 'I mean . . . it was early this morning.'

'Ah.'

'There were complications,' she said.

'I see.' I didn't know what that meant and I realised that I'd never known what his problem was. Had he undergone surgery? Was it an infection? What kind of complications did she mean? I thought of asking, but she began speaking again before I could say anything.

'We thought you were arriving yesterday,' she said. '*I* thought –'

'My flight was delayed,' I said, but I don't think she heard me. She was starting to tell me something, something she had gone over already in her mind – and I wondered what time it had been that morning when Arild Frederiksen had died, and whether she had been at the hospital all along.

'I didn't tell him,' she said. 'Not till you confirmed you were . . . I didn't want to get his hopes up.' She closed her eyes, and it reminded me of something, the way she did it. She closed her eyes and kept talking, and I remembered that it was something one of my teachers had done. I could see the woman's face, and I remembered that she had taught Literature, but I couldn't remember her name. What I did remember was how irritating it had been. 'He wanted to see you,' she said. 'He talked about you often, these last few weeks, but he didn't want to ask . . .' Her eyes opened suddenly – and I remembered that *that* was what I had disliked so much in that Literature class. It had felt like a trick, in school, as if the teacher – her name came to me, then: it was Mrs Olerud – it was as if by closing her eyes this Mrs Olerud was wishing away the inferior version of the person she was talking to, and then, when she opened them again, was hoping to find somebody better. Somebody capable of understanding what she had to say. 'It wasn't his idea, to write, and I didn't tell him that I was getting in touch. Not till I knew you were coming.'

'I'm sorry,' I said – and I hoped she understood that I wasn't apologising. That I was – offering her my condolences. In American films, they had a way of saying that – *I'm sorry for your loss*, they said, when somebody died, or when the policeman has to interview the dead man's wife, just hours after they find the body. *I'm sorry for your loss* – it was a neat, clean phrase, but it sounded too easy and I didn't say it. I didn't say anything else, in fact, because there was nothing I could say. The loss was hers, not mine, but for either of us to acknowledge that, I knew, would be a mistake.

She turned away. There was nothing more to say, though, obviously, we couldn't just leave it at that. We didn't know each other, I had never even met Arild Frederiksen and, as I had just been given to understand, I only had her word for it that he had ever wanted to meet me in the first place. He hadn't asked her to write to me, he hadn't asked her to send me copies of his books. Through all the years I was growing up, he had made no effort to find me, or to come and visit. He hadn't even written a letter – so I had no way of knowing if he had really agreed to Kate Thompson's approaching me. Perhaps he had said he did, for her sake. To honour her good intentions, perhaps. He probably didn't even know about the phone calls, or the messages on Mother's answering machine. I waited. The situation seemed to demand something from her, some indication that she accepted that there was nothing more to say, some sign that it would be acceptable for me to leave. She wasn't ready for that, though. She needed something more. She stood for a long moment, gazing out at the hospital grounds; then she turned back to me. 'Perhaps you'd like to see him?' she said. Her voice was very quiet and I thought I detected a trace of doubt – enough, at least, that I knew she wouldn't insist, when I rejected the idea. 'I could ask,' she said. 'If you felt you'd like to see him. To say goodbye.'

I shook my head. I wanted to say – I wanted to shout at her – that Arild Frederiksen was dead, and that I had never even met him, so how was it possible for me to say goodbye to him? I wanted to shout that I didn't know him, and I didn't know her either. She had taken it upon herself to intrude upon my life, but that was all. I wanted to shout at her that she should accept things as they were – but I didn't. I didn't shout; I just shook my head and said that what she had suggested wouldn't be necessary. That upset her, of course, but she didn't say anything. She lowered her head, and I thought she might be on the point of tears, so I waited for her to regain control of her emotions. I was still hoping she would say or do something that would allow me to go, but she didn't speak, or look up, for a long time and, gradually, I sensed that she was drifting into some private train of thought, some memory that had nothing to do with me. It wasn't exactly the sign I had wanted, but I decided that it might be enough. I cleared my throat, to get her attention. 'You must be very tired,' I said. 'I should go, and let you rest.'

She lifted her head. Her eyes were dry and her face seemed, if anything, unusually calm. She didn't say anything, though, she just looked at me – and I realised that she either hadn't heard or hadn't understood what I had said.

'You've been up all night,' I said and then, for some reason, I looked at my watch. There was no reason for this: I didn't have any place to be, and I didn't remotely care what time it was. It was, I think, an involuntary movement and nothing

185

more – but she noticed the gesture and, as slight as it was, it upset her.

'What are you saying?' she said. Her voice came out hard, so I thought for a moment that she was angry. 'Do you have to be somewhere?'

'No,' I said. 'It's just . . . I thought I would leave you to . . .' I didn't know what came next. I think I was going to say that I would leave her to her grief, but I knew that *that* wasn't appropriate.

'No,' she said. Her voice was softer now, but she still seemed angry. Or maybe she was unhappy at how awkward it was turning out to be. 'I don't understand.' She stared at me, not so much angry as dismayed. 'I mean . . . You only just got here,' she said.

'Yes,' I said. 'I'm sorry I was too late to . . .' It was hopeless. What was I supposed to say? I just wanted to shake her hand, or sign a paper or something, and get out of there – and my desire to get away was apparent to her.

'He was waiting for you,' she said. 'He was trying so hard to hang on. Even the nurses noticed it.' She shook her head in wonder, presumably at Arild Frederiksen's tenacity – and also, I thought, at my apparent callousness. To her, it was quite straightforward: my father had been dying, and I had been hurrying to his bedside. Only I hadn't hurried fast enough – and maybe I hadn't hurried at all. 'We'd thought you would get here last night,' she said again, and this time it was an accusation. She was watching me closely now, studying me as if she had just discovered a new life form that she wasn't quite familiar with – and I felt a sudden rush of apprehension, something like the apprehension you feel when you find yourself with someone who wants to say something you don't want to hear. A sincere person who is just about to say something,

186

but hasn't quite found the words yet. Someone who might reach out and touch you, someone who might take hold of an arm or a hand. I stepped back, and she sensed my apprehension. She sensed that I didn't want to be touched, or made to feel guilty, and she decided to be gracious. 'Anyway,' she said. 'If you have nowhere else to be, I thought we might get a coffee. I mean, now that you're here, I thought you might want to talk.'

'What about?' I didn't know what she meant. She had told me what she had told me, and there really wasn't anything else to say. What more did we have to talk about? I had come too late and Arild Frederiksen had died before we could meet. That was unfortunate, but it wasn't anyone's fault. There was no need for explanations, or reminiscences, or some cosy heart-to-heart. In fact, there was no need for any kind of talk at all.

'Well,' she said – and I could see that she was surprised by my question. 'I could tell you . . . I thought you might want to hear about him, since you never had the chance to get to know him . . . That's if you have the time, of course.' There was a trace of resentment in her voice, but it wasn't put on – if anything, she was trying to hide her feelings. It bothered her that I had taken so long to make this visit and now it bothered her even more that I seemed in such a hurry to get away, but she didn't want to come across as judgemental, in spite of all that. 'I thought you might like to . . .' She considered a moment. 'You didn't have a chance to get to know him,' she said. 'That was a source of unhappiness to him . . .' She ventured a thin smile. 'I thought I could tell you something about him. He *was* your father, after all.'

I didn't know what to say. I didn't want to listen to her stories about a man I had never known, and I was bemused

187

by the fact that it meant so much to her. I felt unhappy and imposed upon, and I wanted to refuse this apparent kindness that wasn't a kindness at all, but I didn't know how. It's an art, refusal. At the time, I hadn't mastered it, not the way Mother had, and I was hampered by awkwardness and a desire not to seem impolite. 'What about you?' I said. 'Were you –' I wanted to say *close*, but she was annoyed with me now and, though she wanted to conceal her annoyance, she couldn't stop herself from jumping in.

'Were we? What – lovers?' She laughed. 'Well, after a fashion. After his fashion, I should say.' She smiled, then looked away. There was a long pause. 'Arild was a real Aquarius,' she said, still not looking at me. 'He was so busy loving the whole world, he didn't get round to specifics . . .' She glanced back at me quickly, then she smiled again – but I could see that the smile was a cover and that she was, in fact, close to tears. A long moment passed, as she fought off some unwelcome feeling. An unwelcome feeling of – what? Grief? Betrayal? Disappointment that they hadn't been closer? 'Well, I'm sure you don't believe in that sort of thing,' she said.

'What sort of thing?'

'You know. Astrology. *That* sort of thing.'

I shook my head. 'Ah,' I said.

She gave a soft laugh. 'Why?' she said. 'What did you think I meant?'

I didn't answer – I felt caught out somehow, but I didn't know why – and she seemed amused by my apparent confusion. 'The cafe's just over here,' she said, turning to lead the way. She was confident, now, that I would follow. 'It's quite nice. I'm sure you could do with a coffee, after your journey.'

*   *   *

The cafe wasn't *nice* in fact. It wasn't really a cafe at all, it was just a section of the main concourse that had been blocked off and furnished with tables and chairs, so you could watch the people coming and going as you drank your coffee and ate your iced doughnut: nurses in uniform, porters wheeling trolleys, visitors with bunches of carnations or fruit baskets. The coffee was thin and weak, and it came in a polystyrene cup with a garish purple logo on the side. Still, it wasn't as if I was there to drink coffee. Kate Thompson found a quietish table in the corner and sat down. 'There's milk over there, if you want it,' she said, and I realised that she had sat at that table once or twice before.

I shook my head. 'Black is fine,' I said. I sat down opposite her. The tables were small and rickety, and I felt that we were too close, but there was nothing to be done about it. It was, at least, quieter than the waiting area had been and, from where we were sitting, I could see a patch of greenery, at the far end of a wide grey-and-white corridor. After the previous day's rain, the trees and shrubs were still wet, but now the sun was poking through the clouds and, for the moment, everything in that bright square of greenery was sparkling.

'So,' Kate said, with the air of someone good-naturedly changing the subject. She had put aside her annoyance and, now that she had me where she wanted, she was ready to start over. I wondered, again, why talking about Arild Frederiksen meant so much to her. 'What does it mean: *Liv*?'

'I'm sorry?'

'Your name,' she said. 'It sounds like it ought to mean something. Like – I don't know, *life* or something . . .'

I shook my head. 'It's just a name,' I said.

'So Liv isn't *life* in Norwegian,' she said – and for a moment, it seemed she was challenging me, or maybe asking me a trick

189

question, the way the class show-off used to do in school. She smiled. 'I thought it was *life*,' she said.

I shook my head. 'I don't think I've ever thought about it. Not like that,' I said. 'It's just a name. Do names have to mean something?' The question annoyed me. It should have been obvious to her that I didn't want to be there any more. I hadn't wanted to be there earlier, when we were in the corridor, but now things were different – and I sensed something ugly was coming. The proving of a point, perhaps, or the justification of something that, as far as I was concerned, didn't need justifying. Then, as if she had read my mind, her manner changed. She sat back in her chair and gave me a kindly, even sympathetic look, a look that, as I saw it, deferred rather too obviously to the grief I ought to have been showing, as if to say that it wasn't her place to question my apparent calm – and I saw that she was trying to imagine, not that I was some heartless creature who felt nothing, but that I was hiding this grief, not only from her, but also from myself, out of some misplaced sense of loyalty, or *amour propre*. 'I'm sorry,' she said. 'But I don't know what your mother told you about him, and I have to ask, because I don't want to go over things you already know –'

'She didn't tell me anything,' I said.

That surprised her, of course. Not only the fact, in itself, but that I could admit so calmly that I'd had no idea who my father was. She swayed forward, then leaned her elbows on the table and looked into my face. 'You mean you didn't know *anything* about him? Who he was, what he did . . .'

I shook my head. 'I didn't even know his name, until you wrote to me,' I said. 'And even then . . .'

'Even then?'

I sat back in my chair, away from her. I didn't wish to be

scrutinised. 'Even then,' I said, 'I couldn't know for sure that he was who you said he was.'

She bit her lip. She was scandalised now, scandalised and *offended* by my lack of emotion, which she no doubt considered unnatural – but she was also enjoying this. Everything she had imagined about Mother was being confirmed. She had probably read articles and searched for Angelika Rossdal on the Internet, and she would have loved the image of the cold recluse who only cared about her work. She was the kind of person who took up other people's pain, holding the grudge that they were too hurt or self-deceived to hold themselves, and she no doubt imagined that, whatever had happened all those years ago, it was Mother's fault. Oh yes; she had to be enjoying this – though I think now that some part of her was trying not to. Or rather, some scrupulous part of her, at the front of her mind, was trying not to relish what had just been confirmed to her secret and slightly craven satisfaction. 'And your mother never spoke about him?' she said.

'No.'

'She never spoke about their life together, in Oslo?'

'No.'

'Really?'

'I can't imagine there was much to talk about,' I said. 'It wasn't a lasting relationship –'

'Ah. So she told you *that* much?'

I shook my head. 'She didn't tell me anything,' I said. 'She had left all that behind. She's happy now, where she is –'

'Happy?'

'Yes.'

'How's that?'

'I'm sorry?'

'How is she happy?'

I shook my head again. I felt offended for Mother's sake, because a judgement was being made that I didn't think was fair, but I had no intention of allowing her to upset me. 'I don't know that that's any of your business,' I said.

Her mouth hardened and she sat looking at me for a long moment before she spoke again. 'You're right,' she said, finally. 'It's not my business. But it is *yours*. It *was* yours.' She was visibly upset now, but I couldn't tell if she was genuinely angry, or whether she was just pretending – to herself as much as to me – to keep from being overwhelmed by some personal and perhaps slightly shameful sadness that she didn't want me to see. 'He was your *father*,' she said. 'And that was *your* business. You can't tell me that it was all right, just to erase him ... That it was all right for you both to pretend he didn't even exist –'

I shook my head. 'Nobody *pretended* anything,' I said. 'He went away, and that was that. He was forgotten –'

'He went away?'

'Yes.'

'Is *that* what your mother told you?'

'Yes.' I thought for a moment. It wasn't true, of course; she hadn't told me anything. I had just assumed – but it was a reasonable assumption, all things considered. I looked at her. She was watching me closely now, and I felt uneasy, because I knew she was trying to read something in my face, trying to find a way through what she must have thought of as a lie.

After a moment, though, something in her expression changed, and she sat back in her chair again. Something had occurred to her – some private memory, or half-concealed realisation – and now the scrutiny was done with, and so was the anger. Now there was just – not sadness exactly, but

192

something like it. Resignation, perhaps. A feeling that there was no point any more in telling what she knew, because, now, Arild Frederiksen was gone. She had loved him, of that there could be no doubt, but I was beginning to suspect that he had loved her less than she had hoped or wanted – and *that*, I realised, was her personal sadness, *that* was her secret shame. She had loved him, but he had been too much of an Aquarius to love her back. Or to love her as much as she had wanted. I looked at her hands. There were no rings. I realised this, I understood it, at that moment – and at that moment, I think, she saw that I had understood. I thought that she would be angry, then, or upset, but she wasn't. Instead, she gave a soft laugh and shook her head – and it wasn't a pretence. It wasn't a cover. She'd had years to get used to her condition, years to learn how to give up on false hopes, years to relinquish the story she had hoped would unfold with Arild Frederiksen – and she *had* got used to it, she *had* given up her fondest hopes, and she had done so, I suspected, with enough grace that she could feel proud of herself. No doubt she had even managed to convince herself that, by giving up the most obvious thing, she was gaining something far subtler and richer; no doubt she had told herself that the romance she had hoped for was banal, or unsustainable, and that what she had won was far better. More honest. More realistic. 'He was a good man,' she said. 'If you had been able to meet him, you would have been able to see –'

'I'm sure he was,' I said.

'But you didn't get to meet him,' she said. 'And I think it would be good – for you, as well as him – if you would let me tell you something about him. Since your mother . . .' She pulled herself up and reconsidered. She didn't want to drive me away, I could see that, and she genuinely believed that I needed to know about this man, this *father*, but that wasn't the main reason she wanted to keep me there. She wanted to repair something that, in her opinion, needed to be repaired, but the main reason for this conversation was that *she* wanted to talk about him. She *needed* to talk about him – and, no matter how good her intentions might have seemed to her, I couldn't help thinking that she had chosen me for this conversation because she had nobody else. I had no proof of this – I knew nothing about her, or the life she and Arild Frederiksen had lived together – but I suddenly had an over-whelming sense of loneliness, a sense of a sad, slightly dismayed couple, washed up in a quiet, moderately comfortable back-water and doing their best to fill the days with purpose and interest. I had a vision of Arild sitting at home with his type-writer, while Kate went off to yoga, a raincoat over her leotard, and I knew – I don't know how I knew, because I hadn't given it a moment's thought before we sat down in the hospital cafe, but I *knew* that they had come together, not because of some-thing they had shared, but out of a common sense that their best days were over, a common feeling that whatever they had wished for in life hadn't quite materialised. 'I thought you'd want to know what he was like,' she said, with a slightly defeated air that, because I didn't think it was put on for my benefit, I couldn't help sympathising with.

I nodded. What I felt wasn't the agreement or curiosity she thought she had won; no, what I felt was resignation. 'I read the book you sent,' I said. 'He obviously travelled a good deal.'

That must have sounded lame to her, but she didn't let it show. 'All over the world,' she said, allowing herself a faint, somewhat tentative smile, as if she thought I might want her to apologise for something – for detaining me, I suppose – then she launched into a story that she had obviously thought about for some time, a prepared narrative that was so obviously designed to show Arild Frederiksen in the best possible light that I couldn't help but find it touching. 'Every journey was supposed to be the last,' she said. 'I was always waiting for him to come home. But it was something he felt he *had* to do. He was trying to change the world, in his own way. Or maybe not to change the world, but he wanted to make something happen. To give something to people . . .' She looked at me – and for a moment it was as if she wanted to ask if I was one of those people. No doubt she had already drawn her own conclusions with regard to Mother.

'That must have been lonely,' I said.

She smiled. 'It was,' she said. 'But I had no complaints.' She was lying, of course – she had been miserable, I was sure of that – but she was proud of him and it was part of who she thought she was, who she wanted to be, that she never once questioned his decisions. And I could see, too, that she was happy now, because, now, she was telling the story she wanted to tell, the story of a selfless man who worked tirelessly for the environment, a man who could wander for three days through bandit country, without food and with only a limited supply of water, in search of the giant buttercup of the high Andes, a man who, when Salvador Allende was assassinated, had to walk out of Chile over the mountains, crossing into Argentina under cover of night, with a backpack full of rare seeds and herbarium specimens. The man who had zigzagged back and forth through war zones in search of endangered tulip species and talked his way out of captivity, or worse, in the no-go areas of countries that didn't even exist any more. The man who had been praised, not just for his heroism, or for the contribution he had made to our under-standing of remote ecosystems, but also for the modesty and self-effacing humour that informed his not quite best-selling, but once fairly popular, accounts of his various journeys and of the people and plants he had encountered. 'He took so many risks,' she said. 'He was shot at, he went for days without food and water. Once, he was arrested by some warlord and he spent several days in a narrow cell with nothing but a pocket chess set to divert him. He'd lost the white queen, apparently, and he had to play without her, memorising her position on the board as he went along. He had nobody to play with, so he played against himself, and that was how he passed the time . . .' She smiled. 'He didn't tell me about that for ages afterwards. He could have been killed and he just sat there, remembering where the white queen was, playing chess against himelf.' She looked at me, expecting, or at least hoping, for some kind of response.

I shook my head in more or less genuine wonder. 'That's . . . remarkable,' I said.

She accepted the compliment on his behalf, then continued with her account. 'He said once that the reason he wrote was that he wanted to take us all into a deep forest and leave us there, so we could see how beautiful it was. He wanted to carry people off to remote islands and the slopes of active volcanoes so they would stop what they were doing and start to *care* about the world. He wanted them to switch off the television and the piped music and see what was *real*. The plants were just a pretext.' She smiled happily, and I think for that moment she was close to forgetting that the man she was describing was dead. 'I know it's corny,' she said. 'And it's defi-nitely a bit Age of Aquarius. But he really did care. He wasn't in it for money, he didn't want to be recognised. Well, not in the usual way . . .' She stopped talking and then, delicately, in the way somebody might do it if they were alone, she selected a sugar cube from the bowl in front of her, and lifted it to her lips. She held it steady for a moment, then she put it in her mouth and sat back in her chair. And this time, when she closed her eyes and sat for a time in complete silence, it wasn't me she was shutting out, it was everything.

I didn't speak. I thought of leaving her there – what difference did it make now, my seeming impolite? At the far end of the corridor, the light had dimmed on the hospital gardens and it looked like it might rain again, but I didn't care. I wanted to be outside. I wanted to be gone. 'I think –'

Before I could say anything else, Kate Thompson sat forward and began speaking again in a soft, but oddly argumentative voice. 'Of course, he got depressed sometimes,' she said. 'That's what you Scandinavians do, isn't it?' She thought for a moment, searching for the right word. 'You *brood*,' she said, but she wasn't satisfied and I could see that she was talking about something that she didn't want to fully acknowledge but refused, at the same time, to gloss over completely. She pulled back again and smiled understandingly, as if, whatever his condition was, I almost certainly shared it. 'He was a good man,' she said again. 'But he went through so much, and he risked his life, many times, for his work. It tired him out and it made him unhappy, because *nothing* changed. He always said you had to keep going, you couldn't give up, no matter how hopeless it seemed. But he was exhausted.' She looked to see if I was following her. To see if I even knew what that kind of exhaustion meant. 'And then,' she said, 'all of a sudden, he came home. He didn't say anything. He didn't make any promises. He just walked about the house, looking at all the stuff he'd brought back from all the different places he had been to. Shaman masks. Stone carvings. Old maps. It was like he'd come home and suddenly realised that his house was a museum . . .' She looked at me again, not to see if I was following, but to reassure herself that she was holding my attention. Because, if she wasn't, then I didn't *deserve* this story. I was just one of those others, the ones who didn't change, the ones who stayed at home and watched TV while the forests and the meadows and the mountain slopes were destroyed forever. And, even though I had wanted to get away, even though I didn't really like her, I *was* following. It was the one real story she had, I suspected, and though she hadn't quite got to whatever was interesting or tragic or life-affirming about it, I sensed that something of that nature was coming. Some decisive moment, some twist maybe, was on the horizon. What she was afraid of was that, whatever that twist or turn in the narrative signified for her, it might mean nothing to me.

'Yes – he was a good man,' she said, yet again; but this time even she noticed that she was repeating herself and she didn't say anything else. For a minute or more, she sat quietly, staring at the sugar bowl. I thought she was working on her story, finding the right way of coming to the significant detail or plot segment that would make me *understand*. The moment of revelation, the point at which everything changed. I could see that what she was about to say mattered to her in ways that I didn't begin to appreciate and, so, I waited. But nothing happened. I'm sure she started out with the plan of continuing with her account but, somewhere in the midst of that chain of thought, something shifted and, for some reason, she decided not to tell me the rest of the story – or at least, not yet. She wanted to make me wait. She wanted me to come back. It was a gamble, she knew that, but it was a gamble she had to take, because it was also a test. She sat upright and looked at me. 'Well now,' she said. 'I have talked long enough, and I'm sure you must be . . .' She shrugged. 'I'm sure you're hungry,' she said, in a tone that made the very idea of food seem outlandish, or quixotic. 'I have some things I need to do, but maybe after . . .' She hesitated, then she made up her mind to trust me. 'Maybe this evening, you could come to dinner,' she said.

I didn't want to have dinner with her, but I couldn't refuse her invitation. Not in so many words. She was letting me go, and if I didn't come back, there was nothing to be done about it and she would know that I wasn't worthy of Arild Frederiksen's memory. And I thought, at the time, that she probably wanted me to come back, but that there was also a part of her that didn't. Maybe she had said all she needed to say. Maybe she *wanted* me to be unworthy. Either way, I couldn't refuse her invitation; though I felt sure that I couldn't accept it, either, so I didn't say anything.

She smiled. At that moment, I think, the outcome was irrelevant to her anyway. 'I have some things at the house that he would want you to have,' she said. 'You have my address, don't you?'

'Yes,' I said.

She waited, but when I didn't say anything else, she plucked another sugar cube from the bowl and stood up. 'If you can make it,' she said. 'I'll see you around seven.' She slipped the sugar cube into her mouth and, before I could answer, or even get out of my seat, she turned and left me to the half-empty coffee cups and what was left of the sugar.

It didn't come to me until later that she had been dismissing me by walking out like that. Or, rather, that she had been rehearsing a dismissal that might come to be necessary, if I failed to keep my appointment. At that moment, however, I didn't even know if I would go to dinner with her or not, because I hadn't decided yet and I didn't give it another thought because, at that moment, all I could think about was food. It hadn't been long since breakfast and I had eaten well that morning – certainly more than I usually ate at home – but, as soon as Kate Thompson disappeared, making her way back to some dim upper room where someone official would no doubt require the appropriate forms to be signed, and the necessary personal items to be taken away, I realised that I was very, very hungry. They say that exposure to death makes you feel more alive and, though I can't really say that I'd been directly exposed to anything much, I was overcome, as soon as I was alone, not only with a ravening hunger, but also – I am not quite sure exactly how to put this – with a sense of excitement, an almost feverish sensation of urgency. All I wanted was to get out into the open air and find something to eat. I didn't want the damp sandwiches wrapped in cling film that the cafe had to offer, I didn't want the slices of gelatinous apple pie laid out on shelves in the cooler on waxed paper plates, or the transparent cartons packed with pale carrot wedges and slick pastes, I didn't want bags of crisps and packets of mini crackers, I wanted fresh apples and newly baked bread; I wanted sweet, creamy cheeses; I wanted cloudberries, soused herrings, gulls' eggs, *gjetost*. Most of all, I wanted *sjørøye*.

I stood up. I felt a little dizzy, but it was a pleasant dizziness, like the feeling you have when you lean far out over the side of a fast-moving boat and, as I made my way back along the corridor, gliding through a tide of people who, like me, were on their way home from visits or outpatient appointments, glad to be free and empty-handed, going out all together into the fresh, damp air, I decided that I would do as Mother

200

had suggested and make a holiday of what was left of the trip. I took a taxi into the centre of town, found an old-fashioned greengrocer's shop and bought a bag of apples, which I ate immediately, one after another, while I wandered about the high street, searching for a place to buy cheese. Finally, I came to a tiny delicatessen, with a narrow shopfront that gave on to a long, dim space full of bottles and jars and wicker baskets packed with crusty bread and boxes of oatcakes and panini and, for almost the entire length of the shop, a high marble-effect counter piled with cheese rounds and boxes of apples. It was the first shop I'd found selling real food, but there was only one other customer there and the assistant – a tall, dark-haired man with the slightly self-congratulatory air of a superior tour guide – waited patiently while I wandered about, choosing one thing, then another: more apples, a chunk of Comté, a half-dozen crusty rolls, some herrings in dill sauce, a few thick slices of cured ham. Finally, I was satisfied that I had enough for a decent lunch. They even had *gjetost*. As he was taking my money, the man smiled and asked if I was Swedish.

'Norwegian,' I said.

'Ah.' His smile broadened. 'That would explain the *gjetost*,' he said.

'You don't like it?'

'It's a little too sweet for my taste,' he said.

I nodded. I suddenly felt very calm. Very calm and strangely happy. 'But it's supposed to be sweet,' I said, as I watched him wrap the sliced ham in waxed paper. 'That's what makes it *gjetost*.'

He laughed at that and handed me my purchases. 'Enjoy,' he said.

*   *   *

201

I ate my food in a little park near the slow, charcoal-coloured river that ran along the edge of the town centre. The rain had stopped, but the sky was still heavy and dark and nobody much came by as I sat on a wooden bench in the shelter of a willow tree and worked my way through the contents of my bag. Even though I had finished off the first batch of apples, I was still hungry and I didn't stop till I had consumed everything, breaking the cheese and rolls into pieces and fishing the herrings out of their pot with my fingers. Then, as soon as I had eaten the last of the *gjetost*, I realised that I hadn't bought anything to drink. I had been so hungry for food, it hadn't occurred to me to pick up a bottle of mineral water or orange juice in the delicatessen, though I had seen them set out in rows on a cold shelf by the counter.

I dumped the rubbish and leftovers into a bin and headed back towards the high street. I had seen a poster on a noticeboard earlier for the town museum and art gallery and I remembered Mother telling me once that if I was in a strange place and couldn't find a good cafe, the best alternative was an art gallery, because they usually had decent coffee and the surroundings were less shabby than you might find elsewhere. I didn't know if there was any truth in this, but I was in a strange place and far from home, so far that I felt – sentimentally, no doubt – that taking Mother's advice was the next best thing to having her there. I can't explain it, quite, but at that moment I felt guilty towards her. I didn't know *why* I felt guilty, but I did – and I remembered the sensation I'd had the night before, when I'd heard her voice on the answering machine, and she had seemed so far away and unlike her usual self. And I know, if I say it like this, it's not exactly right, but the feeling I had, the feeling of guilt, was similar in some way to the sudden understanding I'd had as a child – I can't remember how old I was, maybe six, maybe younger – the sudden realisation that she, my perfect mother, would die one day, and I would continue without her, in her house, in her garden, with her things all around me. Until that moment – I don't recall the exact details, but I have a sense of our being out walking, at the end of the summer – until that moment, it hadn't occurred to me to think of her dying, though I knew that people died, and I was shocked by the certainty of the fact. I recall looking up and seeing her there – she was searching for something in the long grass, off to one side, with her back to me – and the inevitable fact of her mortality hit me like a blow to the throat, so I wanted to catch hold of her and pin her down, to keep her from slipping away – and yet, at the same time, there was something beautiful about it. I didn't really know, then, what she had done when she moved to Kvaløya. I didn't know that she had left her old life behind to start again in the north, with no one to turn to and nowhere to go back to if it all went wrong, but I sensed her solitude and, at that moment, I felt that solitude and the fact of her coming death were somehow linked – and *that* was what made it beautiful. I knew that, even though she was going to die, she had *chosen* something lonely and difficult and, though I didn't know what it was, her choosing it seemed beautiful to me.

Now I was experiencing a similar sensation, combined with a suspicion that some kind of betrayal had been, if not enacted, then at least contemplated, that morning at the hospital. I couldn't have said what form that betrayal might have taken, but I knew it was there and I wanted to go quickly and find a museum cafe, where they had decent coffee and the kind of cakes that would smell of dough and burnt sugar, just like our dining room on a Saturday morning. It took me a while

203

to find the place but, when I did, I remembered why I had noticed the poster earlier. It wasn't a large gallery, and I couldn't imagine it was a very important one, but, as luck would have it, on that particular day, in that particular town, a travelling exhibition had just opened, and the poster I had seen – now I recalled that it had stood out among the others on that noticeboard, because it was new and bright, while the others had been weathered and faded – the poster I had seen announced the opening, only a few days before, of an exhibition called *Wild Reckoning: Art and Nature from 1850 to 1939*. Rather a dusty, academic-sounding title, no doubt – I wondered for a moment why those particular dates were significant – but I was intrigued. I ran up the steps to the gallery and got inside just as it began raining again; then, in the ornate, brick and marble foyer, which must have dated from the mid-Victorian era, I bought my ticket from a pretty Asian girl in a red scarf and a dark blue blazer, politely refused the offer of an audio guide, and made my way into a long, high-ceilinged room where the first set of pictures had been hung.

What do we mean by 'wild'? What is it in the natural world that seems alien to us, alien and yet, at the same time, essential? What is it we are missing, when we go into the woods? Why do we feel so nostalgic for landscapes we have never inhabited?

I read the first few lines of the exhibition guide the Asian girl had given me with my ticket, then I folded it carefully and put it away. It was immediately obvious that *Wild Reckoning* was one of those exhibitions that seek to inform and, at the same time, provoke serious thinking about what art is all about and I couldn't be bothered with that. I wasn't interested in art history – though, as I walked from exhibit to exhibit, I was surprised at how many of these images I already knew from Mother's books – what I wanted was the atmosphere these pictures created, en masse, an atmosphere that reminded me of home. The paintings were mostly minor works by artists whose names were only vaguely familiar, but that didn't matter; in fact, what I liked most was their quietness, the fact that they were, on the surface, nothing more than representations of some anonymous meadow or pine wood that, for reasons that no one else would ever understand, had beguiled the painter enough to halt him in his tracks, at the edge of a wet field, or on a windy beach, and hold him there for hours, his fingers numbed to the bone, as he worked to capture something that, for most people, was neither here nor there. There were several rooms, each with a larger painting at its centre, and I walked slowly from space to space, absorbing the fields of reimagined colour and light all around me, until, finally, after a series of minor Impressionist orchards and gloomy English seascapes, I was brought to a sudden halt by a large, brooding canvas that had been given pride of place in the last room of the exhibition. I knew it immediately, of course, but I had never seen it in all its glory and I was stunned by how beautiful it was. I was stunned, yes, and not just by its beauty but also by the fact that *this* painting, one of Mother's two or three favourite works of art, should be *here*, of all places – and the dizziness I had experienced earlier returned, even though I saw, immediately, that it was this, exactly *this*, that I had been expecting all along.

I looked around. Nobody else was there, not even a security person, but in the middle of the room, there was a low bench, on which some previous visitor had left a grubby and slightly scrunched-up exhibition leaflet. I walked over immediately and sat down, then I looked back to the exhibit. It was an oil painting, by Harald Sohlberg, of a small house at the edge of the sea, an isolated white *hytte* glimpsed through pine woods, its windows illumined with a soft, golden light, its roof almost black, like the pines and the dark water beyond. Had it been done by anyone else, this would have been taken for a night scene, but Sohlberg had painted the sky – a distant-seeming sky, far beyond the inky reach of the Sound – in a pale, eerie blue, an almost powder blue, like the gloaming of summer's end, and the little white house, with its faint gold lights, looked like it was part of a theatre set, impermanent, provisional and only temporarily inhabited. The sign on the wall gave the name and date of the work in Norwegian, *Et Hus Ved Kysten* (1907), and then in English, *The Fisherman's House* (1907), which wasn't entirely accurate as a translation, though it was close enough. It was a work I had seen often, a work I had known for as long as I could remember – Mother had a framed print of it, from an old National Gallery exhibition, on her studio wall – and to find it here, in this English market town, on this particular occasion, struck me again as utterly absurd. It was like being haunted – by Mother, of course, and by the landscape I had only just left and was already missing, but also by the Sigfridsson boys and by the white nights of home, full of shapes and spirits that were, I suddenly understood, quite alien to those who had never dwelt in the north. Under the picture label was a rectangular printed display card, with some basic facts about Sohlberg's life and career; it came as a surprise, in fact, to see how basic it was. Obviously, whoever had curated this exhibition had assumed that few visitors to the gallery would be in any way familiar with Sohlberg's works, and it reminded me of Mother's old complaint, that nobody abroad knew anything about Norwegian art, other than *The Scream*. But what was worse still, what would have annoyed her more, was that whoever had written the copy for this exhibition had decided to portray Sohlberg as an obsessive, solitary figure who had turned his back on his contemporaries, so that, by the time he died he was alone and forgotten.

I don't know how I sat there, gazing at *Et Hus Ved Kysten*, but I do know that, no matter how hard I studied the painting, I wasn't really seeing it – or not, at least, as a work of art. I wasn't looking at a canvas, I was looking at an illustration – an image, not of something Harald Sohlberg had imagined but, in spite of the pines and the shape of the land, so much rounder and gentler than the far side of Malangen, a scene that corresponded almost exactly with the image of Kyrre Opdahl's *hytte* that I had seen in my nightmare of the night before. I sat there for fifteen minutes, or longer even, but I wasn't in that gallery, in that English market town any more, I was *home*. Not just home, on Kvaløya, but home in my own head, in the place where dreams happened. I was in a place that nobody else could ever see, and I was completely alone there.

It was some time before I emerged from this reverie and, as soon as I did, I became aware of a feeling that I was being watched. I looked around. There really was nobody else in the room – and there had been almost nobody in the gallery from the moment I came in – and yet the feeling didn't leave me, even though it was obvious that I was alone. Which, in itself, was odd: in the previous rooms, there had been a member of staff, someone in a grey uniform sitting on a folding chair in the corner, pretending not to be there while I walked around looking at the paintings, but in this room there was no one. There was *no one*. I was completely and assuredly alone, but the sense of being watched was, if anything, stronger now than it had been before – and I have no explanation for this, because it was a trivial matter, but I felt a sudden and acute sensation of fear, or panic, and I walked quickly back to the arch between this last room and the one before – into a space that was just as empty as the space I had left – and then into the one before that, where two attendants, a middle-aged man and a young woman, were standing in front of one of the paintings, talking. They turned quickly when I came in and it was immediately obvious that I had interrupted something – from the look of it, a secret romance, though they seemed so mismatched, the man in his fifties and slightly paunchy, with dry-looking reddish hair and very pale skin, the woman not much older than me, her thick dark hair pinned up to expose her neck, making her seem even more slender than she was. They didn't go together, but it was obvious that, whatever they had been talking about, it was an intimate matter, something so private that they would never have discussed it unless they were sure they were alone. Now, trying to hide the awkwardness of my having interrupted a conversation that he probably considered inappropriate – he had a married person's air about him – the man took a step towards me. 'Can I help you?' he said.

I shook my head. 'Oh, no,' I said. 'I was just looking for the cafe.'

He smiled. It was a surprising smile, one that lit up his face, utterly transforming him from the plain creature he had seemed a moment before – and I could almost see what the girl saw in him. 'Go back to the foyer,' he said. 'Turn left just before the main doors and you'll see it right away, just opposite the cloakroom.'

I nodded and glanced at the younger attendant. She smiled happily too, as if to show that she didn't mind my having been included, for a few irrelevant seconds, in the story that they were caught up in. Whatever that story was. 'Thank you,' I said, then I turned to the man and thanked him too. I didn't know why but, even though I knew nothing of their circumstances, for one fleeting moment I felt sorry for them and, to avoid their noticing that fact, I turned and walked quickly back to the entrance and out into the rainy street, without stopping for coffee. I didn't see anybody in any of the rooms as I passed through – and I realised with some surprise that, apart from the staff, I really had been alone in the gallery for some time. No one had been watching me. I had imagined it.

Yet even outside, away from the confined space of the gallery, I couldn't shake off the sensation of being observed. I looked around. A group of men had just come out of a large, mock-Tudor building opposite, and one or two them turned to look at me, no doubt wondering why I was standing alone in the rain, which was fairly heavy now, and I began walking quickly, not at all sure of where I was going. I glanced at my watch. It was four o'clock – which surprised me, because it seemed no more than an hour since I'd had my picnic in the riverside park. I walked on and, with each step, the rain got heavier. I didn't know what to do. It was still daylight, but the sky was low and dark, and the rain made everything so grey that there were lights on in some of the shops. The street was empty, apart from the gang of men by the Tudor building – which I now realised was a bar – and a few women with umbrellas, hurrying to get home and out of the rain. I looked for a taxi rank. I needed to get back to the hotel, to get dry. I remembered Kate Thompson's invitation, but I had already decided against going to her house – had decided, without a second thought, that I didn't want Arild Frederiksen's things. No: all I wanted to do was get inside away from the rain and the sense of being looked at – so I gathered myself together and hurried to the far end of the street, towards the little delicatessen I had visited earlier. If I couldn't find a taxi before I got there, I thought, I would ask directions from the man who had served me earlier. He had seemed friendly and, at that moment, I felt the need of someone I could trust. By now, I had left the gallery and the Tudor bar far behind, but all the way to the little shop, I still felt that someone was there, watching me from close by and, several times, I stopped walking and looked around. No one was there. I was tired, of course, and I reminded myself that it had been a difficult morning, so it wasn't surprising that my mind was playing tricks on me. Yet, no matter what I told myself, no matter how thoroughly I scanned the street and the shopfronts around me, I felt sure that somebody was there, just out of the corner of my vision – and, once again, I felt something close to panic, a panic that increased, for no good reason, when I remembered that I hadn't spoken to Mother since I'd left home.

I found the delicatessen. I could see the man I had spoken to earlier, clearing away the cheeses and baskets, while another man, whom I hadn't seen before, stood at the till, apparently cashing up – but I didn't have to go in because, just as I was about to open the door, a taxi drew up alongside me and a very tall, thin woman got out. As she exited the car, calling goodbye in a tone that suggested that she and the driver knew one another, I stepped over to the passenger-side window and signalled to the driver. The woman looked at me – I saw from her expression that I was much wetter than I had thought – then she turned back to her friend. 'You've got a wet one here,' she said.

The driver studied me through the window. 'I've had wetter,' he said.

For some reason, this amused the woman, and she laughed outlandishly; then, leaving the door open for me, she ran into the delicatessen out of the rain, while I ducked down and slipped into the back seat. 'I'm sorry,' I said. 'I really am pretty wet.'

The driver smiled at me through the rear-view mirror. 'Not a problem, love,' he said. 'Now. Where would you like to go?'

By the time I got out of the taxi, I was close to exhausted. The driver talked all the way, asking where I was from and whether I was on holiday, and I'd managed to keep up my end of the conversation, pretty much, but it had become more and more difficult as the journey went on and, what with the rain and the traffic, it had taken some time to get back to the hotel. By then, I just wanted to go to my room, have a bath and get some sleep – but all the way back from the centre, even while this conversation had been going on, I had been convinced that the person who had been watching me before was now waiting in the hotel lobby and, to begin with, I was reluctant to go in, standing in the gravel courtyard where the taxi had left me and getting steadily wetter and wetter as I forced myself to accept how ridiculous that notion was. I had no idea who had been following me. For several moments, when I was still on the high street, I had imagined it was Kate Thompson: I decided that she had only pretended to dismiss me at the hospital and that she had tailed me when I left, tracking me to the delicatessen and around the art gallery, an invisible presence stalking me from place to place, watching my every move, unable to surrender the right to judgement that she thought she had won. But that was absurd. Why would she do such a thing? What was in it for her? At that very moment, she was probably at home, in her kitchen, sipping on a glass of white wine and chopping leeks for the dinner she already knew I wouldn't turn up for. Besides, even while I was still allowing myself to suspect her, I knew, way down in the dark of my mind, that she wasn't the one – I *knew*, for certain, because, as soon as I'd felt myself being watched, a name had come into my head and though it was even more preposterous to imagine that it was Maia who had tracked me from the park to the art gallery and then from room to room, studying my face as I stopped before the Sohlberg before she vanished, into thin air, it was *her* name that had come to me. Which really was beyond belief, I told myself, as the rain trickled through my hair and ran down my face, and I continued to stand there getting soaked, just three steps from the shelter of the hotel lobby. Three steps and a flight of stairs from my room, I thought. All I had to do was walk through that door.

Finally, a couple came out of the hotel and hesitated a moment in the doorway, the man wrestling open a huge umbrella while the woman looked me up and down with something that seemed more like amusement than concern. Oddly enough, she looked very similar – in the grey light of the rain – to the woman who had got out of the taxi, just fifteen minutes earlier and, though I knew that it wasn't the same person, it seemed to me that the two women could have been sisters. She looked at the man, who had now raised the umbrella over their heads, and then back at me. 'Are you all right?' she said – and her voice sounded just like the other woman's voice. 'Are you looking for something?'

I shook my head and forced a smile. 'I'm sorry,' I said. 'I was miles away.'

212

'Well, you'd best get in,' the woman said. 'You'll get drenched out here.'

I nodded, but they were already moving away. I heard the man say something, then the woman laughed, and I knew that she was laughing about me, but I didn't care. I didn't mind the rain either, but I went inside because, now, the spell that had held me there in the rain was broken.

The lobby was empty, but I could hear a woman, or perhaps a girl, talking somewhere, off in a back room where only the staff could go. I wondered if Mother had called while I was out, but I didn't want to stop and find out. I wanted to get to my room right away and shut the door behind me. I wanted to get out of my wet things and have a hot bath, then lie on the bed watching television till sleep came. I started for the stairs – but then the young woman who had been on duty the night before, the one with the Irish-sounding voice, emerged from the back room and saw me. 'Miss Rossdal?' she said. Her voice was higher and lighter than it had seemed the night before, almost a sing-song, and when I turned, it was apparent from the expression on her face that she had just been talking to someone she liked, and hadn't quite regained the more formal attitude she usually assumed for her job. The person she liked was still in the back room, and she had only just left that person – maybe it was a friend, or a colleague she particularly liked, though I found myself suspecting, for no good reason, that this person was her lover. When she saw that she had my attention, she picked up something from the desk behind reception and held it out. It was an envelope. 'There's a message here for you,' she said.

'Ah,' I said. I assumed that it was a message from Mother – what else could it be? – and I walked back to the desk to take the envelope – and she gave it to me, almost right away, but not before she allowed herself a moment of hesitation, as if she wanted to play with me. To tease me. She smiled – and I saw an insinuation in that smile, as if she knew something about me that I didn't know myself, or maybe it was something about the contents of the envelope that she knew. I took the letter – and it wasn't a message from Mother, after all; it was a sealed envelope, with my name and the name of the hotel printed on the front. 'Thank you,' I said, ignoring her little game. I sensed a complicity with the person in the back room, then, as if the ploy with the letter had been performed for their benefit, but I had no intention of getting dragged into whatever it was they had in mind.

The girl's face became serious, as she readopted her professional manner. 'You're welcome,' she said, then, without speaking another word, she returned to the back room.

> First, the desert is the country of madness. Second, it is the refuge of the devil, thrown out into the 'wilderness of Upper Egypt' to 'wander in dry places'. Thirst drives men mad, and the devil himself is mad with a kind of thirst for his own lost excellence – lost because he has immured himself in it and closed out everything else. So the man who wanders into the desert to be himself must take care that he does not go mad and become the servant of the one who dwells there in a sterile paradise of emptiness and rage.

Like the envelope, the contents of the letter were typed and there was nothing to show who had sent it. Nothing at all, in fact, but this one paragraph, printed in the middle of the page. I read the words carefully, then I read again:

So the man who wanders into the desert to be himself must take care that he does not go mad and become the servant of the one who dwells there in a sterile paradise of emptiness and rage.

It was absurd. It meant nothing at all, but I knew that whoever had sent the letter had intended me to understand something very specific. But who had sent it? I didn't recall telling Kate Thompson which hotel I was at, and there was nobody else within a thousand miles of the place who even knew my name. Besides, if these words were intended for someone, surely they should have been sent to Mother, not to me – after all, she was supposed to be the recluse, she was the one who had taken herself off into the desert, not me. Though it was only a desert to the untrained eye and Mother's presence there was purposeful and necessary. It wasn't a retreat, it was an act of faith. Faith in her work, and in her own mind. And it certainly had nothing to do with the devil.

Who had written these words? And who had typed them out and sent them to me? Was it the same person? I didn't think so. These lines were from some great book, some classic of theology or literature – and I felt sure that, if I could have shown them to Mother, she would have told me the author's name right away, without even having to think about it. They even seemed familiar, a quotation from something that I already knew, though they weren't familiar enough for me to be able to place them. I read them again – and as I did, I felt sure I had seen these words before. But where? When? And who had typed them out so carefully and sent them to me? Had I said something to Kate Thompson that gave me away, not the name of the hotel, but some hint or clue that allowed her to work out where I was staying? I didn't think so – but then, nobody else could have done this. Nobody, other than Mother, even knew where I was.

I picked up the phone and dialled reception. It rang several times, then the girl picked up. 'Can I help you, Miss Rossdal?' she said. She sounded formal and distant, not at all sing-song, and I wondered if her friend had gone.

'I just . . . I wonder, were you there when the letter arrived?' I said.

'The letter?'

'Yes,' I said. 'The letter you gave me just now.'

'Ah, yes,' she said. 'The letter.' She was silent for a moment. 'No,' she said at last, without the least hint of regret in her voice. 'It was Renate who took the letter.'

'I see. Is Renate there now?'

'I'm afraid not.'

'Well, did she say anything?' I said.

'What do you mean, Miss Rossdal?'

'I mean, did she say anything about the letter? About who left it.'

'I'm afraid not,' she said. There was a short silence before she spoke again and I sensed that her friend hadn't left, but was standing right next to her, listening in. 'Can I help you with anything else, Miss Rossdal?'

'No,' I said. 'I'll ask Renate tomorrow –'

'Renate won't be here tomorrow,' she said quickly.

'She won't?'

'It's her day off,' she said – and now her voice wasn't professional any more. There was a slight – a very slight – hint of mockery, or amusement in it, and I sensed that the person she had been with earlier, the person standing right next to her at that moment, was, in fact, Renate, and I knew, then, that it was impossible. They were playing a game with me,

216

though I couldn't think why, and the letter was part of that game. And maybe not just the letter.

'What is this?' I said. 'What are you playing at?' and I waited a moment, for her to answer, but she didn't say anything, and I could see her, standing at the desk, holding the phone away from her ear, so the other one could listen. Then, when I was certain that she had no intention of answering me, and was just waiting to hear what I would say next, I hung up.

It rained all night. I had felt so tired, getting back to the hotel that, in spite of the letter and the lies Françoise had told me, in spite of the sense I'd had of being followed, in spite of the near panic I had drifted into, first in the doorway of the hotel and then, later, a few moments after I had put down the phone – in spite of all these things, I had expected to fall asleep right away and not wake till morning. But I couldn't sleep. I ran the bath as high as I dared, then I called home, but there was no answer, so I took off my wet things and lay for a long time in the hot, steamy water; then I put on the thick terry cotton dressing gown in the wardrobe, called Room Service and asked them to bring me a Steak Sandwich, a Chicken Caesar Salad – the one on the menu, not a side order – and a large bowl of Nachos with Hot Salsa Dip, then I ordered Crème Brûlée and a selection of local cheeses to follow. I was hungry again, and I wanted to order everything on the menu, the Burger and Home Fries Special, the Turkey, Brie and Cranberry Baguette, the Apple Pie with Cornish Clotted Cream and/or Vanilla Ice Cream. I wanted to eat it all, and then sleep for days, alone in my room, with the DO NOT DISTURB sign on the door and nobody there to see me. It was twenty minutes before the waiter came and it was obvious, as he set the tray down on the little table in the corner, that he

217

was surprised to find only one person in the room. He didn't say anything, though, he just started fiddling with the cutlery. I waited for him to go, then I began to eat. It was three or four times as much food as I usually had for dinner, but I ate it all. Every last nacho, every last drop of salsa, every crumb of cheese. When I was done, I felt calm again, just as I had earlier, when I'd bought the stuff at the delicatessen. I lay down on the bed and closed my eyes – and for the first few minutes, it seemed that I was about to drift away. I was so tired. I lay still and felt my arms and legs sink into the duvet, and my mind began to swim. I think I even slept for a few seconds, before something clicked – inside my head, somewhere in the room, or further away, I couldn't say – and I opened my eyes. There was nothing there, and no other sound, but I had heard *something*, and though I tried to let it go, before it was too late to slip back into the slumber I had almost achieved, I couldn't. I lay a while longer, then I stood up and went to the window. Outside, the garden of the hotel was empty, nothing but rain falling into the circle of orange street light, but for one instant – one fleeting instant and no more – I thought I saw someone in the play park opposite, a girl or a woman, I thought, with her face tipped up into the rain, her eyes fixed on the light from my window. It was only an instant and, when my eyes got used to the darkness, I saw that I had been mistaken. It was a trick of the light, a reflection on the wet surface of the play area. It was understandable, given how tired I was, that my eyes might deceive me, and I realised, quite quickly, that there was nothing there. I stood a moment longer, aware that I was wide awake now, then I forced myself to go back to bed, creeping in under the covers this time and switching off all the lights save one small lamp in the corner, but I knew, even as I did, that sleep wouldn't come. It was impossible, now. I wasn't afraid, I wasn't suffering from anxiety or the panic I'd felt earlier, but I couldn't get myself settled either, and I lay awake for hours, wishing I could just get up and go home. I don't know what time it was, when I finally did drift away, but I know it was late, and what sleep I did get was short, dreamless and empty.

I went down to breakfast early the next morning. Nobody else was there, so I took a table by the window and sat staring out at the park across the road, while I waited for someone to come and take my order. I waited for a long time, maybe ten minutes or more, before a girl in a black skirt and a white sateen blouse emerged from the kitchen, carrying a basket of croissants. She didn't see me to begin with; then, having deposited the croissants on a long buffet table by the far wall, she turned and made a great show of hurrying over. She was tall and thin, with very white skin and – just like Françoise and Renate – her long dark hair was pulled back tightly into a ponytail. 'Good morning,' she said. 'Can I take your room number?'

I told her the number and ordered some coffee, then I helped myself to a plateful of croissants, a couple of cold boiled eggs and some bread from the buffet table. When the girl came back, I ordered the Full English Breakfast, then I sat staring out at the wet gardens. Everything was wet from the rain still, and the sky was overcast; there was nobody on the street outside, though the odd car swished by, splashing through a puddle that had formed just outside the hotel gates and disappearing in the direction of the town centre. I stared out at the play park. To begin with, I thought it was empty; then I noticed a girl, maybe six or seven years old, standing by the metal fence that ran around the play area. She was wearing a thin cotton dress and a skimpy cardigan and she seemed to be alone, which struck me as odd, at that time of day, but I guessed she must live nearby, and her mother was keeping sight of her. Still, it seemed wrong for her to be out there, with it being so wet and more rain threatening, and I was looking around, trying to see where the mother was, hoping she would come and bring the girl a coat or take her away to where it was dry and warm, when the street and the fence around the park lit up unexpectedly, as if someone had switched on a lamp in a far room, and I saw that the girl had come closer to the fence and was staring back at me through the sudden light, her face bright like the face of an angel in some painting by Raphael – except that, now, I saw that her expression wasn't angelic at all, it was spiteful and cruel and that cruelty was directed at me, for some reason. I had never seen her before but, as she advanced towards the fence, the look on her face turned to a grimace of utter, violent hatred, not just of me, but of everything and everyone. This girl – this thin, cold child in a hand-me-down cardigan and faded dress – hated me, not for anything I was or had done, but because I *existed*, in *her* world, and she didn't want me there. And the oddest thing was that, as she came closer, and I could see her just a little more clearly, she seemed familiar. I had encountered this girl somewhere before, I was quite sure, though I couldn't have said where and, in retrospect, I can see that she was too far away from me to make her out properly. Now, I can say that she could have been anyone, and that the look on her face was just the look that children sometimes put on, when they don't get everything they want; but at that moment I was sure I knew her and I was trying to work out how – trying desperately, because, all of a sudden, it seemed vital that I work this out – when the waitress came with the cooked breakfast. She had slipped into the professionally pleasant manner that all the women who worked at this hotel seemed to have adopted; she was even close to smiling, in fact, when I heard her and turned from the window – but something must have been visible in my face, some reflection of the girl's rage and loathing, because her expression changed right away and she came to a dead stop. 'What is it?' she said. 'Are you all right?' She appeared to be frightened, rather than concerned – frightened for herself, in fact, and not for me.

'It's all right,' I said. 'It's just . . .' I turned back to the window, and she turned too and looked out. 'I was startled by the girl,' I said – but now I could see that there was nobody there, just a thin figure hurrying away towards the far side of the park, a figure that could have been the girl I saw, but could just as easily have been someone else entirely, as it disappeared from view.

HULDRA

Mother picked me up at the airport. She was wearing her long blue jacket and the velvet scarf that I had given her the previous Christmas, the one with the poppies. She loved that scarf, and she had been surprised when I gave it to her, because I don't think she had been expecting anything so fine. And, as it happened, she was right to be surprised, because Ryvold was the one who had chosen it, not me. I had run into him in town while I was Christmas shopping, and he had pointed it out: a luxurious, charcoal-grey scarf with a red-poppy motif, the velvet thick and secretive, like the fur of some live creature, the colours almost too vivid, like the colours in a Sohlberg painting. I had known immediately that he was right, of course, but the fact remained that it hadn't been my choice, and some part of me still felt guilty that I had passed that gift off as my idea. It was the first time I had given her something she really liked – and though she had done all she could to conceal her surprise, I had sensed it nevertheless, and she understood that she had let something slip. That was why she had only worn it once or twice since, and that was why she was wearing it now, as a sign, as a welcome. She wanted me to know that nothing had changed between us, or not for her at least: she was still my mother, and I was still her daughter, and she wanted me to understand that she was happy about that. It didn't matter that we had almost nothing in common. What mattered was that she was happy, and she wanted me to be happy too.

She knew right away that something was wrong, of course. How could she not? After my vision in the play park, I had gone upstairs and stayed in my room till it was time to leave, eating nothing, trying desperately to fall asleep and, at the same time, worrying that, if I did, I wouldn't wake up in time to get my connection back to London. After a day of ravening hunger, I had completely lost my appetite; now, all I could do was drink water and lie on the bed, hovering between sleep and waking and listening to the world going about its business all around me. Then, when it was time to go, I packed my bags and hurried downstairs. There was a new girl on reception, not Françoise, not Renate; this one was a blonde, moon-faced Englishwoman who ran up my bill and asked if everything had been to my satisfaction with a look on her face that said she would have been happier anywhere else than there. The bill paid, she called me a taxi, and I started out on the first leg of my journey in brilliant sunshine, the trees and hedges still wet from the rain, but sparkling in the morning light as the car headed for the station. It was sunny all the way to London, it was sunny at Heathrow, it was sunny in Oslo. When I got off the plane at Tromsø, the sun was on us as Mother walked me to the car, and it felt like a spotlight on my face, picking out every shadow, and Mother noticed, but she didn't say anything, other than to remark that I looked tired and that I should go straight to bed when we got back.

She didn't ask about Arild Frederiksen. She didn't want to know what had happened or whether he was all right. She didn't want to know why Kate Thompson had suddenly decided to contact me on his behalf, after he had stayed away for eighteen years. She didn't want to know anything – though she left a small, rather tidy space between us for me to say what I wanted to say, if I should choose to talk about it. She must have known that he, or Kate Thompson, would tell me his side of the story and she must have wondered how I would react, but she would never have admitted – to me, or to herself – that she was capable of giving such matters even a moment's serious consideration. I think she wanted to leave that neat space around an experience that was mine and mine alone – and I understood that this decision was symptomatic, not of what Kate Thompson would have taken as coldness, or indifference, but of an exaggerated, almost entirely formal delicacy on her part. After all, she had encouraged me to make the trip, she had needed to let me go, she had bought the plane tickets and paid for my hotel, but she had no wish to intrude upon the experience. At the same time, she wanted me to understand that she would listen, if I wanted to speak, or answer any questions I might have, or give advice if advice were needed. The man I had gone to see was nothing to her now, but he was, or he might be, something to me, and she wanted me to understand that she knew that. And of course, I did. I understood completely. When I saw her standing there, in that red-poppy scarf, I knew that she wasn't at all interested in what anyone else might say about what she had done or failed to do in a long-ago past. She knew, without a doubt, that she had nothing to answer for, and no other concern than my well-being. Her behaviour was perfect – *she* was perfect – and it troubled me, all the way home, that I would have doubted that perfection on the say-so of a woman I barely knew. A woman who had judged her years ago and decided, as such people do, that she was heartless and self-involved. I had seen that judgement, and even though I had never for a moment accepted it, I was afraid that Mother might think otherwise. I was worried that she would guess what had been inferred from what I had told Kate Thompson about her and I was afraid, suddenly, of hurting her. I wanted to say something to allay any possible suspicion, but during the drive home and, then, during the quiet, slightly ashen days of bed-rest and self-recovery that followed, days of exaggerated kindness and good grace with one another that made it seem all too obvious to me that something was in the process of being concealed, not only for now, but for always, I couldn't decide what to say until so much time had passed that I couldn't say anything.

On the fourth day, I couldn't stand being indoors any more, so I took myself out and away. Mother had been concerned for me, when I first got back, but I think she saw it as a good sign, my wanting to be outdoors. Besides, she was still busy, even though the work for the new show had gone to Oslo, and she was too preoccupied with work to realise that, if I was spending so much time out of the house, it wasn't because I'd been homesick and needed to reconnect with the meadows and the birch woods, but because I needed to avoid her for a while. Or maybe she did and was carefully hiding the fact, because – of course – she would have been just as concerned about saying or doing something that would make me feel bad. Or no: that wasn't it. What I really mean to say is that she would have been careful not to give *me* the chance to do or say something that would cause pain, not to her, but to myself – because *she* was still in control, *she* had already considered and decided what must be done, whatever might unfold between us after my time away. Of course – and she was right, I have no doubt – *I* was the possible weak link, the awkward teenager, the clumsy child. That was what all the kindness and care were about, in those last days of the summer: she didn't want me to make a mistake and upset myself. And how could I fail to appreciate that? The last thing I wanted was a meaningful conversation about Arild Frederiksen's death, or one of those awkward silences in which everything goes awry. What I wanted, in fact, was to be left alone, because I didn't want anyone, least of all Mother, to see that I hadn't quite recovered from whatever it was that had plagued me during those two or three days in England – because, for a short time, it appeared that I had come close to losing my mind and, though I felt better now, I was afraid that, at any moment, I might slide back into the panic that had overtaken me in the art gallery.

Meanwhile, it seemed that the summer – the true summer – was coming to an end. That true, warm, tragic and at the same time almost miraculous summer was disappearing, day by day, and I didn't want to miss a moment of what was left. I wanted to walk in the meadows and sit out among the birch woods when the night gloaming seeped out from the interior; I wanted to stand on the shore and watch the big boats slowly make their way to the open sea; I wanted to go to Hillesøy and gather *kråkebolle* on the rocks, or pick handfuls of cloud-berries at what sometimes felt like the edge of the world, alone and silent but for the shorebirds and an occasional gust of wind. I didn't want to be indoors, and I didn't want to be with *people*. I certainly didn't want to have anything to do with Martin Crosbie. Or not at first, anyhow. During those first few days, I kept well clear of the *hytte* on the shore; I did everything I could to remain unseen – and unphotographed – and I didn't *spy*. And then, unexpectedly, without meaning to, I saw him. I don't suppose I had expected to avoid him forever, and it wouldn't have come as a surprise, if he'd been alone, but he wasn't alone, he was with the *huldra* – and I could see right away that they were together. It was ridiculous, not only that he and Maia had found each other, but also that it had happened so quickly – yet as soon as I saw them, I knew it was true. They were out on the meadows, walking side by side: not actually touching, but *together* in a way that was unmistakable, the way people from school would be together, in couples, when you saw them on the street in Tromsø, not touching, not doing anything, but linked, of one mind, in their own shared space. That was how Martin and Maia seemed, when I saw them that day. I didn't know, then, how long they had been in that separate world, but it was obviously a new thing, something that still pleased and mystified them – or should I say, something that still pleased and mystified Martin, who was, no doubt, amazed at a turn of events that had brought him together with this beautiful, strange girl from the north, something he had never expected, and couldn't have hoped for. Yes, this affair was new: it had started on the very day I had left for England and, from that first moment on, it had blossomed.

Blossomed. Not the right word, perhaps, yet it did have that inevitable quality to it, like a flower opening. A rose, say, or one of Harstad's Arctic poppies, turning perpetually to gaze into the sun. As soon as I saw them together, I knew that something was going on – which was odd, because they really weren't doing any of the things that lovers do when they think they are alone. They weren't touching each other, they didn't stop halfway along the strand to kiss or gaze meaningfully into one another's eyes, and there was a distance between them, a distance that was so correct, so very precise, you would have thought they had measured it out beforehand. On that first sighting, I could see that Martin was talking, turning every now and then to glance at Maia as they walked, and every now and then she would turn towards him, almost but not quite looking into his face, before turning away and gazing out across the Sound. She wasn't being evasive, however; if anything, she seemed comfortable: happy to be there, perhaps, happy and even hopeful of something – and it was almost touching to see how happy Martin Crosbie was, walking on the shore with this pretty girl, who could have been one of the girls in his library of images, fresh from school and warmed by the summer sun, the beautiful innocent of his lonely fantasies. I didn't think, then, what I had thought before. I gave him the benefit of the doubt, because, at that moment, I could see that something had changed in him. Naturally, the question of whether they were sleeping together crossed my mind, but only for a moment. On that visit to the *hytte* when I found the pictures, I'd assumed that his interest in those girls was sexual, plain and simple, but now I wasn't so sure. It all looked so innocent, so – romantic. And that was why I gave him the benefit of the doubt: because he looked like a man in love – as if a man in love couldn't also be dangerous, as if a man in love couldn't cause anybody any harm.

At the time, though, I didn't give Martin's new romance much thought. All I wanted was to be left alone, so I could devote myself to not thinking about *anything*. So, considering my need for solitude, it seems odd that I would have sought out company, especially the company of Mother's suitors, but on the first Saturday after I got back, for reasons I wasn't quite sure about, I invited myself to the morning tea party. I'd sat

231

in before, of course, but I'd quickly get bored and leave, and the suitors had tolerated me, because they knew that I never stayed long. That morning, however, I lingered for much longer than usual, because Ryvold wasn't there, and that was odd. Ever since he'd first arrived in the group, he had come every week, without fail. He was a permanent fixture and, though it was never acknowledged, the truth was that everything revolved around him. There were times when he didn't say very much, but what he did say, or what he *might* say in certain circumstances, had always set the tone of the discussion – and I can see now that Mother depended on him for whatever pleasure or entertainment she got out of those mornings. She loved Rott, I think, the way you love a puppy, but Ryvold came as near as any outsider could come to being *real* in her world – and that morning, as the suitors gathered around the table, Ryvold was conspicuously absent.

He had been absent the previous week, too, while I was away. Nobody had thought anything of it at the time – one of the others thought he'd seen him getting out of a taxi outside the airport in Tromsø, and they had agreed to assume that he'd probably had to go away suddenly on business. It would have to have been very sudden, though, because Ryvold wouldn't miss a Saturday morning without letting Mother know that he couldn't come. Nobody would have imagined him failing to appear without some kind of explanation – but now, for the second week running, he had.

And now, for the first time ever, I was a full member of the Saturday-morning tea party. Not just a drop-in visitor on the way to something else, but a stubborn presence in the suitors' midst. There were four that day: Rott, Harstad, a very thin, rather distinguished-looking man named Nilsson who didn't come very often, and a man with very blue eyes and oddly gull-like features whose name I didn't even know, though I'd seen him a couple of times walking up the front path. They couldn't figure out how to deal with me, not after the first twenty minutes or so had passed and I still hadn't made my excuses and left. It was as if I was there in Ryvold's place, come to sit in for him during his unexplained absence, and that made them restless and ill at ease. Mother didn't know why I was lingering either, but she was enjoying the discomfiture of her guests, a discomfiture that became more and more obvious, the longer I stayed in my chair.

The conversation was general, at least to begin with. Nobody mentioned Ryvold, of course. Polite interest was shown in my plans for the future – what was I going to do, now that I had finished school? How did the exams go? Was I going away to college or had I something else planned? – but I didn't mind that, for once. I was curious about Ryvold, curious about what he had said the last time he had come to the house. I had forgotten to tell Mother, at the time, about that un-scheduled visit – the discussions about my trip to England had distracted me – and now it was too late to explain. Not that I would have tried to, with the suitors present. I hadn't suspected, when Ryvold came to the house, that he had come to say goodbye. Yet, apparently, he had and, as we all sat round the dining table, eating Danish biscuits and napoleon cake – it takes great artfulness and physical tact to eat a napoleon cake in public, something Rott had never realised, though he'd eaten enough of them – I could see that Mother was perplexed. Not so much by his absence, which I'm sure she still believed would be explained, sooner or later, as by the question of how to get through another Saturday-morning gathering without him.

The conversation was general, and it was dull: when

conversation is general, it usually is. I kept waiting for someone to mention Ryvold, but nobody did. I looked at Mother. Was she annoyed by his unexplained absence? Did it even matter to her, one way or another? She didn't seem upset; if anything, she appeared to be enjoying the situation. As time passed, though, her interest flagged. Everybody was uncomfortable by then, and not just because I was lingering beyond my allotted time. No: they were missing Ryvold. It bothered them that they didn't know where he was, or when he would be back – and it soon became obvious that they missed him, each man in his own heart, because they didn't know how to conduct themselves in his absence. Without Ryvold there, setting the tone, each of them was afraid that he would do or say something foolish. Yet they continued stolidly to pretend that nothing unusual was happening. Eventually, I couldn't bear it. I looked around the table at them all, then I turned to Mother and said, quite casually, 'I wonder where Mr Ryvold is?'

She looked surprised. She studied my face for a moment, as if she was trying to work something out, then she shook her head. 'Nobody knows,' she said. 'He's simply vanished from the face of the earth.' She smiled. 'Isn't it curious?' she said, to the suitors as much as to me, though she wasn't really talking to any of us. She had taken my question as a provocation, a tiny piece of childish theatre – which it no doubt was – and she was delighted.

The others were far from delighted, however. In fact, Mother's response made them more uncomfortable than ever. Nobody said anything and nobody looked at me and, for a long moment, there was silence – that moment when, as the French say, *un ange passe*. An angel passes. Though I suppose that expression denotes a natural, easy silence, rather than the awkward hiatus that lasted for just too long, before it was broken by Rott, who craned forward suddenly and, obviously overcome by the allure of the last napoleon cake sitting lonely on its willow-pattern cake stand in the middle of the table, lifted it carefully, between thumb and forefinger, and transferred it to his plate with a tiny and almost imperceptible sigh.

The tea party was still in session when I left, but I couldn't imagine it continuing for very much longer. Mother was bored, and though she was too gracious a hostess to let her guests see it, she wanted them gone so she could get back to the studio. I had realised, by then, that she was surprised at how much she missed Ryvold and I think, looking back, that she had already started wondering why she bothered with these Saturday mornings. With Ryvold there, they had been pleasant; without him, they were awkward and dull. And I believe that did surprise her. It surprised her that, in some area of her life, no matter how inconsequential, she had come to rely upon someone else.

As for me – well, I would have liked to know more about what was going on, but it was obvious that I wouldn't learn anything by lingering at Mother's table, so I excused myself and went off to spy on Martin Crosbie and his girl. I thought I would find them walking on the shore, or sitting on the lawn by the boathouse, having tea or eating ice cream, but when I got to the meadows, the *hytte* looked to be deserted. Martin's car wasn't parked in the usual place, and there was no sign of activity, other than the seabirds floating in above the meadow and then out again, over the beach beyond. I wondered if Martin had taken Maia on an outing, maybe over to Andøya; or maybe they had gone on the trip north he'd talked about. It was a grey day, but it was dry, and I remember being aware of that effect I liked so much on certain late-summer afternoons, the sense that the land had started to separate out into distinct zones of light and dark, a patch of deep shadow here, an unlikely glimmering there, near black-ness along the line of the narrow stream that ran by the edge of Kyrre's field and trickled out on to the beach below, a faint shimmer streaked through the grass around the boathouse, where the meadow met shingle. It happens like that, some-times, on days when there is no sun, yet the cloud cover is high and thin, and it makes the whole world look like one of Mother's paintings, or the landscape in a fifties movie. It's as if the land can't decide whether it's in colour or black and white and so settles for something that is neither one nor the other.

I've always loved the meadows in late summer, when the wildflowers are all in bloom, more or less together, and every-thing – plants, butterflies, shorebirds, the minor nations of animals and insects – everything that lives here is hurrying to grow and multiply before the cold returns. There's something miraculous about these short summers, the way life continues, laying up just enough fat and seed to carry it through another dark time. Everything works together, and nothing is lost. It still surprises me, now and then, to think that Mother goes to such lengths to grow the big, showy flowers that populate her inner garden – the peonies and opium poppies, the wild roses, the penstemons and delphiniums that barely flower against the south wall before they are gone, the black-eyed Susans and marguerites that have to be renewed every few weeks – I can't believe she would work so hard at *that*, when the meadows are here, all around us, full of the wildflowers and grasses that belong to this place. It would seem more logical if the garden featured in her art but, apart from the odd watercolour, it's the world outside our perimeter that haunts her canvases, the world of wind and salt water and rock-splitting frosts that she works so hard to exclude from the half-acre plot that immediately surrounds us. I don't know why that is: to me, the garden is really another room of the house, an outer sunroom whose decor can only be maintained by endless expense and painstaking work. It's so unlike Mother; so profligate. Even in the summer, things die all the time and are constantly having to be replaced, while in winter, almost everything dies, and very little of what survives one summer makes it through to the next. Yet when Mother was choosing an emblem for one of her catalogues, she chose the Arctic poppy, the flower she has often said, in exhibition notes and to curious journalists, is her favourite. A plant that belongs here, yet probably wouldn't survive in her overly cultivated plot, a plant that lives out in the open, turning around and around to follow the midnight sun, in a patch of moss and stones, somewhere on the Finnmarksvidda. She is, as Ryvold used to say, a mass of contradictions, this woman – though I'm not sure that he is right when he would add, as he always did, that this is why we love her.

I don't want to suggest that I dislike the garden, however. It's beautiful, of course it is, and I often find myself carrying one of the sunroom chairs out into the rock garden, to sit amid the colours and scents that Mother works so hard to contrive. It's just that I prefer being out in the open, out on the meadows with the salt wind blowing up from the shore, out with the birds and the clouds and the line of the horizon. For me, Mother's garden is too sheltered. Too sheltered, and too enclosed, hemmed in by the birch woods and the carved rocks that rise on the north and west side. You can't really see into the distance – or rather, in those places where you can see, it feels like a calculated illusion. A vista. Out in the open, I can turn and and see the whole world stretching away to the horizon and, at the same time, I feel myself in heaven's eye.

I could see all around me, but I didn't see Maia until it was almost too late. I'd assumed that, because Martin's car was gone, she would be gone too, but as I made my way across the upper meadow, I saw her – just a flicker of movement at first, then a human form, crossing the space between the lush meadow and the stark line of the shore. I didn't think she had seen me – though later, when I took the time to reflect on the moment, I couldn't help thinking that she'd probably noticed I was there long before I was aware of her, and had chosen to pretend she was alone. And if that was true, then she was showing me something. I can't swear to it, but I think she wanted me – or not me, so much, as some random witness – to see that she had changed. And it was true, without a doubt: something really was different about her. That game she had played, that old tomboy bluff, was gone, replaced now by an immense, dark calm. Or not calm, so much as the air of someone who has seen the worst and feels the relief of knowing that it isn't as bad as she had expected. A relief – and a sudden realisation that, now, she could do anything she liked. Once, she had seemed lost – an unwanted child, reduced to anger and pride and the limited satisfaction of putting a brave face on it; now, she had seen how magical it was, this feeling of having nowhere to go. Something was different – and, for a moment, I was frightened for her. She had lost her bounce, it was true, and she had started to relax – but she was relaxing into something terrible, and she was going about the world in a state of complete indifference to whatever might come, a wild girl with dream patterns and faint, dark animals etched on her skin, a creature who had passed beyond fear and was, therefore, beyond saving.

So, when I saw her that day, I confess that I was afraid for her – yet, at the same time, I couldn't help thinking there was something a little sinister about her too. Seeing her in that place, in that eerie play of light and dark, I could almost understand Kyrre's suspicions, even though I tried to keep in mind that what he had called the dark cast in her was mostly put on, an effect striven for and achieved by a combination of self-belief and the gullibility of others. Maybe, at one time, Maia had discovered in herself a certain shadow quality, a fleeting hint of tender malevolence that she had enjoyed enough to linger upon; maybe, looking into a mirror on some white midsummer night, she had seen something she liked, something that seemed immune to the ordinary neglect she must have suffered at home. I can well believe that, sensing a hint of the devil in her reflection, she had decided – consciously, or not so consciously – to cultivate it. But it wasn't real – and, that day, it didn't seem to me anything like what Kyrre thought it was. Oh, I don't doubt that there was malice in her – how could she have lived in that house all her life, and not be soured a little? But it wasn't enough to do real harm. Or that was what I wanted to believe, seeing her there, alone on the meadows. That malice, that sinister quality, was play-acting, I told myself, and as she held the pose for just a minute too long, I shook my head and turned away, saddened and ashamed for her – and I didn't look back once, all the way up the track and across the road to Mother's bordered domain. I didn't look back, in fact, till I got to the stand of birch trees, at which point I turned, just slightly, and glanced over to where she had been standing, out of the corner of my eye, only to find that she had vanished.

I wondered where she had gone, but I didn't look back again and I didn't think she had disappeared, as if by magic, as she had the last time we'd met. Now, I thought, she was only hiding, playing a trick, trying to catch me out, and I told myself that she was harmless, just a girl who had discovered a convincing pose, partly – mostly – by living up to what others saw in her. I didn't look back again, because I didn't want her to see me looking – and yet, for ten, maybe twenty yards of that walk back up the track, I could feel something behind me, something dark and heavy hovering at my shoulders, like some great bird of prey about to strike, and I have to admit that this feeling was both vivid and frightening. Of course, that bird of prey was nothing more than the product of my own imagination, I knew that; but knowing it did not diminish the fear I experienced, if only for a few thrilling seconds – which goes to show, not only how well she had learned to play her chosen role, but also how superstitious I had become. That was Kyrre Opdahl's doing, of course, and as I walked up our drive and opened the inner gate that led to Mother's gaudy and improbable garden, I remember wondering why I had fallen into this complicity with him, like some loving child who doesn't know how else to please an eccentric, even half-mad grandparent, other than by sitting obediently by the fire of an evening and listening to his tales of sprites and devils, going into a strange and frightening place for no other reason than that he was going there, and this was the only way to show him that he was loved.

We went out to the end of the earth today. It isn't far, just a short drive to the far side of Kvaløya, then over the bridge and the causeway, out to the furthest point on Hillesøy, where we always find *kråkebolle*, half smashed on the rocks, powder green and white, or touched with pale blush pink, the urchin inside long gone, gulped down by the gull that had plucked it from a pool then let it fall to smash the hard shell on the rocks below. Mother did a study of one of those sea urchins, when she first came here, carrying the broken shell back to the studio and setting it out on a white tablecloth and, somehow, she managed to make it seem newly shattered, the breaks clean and a glisten of entrails inside, entrails and salt and water, at once thick and translucent, like oyster milk. She did a good number of still-life pieces when we were first here and, though I barely noticed at the time, I think, now, that *that* was how she made the transition from portraits to landscape. So it's interesting that she hasn't shown those pictures. Many are little more than sketches, of course, but there are some finished works – almost all of them of damaged things, like these broken urchins, or a nest of broken eggs she found on the shore, just below Kyrre's *hytte* – that stand alongside anything she has done.

Today, however, she didn't go looking for urchins or broken shells. She simply walked to the end of the earth and stood a while, looking out over the water. It's our private name: *the end of the earth*; we use it whenever we speak of this place, an entry in the common ledger of word games and in-jokes that any family shares and it's an expression – a reinforcement, no doubt – of our shared fondness for the days when we first arrived here, a woman and a child come to a strange place where they knew nobody and had no certainty of a future, days when this spot, as far west as a person could walk, really was the end of the earth. Or it was, at least, to my child's mind, and I was the one who gave it the name, thinking partly of a real place and partly of the true remoteness in some old fairy story, where ships sailed off the edge of the sea and strangers appeared, washed up on the shore, from the next world but one. For the first year or two, we came here often, and I know it was a place where Mother found refuge, or solace, or whatever it was she needed to work out how she would proceed. After that, it was there when we wanted it, no longer necessary, but still touched with significance, like a ruined castle, or a place of pilgrimage.

Mother is more alone than ever, now that Kyrre Opdahl and Ryvold are gone, but that seems not to trouble her. If anything, she is happier – and I feel closer to her, now, in that solitary happiness. Before, I was her child: I depended on her. She couldn't quite leave go of the world, for my sake; she had to live as if she still belonged there, in case circumstances forced her back. Of course, I was one of those circumstances because, for as long as I was growing up, she didn't know what I would choose and, now that I am past the point of asking her to do so, I am quite certain that she would have gone back in an instant, and without a word of argument – if I had. On the other hand, now that I *have* chosen, and we have both relaxed into an unspoken agreement that we will stay here for the rest of our lives, she betrays no sign whatsoever that she is glad, or relieved, that this is the case.

In the old days, Mother used to bring us out here. Now, I am the one who suggests it, and I am the one who drives us, leaving the car by the last, lonely house – the one with the ruined boat shed off to one side, its walls stripped back to bare timber by the wind. From there, a narrow track – one of those paths that twists and winds through the scrub and rock, following intentions more animal than human – leads away to the far side of a low knoll and, from a perilous edge-line splashed by a cold tide, a view of empty sky and a sea that ranges from near-black to the blue of crushed velvet. I don't know what Mother is thinking when we come out here – and I don't ask – but, every time, a brief and no doubt absurd notion passes through my mind, the notion of how all this was before we were here, not just Mother and me, but everyone – humanity, people, that self-designated world which, for so long, would have drawn us back to it, had we been willing to go. It's a notion of some inconceivable Before: the seas empty of ships, the land of houses and roads, the shore from here to Africa one long, uninterrupted flock of feeding birds, sandpipers and terns and oystercatchers, curlew, godwit, ibis, vast herds of reindeer and elk wandering from feeding ground to feeding ground, all the way to Siberia, the birch woods bright and articulate with song, wolverines and wolf packs calling to one another over the high snow. I can't really imagine that time, I know, and it's only a notion that comes flickering through my mind for the briefest of intervals before it is gone, but I regret that lost state, and I regret the lost connection with it that the old stories seemed to perpetuate. For as long as we believed those stories of trolls and sea-trows, they offered us jagged and uneven trails back to that time, and somehow, here and there in the fabric of the tale, memories of a place we never saw – *could* never, by definition, be party to – came ghosting through our heads. Now, though, the stories we tell – or, at least, the story that *I* have to tell – seems merely curious, a grotesque and utterly unconvincing account of a series of tragic coincidences, told by a solitary woman who, by her own admission, has a history of *seeing things*.

I went back to spying gradually, possibly because it was familiar territory and, after my trip to England, I needed familiar things. To be honest, though, I wasn't really that interested in

Martin and Maia's domestic arrangements. I saw them together on the meadows, I saw them get into his car and drive off together, I saw them sitting out late in the evening, when it was obvious that Maia wasn't about to go anywhere else, but I didn't care, now, if they were lovers and, truth be told, I have to confess that I was a little disappointed in them, for not continuing with the old, tragic story that I'd had in mind. Nevertheless, I continued to spy on them, off and on, as the summer wound to its end. I needed a distraction, I suppose: I had come back from England quite determined to put Kate Thompson out of my head, but that was proving harder to do than I'd expected. I'm not saying that I was terribly upset by Arild Frederiksen's death – but I did feel – what? Touched. Tainted. Yes, that was it: at some point during my conversation with Kate Thompson, I had allowed myself to feel sorry for her and, even if this pity didn't last, even if it had dissipated the moment she walked away, the memory of that ghastliest of emotions bothered me. At the same time, I knew that I wasn't genuinely concerned about her. No doubt she had gone home that evening – after delivering a note to the hotel, perhaps – and she had stood in her kitchen with a glass of wine, cooking a meal that I wouldn't turn up for, and judging me, judging Mother, for our lack of kindness. But it wasn't that *that* bothered me – it was the implication that Kate felt – or rather, *knew* – that Mother had deceived me in some way, if not with actual lies, then by a series of careful omissions. Which was preposterous, of course. For even if Arild Frederiksen hadn't abandoned her when she was pregnant with me, as I had always assumed, even if he had been the *good man* that Kate Thompson had presented in her account of him, it was still the case that Mother hadn't lied. It naturally occurred to me that I had known Mother all my life and had never been given cause to think of her as deliberately deceitful, whereas Kate Thompson was someone I neither knew nor liked – but the thought wasn't enough. Not without faith. Even though the doubt had endured for no more than a matter of seconds, it had arisen, and the sour taste of it was there all through the trip home on a half-empty plane; crossing the snowy mountains, then watching the western islands slip by below, I'd found I didn't quite know what to believe. Of course, I was exhausted by then, and upset by the mysterious note and the strange imaginings that had gone through my mind and, even though I had tried to put it all down to lack of sleep, the confidence that I'd always had in the few things I depended upon – Mother, my sense of home, the history that she and I shared – had been badly shaken. That was why I needed a distraction – and the only thing I could think of was to fall back on the things I'd always done to distract myself. I spied on Martin. I looked at pictures. I went walking. I sat in Kyrre's kitchen, drinking coffee. It didn't occur to me that I was waiting, until the thing I had been waiting for arrived; but I knew, as soon as I saw Kate Thompson's parcel, that I had been expecting it all along. I was only surprised that it had taken so long.

Mother took delivery of the mail that day, so she had seen it too, but she didn't say anything. She just left it on the kitchen table, so I would find it, and went off to the studio. She had been extraordinarily tactful about the trip, anyhow: we hadn't touched on the subject once since the drive home and I felt sure that she wouldn't bring the matter up again, unless I did – which, of course, I had no intention of doing. The parcel was quite large, and I knew it contained the *things* that Kate Thompson had mentioned, the ones she had decided Arild Frederiksen would have wanted me to have. I didn't want those things, I didn't want them in the house and I didn't want Mother to have to see them – and, to begin with, I considered throwing the parcel away, or maybe burning it. After a long moment's hesitation, however, I decided to get it over with and I carefully undid the wrapping and removed the contents, one by one. There were five items in all, and each was more beautiful than the last – in spite of everything, I could see how beautiful they were, and I was just as taken with them as Kate Thompson had presumably hoped I would be. They were things Arild Frederiksen had no doubt picked up on his travels, things that he had been given as tokens of friendship, perhaps, or had bartered for in mountain villages or crowded bazaars in South America or Mongolia. A red enamel box, with an exquisitely detailed painting of a bird on the lid; a piece of carved bone or tusk, worn smooth with age, on which I could only just make out three rowing boats full of hunters or fishermen; a small painted mask, too small for anyone but a child to wear, with a black-and-white zigzag pattern across the cheeks; a clay figurine of a running horse, which looked like it could have been a thousand years old. The last object, a piece of what I took to be jewellery, was the most beautiful of all, though I couldn't quite make out what it was. It might have been a fragment of some larger piece. It was a flat object, about three inches square, and it was made of solid silver, with six parallel slivers of a blue stone – lapis lazuli, I thought – not so much set in the metal as growing through it, so it seemed more the result of a natural process than deliberate craftsmanship. I was taken aback by how beautiful it was, by how it felt to hold it and by the beauty of the work, and as I stood there in our kitchen, wondering what to do with it, I couldn't help thinking how much Mother would have liked it. Of course, I couldn't give it to her – and I was angry, then, that Kate Thompson had given it to me, because it was so precious, and she would have known how difficult it would be to get rid of it. But then, she didn't want to give me something I could get rid of: she wanted to insinuate Arild Frederiksen's existence into my life with this talisman, she wanted him to be a part of the fabric of my days, so I would never be able to forget him. Once I had everything unpacked, I went through the items, and then through the packaging to see if she had sent a letter, or even a note, but there was nothing – which was a surprise at first. And then it wasn't. There was nothing for her to say, now: the contents of the parcel said everything. They were mysterious – there was nothing to say where they had originated, or how Arild Frederiksen had come by them – and they were too beautiful to throw away, so, at the very least, she had presented me with a problem. And I really didn't know what to do – all I could think of, when I heard Mother moving about above me, and then, slowly, starting down the stairs, was that these beautiful things had to be concealed from her, and I quickly put them back into their wrapping and carried them out to the garden room, where I put them inside a large plant pot that had been sitting in the far corner of the highest shelf for years, undisturbed.

I thought about Kate Thompson's package all the rest of that day, but I still couldn't decide what to do with it. The idea passed through my mind that I could give it to Kyrre Opdahl, but I couldn't rule out the possibility that he might show it to Mother. The thought of taking it all down to the Sound and throwing it into the water was one I considered for a long time, but I couldn't quite resolve to throw away something so beautiful as that piece of jewellery. I had to get it out of the house, though – so I waited till Mother went off on her walk the next day and I went out to the garden room, took the parcel from its hiding place and was just about to carry it out into the garden – I had it in mind that I would dig a hole, out at the edge of the birch woods, and bury this secret treasure trove by one of the carved stones – when I heard the front door open and a man's voice calling out along the hallway. 'Hello. Is anybody home?' the voice said, and then I heard the man stop and listen. He was alone and he sounded nervous or wary and, to begin with, I didn't recognise him. Then he called again, and I put the package back into the pot and walked through to the hallway, where I found Ryvold, who seemed just about to turn and leave, possibly relieved that he'd found the house empty. There was a package on the hall table, that hadn't been there before: it looked like a small box in a plain brown wrapping similar in colour and texture to the paper that Kate Thompson had used. As soon as he saw that I had noticed it, Ryvold picked it up and held it out to me. 'I brought something for your mother,' he said, as if he felt he needed to explain himself.

'She's not here,' I said, not taking the box. This was getting to be too familiar a scene and I wondered if he really had expected to find her at home 'But come into the kitchen and wait. She'll be back soon.'

The idea of waiting seemed to worry him. 'I don't have much time,' he said.

'Come in for a moment, then,' I said. 'I was just about to make some coffee.' He hesitated; I could tell that he was remembering the last time he had visited unexpectedly, and he didn't want to play that scene over again. He was the type of person who hated to intrude, or push himself forward, and now, for the second time, he was, in his own mind at least, doing exactly that. Any other time, I would have let him go,

248

but I was curious to know why, after missing several Saturday tea mornings, he was here now, bearing gifts, so I started for the kitchen without saying anything else, knowing that he wouldn't have any choice but to follow. I think I had already guessed that he had come to say he was leaving, but I didn't know why and I wanted to give him time to tell me. Of course, Mother would probably be gone for hours yet, but he didn't know that.

He was still nervous. We made small talk, while I prepared the coffee and he sat at the kitchen table, clutching his brown-paper gift, but neither of us took it very seriously – we were both waiting for the real conversation to begin, the one where he said what he had come to say. The one where he explained his absence and made whatever announcement he had come to make. 'So, I heard you were in England,' he said, as I brought the things to the table.

I nodded. 'Only for a short while,' I said, in a tone that suggested, I hoped politely, that I didn't much want to pursue *that* line of conversation.

'And all the work for the show has gone off to Oslo?'

'Yes.'

'That's good.' He sat quiet for a moment, not knowing what to say next; then, when he did speak, his voice sounded different, less nervous, more relaxed, as if he had worked out that Mother wouldn't be coming back any time soon and he could leave his gift, and whatever message he had, with me – because it was obvious, now, that he was afraid of seeing Mother. There was something he wanted her to know, but he would be happier not to have to say it to her face. He smiled. 'So what else is new, out here on Kvaløya,' he said. He made it sound far away, a part of his past already, and it made me uncomfortable, for Mother's sake, to know that he had already begun the process of putting this part of his life behind him.

'Nothing much,' I said.

'That's good,' he said, relaxing a little more. 'Too much has happened already. Those boys drowning like that . . .'

That surprised me. For some reason, I had thought that what had happened to the Sigfridsson brothers hadn't registered with him – or not, at least, enough that he would choose it as a topic of conversation. 'It *was* odd,' I said.

'Yes,' he said. 'It was a terrible coincidence, their being brothers and –'

'Kyrre Opdahl doesn't think it was a coincidence,' I said quickly, surprising myself. I hadn't intended to talk about Kyrre, but it was all I could come up with – and I saw that I was casting about for some way of extending the conversation because, now, for no reason that I could think of, I didn't want him to just hand me his box and leave. It was too casual, too unceremonious.

He smiled. 'Ah,' he said. 'I'm not sure I want to know what Kyrre Opdahl believes. But no doubt you'll tell me anyway.'

I smiled at that. He was, I think, rather fond of Kyrre Opdahl, and had a higher regard for him than he pretended – though he knew perfectly well what Kyrre thought of him. 'He thinks they were *taken*,' I said.

'What do you mean, *taken*?'

I shrugged. 'Taken by the *huldra*, I think,' I said.

I expected him to laugh at that, but he didn't – and for the first time, I understood that he was concerned about my friendship with the old man. Concerned about what nonsense Kyrre might be planting in my head, with his crazy stories. He collected those crazy stories himself, of course, but for him it was purely academic. It wasn't a matter of faith, the way it was with Kyrre. 'Why does he say that?' he said.

'Well,' I said, 'you said yourself, it's an odd coincidence . . .'

He shook his head. 'Well, you're right,' he said. 'It probably wasn't a coincidence.' He studied my face while he thought about what he was saying. I didn't know why, but it was obviously important to him to say what he wanted to say in very precise and unambiguous terms. 'No,' he said. 'It wasn't a coincidence. But it wasn't the *huldra* either. Or not what Kyrre Opdahl means by the *huldra*. The *huldra* is an idea. It's not a person, it's not a monster. It's just a way of saying those boys were – *susceptible* . . .' He paused and shook his head. He was unhappy with himself, that he couldn't find the right words. 'They were too susceptible to the world around them,' he said. 'Probably they always were, but over this last while, something shifted –'

'What do you mean, susceptible?' I said. 'Susceptible to what?'

He shook his head again. 'I don't know,' he said. 'But the old folk would have said that the susceptible person is drawn in because he wants things that he shouldn't even be thinking about. A man goes out and he's looking for someone – he's looking for someone to love, but he doesn't want just anyone. He wants somebody special, somebody – unnatural. No ordinary woman will do for him – and when he meets the *huldra*, he sees that she's beautiful, and, yes, he falls in love with this beautiful girl, but he already knows that she's something other than that, and he's drawn to that other thing. Not the space she conceals at her back, and not the animal – not that – but the mysterious creature he sees in her –'

'And she's irresistible –'

251

'Yes, but only because he collaborates with her. He *could* see her as she is, he could expose the illusion, but he doesn't want to –'

'Why not?'

'Because that would dispel the illusion. That's what gives the *huldra* her power – she is the keeper of the illusion –'

'I thought you said it wasn't the *huldra*?'

'It wasn't,' he said. 'Not like that. Not the way Kyrre Opdahl means it –'

'How do you know what Kyrre Opdahl means by it?'

'I *know*,' he said. He seemed almost annoyed by the question, and that was surprising, because I had never seen him annoyed before. In fact, I had never seen him show any kind of emotion. 'The *huldra* is an idea,' he said. 'People in the old days, they knew that. They could tell that story *because* they knew. They didn't really think there were women with cows' tails roaming around the countryside, luring young men to their deaths. But they did think that some people were . . .' He thought for a second.

'Susceptible,' I said.

He looked at me – and the annoyance was gone. He smiled. '*Akkurat*,' he said – and when he said it, he sounded just like Kyrre Opdahl.

We sat silent for a moment. I could see that he was dissatisfied with himself, for having been annoyed; he was also trying to work out a way of raising the subject he had come to talk about – and it seemed a small courtesy to help him on his way. 'So,' I said, at last. 'What's new with you?'

He looked startled for a moment, then he smiled – a little sadly this time, I thought. 'It's hard to say,' he said. 'I've been coming to this house for so long, I know I'll miss it . . .' He picked up the little box that he'd set down on the table when

I gave him his coffee. 'I'm going away,' he said. 'I'm starting a new . . . I'm making a fresh start.'

'Where?'

'In Bergen,' he said.

'This is sudden,' I said. 'I always thought you liked it in the north –'

'I do,' he said. 'I've enjoyed my time here. But . . .' He considered for a few seconds, before beginning the next part of his story. The part he wouldn't have told to Mother, I think, but could tell to me because, as far as he was concerned, I was a neutral party – and it was obvious, as he began his story, that he wanted to tell it to someone. 'It's strange how things turn out,' he said. 'I would never have expected it, but . . . Well. Years ago, when I was very young, I met someone . . .' He smiled and shook his head slightly, as if amused at his own foolishness. 'This was when I was still in Telemark, just after I finished college and had my first teaching job,' he said. 'We weren't together for very long – a few weeks, really, and we were both young. I wanted to be with her, but I was stupid and I didn't understand . . .' He gave me an odd, somewhat quizzical look and I remembered what I had thought about him once before – remembered that he was someone who had taken to collecting stories because he found people puzzling, and the stories allowed him to put their strange actions into some larger context. 'I was – cruel,' he said. 'And she left. She went to America . . . To Wisconsin. Which seemed to me hugely exotic at the time. I tried to picture her there. I had this picture in my mind of snowy forests and endless roads running across America, and I wanted to go after her . . . But I didn't.'

The sad smile flickered across his face again, but I didn't say anything. I couldn't imagine him as cruel. I suppose, all

that time, I had thought of him in a quite different light –
not as a victim, perhaps, but as someone who, to some extent,
had been burdened by the pain, or at least by the disappointment, of wanting something from Mother that she
couldn't reasonably give. As a suitor, in other words. As
someone who was, in his own way, susceptible. 'And now?' I
said.

He looked back at me, and his face was serious, but I could
tell that he was – hopeful. I had never seen that in him before
and I realised, then, that I'd always thought that he preferred
to live without hope. 'It was too much of a coincidence,' he
said. 'Our meeting again. She's come back to Bergen to live
and . . . Well . . .' He smiled – at himself, mostly. 'We're going
to give it a try. See where it leads. It's early days, but . . .' His
expression grew serious again. 'I need a change,' he said.

'I see.' I was disappointed in him now, and I couldn't resist
the impulse to let him see that I was. 'And I always thought
it was Mother you were in love with.'

He gave me a sad, somewhat accusing look, as if I'd just
hit him with something. 'Ah,' he said. 'Well – that's true, I
suppose. Though maybe not in the way you imagine. We're
all in love with her, I think, in our different ways, but . . . if
she came to any one of us and said, all right, I'll marry you
. . . I hope you won't take this the wrong way –'

'Why would I?' I said.

He considered a moment, then he decided not to pursue
the point. Instead, he held out the box and waited for me to
take it. 'This is for her,' he said. 'It's a goodbye gift – and a
thank-you, too . . .'

I took it from him. 'Don't you want to give it to her yourself?' I said. 'She won't be long now.'

He shook his head. 'I don't think I can,' he said.

254

'Why not?'

He smiled. 'I thought, before, that I wouldn't be able to explain,' he said. 'But I realise now that I wouldn't have to, because she wouldn't ask.' He looked me in the eyes to see if I understood, fully, what he was saying – and he must have been satisfied, or he wouldn't have continued with what he wanted to say. He would have gone away and left us to forget him. 'Your mother is an astonishing person,' he said. 'A great artist, without a doubt, and a great spirit too. You could say that she lives up to her name. But the more angelic a person becomes, the less room there is for the merely human, and I . . .' He thought for a moment, though he knew what he wanted to say. He knew what he wanted to say and he felt right in saying it, but I think he also wished that it wasn't true. 'For my own part,' he said, 'I find the merely human a little less . . . difficult . . .'

I nodded. I understood what he was saying, and I didn't think less of him for it, but I didn't want him to be there any more. Now that he had said what he had to say, I needed him to leave, before Mother got home. 'Thank you,' I said. 'I'm sure –'

He shook his head. 'It's all right,' he said. 'You don't have to say anything.' He stood up and made ready to go – and I didn't try to detain him. I felt sure that we would never see him again, and I knew Mother would miss him for a time – but only for a time. He knew it, too – but that didn't matter now. His mind was elsewhere – and that felt, for a moment, like a betrayal, not of Mother, but of himself. As if he had settled for something less than he deserved, something he merely *wanted*. As I opened the door to see him out, he paused a moment and looked at me, one last time. 'There's more than one way to live,' he said.

255

I thought, at first, that he was talking about himself; then I saw that he meant something else – that, in fact, it was *me* he was talking about. 'I don't know what you mean,' I said. I did, though – and for the first time, I was angry with him.

'You're her daughter, but that doesn't mean you have to *be* like her,' he said. 'You have your own life.'

I shook my head. I didn't want to hear any more. He was letting himself down and I needed him to stop. 'Thank you for coming,' I said. 'I'll tell Mother you said goodbye.'

He didn't move for a moment – and I think, for that one moment, he thought I might have misunderstood him. Or maybe he was upset with himself, for blurting out what he'd obviously been thinking about since – since when? Since the time we had skipped stones on the beach? Since he'd fallen in love with a mere human and started looking at Mother with new eyes? I didn't know, and I didn't care – and when he saw that, he made the only choice he could make, which was not to say anything else, but leave his gift and go.

I can't say for certain, but I'm pretty sure it was that same night that Martin drowned. I almost missed what happened, because I fell asleep in my room right after dinner, and I didn't wake up till after ten o'clock. Mother and I had prepared dinner together, and I had told her about Ryvold's visit and given her the gift, but I didn't say anything about the girl from Wisconsin or Ryvold's attempt to offer me advice. I just told her the basic facts – and I could see that she wasn't surprised. She didn't seem to be particularly upset either. She opened the box – it contained a brooch whose design suggested that Ryvold had chosen it to go with the poppy scarf – then she set it aside and we had dinner. 'How was your afternoon?' she said, as she passed me the potatoes.

'Fine,' I said. 'How was your walk?'

'Good,' she said. 'I ran into Kyrre Opdahl down on the shore. He says you haven't been to see him since you got back from England.'

It was true. I hadn't been to see him, and I knew he would be waiting to hear all about the trip. And that, probably, was why I hadn't been down there. I didn't know what to say. I felt awkward, because of what Mother had told him, and I didn't want to have to talk about what had happened with Kate Thompson. I didn't want to have to tell him that I had arrived at the hospital too late – and I didn't want to have to tell him that my father was dead, because that would upset him. It would upset him for my sake and he would be hurt by the fact that I wasn't upset.

Mother shook her head. 'You should go and see him,' she said. 'He's very fond of you, you know.'

'I know,' I said. 'It's just –' I broke off. I didn't know how to say what I wanted to say without making it sound like an accusation. The truth was, I'd been annoyed when she said I was going to England to visit my father. 'It's just that . . . He'll want to know all about the trip and . . .'

'And what?'

'I'd rather not have to talk about it.'

'Well, don't.'

'I can't do that,' I said.

'Why not? You don't have to talk about it if you don't want to.'

I shook my head. 'Not everybody is like you,' I said.

She laughed. 'What does that mean?' she said.

I didn't say anything for a moment. She hadn't asked me about my father, she had left it to me to tell her as much as I wanted in my own time, which is exactly what I had expected of her. She didn't even want to be reassured that the phone calls wouldn't continue. 'He died,' I said.

She didn't react right away, though I could see that she had taken the information in. Then she put down her fork and looked at me. 'I'm sorry,' she said.

'Don't be,' I said. 'He was a stranger to me, after all.' I was wondering, now, what she felt – because, even if she didn't show it, she had to feel something. She, at least, had known the man Kate Thompson had described, whereas I hadn't. 'I didn't even get to see him,' I said. 'He died before I got there.'

'Ah.' She put her hand over mine. 'Are you all right?' she said.

I nodded. 'Perfectly fine,' I said. 'As I say, I never knew him.'

She studied my face for a moment, then she took her hand away and sat back. 'Well,' she said, 'that's – unfortunate.'

'Is it?'

'Yes,' she said. 'He was a good man, I think. And he loved his work –'

'Was that why you didn't get married? Because of his work?'

She didn't answer right away, and I could see that she was puzzled by the question. 'Married?' she said. 'Oh no . . . I never had any thought of getting married.'

'Why not?'

She was quiet for a moment and, for no more than a second or two, she had the air of someone who was carrying out a simple and rather familiar calculation in her head. 'I didn't want him,' she said – and then, when I waited for her to say something else, she nodded ever so slightly and said it again. 'I didn't want him.'

'And did he want you?' I said.

'I don't know,' she said. 'It wasn't a question that came up.

258

I didn't want him, because I didn't want anybody. No way to explain it. I just didn't want that kind of life.'

That was the end of the conversation – but I was still thinking about what she had said when she went to the studio and I headed to my room to look at picture books. I was tired, though, and I hadn't lasted long; so it was ten, maybe later, when I woke up and looked out across the meadows and, by then, something had already begun – some story that belonged, not to the world that I knew, but to some other place, where the logic was different – and what I saw that night was just the very last act in what must have been a long chain of events, a sequence of words and looks and silences that led, inevitably and inexplicably, to the scene that I was unlucky enough to witness, quite by chance, when I woke. Not that I can be entirely certain of what it was that I witnessed that night. I was still a little woozy when I got up and went to the window and everything that happened afterwards seemed to contradict my version of events – but I saw what I saw, nonetheless. I didn't imagine it all and I'm not crazy. I would happily believe that, if I could, because it would be an explanation, of sorts, for something that is otherwise impossible to explain. I saw what I saw, that night, and I saw what I saw later, when the *huldra* claimed her last victim and I can't explain it away, no matter how much I would like to. It's impossible.

I'd not intended to sleep, and I didn't remember having lain down on the bed, fully clothed. And it does seem odd to me, now, that the first thing I did when I woke was to take the binoculars from my desk and train them on the *hytte*, but I know that that was exactly what I did, even though I had decided earlier, once and for all, that I was bored with Martin Crosbie's tawdry romance. I picked up the binoculars and trained them on the shoreline, pretty much from habit, and I saw them immediately, Martin and his girl, down by Kyrre's boathouse. I singled them out right away, and I saw that they had taken Kyrre's boat out, and they were dragging it towards the water, but that didn't alarm me, or not to begin with anyway. Maybe I was still half asleep – I asked myself that question over and over again later: was I still asleep? Did I dream what I saw? – but it didn't occur to me that there was any danger. It was just two people taking a boat out on a summer's night – a boat that didn't belong to them, of course, and I should have remembered how careful Kyrre was about that boat, and how he never allowed his guests to use it. But I didn't remember anything. All I saw was a man and a girl dragging a boat down the shore and then, when they'd got it out into the water, pushing it out into the tide. There was a moment of quiet, and total, unnatural stillness, like in some old painting of a fishing scene by Christian Krohg, then I heard the outboard motor kick in and I saw, as the drama started up again, that Martin Crosbie had jumped into the boat and was heading out into the Sound, while his companion stayed behind on the shore. That seemed odd to me, and I was puzzled as to what might be happening, which is absurd, of course, considering what I already knew. But I really didn't see it, not when the boat puttered out into the water and came to a stop, less than twenty metres from the strand, and not when Maia went and stood on the little lawn by the *hytte*, the better to see, I suppose, as the boat halted in the channel, the motor chugging away softly now on idle, and Martin Crosbie sitting there, looking for all the world like someone who'd been doing this all his life. Only, he hadn't been doing this all his life and there was no reason for him to be out on the Sound. He had never shown the slightest interest in Kyrre's boat and now, for no reason, he was taking it out into the white, calm water, where he had no business being – and Maia was watching, her hand raised, as if in some corny wave, all innocence and lovestruck stupidity.

And then, suddenly, he was gone. About ten or fifteen metres out, certainly no more than that, and hardly in the kind of water that could claim a grown man, he stood up and, raising his hand as if to wave back, flickered a moment, like a character in some grainy old film from the 1920s, and, soundlessly, with no apparent effort or intent, he vanished. Later, there was no evidence to prove that this was what had happened – unlike the Sigfridsson boys, he didn't drift down-shore with the tide, or wash up by a jetty to be hauled in by a passing fisherman – but he vanished nevertheless, and I was there, spying on him through the binoculars, when he went into the water. I was there, and I saw – or rather, I almost saw – what happened. I only looked away for a moment, a hurried glance, to where Maia stood watching, but it was in that moment, when I glanced away, that he disappeared. The last I saw of him, he had been standing, looking back, and though I couldn't really see his face, not even through the binoculars, I had the sense, for one brief moment, that he was happy. And I think that Maia was happy too: I *had* seen her face, and I could all but swear that she was. Happy, that is, for Martin Crosbie, and not for herself. Not for having succeeded in tricking him into the water, the way the *huldra* in the old stories might have been, at the moment of truth: no; as absurd as it might sound, I still believe that whatever happiness each of them felt, for whatever perverse reason, it was a shared happiness and, when I saw that Martin Crosbie was gone, I knew right away that Maia would do nothing to save him. She would watch and she would let him go into the tide. No attempt to help or raise the alarm: she was happy, and what was happening was something that had been intended, something that should not be interfered with. The problem for me, however, is that, for the first few critical seconds, I did nothing either. I just watched as the boat drifted a little further and came to a stop, turning slightly in the tide, just twenty metres from the shore.

I stood frozen for a long moment – a moment from a story-book in which decades pass – and then that moment was over and the spell was broken. Until then, I hadn't been able to take in what I was witnessing – and I have to imagine that it was shock, shock and stunned disbelief, that held me there so long, unable to move as the boat drifted and the man who had been visible a moment before disappeared into thin air. I say thin air, because that was how it seemed to me. It wasn't so much that he stepped out of the boat into the water – I didn't see that, and I had no sense of it happening – it was more that he quite simply vanished, cancelled out by a grey light in which the surface of the water and the air above the boat were indistinguishable. And until that moment, I hadn't been able to move. Martin had been there, I had seen him raise his hand, as if to wave and, when I turned to see how Maia would respond, he must have gone into the water, with that odd, rapt look on his face: rapt, happy, I didn't know what it was, but that was how it seemed through the binoculars and maybe I turned away because that look, that simulacrum of happiness, was too awful to have to witness. It's not as if I turned to see who he was waving to – I knew who else was there – but I did turn, just for a moment, and when I looked back, he was gone. And I suppose that was when I cried out. I didn't know at the time that I had uttered a sound, but Mother told me later that that was what alerted her to the fact that something was wrong – and at the same time that I let the binoculars fall and stared out into the hugeness of the white night, everything suddenly far away and strange-seeming, too small and too wide to be real, she stopped what she was doing in the studio to listen. I think I believed that I had been tricked in some way and that the binoculars had something to do with that, but even with the naked eye, taking in the entire scene, I couldn't see anything in that shimmer of grey and silver, and when I looked back to the lawn outside the *hytte*, Maia was gone too. Gone, as if she had never been there. As if neither of them had ever existed. I suppose that confused me, and I didn't know what to do, or even whether I had imagined the whole thing – and then I was running, running downstairs and out through the front door, not because I thought I could help Martin Crosbie, but because I had to see for myself what had happened. I had to break the spell that had been cast. I believe I thought that if I ran to where the boat still sat, turning ever so slightly in the water, then this dream would end and I could tell myself that I had imagined everything.

I didn't know that Mother had heard me cry out, or that my leaving in such a hurry had startled her into following. It hadn't even occurred to me to go to her for help, or to stay and call the police, or the coastguard, or whoever it is you call when something bad happens. I just started to run when the uncertainty of that empty boat and the unbroken grey of the water became unbearable. I didn't know, as I ran down through the birch woods and across the open meadow, that Mother was just twenty metres or so behind me, not running, but walking in that quick, deliberate way of hers; I must have thought that she was in the studio, shut away in her separate world, and I had no idea that she was aware of anything until we got to the *hytte* and found Maia standing by the door of the little woodshed, with something – a shawl, or maybe a veil, I had the impression of fabric, of something silken – in her hands. I only knew, in fact, when I saw in Maia's face that she was aware of someone behind me, someone whose presence on the scene surprised her, at least for a moment. I saw in her face – like looking in a mirror and seeing a flicker of movement away to the left somewhere – that someone else was coming and, for a moment, as I looked back with the sudden, uncomfortable sensation of standing between them, I felt that I had wandered into some zone where I did not belong. It only lasted for a moment, that sensation, but it was disconcerting for all of us. Even for Maia.

Mother had been following me, and she only saw Maia at the last minute – only saw her, I think, when she saw herself being seen – and when she did, she stopped walking. She was about ten metres from Maia, and I was between them. For a second, no more, we stood, like figures in a tableau, each of us surprised by the fact of the others' presence in the world – and then Maia went into an act that I cannot help but think was prepared, her attitude and gestures oddly rehearsed-looking, chosen to seem appropriate to the events that were unfolding, even though they weren't appropriate in the most obvious way. She wasn't frantic or tearful, she didn't run to us the moment we arrived on the scene and appeal for help. She wasn't even visibly upset, the way a character in a film might be in that situation. No: she was calm, and she was very still, though it was a stillness that could have been taken for shock, or stunned horror, and that – I thought this at the time, in spite of all that was going on – that was astute of her, because that was the most likely reaction for someone in her situation, her relationship to Martin Crosbie ambiguous, her being there at all a surprise. She had been standing in the middle of the lawn, where I had last seen her through the binoculars. After that, she must have walked away, to end up by the *hytte*. Now, however, she took several steps back towards the beach, back to where the boat was clearly visible, turning around in the open water.

Mother followed her. 'What happened?' she said. She was calm, and her manner was deliberately reassuring, but I could see that she didn't quite know what to do. She looked out towards the boat and something dawned on her, and she took Maia by the arm. 'Is somebody out there?' she said.

Maia turned and gazed into her face, but she didn't say anything.

Mother looked back to me. 'What did you see?' she said. I tried to speak, but I couldn't say anything and I suspected that this had something to do with Maia, who had turned away from Mother and fixed her eyes on me. Mother waited for me to reply and then, when I didn't speak, she took another couple of steps and gazed out over the water. The Sound was calm, silvery, very still. Mother scanned its shimmering surface as if she thought that she could raise whoever was out there up from the depths by some effort of attention or will. Then she turned back to Maia. 'What's going on here?' she said, her voice slightly more urgent now.

Maia shook her head like someone who suddenly feels dizzy and is trying to regain control of her thoughts but, once again, she didn't say anything.

'Have you called for help?' Mother said.

The girl looked puzzled – and then, just for a moment, I thought she was going to laugh. Not a hysterical laugh, but the laughter of someone who has been keeping up a pretence for too long and can't sustain it any more. She shook her head.

'There's no phone here,' I said. I hadn't intended to speak and I felt an ugly shiver of surprise, as if I'd been made to do something against my will. I looked at Maia. I didn't believe in her. I *knew* she was pretending. But that wasn't the only reason I wanted to stay clear of her. There was something else, something I can only think of now as a fear of contagion. It's ridiculous, I know, but she seemed to me contagious in some way. I'm not talking about illness here, I'm not talking about a virus. Or maybe I am. A virus. An infection of the will.

Mother turned. 'There's no phone?' This seemed to annoy her, though only for a moment. Then she seemed to give up on us altogether and walked right to the edge of the water, her eyes fixed on the empty boat. 'What happened here?' she said again, but she was suspicious now, because something didn't add up.

I went with her, my eyes still scanning the water. I had no hope of seeing anything, I didn't expect Martin Crosbie to bob up suddenly and start flailing about in the tide, but I didn't want to be left behind, so close to Maia – not because I was afraid of what she might do, but because I didn't want her to look at me. It was ridiculous, I can see that now – I even thought so at the time – but I was afraid of her. I was afraid that she would look at me while Mother's back was turned and laugh in my face, or say something to show that she knew I suspected her. And, yes, as absurd as it sounds, I was afraid that she would *infect* me in some way and then I would never be rid of her. 'Martin Crosbie was in the boat,' I said. 'I saw him –'

'Martin Crosbie?'

'From the *hytte*,' I said.

'You saw him?'

'Yes.'

'So what happened to him?' Mother was puzzled now. She could tell something was wrong, but she seemed not to believe what I was saying. How could Martin Crosbie have been there, when he was so obviously *not* there now? If he had fallen into the water, he would have struggled, called out, tried to save himself. And he hadn't. There had been no cry, no struggle. I knew that too, and for the first time, I started to doubt myself. What had I seen through the binoculars? What had I imagined? Had I been dreaming? 'He can't have just disappeared . . .' Mother turned back to appeal to Maia for her version of the story – and I understood her line of reasoning. Whatever I had seen, I had seen from far away, while Maia had been there all the time, and she would have seen everything.

But Maia was gone. I knew it right away from the look in Mother's eyes when she turned – a look, not of surprise, so much as puzzlement – and when I turned I could see that we were alone now. Mother frowned. Maybe she was beginning to suspect this was some childish prank. She looked at me. 'Who was that girl?' she said. 'Do you *know* her?'

I shook my head. I didn't want to talk about Maia, not there, at the edge of the water, with the boat still turning slowly in the current and the sense that Martin was somewhere under the surface, just ten metres away and beyond saving.

'Well, do you know her?' Mother said again. She sounded so casual, as if nothing serious had happened.

I looked at her. 'Yes,' I said. 'She's the one . . . she was a friend of the Sigfridssons.'

She stared at me. 'The Sigfridssons?'

'Yes,' I said, and I suddenly knew why she was so calm. She had begun to suspect that this girl had played a trick on me. She thought that, with Maia's help, I had imagined the whole thing, that I'd been affected in some way by the mysterious deaths of my school friends and by the stress of exams and not being able to decide what to do with my life. Which was ridiculous, of course – and she had to have known that Mats and Harald weren't my friends, because I didn't have any friends. And that was something else she knew. She knew and she had let it pass all those years, which suited me well enough, but surely it should have seemed odd to a parent that my only friend was an old man who lived along the shore and told crazy stories about farm boys who went out to fetch water in the broad light of day and never came home and babies stolen from their beds by the troll people. She was watching me carefully, and I knew, before she said it, what she was going to say next. I don't say that she wasn't concerned for me, but that wasn't the point. Her not believing was the point. 'Are you *sure* you saw –'

'Yes,' I said.

'These summer nights can play tricks on you –'

'I saw what I saw.'

'All right,' she said. She put her hand on my arm, just below the elbow. 'We have to go back to the house now,' she said. 'You've had a shock –'

'No. We have to call someone –'

'Back at the house,' she said. She started away – and I knew that she didn't believe me. She was remembering how I'd seemed when I came back from England, and she was already deciding that I wasn't well. Because, of course, there was no other explanation for what I had seen. No explanation at all, in fact, apart from delusion.

I didn't know what to say. She was right, of course. It made no sense to linger on the shore, gazing out at the empty water

– but I didn't want to go back. That was like giving up. Like letting go of a drowning man's hand and turning away as he slid beneath the surface. I looked out to where the boat sat bobbing in the water. How could it be so calm, after what had just happened? How could it be so beautiful? 'But can't we *do* something?' I said.

Mother didn't answer. Somewhere off to the side, I heard a noise – a soft, sweet call, like a bird in the near grass – and I turned. I half expected to see Maia out there among the willowherb, or on the bank of the stream that crossed the beach a few metres further downshore, but there was no one. It was utterly still. I turned back to Mother. 'But can't we do something?' I said again, but my voice was thin and far off, even to me, and she would have known that it wasn't really a question.

She answered, though. I don't know what she believed at that moment, but I suspect she just wanted to get me back to the house. She didn't believe anyone was in physical danger – though she was worried that I might be experiencing some kind of psychological crisis and the best way of dealing with that was to get me home. 'No,' she said. 'There's nothing to do here.' She shook her head. 'We have to go back to the house.' She smiled sadly – a smile that reminded me of the early days, when she would get me ready for bed and tell me stories from one of her big picture books. Stories about heroes or street urchins who made good, stories with no darkness in them at all.

I shook my head but, after a moment's hesitation, I started back with her to the house. I knew, now, that she didn't believe I had seen anything, but she didn't want to press it, she wanted to go slowly, putting the pieces of the puzzle together carefully till she understood what was going on. She had decided that I was seeing things – and, at that moment, the whole thing seemed ridiculous, a trick my mind had played on me, a leftover from one of Kyrre's old tales. After all, why would a grown man take a boat that wasn't his, then steer it out into the current and slip overboard? Which was something I hadn't seen him do, anyhow. I had *inferred*, but I hadn't *seen*. How could I be a witness to something that I hadn't actually witnessed? Of course I understand, now, that she wasn't concerned about what had or hadn't happened, she was concerned about me. There I was, talking about how Maia was the one who had drowned the Sigfridsson boys, and now, by some strange enchantment, had forced Martin Crosbie out into the Sound, to die as they had, in cold, calm water. How could a mother not worry, when her child talks like that? She was my mother, and it was me she had to take care of, not some lost girl or some phantom suicide who might not even be real. And that was what she did. She took care of me. She got me back to the house and sat me down in the kitchen. Then she went to the phone and called someone. I never discovered who, but it was a real call, to someone who asked questions that she answered and then, it seems, reassured her about something. It was a brief call, but she made it. Then she gave me some *akevit*, which I surprised myself by drinking, and sat with me till I agreed to go to bed. I could see that she was worried, but I could also see that she was working to a script: calm words, a little alcohol, sleep. Things would be better in the morning. Everything would be explained. In the morning, I would wake and, like Alice, I would see that it was all nothing more than a curious dream.

It wasn't a dream, though. Late in the summer, with the first suggestion of returning night, cool pockets of darkness formed along our garden walls in the small hours, a soft, almost powdery shade gathered in pools here and there on the blown meadows, and Martin Crosbie disappeared into Malangen Sound, while three people did nothing to help him. I was one of those witnesses, and though, when he fell, I was too far away to do anything, I didn't even try to save him. Then afterwards, when he was gone, I didn't even try to testify as to what happened, or the part that Maia must have played in his death. Why? I know I couldn't have saved him, but I could have told someone other than Mother about what I had seen. But I didn't, and that wasn't because Mother doubted me, or because I was reluctant to cause trouble for Maia – her sudden disappearance, which Mother had also witnessed, surely implicated her in what had happened, and even if she had done nothing to cause it, she certainly made no effort to prevent Martin Crosbie's death. No: the reasons weren't even that logical. The fact is that I didn't say anything because I was confused: confused by the calm on the water, confused by the light and the unreality of it all, confused by that sense I'd had, watching him go out in the boat, that Martin had been happy during the last minutes of his life, happy as he hadn't been in years, and maybe happier than he had ever been before. I was confused because I couldn't shake off the idea that he'd done what he did because he *wanted* to drown, and whatever it was I thought I had seen, and whatever I could have said that I had witnessed – which was, I realised, something altogether different – it was only the shell of the experience, a purely external matter that had nothing to do with the essential story: a story that was neither a murder, nor a suicide, but a natural event, like a rainstorm, or a bird migration.

The next day was rainy and overcast, and there was a darkness over the meadows that made everything seem on the

271

point of vanishing, shorebirds flickering out of the grey air and gliding a moment before they disappeared, like the props in some old-fashioned magic trick, gusts of wind taking form as they rippled through the grass, only to melt away at the fence lines and verges, something then nothing, the entire coastline and everything on it an illusion, from the dripping birches at the edge of our garden to the mountains on the far shore of the Sound. On days like those, I was happiest at home, curled up on the chair with a picture book and listening to the sound of the rain dripping from the eaves. Or I would sit in the kitchen, drinking coffee and staring out at the grey sky, enjoying the stark cleanness of it all, the whole world streaming with water, the colour bled from every leaf and blade of grass till there was nothing but white and grey, like a Hammershøi painting. That day, though, I stayed home because I didn't want to go out and risk seeing Maia again. I had tried telling myself that she would surely have left the island, now that Martin was gone and she had nowhere to stay, but I couldn't be sure of that, and besides, where else would she go? Her mother was a drunk and her father had run away, so what else did she have, other than this *hytte* and its recent memories of a man she had watched drown himself, a man she had presumably loved, after her fashion? I had seen that look on his face, as he stood up in the boat, preparing to vanish into the cold water, and I had no doubt that Maia had seen it too. Everything I had seen told me that Martin Crosbie had been happy when he died – and I could think of no other cause for that happiness than the girl who had stood calmly on the shore, waiting for him to vanish into the water.

She had watched for a long time after the last ripple faded – and I know now that I should have understood much sooner what was happening. After what had happened with the Sigfridsson boys, I should have guessed the danger Martin Crosbie was in. As soon as I saw the boat, I should have acted. I should have run down to the boathouse or even called out across the meadows and broken the spell that seemed to have fallen over them both, maybe scared her into calling him back – though I already knew, even as I watched them slide the boat down the beach and into the water, that there was nothing to be done. And, if I am honest, I have to admit that, even then, even in that first moment of realisation, I didn't want them to know that I was watching. I didn't want to be a *witness*. From the very beginning, or at least, for as long as I could remember, I had understood that *this* is the first law of the observer: never be a witness. The true observer is permitted to see what no one else sees on one condition, and that is that she *never tells*. This is what distinguishes her from the witness, or the casual passer-by. I can even say that this is what distinguishes her from the painter. Because painting is also a way of bearing witness. When Mother shows her work in some gallery in Oslo or London, she is giving away what she has seen, and so the secret is betrayed – and it strikes me, now, that she knew that all along, and *that* was why she stopped painting portraits. Or rather, that was why she abandoned the portrait she had set out to make of me. She wanted to keep *that* look a secret.

I didn't want to be a witness and I knew, anyhow, that Martin Crosbie was beyond help – but the real reason, the secret reason why I didn't do anything, was that I desperately wanted not to be seen again by that girl. By Maia. I didn't want her to know that I had been watching them all along and I didn't want her to think of me as a witness to something that, for whatever reason and according to whatever

273

twisted logic, belonged to her and to Martin Crosbie and nobody else. I didn't want her to see that I had seen, because – and this is the terrible thing, this is the one thing that I cannot get out of my head, even now – I didn't want her to know that I had understood, not only that Martin was happy at the moment when he let go of the side and vanished into the still, pearl-coloured water, but also that she, Maia, the pretty tomboy I had seen around town all my life, the waiflike girl we all avoided and felt sorry for, had been transformed, at that moment, into someone – or something – unreasonably, and quite inexplicably, *beautiful*. It sounds ridiculous, now, but I know what I saw. I cannot forget it. For as long as she stood there, at the water's edge, looking out to where the empty boat now sat bobbing slightly in the white night, she was beautiful in a way that I have no words to express. Then, when Mother and I arrived and found her by the *hytte*, she became herself again, just Maia, the pretty but slightly odd-looking girl that she had always been.

Yet, in spite of all this, I wonder, now, why I didn't do more. Why I didn't say anything about what a coincidence it was, that Maia had been so friendly with the Sigfridsson brothers, just before they died, and then, shortly before he also disappeared – they never found a body, so nothing was proven – she had moved into the *hytte* with Martin Crosbie? But then, who would have believed me? Martin Crosbie had disappeared, that was clear enough, but there was no evidence to say he was dead. On the contrary, all the evidence suggested that he had simply upped sticks and gone back to where he'd come from. No body was found, there was no sign of foul play, as they say in the crime books, and his bill with Kyrre Opdahl was fully paid up. Even more significant was the fact that his car had also disappeared by the time Kyrre Opdahl

274

went down to the *hytte* the morning after I witnessed – or rather, failed to witness – his fall from the boat. Kyrre had known something was wrong too, it seemed, and he had gone down there to see what was going on, but the place was empty. Martin Crosbie was gone, and there was no sign of the *huldra*, either. There was no sign of anyone ever having been there, in fact. It was as if the whole thing really *had* been a dream, the Red King's, or the crow's, or somebody else's.

But it wasn't a dream, it was a story – and that's different. A story stands in for everything that cannot be explained and, though there are many stories, there's really only one and we can tell the difference because the many stories have a beginning and an end, but the one story doesn't work like that. Ryvold used to say that stories are really about time. They tell us that once, in a place that existed before we were born, something occurred – and we like to hear about that, because we know already that the story is over. We know that we are living in the happily ever after, which means that nothing will ever happen again – and this is the key to a happy life. To live in the ever after of the present moment: no past, no future. Or so Ryvold said, anyhow, and perhaps he's right. When I think about it now, I believe he might be. Back then, though, I didn't care about happiness. It seemed unreal to me – unreal and irrelevant, like romance, or success, or the God you see in old paintings – but that was because I didn't know what happiness was. Now that I *am* happy, the sheer fact of it surprises me every day, because it's so much darker and less finished than what I was led to expect – and I think that was what Mother wanted to tell me, all the while I was growing up. Happiness is a secret: it's quiet and personal and beyond telling. It can't be told and, no matter what they say, it can't really be shared either. When you see two people together who are happy, you know that they each brought that happiness with them – they didn't find it together, because happiness, like peace, or the Holy Spirit, is something you can only find when you are alone.

My memory of the next few days is hazy. It had taken one white night for me to become totally unsure of myself, unsure of what I knew, unsure of what I had seen. For a time, I couldn't bring myself to go out – I kept to my room, and Mother encouraged me to rest, looking in on me from time to time, bringing me soup and neatly cut sandwiches like the ones she served to the suitors on Saturday mornings. I wasn't resting, of course, but I let her think I was – and finally, after two or maybe three days of near insomnia, I fell into a deep sleep at around midnight and didn't wake up till close to three the next afternoon. As soon as I did, though, I knew something was different. Someone was downstairs with Mother. A stranger. I couldn't hear anything, but I knew that someone else was in the house and, right away, the very moment I woke, I felt a surge of panic. Real panic; actual terror. Someone or something was in the house and I immediately sensed danger. The sensation only lasted for a moment, but I remember, still, how strong it was. After a moment, it was gone, just like that, and I stood up and went to the door. I listened, but I couldn't hear anything. Then I heard the front door clicking shut – and I realised that someone had just gone out. I ran to the landing window. I already knew what I would see, but I didn't believe it, because it wasn't possible. It wasn't possible, not that Maia would come to the house, but that Mother would let her in if she did. But she must have done – because it was Maia I saw, making her way calmly down the path towards the gate, as though she had just popped round for afternoon tea.

I almost ran down the stairs. I knew Mother was in the kitchen: I felt her there. I felt her attention, an attention that had been given to the *huldra* for – how long? A few minutes? An hour? The entire day? I couldn't help but see, the moment I entered the room, that it had been more than a few minutes. There were two cups on the table, and there was a strange scent in the air. I stood for a moment, in the doorway and stared at Mother. She was standing by the sink, holding the kettle, and I – I was shaking with anger, anger, and also fear, still, so that, for a moment, I couldn't even speak. Then the words came. 'What was *Maia* doing here?' I said.

Mother closed her eyes for a second, the way she sometimes did when she was trying to think, then she gave me a kindly, concerned look. 'You're up,' she said. 'How are you feeling now?'

I wouldn't be diverted, though. 'Why was she *here*?' I said. 'What was she doing in *this* house?'

She didn't reply for a moment, but turned to the sink and filled the kettle. Finally, without looking round, she spoke. 'I'm painting her,' she said.

'*What?*' It should have been a cry of justifiable outrage, but it came out as a whisper, so quiet I could barely hear myself.

Mother turned round. 'I'm *painting* her,' she said. She was perfectly still, perfectly calm – and that calm was intended, I knew, as a challenge to me, the way a parent challenges a child to behave, if it wants the parent to cooperate. That *you won't get anywhere if you don't pull yourself together* tone.

And I did pull myself together, after a fashion. Enough, at least, to speak in a normal voice. A voice that wasn't meant to sound ironic, or bitter, or childish, though it came across, I imagine, as all these things. 'You're *painting* her?' I said.

Mother nodded, but she didn't say anything.

'You mean a portrait?'

'Yes.'

'I thought you didn't do portraits any more?'

She hesitated – and I thought that her composure was about to break. Or maybe she was just thinking about the question, but she didn't respond immediately. Then she gave me a bright smile. She obviously hadn't thought about it in that way, before I asked the question in so many words; now she allowed herself a moment's happy surprise. 'So did I,' she said. She didn't appear to see any irony in the situation: on the contrary, she was obviously happy, the way she always was when she was working on something new. She smiled at me a moment longer, then she went back to making the tea. 'Apparently I was wrong,' she said.

I didn't know what to say to that. She seemed oblivious, as if something in her had been switched off. I took a few steps into the room – and I felt cold, all of a sudden. The strange scent was still there, a soft, sweet sootiness on the air that I couldn't place, but I knew it had come from Maia. It was alien to our house, an intrusion, a contamination. My anger was draining away, and all I felt now was dismay. I watched in silence as Mother set a cup in front of me, then sat back down where she would have been sitting when Maia was there. Finally, I gathered myself together, and spoke. 'Is it going well?' I asked. It was a test, I suppose, a test to see if she really did have no idea what she was doing.

She pursed her lips and considered for a moment – and I could see that she really did have no idea of what she was doing. She had found a subject that she found interesting, and that was that. 'Too soon to say,' she said. She got up, went to the cupboard and brought out the big cake tin, the one that usually only came out on Saturday mornings.

'Can I see it?' I said.

She set the tin down on the table and opened it. She must have noticed the hardness in my voice, and she must have been aware of how upset I was, but she didn't look up and she didn't rise to the challenge. 'No,' she said, lifting the lid off the tin carefully and placing it on the table. 'It's not done yet.' She looked up. 'Would you like some cake?' she said.

I shook my head. 'Is she going to be here again?'

She turned round and fetched the big knife from the drawer by the sink. 'Why do you ask?' she said. 'Don't you like her?'

I laughed. '*Like* her?' I said. 'Don't you remember what happened . . . ?' And then, of course, I remembered: Mother didn't believe that I had seen Martin in the boat, she thought I was imagining things, and no doubt Maia had told her some other version of that night's events, a story that must certainly have made more sense than mine. I felt something fold inside me, and I had to sit down. 'Something happened,' I said. 'I'm not sure what, but whatever it was, she was responsible –'

Mother shook her head. 'Come now, Liv,' she said. 'That girl's had a shock too, you know. She thinks something terrible happened that night, but she seems to believe, now, that it happened to *her*. She's not quite over it yet, to be honest. It had something to do with that man . . .' She looked at me, but I didn't answer. I was stunned. Surely she had seen what I had seen, down at the *hytte*. Surely she didn't really believe what she was saying. What was Maia accusing Martin Crosbie of?

'Really?' I said. 'So what *happened* to her, then?'

She would have heard the contempt in my voice, but she didn't react. 'I don't know,' she said. 'But *something* happened to her. You can see it in her face.'

'Really?'

'Well, of course –'

'And what is it *you* see? In her face?'

She looked at me and considered the question. 'I don't know,' she said, at last. 'I'll have to finish the picture to find out.' She inclined her head slightly in the direction of the cup. 'Drink your tea,' she said. 'You have to rest and stay calm. You shouldn't be getting all worked up. Drink your tea and I'll make you something to eat.' She didn't say anything else, but quietly set about preparing a plate of sandwiches and sliced apples. I knew this was her way of bringing the conversation to an end – and, because of what happened next, it was several weeks before I was able to ask about the portrait again. By then, Maia was gone and I had started to wonder if I had made a mistake about her – to wonder if she was just as much a victim of the *huldra* as the Sigfridsson brothers and Martin Crosbie. So I asked what had happened to the painting, because I knew, I knew for certain, that whoever the real Maia was, Mother would have captured the truth of her in the work she had done over those last few days. I should have known, though, that she wouldn't let me see. It was for my own protection, of course – she couldn't risk having me relive the events of those days – but I was still taken aback by the lie she told me. The portrait hadn't worked out, she said, and she'd needed canvas for something else, so she had painted over it. Naturally, I was shocked by that, not just because I knew it wasn't true, but because I understood why she wanted to hide that painting from me – and it had nothing to do with my sanity. It was because the painting hadn't failed at all: she had captured the gaze of the *huldra* and, as terrible as it was, she couldn't bring herself to destroy that image. She had kept it, and I knew that, even as she stood in our kitchen lying to me about it, that portrait existed somewhere – if not in the house, then in a

280

storeroom at Fløgstad's gallery, or on the wall in some collector's house in Oslo, or Los Angeles: the cold eyes of the *huldra*, gazing out from the face of an ordinary girl, a girl who could have been the artist's own daughter, or a family friend, sitting patiently for hours in a bare studio with the last of the summer light falling on her face, revealing her terrible secret and, at the same time, making it beautiful.

Over the next two days, Mother went on treating me like I was some kind of invalid, bringing soup and crackers or cups of sweet milky coffee to my room and doing all she could to keep me there, telling me that I wasn't well yet, that she was worried about me, I'd had a shock, all the usual things you say – not to make too fine a point of it – to someone you suspect of having come close to a nervous breakdown. And it was true: I did feel that I'd had a shock, though it wasn't exactly the shock she meant, and I felt shaken and weak, but that didn't mean I was unaware of what was going on downstairs, any more than it prevented me from suspecting Mother of keeping me out of the way for her own motives. I could see it in her face when she brought the soup: a kind of appeal, under the calm surface and, behind the appeal, a determination that she would continue working on the portrait, no matter what. It was too important to her, now, to finish what she had started. Later, I saw the painting that came out of those few days with Maia: a terrifying image of a cold, manic child in something that approximated, but didn't quite match, a woman's body – and that day, long after the *huldra* had disappeared into the darkness of summer's end, I was stunned by the realisation that, whatever Mother saw in Maia's face, the subtly fantastical figure she painted wasn't that much different from the figure of the *huldra* in Kyrre's stories. I even

281

think she saw this figure on that first night, when Maia had just turned away from watching Martin die and she had asked about the girl, not because she was concerned about her, but because she saw the cruelty and tragedy in that face, and she had been fascinated.

It wasn't the appeal in Mother's eyes that kept me in my room for the next couple of days, however. It wasn't fear, either. Or not fear of the *huldra*, anyhow. It was a bitter and unseemly curiosity. I wanted to see how long Mother would keep up her pretence. I wanted to see what would happen when she was done with the painting and sent Maia away, without a second thought – because I was quite sure she would do exactly that and, even though I was worried for her, something in me refused to acknowledge that concern. I wanted to see what would happen. I wanted to see how Maia would react to the inevitable rejection, and how Mother would react to her reaction. And, yes, at some ugly, defiant level, I thought the two of them probably deserved each other. They had been destined to meet from the first, in fact. It was part of the story. I didn't love Mother any less – quite the contrary – but I wanted to see what would happen.

So I waited. I waited for two more days – at which point I knew that the painting was finished. I could hear Mother in the studio, clearing up, doing the small practical things she always did when she'd just finished a piece – and that was enough to tell me that she had no more use for Maia. So I got up, dressed quickly, and hurried downstairs. I knew better than to disturb Mother at that stage in the process; besides, what I wanted, then, had nothing to do with her. It was about the house. Everyone thinks of this as Mother's house; everyone, including me, sees how artfully she has made it, how she created it as a shell for her inward existence, how the careful illusions of the garden and the ground floor are so perfectly maintained, saying so much about the skill of their designer, and so little about her true self, but they forget – we all forget – that this is my house too. It is my house and, for those few days, Mother had allowed it to become contaminated by a stray from one of Kyrre's old stories. Now, I thought, it was time to claim back what was mine – or rather, to claim my share of a place that I had never fully inhabited until then. I wanted my home back and, as I hurried downstairs and went from room to room, scenting the air like a dog, checking for any sign of the *huldra* that might remain, I was careless enough to assume that, just because the kitchen and the dining room and the downstairs study were empty, my place in the world could be salvaged so easily. Yet the sweet, smoky scent was still there – it didn't clear for weeks after – and it led me down the hallway and out through the open door to the garden. The sun was out, I remember, and it was very warm for that time of year, more like the beginning than the end of summer, and the scent of the *huldra* was sweeter, here – sweeter and, at the same time, stronger, a maple-syrup smell touched with dust and lanolin, though there was something else there too: a faint suggestion of milk, or was it the sickly cleanness of the stark white threads that run through leaf mould, sprouting new, misshapen forms in the birch woods? Whatever it was, I should have seen it for the warning it was, but I followed it all the way outside, all the way to the *huldra*.

She was sitting on the wide stone in the middle of the rock garden. She looked completely at ease, her face very calm, her eyes half closed, taking the sun as if she had lived here all her life, the second daughter Mother never had, my inverse sister, brighter and darker than me, more light to her, and more shadow – and yet, for a moment at least, when I first caught sight of her, it seemed to me that she was only pretending to feel at home in Mother's garden. The calm, the apparent pleasure she took in her surroundings – it seemed to me that it was all an act, a bluff; but, if it was, who was it for? Who was she trying to convince?

She didn't see me for a split second; then, when she did, the smile that ghosted across her face had something of anticipation in it, a hint of sly mischief that made me think again of some ugly and unnatural sisterhood. It was the smile of a younger child who knows the grown-ups aren't watching, and decides to have some fun. She stood up and took a couple of steps towards me. 'I love the garden when it's like this,' she said. 'Don't you?'

It wasn't difficult to see what she was doing, but she was wasting her time if she thought she could provoke me. I wasn't angry with her for being there, I was angry with Mother for letting her in. 'I'm sure you do,' I said. 'But don't get too comfortable. You won't be here for long.'

She smiled sweetly. 'It's lovely and warm – *out here*,' she said. 'But why is it so *cold* inside?' She stepped closer, so she was only a couple of feet away and lifted her hand, till it was level with my chest, so that, for a moment, I thought she was going to touch me.

'We like it cool,' I said, making an effort not to draw back. I didn't want her to touch me, but I didn't want to give ground either. 'If you keep it too warm, it draws in all the vermin for miles.'

She laughed at that – and, even though she was standing right next to me, her face too close to mine, the laugh sounded far away, coming from somewhere at one remove from us, like the laughter you hear sometimes on a recording, when someone in the studio does or says something funny that you can't hear, and people laugh in the background, far away and close at the same time, and privy to a secret that you don't share. 'Maybe,' she said. 'But maybe there's another reason.' She waited a moment to see if I would respond, but I didn't say anything. She smiled. 'They do say a house takes on the qualities of the people who live there –'

'It's fortunate that you don't live here, then,' I said.

She laughed again. 'It probably is,' she said. 'That really would be confusing.' She stepped away, turning slightly to look back towards the front door, which was standing open on a whitish patch of sunlight, right at the threshold, and a dark, brownish area of shadow in the hall beyond. 'Tell me,' she said. 'Did you ever *fuck* anybody?' She glanced at me sideways, still smiling her sweet, practised smile. 'Or are you just as cold as your nice, cold house . . . ?'

I shook my head. I wasn't going to be angry with her. I wasn't about to give her the satisfaction. 'Have you got some business here?' I said. 'Will Mother be – using – you again today?'

That drew a hard, bright laugh, but she couldn't quite hide her annoyance, and I understood that what I had thought before – that Mother had finished with her – was true. The picture was done and Mother was already beginning to detach herself, not just from the portrait, but also from its subject. Besides, it had never really been *Maia* she was painting. It was something else entirely. Something she had seen in the girl's face that didn't quite belong to her: a phantom that had taken up residence in her eyes for a while, and would soon move on.

Maia looked down at her feet and, just for a moment, I thought she was biting her lip. But that was all pretence too. Everything about her was pretence and I felt that, if I could only reach out and push against her, all that knowing, cocksure facade would crumble. There was nothing behind her but empty space. Nothing to her, other than a careful illusion. I didn't reach out, though, partly because I wasn't sure, but also because I didn't *want* her to crumble. It was easier to dislike her for a while, than to watch her become the lost girl who might be hiding inside that facade. If you allow people to keep up appearances, then you can leave them to their own devices, but if you probe too far and the pretence falls apart, there's always the risk of being implicated in the mess – and I didn't want to be implicated in *anything*.

Though there was no danger of that – or not yet. Maia kept up the pretence for just long enough that I was almost convinced I'd hurt her feelings, then she looked up and grinned. 'As a matter of fact,' she said, 'I actually *do* have to go – for a while.' She looked at the house wistfully, though it wasn't clear what she regretted. 'Your mother has some things she needs to think over,' she said, though it seemed she wasn't talking to me any more. 'She's a complicated woman.'

I almost laughed out loud at that. There were no limits to the girl's presumption. 'You think so?' I said.

She turned back to me and her face brightened. 'Oh yes,' she said. 'She's a puzzle, that one.' She sounded like Kyrre Opdahl.

'Well,' I said, 'I won't keep you.' I studied her face for a moment, hoping that no sign of triumph showed in my face – I couldn't allow her to see that because, then, she would know that I hadn't been assured of winning all along – then I stepped away carefully and, without turning my back on her, took a few steps towards the house. I didn't want to have to look at her any more. It wasn't that her rudeness annoyed me, or even that I found her pitiful, though for a moment I had, and that, too, felt like a triumph – a triumph that shamed me, rather. Still, triumph or not, I was still afraid of her – and that day, I at last understood why. As she had guessed, I was afraid that she would touch me. Nothing worse than that: just a touch. She would touch me and I would be touched forever – and I couldn't say anything more until I was out of range of that possible touch. When I was, I could turn and leave her there, alone, watching me, that bright, amused look on her face still. As soon as I had taken myself safely out of reach, I could have been magnanimous and let things go, I could have told myself that, very soon, she would be gone to who knew where, and I would never have to see her again. I still believed that, and while I was angry that Mother had let her in at all, I was reassured by the conviction that she would just as easily send her away. It was possible that Maia saw her relationship with Mother as something real, perhaps even personal, but I knew better. Mother looked on her as a subject, nothing more, and now that the painting was done, she would move on to another subject. All of which was enough to allow me, at that moment, the possibility of being kind. I could easily have said nothing, and left her with whatever pyrrhic victory she seemed intent on winning. But I didn't. 'I wonder why you don't get back to your own house,' I said. 'I imagine it's lovely and warm *there*.'

Her face hardened. It only lasted for a second, but I saw it. She was genuinely angry, or upset, if only for that briefest of moments, and not only did I see it in her eyes, but she saw that I had seen. She recovered quickly, however. 'Well,' she said, the brightness returning, 'you know what they say.' She paused, expectantly, as if I really *did* know what they said. Then she laughed – that same laugh again, far away and knowing, not mocking, just enjoying a joke that was not only

287

private, but beyond sharing. Or beyond sharing with the likes of me. 'My home is in the wind,' she said, quoting from something, though I didn't know what. 'And I go where the wind goes.' She studied my face a moment longer, then nodded slightly, before she turned away. It was the slight nod of someone who has just received good news, or a rare compliment, but it was also the calculated, if almost imperceptible gesture of the victor in some subtle game that, for a time, and wholly for her own amusement, she had tricked me into thinking I could win. Now, I saw that she could never have been defeated and, though I didn't know what her victory actually consisted of, I turned away quickly and made my way back to the house – and all the way, just as I had when I'd met her in the meadows, I was chill with the fear that she was following and that, if I stopped, she would be right there, reaching to touch my face if I even dared to look back. I didn't lose that fear until I crossed the threshold and, turning to close the door, I saw her walking away, that old bounce in her step as she passed through the gate and disappeared into the birch wood, following the path down to the Brensholmen road, for all the world like some ordinary girl, out for a walk on a sunny day – and if he hadn't moved at that exact moment, I would have been too preoccupied with her to notice Kyrre Opdahl, who was standing, half hidden in shadow, among the birches at the far edge of the garden. I don't know how long he had been there but, when he saw me, he gave a slight shake of the head before he turned and stepped away. I knew, then, that he had been watching all along, and that this tiny, almost imperceptible movement was a sign to me, though whether it was a request that I didn't say anything about his being there, or a signal of his unhappiness at having witnessed the *huldra* leaving our house as if she had every right to be there, I couldn't have said and, a moment later, he was gone, stepping back into the full shade and disappearing quickly into the cover of the trees.

When I was sure Maia was gone, I went up to my room. Not because I felt ill, or frightened, but because I wanted to be alone. I kept to my room for the rest of that day, but I didn't do any of the usual things I did when I was alone: I didn't look at books or think about what the future would bring, I just sat by the window, looking out towards the Sound. I think, now, that I was trying to make sense of what had happened, going over the details in my mind and attempting to put it all into one convincing narrative, but no matter what I did, nothing made any sense. I must have thought, at the beginning, that I wouldn't give up until I had an answer but, late that afternoon, when nothing that even remotely resembled an answer had arrived, I went to the window and saw Kyrre Opdahl's car out on the road at the foot of our drive. I thought, for a moment, that he was coming to us with news of Martin Crosbie, but he turned and rolled slowly down the grassy track that led to the *hytte,* and emerged with a large plastic box in one hand and a roll of dustbin liners in the other. Even from that distance, I sensed that he was tired and weary – and I knew I had to go down and help him with whatever he was doing. I hoped he wouldn't say anything about what he had seen – I felt, now, that Mother's association with Maia was even more a betrayal of him than it was of me – but, if he did, I resolved to tell him that Mother had finished with the portrait, which I felt sure was true, and that Maia would soon be gone for good.

Mother always says there is nothing so beautiful as a wet meadow. That's why it is so hard to paint, she says, because it *is* beautiful, and obvious beauty is almost impossible to work with. That morning, I saw what she meant and, as I headed down the track, I realised that I was actually walking in one of her paintings, a work she had spent weeks on, when I was fifteen or so. That painting had been possible, she said, because the beauty had been softened by the season: at the end of the summer, the first hint of decay had stolen in, tingeing a seed head here, or a blade of grass there, with grey, or brown, everything glossed with the rain, glossed, but not freshened, limned with hints of rust and charcoal, at the moment that comes *after* the last flourish, but before the descent into nothingness. That was how it was, that day – and I was surprised, because I hadn't seen it coming. In a week or two, an autumnal cold would set in, the headland along the shore would be nothing but dry, wiry scrub, spotted here and there with the last of this year's berries and the chalky, mint-green *kråkebolle* that the gulls had carried to land to smash upon the rocks. It seemed to be coming too early that year – yet I didn't mind and, to my shame, I caught myself thinking that, soon, it would be too cold for hauntings, too windy, out on the foreshore, for ghosts and spirits. Out there, I thought, winter was inhospitable to everything, even the *huldra*.

When I reached the *hytte*, the door was open. I knocked, as usual, then I walked in. Kyrre Opdahl was at the table by the window, surrounded by piles of crockery and glassware. In one corner, there was a stack of boxes and it was obvious, right away, that this wasn't the usual end-of-season chore. This was something unusual, something final.

'What are you doing?' I said.

Kyrre looked up and I could see that he was surprised to see me there. Surprised – and not at all happy – and I realised, at once, that he wished I hadn't come. He pursed his lips, in that way he did, then he went on with his work. 'It seems that my summer guest has gone away,' he said at last.

'What do you mean – gone away?'

'He left. Didn't say a word, just packed up and left –'

'How do you know he left?'

He looked around the room. 'Because he's not here,' he said. 'His car's not here. His things aren't here. He's gone –' He nodded to himself. 'Yes, he's gone all right – which is fine by me. I just don't want to make it easy for anyone else to move in.'

It's the end of the season. I said. 'Nobody's coming now.'

He went to the cupboard and took out the next stack of crockery. 'You know what I mean,' he said.

I did know, of course; but I didn't say so.

'Besides,' he said, 'I'm not sure I want to let it out again. Not now.'

I couldn't say anything. I had always treated his *huldra* story as just that – a story – but I knew better now, because, now, I knew that something out of the ordinary had happened in this very place, and I nodded – or maybe it wasn't quite a nod, but a slight shake of my head: just the hint of a movement, in spite of myself. I wanted to tell him what I had seen, but I didn't know how. Besides, there was too much that I couldn't explain. The absence of a body. The missing car. Mother's disbelief. None of it made any sense.

Kyrre's lips tightened. '*Akkurat*,' he said, quietly, in that grim way of his, though I hadn't spoken a word. He opened another box and started loading it with books. They were old storybooks and paperback novels, most of them for children, with a few crime thrillers for the grown-ups. Some of them were familiar from my childhood. Fairy stories, picture books, a fat volume of rhymes and songs called *Den Store Barne-Sangboka* that I remembered singing from as a little girl. He smiled sadly. 'Some of these books have been here for twenty years,' he said. 'And I'll bet they've never been opened in all that time.'

I nodded. 'They bring their own,' I said.

He shook his head. 'Nobody reads books like these any more,' he said. He picked one book from the pile and held it up. It was a collection of old folk stories, with a picture of a beautiful girl in a red dress on the cover. 'You know what this is?' he said.

I knew who it was, of course I did. But I didn't want to play that game. This girl in a red dress wasn't Maia, she was just a character from a story, a creature born of the panic in lonely places and a perverse, incommunicable longing. 'I saw him take the boat out,' I said, though I hadn't meant to say it. 'He was . . .' I thought for a moment, and I knew what I was about to say was ridiculous, but there was no other way to say it. 'He was happy,' I said.

'Happy?'

Tears welled in my eyes unexpectedly, but I didn't know what I was crying for. It wasn't for Martin Crosbie. It wasn't for the Sigfridssons. 'Yes,' I said.

Kyrre put down the book and gave me a long look. I thought he would ask questions, try to get at the story – and I could see that he wanted to, because I was a *witness*, the one witness he had to the story he knew was unfolding in this place. Then, slowly, as if he were doing it on purpose, his eyes filled with sympathetic tears. He put out his hand and touched me on the shoulder. 'You poor girl,' he said. I thought, for a moment, that he was going to put his arms around me, give me a hug, try to comfort me – and a thin surge of panic rose in my throat. I didn't want sympathy; I didn't want to be comforted – and he understood that immediately. He hesitated for a moment, his hand on my shoulder, and then his arm fell to his side and he stood there, not saying anything, strangely bereft on my behalf.

I let out an apologetic laugh then and shook my head. 'I'm all right,' I said. 'Besides – it wasn't –' I didn't know what to say. I felt sad, but my tears really *hadn't* been for Martin Crosbie, or for the boys. They hadn't even been for Mother's betrayal, or for the fact that she hadn't even known she was betraying me. No: at that moment, I felt sad for this old man and his clumsy, caring heart – and maybe I was beginning to understand something, about him and about myself, that I hadn't understood before. Of course, I knew the image people had of me, at school. How cold and stuck-up they thought I was, because I didn't have a best friend, or that supposed prize, a boyfriend, tagging along with me on Saturday afternoons in town. They saw that I wasn't affectionate, or romantic, they saw that I wasn't *nice* – but it had never bothered me one little bit what they thought. I didn't have an intimate circle of girls who were just like me, girls who read the same books and watched the same movies and listened to the same music – and I didn't want that. I didn't want friends and I didn't want some pretty, inarticulate boy to run around with and, at the same time, to feel slightly awkward about, knowing that he wasn't quite good enough, but that he would have to do, for the time being. I didn't even have one of those substitute *special friends*, like the ones girls like me have in movies. The gay surrogate. The shy nerd who comes on all heroic in the final reel. I was just me, by myself. The only people I had ever cared about, in any meaningful way, were Mother and this odd, slightly mad old man – and all at once, as we stood there, packing books into boxes, with summer coming to an end and all the stories suddenly too dark and strange for comfort, I realised that it was him, this taken-for-granted good neighbour, this mad, lonely old man, that I had loved all along. He was the father that this place had given me, and he was my only friend, this embarrassing man with his ridiculous true stories about trolls and spirits, and his long, clouded memory, a memory that seemed as old and perverse as the tide.

I looked at him. He peered at me over his glasses for a few seconds, as if in wonder at the odd complexity that had suddenly turned up in a girl he had known all her short life, then he smiled. 'Let's get to work,' he said. 'We'll feel a lot better when this place is all cleared up.'

I don't know how I could have been so naive, but for a while it seemed as if Kyrre's plan had actually worked. It really did feel like an exorcism, cleaning out the *hytte*, and during the days that followed, with Mother alone in her studio again and no sign of Maia anywhere, I even started to believe, or at least to hope, that the summer of drowning was finally over. But three days later, when it had just begun to seem that things had gone back to how they were before, I woke again with an overwhelming sense of dread. It was early. I could hear Mother in the kitchen, going about her usual morning routine, clearing last night's dishes, making coffee, working in a quiet that only deepened for being interrupted occasionally. This was where she got her ideas, she had said once, and though I understood that it was partly something she had thought up to say to journalists, I also believe that she really did treasure those moments, and I think something of what she did in the studio originated in the silence after a kettle boils, or the quiet of turning round and seeing a boat out on the Sound, gliding slowly past the mountains, just far enough away that she couldn't hear it. The quiet before a bird began to sing, then the quiet after; the feeling that came, sometimes, when she was alone in the house, that nothing would ever happen again. No sound, no movement. No passage of time. The studio was where she worked, and the dining room was where she negotiated with the outside world – but, in many ways, her true home was the kitchen, especially on those quiet mornings when she got up early and had a solitary breakfast before she began to paint. Other people passed through from time to time – and I include myself among those others – but when she was alone there, that room was transformed into a space that nobody else could ever enter, a temporary and provisional sanctuary that, for her, was all the more reliable for being imaginary and impermanent.

Naturally, I didn't like to disturb her when she was in that place. She probably never even realised that I understood it so well – when she talked to other people about it, she made light of it, as if it were just some anecdotal detail she was offering them, like a childhood memory or a story about her early career – but, looking back, I can see that I knew much more about her than either of us ever let on. I had learned her ways over years and they had become part of my life too, just as mine had been incorporated into hers. That house we lived in wasn't just a building, surrounded by a garden and birch woods, it was a mapped lattice of rituals and habits that, silently, over years of trial and error and infinitesimal adjustments, we had created together, constantly defining and redefining ourselves and one another as we went. I never really thought about this until recently, but that was what she meant when she used the word *home*. You can't share home, you can't be with others there, not if you are like us. It has to be secret. For us, home is a place that nobody else ever sees, an everyday and, at the same time, mysterious terrain of wind and snow and white nights, with colours out of a Sohlberg painting and faint, faraway cries coming up from the meadows or the shore-line at night, touching us as we dreamed or lay awake in the insomnia of *midnattsol*, before it moved on.

It was my house and it was hers, and to an extent it was ours together, but we had each to decide when to be visible, and when to go unseen – and that morning I waited till she had finished her solitary breakfast and climbed the stairs to begin the day's work before I went down. I had some cereal and a cup of coffee, then I headed out, with my camera and binoculars, to see what I could see. I didn't think I would encounter anything out of the ordinary, though: now that the *hytte* was shut up and the game of the portrait was over, it felt like the afterwards of something. I think I imagined that, because the summer was over, the story we had been telling ourselves those last few months was finished with too. Martin Crosbie was gone, the Sigfridsson boys were buried, and Maia – well, until that morning, I thought Maia had drifted away, driven off the island by the turning weather and what she must have seen as Mother's rejection. I really did think she was gone – so it came as a surprise, as I closed the front door behind me and turned, to see her standing by the gate, looking up at the house as if she were waiting for someone to come out and ask her in. She reminded me, then, of Martin Crosbie when I first saw him – a lonely figure on an empty road, not quite sure how he had come to be there – but, unlike Martin, she seemed to know exactly where she was, and exactly what she had come for. It was all an act, maybe, but then wasn't everything about her an act? Wasn't it all bravado, a bluff she'd learned to show the world, to let us all know that she didn't care that we didn't care about her? That she wasn't going to be a victim? When she saw me, she smiled that knowing smile of hers, but she didn't move. She just stayed where she was and waited for me to go to her. Which I did, of course. Not because I wanted to, but because that smile of hers was a challenge that, at the time, I didn't know how to ignore. Something in me had to show her that I wasn't bothered by what she said or did — but there was also more to it than that. I didn't quite believe it at the time, but looking back, I can see that she had cast a spell on me — ridiculous, I know, but how else can I explain the strange, panicked mood that came over me when I saw her? How else can I explain the fear and, at the same time, the odd longing for some terrible event to occur? How else to explain that change of mood and how else to explain what happened next, when what happened next was so inexplicable? That it had something to do with Maia remains unproven, of course. It was a coincidence, nothing more — but it did seem, at the time, that there could be no other explanation for the fact that, all of a sudden, there were feathers everywhere. I hadn't noticed them when I first saw her and then, in an instant, they were floating through the garden in their hundreds: white down fledging the spider's webs on Mother's rose bushes, odd plumes of charcoal or gull grey here and there among the dried-out grasses and lupins, traces of colour and softness, thin as smoke, clinging to the soft brown fuzz of the Himalayan poppy stems. They weren't all from one bird, like when you find a kill under a hedge somewhere and you can trace it all back to an epicentre of torn beak and innards. No: that day, there were feathers of every kind and almost every possible colour, greys and whites and pale powder blues, as you would expect, but I remember seeing threads of an impossible, delicate pink snagged on the head of a Tromsø palm, and a single wisp of imperial yellow was pasted to the trunk of one of the birch trees by the gate. I couldn't understand it. Maybe they had been there all along, and I just hadn't noticed, but when I did, it seemed that there were hundreds of them, thousands even – soft, very downy feathers, floating on the air, settled in the grass, clinging to the leaves of the birch trees, drifting across the gravel at my feet as I started towards the gate. At that moment, they seemed to be everywhere at once – and the thought came to me that I should go and fetch Mother, so she could see. Only, I couldn't move. All I could do was take it all in as the tide of feathers grew and scattered across the garden. Now, of course, I wish I had gone to find her, because things might have been different if she had been there. I wish I had been stronger, or braver, because that spell could have been broken and, if it had been, the *huldra* might have abandoned us as easily and quietly as the wind crossing a field and dying in the far grass, a small local darkness, gone to nothing in a clump of reeds or a pile of old timber.

I looked at Maia, who was still standing motionless by the gate, but she appeared not to have noticed anything out of the ordinary, and for the briefest of moments, I suspected that it was all an illusion, a hallucination that she wasn't even aware of. A moment later, it was over and, instead of hundreds and thousands of feathers, swirling around me and coating the earth at my feet, there was only a fistful of bedraggled plumes, like the aftermath a cat leaves when it catches a bird and dismembers it under a hedge. I looked around. A moment before, everything had seemed suddenly and darkly miraculous; now, it was the usual garden, the usual, plain light of day.

'What was that?' I said. I'm not sure, looking back, what I expected from Maia, but I think, for one absurd moment, that I hoped to engage her in some shared moment of bewilderment or wonder, as if, by doing that, I could have made a friend of her, somehow, in spite of what we both knew.

'What?' She looked off to the side, as if searching for a clue to what I meant – but it wasn't real. She was mocking me.

'The feathers –' I said, then I forced myself to stop. I was annoyed with the way I was falling into her trap. Annoyed at being so easy to fool. I could see the way she was looking at me, and I was angry that I had somehow ceded the advantage to her. I had wanted to confront her, to ask what she was doing hanging around our house, or maybe remind her, coldly, and without the least trace of annoyance or irony, that Mother didn't have any further use for her. Now she had the upper hand.

She looked down. A few greyish wisps had settled on the path, just by her feet. 'Yes,' she said. 'I see.' She looked at me and smiled. 'You're right,' she said, in what I took to be mock surprise. 'Feathers.'

I shook my head. 'No,' I said – and for one ridiculous moment, I was about to explain, before I caught myself.

All the while, she had been regarding me with that same good-humoured contempt that the teachers had shown Mats Sigfridsson when he was lost for words in the classroom. For a moment, she was silent, lingering on that feeling, letting it sink in. Then she spoke, her voice suddenly bright. 'Going out?' she said. 'Are you sure you're well enough?'

I didn't respond to that; though now that she asked the question, I realised I'd had no idea where I was going, and all of a sudden, I didn't want to leave the house. It may have been fear, in part, that I would be exposed, out in the open – a fear I had never once felt, day or night, in my life – but it was also a reluctance to leave this girl alone, so close to where Mother was working. Because, at that moment, I was afraid for Mother. It sounds ridiculous now, but I suddenly had the notion that Mother really had fallen under the *huldra*'s spell, just as the Sigfridsson boys and Martin Crosbie had done. Why else would she allow this creature into our house? Why had she suddenly returned to portrait painting? Why did she seem so indifferent to my feelings about the intrusion? I could think of no other explanation than enchantment and, while I realise now that, when someone claims they can think of no other explanation, it's only because they haven't really considered the alternatives, I felt sick at heart and hopelessly undecided – which I was desperate for her not to see. But she did see, and she would have prolonged the moment – pretending, say, that she had another appointment with Mother – if Kyrre Opdahl hadn't appeared at that very moment, walking slowly up the path towards us, his face fixed in what he must have imagined was the semblance of a friendly expression.

'Good morning, young ladies,' he said, his voice not like his usual voice at all, the tone strained, the language artificial. I couldn't have imagined him using the words 'young ladies' until that moment and, of course, I knew he didn't think Maia was any kind of lady. 'What a beautiful day it is!'

Maia turned to him – and because I thought, at first, that she didn't know him, it seemed to me, preposterous as it sounds, that she was underestimating him. Because Kyrre Opdahl knew exactly who *she* was. 'A beautiful day,' she said, echoing him, with only the slightest hint of mockery in her voice. '*Akkurat.*'

The word sounded odd, coming from her – and he almost

smiled. Then his expression altered. 'Well,' he said. 'Better make the most of it. Because it won't last much longer.'

Maia detected the change of tone – and at that moment she understood, if she hadn't guessed before, that this old fool wasn't what he pretended to be. She didn't appear to be disturbed by that knowledge, however. On the contrary, she was, or gave the appearance of being, amused by him. 'You're absolutely right,' she said. 'Winter is coming. And what will a poor girl do then?' She was smiling, but there was no mistaking the provocation in her voice – and, of course, I saw then that she knew who he was. She had to know. She'd probably seen him about the place, and she would no doubt have heard about him from Martin. Maybe she'd even seen him come to the *hytte* that day, just after the last drowning, to clear everything out and secure it against intruders. Against *her*, in other words. I wondered again where she was sleeping, and what she was doing for food.

Kyrre shook his head. 'Well,' he said, 'there's shelter down below, for anyone with nowhere else to lay her head.' He wasn't smiling. He said what he had to say, then he stood with his eyes fixed on hers, his mouth set, waiting for her reply – but he wasn't speaking to a young girl, he was addressing the *huldra*. 'It's not much,' he said. 'But there's room enough for a winter guest.'

It was absurd, of course, but that was how he framed his invitation. He just came out with it, and he didn't seem to mind that it sounded completely inappropriate, a transparent case of a dirty old man propositioning a young girl, trying to take advantage of her, when she was at her most vulnerable. And even though I knew what he thought of her, even though I knew that, in his own mind, he was addressing the *huldra*, I couldn't help but notice a trace of excitement – an infinitesimal trace of dark pleasure – that was almost, but not quite, concealed behind that casual invitation. Of course, I knew what he wanted to do right away. He was protecting me, protecting Mother, by playing decoy, putting himself in harm's way to divert the *huldra* from her intended prey – and in that moment I had a sudden glimpse of Maia through his eyes. A glimpse, no more, of someone, or something, as alluring as she was repugnant to him and his assent to this allure seemed, at that moment, as real as his determination to draw her away from Mother and me.

I was appalled. What did he think he was doing? Did he really hope to deceive her? Was he imagining that he could *charm* her? How could he have believed that such a thing was possible? Maia was still smiling, but I could see in her eyes that she was suspicious, too – suspicious, but not afraid, because she had to know that she had nothing to fear from a silly old man who believed in trolls and sprites. Besides, she really did need a place to stay, now that Martin was gone. Maybe she had been trying to win Mother over, by sitting for her, but I can't imagine she received anything in exchange. If she had, it had come to nothing and winter was approaching fast.

There was a moment's pause – and I don't know, now, why I didn't intervene. I wanted to take Kyrre by the arm and lead him away, I wanted to give him a good shake and make him see how ridiculous all this was, but I simply couldn't. I just stood and watched, as he made what he must have believed was a pact with the devil. Then, having taken that moment to work out what was going on – I look back now and I don't think of her as a girl any more, I see what Kyrre saw: I see the *huldra* – Maia laughed. She turned to me briefly, then she looked back at Kyrre, and her manner changed again. A moment before, she had been suspicious, as any eighteen-year-old might be when presented with such an offer; now, she was flirtatious, and quite brazen. 'Well, I don't know,' she said. 'How much room is there?'

Kyrre's head shook almost imperceptibly. 'Enough,' he said.

Maia studied his face. I didn't think she was going to accept Kyrre's offer, but she wanted to know why he had made it. She wanted to know what *he* knew, or thought he knew, about her. 'I wouldn't want to inconvenience you,' she said.

'No inconvenience.'

'Well,' Maia said, 'I'm not sure . . . I mean, I don't even know you –'

'Nor I you,' Kyrre said, 'But that's not a problem, is it? And I'm sure we could come to some arrangement –'

Maia jumped at that. 'What arrangement?' she said.

'Well,' Kyrre said, 'come and have a look. It's not far. We can talk about that while we walk.'

I couldn't believe it. What was happening was grotesque, and I *wanted* to say something. I wanted to stop him pursuing this mad course, but I didn't know how. Besides, I was sure, still, that Maia would refuse his offer. She would string him along, till he did something stupid, then she would show him up and let everybody know what a dirty old man he was – because surely that was what she was thinking, surely she had assumed that he wanted something from her, the one thing that was hers to give, now that she was alone in the world. The one thing that, presumably, she had been able to offer Martin Crosbie. There was no way for her to know how badly she was misjudging him. Or was there? Maybe she knew exactly what he intended and, maybe, she enjoyed the challenge. Maybe, as the *huldra*, she wanted to show him how invulnerable she really was. Maybe she had it in mind to seduce this

303

foolish old man, just as she had seduced the others – and I wasn't altogether sure that Kyrre Opdahl was beyond seduction. I was ashamed of that thought but, considering what happened afterwards, I cannot rule out the possibility that my suspicions were justified. At the time, though, it was nothing more than an idle thought, a flicker of mischief and superstition that would, I knew, be immediately dispelled, when Maia laughed off this bizarre invitation.

Only, she didn't laugh it off. Not at all. She regarded him for a long moment with a mix of suspicion and amusement; then her face softened, and she moved over to where he was standing and took him lightly by the arm. 'All right,' she said. 'I'll take a look at this *shelter*.' She glanced at me, as if we were together in some girls' conspiracy, then she laughed. 'Though I warn you,' she said. 'You don't know what you're letting yourself in for.'

I turned to Kyrre. I could see that he hadn't fallen under her spell. He was clinging to some plan that he had hatched over the last few days, ever since he'd first seen Maia at our house and decided Mother was in danger. I could see that he was up to something and I could also see that his cunning plan was just as obvious to Maia. She had put on a face – an expression that she must have thought made her seem the gullible and needy girl that Kyrre so clearly believed she was not – but there was, in the dark glitter of her eyes, a knowingness that made me afraid, for Kyrre, of course, but also for her. He was pretending that he wanted to help, but he wasn't making a very good job of it, not because he wasn't good at pretending, but because he couldn't care less whether she trusted him or not. All he wanted was for her to go with him, away from this house, away from the only people he loved in the whole world. I didn't know what he intended – did he think he could save Mother from her grim fascination with the shadow that she saw in this disturbed girl, the shadow that he knew, against all reason, was the *huldra*? If he did, how was he going to do it? I don't recall, now, how much I suspected at the time, and how much came later, but I think, even then, when something could still have been done to divert him, I already knew he wanted to destroy her. What was worse was that Maia knew it too. She wasn't deceived for a second – which meant that, for her, whatever Kyrre had in mind was a challenge she was prepared to accept, quite gladly. A challenge that she welcomed. She thought that she was stronger than him. She knew it, in fact, because she was the *huldra*, and he was just an old man.

I don't recall how much of this I believed at the time, but I do know that, just as he had deceived himself, Kyrre had deceived me, because I was thinking of this girl – who, in the plain light of day, seemed nothing more than a lost, possibly abused child with nowhere to go – I was looking at this lost girl and I was seeing the *huldra*, seeing her with Kyrre's eyes, making her a character from one of the old stories, a creature possessed, whether temporarily or intrinsically, by some random wave of malice. Maia had always been strange, and there were questions about her that I couldn't answer; she had invaded my home and she had taunted me with what she must have imagined was a power that I envied; she was inextricably connected to three unexplained deaths, at least one of which she had watched, without lifting a finger to help or to raise the alarm; but surely common sense should have told me that she was still nothing more than a young girl – troubled no doubt, malicious even, but only in the way that damaged children often are. Common sense should have told me that she wasn't the *huldra*, because – why did I forget it, even for a moment? – the *huldra* did not exist. The *huldra* was just a notion, a metaphor no doubt, for something harder to pin down and more painful to consider, an ugly spirit from an old story, told to keep young men in line, or to explain away the darkness. A story, a warning, a zone on the map that allows us to navigate an impossible world.

I looked at Kyrre, and I could see, in the set of his mouth, in the fixity of his eyes, the expression of a man who has made up his mind to do something terrible – and, beguiled by a fairy tale, I did nothing to stop him. Instead, I turned to Maia and, through a fog of doubt and absurd fantasy, I made a desperate appeal to the plain light of day in her that I had already given up on. 'You can't go now,' I said. 'I don't think Mother's finished the painting yet.'

Maia laughed. 'I think she has,' she said, without a hint of regret. 'I think it was finished on the first day. In fact –' she looked at Kyrre and then back to me with a defiant smile – 'I think she knew what she was going to paint even before I sat down in that lovely studio of hers.' She slipped her hand into her jacket pocket – and I knew that she had something in there, something that Mother had given her, or possibly some small treasure that she had stolen. She looked at me, and her face was pleasant, and utterly calm – yet I knew that she had sensed my suspicion and she was hurt by it. 'I think,' she said, and there was no shift in her manner, no shadow of malice or judgement in her voice, 'if I'm not mistaken, your mother began that painting a long time ago, and has only just got round to finishing it.'

That stung me – and, for the first time, I realised that, to sit for Mother, Maia would have had to climb the stairs, to pass the door to my room and cross the landing and, as she did, she would have seen the portrait of me that Mother had begun so long ago, begun and abandoned, without ever offering a word of explanation. She had seen it, and she had seen through it – or so she thought. But what she had seen wasn't the truth. How could it be? I wasn't like her, and Mother knew that. She *knew* – and what she wanted to capture in this portrait was the same thing, more or less, that Kyrre had seen when he decided that Maia was the *huldra*. She would have laughed at the old man's superstitions, no doubt, but what she saw in Maia was a girl touched by a darkness that could have been ordinary bad luck – a talent, almost, for tragedy – but might just as easily have been a form of possession, a weakness of spirit or resolve that allowed the darkness to work through her. A weakness that had allowed her to welcome the darkness in, perhaps unwittingly – and that was what Mother had wanted to capture. *Susceptibility*, in the abstract – not this lost girl.

I shook my head, but I refused to respond to the provocation. Perhaps I saw in it a wish to draw me into whatever was about to unfold with Kyrre, a wish to drag me down with the old man and make me an accomplice in whatever she imagined he was planning. 'I'm sure, when she's finished, she'll let you see the picture,' I said. 'Don't you want to see –'

She burst out laughing then. 'It's all right,' she said. 'I don't have to see it. But you take a look, and let me know what you think.' She turned to Kyrre, with a sweet, absurd smile. 'Thanks to your kind neighbour,' she said, 'I'll just be down the road . . . For a while, at least.'

Kyrre nodded. '*Akkurat*,' he said.

Maia nodded back and made to leave. Then, as if as an afterthought, she took what she was clutching from her pocket and held it out to me. It was money, of course. She hadn't stolen it – and she wanted me to see that my suspicions had been unfounded. It was payment for the sitting. 'Give this back to your mother,' she said, with that same mocking glitter in her eyes. 'I didn't earn it.'

I shook my head again, but I didn't say anything. I didn't want to touch the money. I didn't want to touch anything she had touched – and, at that moment, I had a sense of the house behind me as contaminated, everywhere, by contact with her. With her fingers, her breath, the scent of her and, most of all, those dark, glittering eyes. 'Keep it,' I said, at last. 'You might need it.'

Her hand wavered a moment, then she slipped the money back into her jacket. All this time Kyrre had been standing by, watching, waiting, patient with the dull resolve of the desperate. For a split second, I thought I had one last chance to intervene, one last chance to dissuade – and then even that moment was gone. Maybe it hadn't existed anyhow. Maybe everything was already decided, the way it is in fairy tales. For too long, I had flickered back and forth between that world where nothing can be done and the plain light of day, where reason is supposed to prevail and now it was too late. Ryvold had said, once, that trolls exist, whether we like it or not, but we had a choice about the forms they took, and the powers they could assume. It all depended on whether we allowed ourselves to be deceived, on whether we succumbed to super-stition – but at that moment, and just for that moment, I didn't believe him. And by the time I did, there was nothing I could do.

I watched them walk away. In some far part of my mind, I was praying, or hoping at least, that Kyrre would abandon whatever plan he had made to divert the *huldra* away from us, but I knew it was too late. He was determined to see this through, they both were – and all of a sudden I pictured them together, in that house of his, a few hundred metres along the shore, sitting at the kitchen table over coffee, as Kyrre and I had always done, surrounded by cogs and spark plugs, in a fug of engine oil and white spirit, each waiting for the other to make a decisive move. It was a terrible image – and I wondered what Kyrre thought he was doing, inviting the *huldra* into his house, when he, of all people, knew that she could not be contained or defeated. They walked slowly, side by side, neither talking nor even looking at the other – and yet, for a moment, just before they disappeared, they looked, not like strangers who have only just met, but like kith and kin, family members who, whether they were fond of one another or not, would always be irreversibly united by blood and history. That impression lasted for a few seconds, no more, before they disappeared at the first curve of the track, but it was undeniable. Then, for a long moment, I was gazing at nothing but leaves and air, the birches paler now, and touched here and there with streaks and blemishes of gold, the light thin and unconvincing at the far end of the track, as if something that had been there for years, some high tree or carved stone, had been uprooted overnight, leaving only a gap where substance should have been. I waited there for a long time – several minutes, I think, though it is hard to tell, looking back – and all that time I was in doubt, ready to believe that what I had just witnessed hadn't happened at all, or was, at least, capable of being reversed. Then, with a sense, not so much of having been defeated as of having given up too easily, I turned to go in. I was still there, at the gate, just a few yards from the front door, but I suddenly felt exposed and, as ridiculous as it sounds, in danger – and it took a considerable effort not to give in to that sudden fear, a sense of apprehension that, in the space between one breath and the next, was transformed into blind, unreasoning panic.

I was almost inside, almost out of harm's way, when I heard the scream. It was a sound unlike anything I had ever heard before, a scream, a shriek, a wild cry laced with horror that seemed just inches away for one awful moment, before I placed it, and realised that it must have come from further along the track, in the direction that Kyrre and Maia had taken a few minutes earlier. It was a sudden, high-pitched shriek, the last cry of something that had been caught and pulled down, and it was startling in its finality, but I couldn't have said whether it was the scream of a girl, or an old man, or an animal that some predator had taken, down in the meadows or somewhere in the woods. It could have been any one of those, and it could have been none of them – and in the old stories, certainly, it would have been the cry of no living thing, but the other-worldly shriek of a harpy or a fetch, echoing on the still air of an afternoon that, by some logic that no mortal could follow, had turned out to be cursed.

I try to think that, on any other day, I could have been rational about what I heard. As that shriek died away – though that's not an accurate description for the sense I had of something moving off into the distance, not fading so much as being absorbed into the land for miles around, absorbed by the birches and the meadows and the white air out over the Sound, absorbed so thoroughly that it would never disappear – as that terrible scream soaked into the fabric of the world around me, I should have tried to explain it as a natural event of some kind. A kill, in the far grass, say, where some predator had pulled down a bird or a hare, or the sound a foreign ship might make, as it navigated its way out of the channel into open water. I could have said it was a tyre blowing out, down on the Brensholmen road, or a seabird calling from further up shore. I had heard sounds here that I couldn't explain often enough, odd wailings in the wind in the small hours of *midnattsol,* a high-pitched keening over the snow in the dark time, bird calls where no bird could have been, animal cries in the woods when I was out in the noonday darkness and imagining the wolverine, come down from the far north to track me by my torchlight. No sound is improbable, here – but *that* sound was impossible and, as it faded away, sinking into my skin and my bones as surely as it was soaking into the land around me, I knew it had come from some point along the track between our house and Kyrre Opdahl's. It startled me, that cry, and it held me for a moment, as it faded – but it was only a moment and, as soon as that moment passed, I was running blindly towards it, running out through the gate and along the path towards the scene of whatever crime had been committed within calling distance of the house where Mother was, no doubt, standing in front of a canvas, putting the finishing touches to a picture she should never have begun, and, absurd as it sounds now, I had a vision of her in what Maia had called her lovely studio, smiling at the finished portrait, happy to have captured whatever it was she had set out to capture, in features that were both girlish and inhuman. It lasted no more than a second, that fleeting vision, but it was as vivid as the cry had been – a cry she probably hadn't even heard, at work on the far side of the house, oblivious to everything, as she always was when her work absorbed her.

The ground is steep and uneven on the track to Kyrre's house, but it couldn't have taken me long to reach the place where the cry had originated – and though I found nobody there, and no immediate evidence of violence or harm, I knew

311

it was the scene of whatever had happened. The place, not where Kyrre and Maia were, but where they should have been. Where they *had* been, moments before, when that shriek pierced the air. There was nothing to detain me at that place, or nothing that I could see at first glance, as I hurried along the track, but I felt sure they had gone no further. This was the place where they had stopped, for whatever reason, and it was here that they had disappeared.

There was nothing there, though. Or nothing I could see. Yet if they had stopped there, if they had gone no further, then it stood to reason that they *had* to be there still, and if they weren't, then they *had* to have vanished. They couldn't have just vanished into thin air – and that was what confused me, because *that* was impossible. That was what confused me – that, and the smell. I didn't catch it at first, but then it was everywhere around me, strong and dark and almost over-whelming, just for a moment, so close that I felt dizzy, and I had to bend, my hands on my knees, my head down, not gasping for breath, quite, but suddenly clogged with that dark, water-and-smoke scent, like the smell you get after a doused fire, when the wood is still smouldering here and there amid the wet timber, a chill, dark scent that made me feel – I don't know what to call it, not sad exactly, but disappointed. Disappointed at some extreme, physical level. Or dismayed – yes, that would probably be the right word. Dismayed. Dismay in the pit of my stomach and in the marrow of my bones, dismay in my throat and in that smoke taste in my mouth and nose, dismay that seemed like it would last forever, that had always been there, waiting on that path I had walked hundreds of times, going down to Kyrre's house to sit in his kitchen and drink strong coffee while he sat opposite, working on an outboard motor and telling me stories from the old days – and though there was no evidence that something bad had happened, other than that black, smoky scent hanging on the air among the birch trees, I think that was when I first knew he was gone. I look back and I see that I knew from the first. I knew, even before I smelled that smell, or saw the spots.

I didn't notice them at first. They only became visible when I bent down, eyes closed, trying to catch my breath and then, when I had gathered my strength and opened my eyes again, I caught sight of the first thick, black spots on the grass at my feet. Then, as I raised my head and started breathing again, I saw that they were all around me: on the grass, in the dirt, on the leaves of the trees, inky black spots that, at first sight, looked like soot or dust but, when I stretched out my hand and brushed the tip of my finger over the surface of a yellowing birch leaf, felt oily to the touch. Oily, like something live. Like the traces you find out in the woods after something has been there in the night, feeding or suckling on its prey. I pulled my hand back and looked around. The spots were everywhere, thick and black and sticky, touched with the dark, smoky scent that had forced me to stop at that turn in the path, almost halfway between our house and Kyrre's. I stood a moment, staring, my head filling again with the smell – and then I was hurrying on, knowing it was pointless, but also knowing that I had to check, because nothing here offered an explanation for what had happened. Nothing here made any sense. I knew that Kyrre and Maia had stopped at that very spot, and that the smell and the black spots had something to do with what had happened next, but I also knew that this was ridiculous, and I ran on for several metres, like a lost dog, ran then walked then ran again, my head craning forward to see whatever I might see before it slipped away and, all at once, it was like being in the middle of a huge and elaborate conjuring trick, as if the whole world had been set up to deceive me, but I could see through it, if I could only find the right clue.

So I ran and walked and ran all the way to Kyrre's house – and as soon as I got there, I felt anxious. Now that I was away from the scene, I thought I must have missed something at that turn in the path, and I had to go back right away, before it was too late. There was something I hadn't understood, something I hadn't seen, or maybe something that I *had* seen that hadn't really been there at all, and I had to retrace my steps and catch whoever or whatever was playing this trick on me, catch it out, see through it, find the real explanation. Even before I got to Kyrre's house and looked in at the kitchen window, I could see that nobody was there, and I realised that, in my hurry, I must have tricked myself, at the turn in the path – and I started back, running now, in a panic, I suppose, and close to tears, not because I knew Kyrre had gone, but because I had been tricked, and I was upset at not knowing how. It was like being in school, doing some complicated equation and not being able to get an answer: you go over it again and again and when nothing comes this astonishing anger rises up in your blood. That was what I felt then: that same anger. I came back to the place where I had seen the spots of black ash on the grass – and at that very moment, quite unexpectedly, it started to rain. That far northern rain, the kind that comes out of nowhere and goes on for days, without stopping. Huge, cold drops, inky and black and sudden, loud on the rooftops, cold on your face and hands, chaotic out among the trees, pouring through the branches, bouncing off leaves, washing everything clean, every trace of warmth, every stain, every mark of what has been and gone over an entire summer, till nothing at all remains. I stood still, unable to move, watching as the black stains on the leaves were washed away. And I couldn't move. I still felt angry, but I was frightened now too, because I knew that, whatever had happened to Kyrre and the *huldra*, it wasn't a trick. I stood a long time, perhaps several minutes and then, when I had started to gather the resolve to make my way back to the house, I heard a sound off to the right, in the birch wood. A soft, rustling sound, like someone coming through the trees towards me. I turned. I thought it was a person – and I suppose I must have thought that it was Kyrre Opdahl, because I took several steps in the direction of the sound, scanning the gaps between the trees, expecting to see a human shape coming through the birches. I didn't see anyone, though. I could still hear the noise – a soft, creeping sound – but there was nothing there that I could see. Or not at first. I had taken five or six steps into the birches, certainly no more, before I came to a stop and stood there, watching, listening, but I was looking for something at eye level, I was looking for a person, and it was only when I heard the sound – a soft, plaintive snuffling, like a dog trying to find its way into a hole where something is hidden – that I looked down. There, ten or maybe twelve metres away, I saw what I took for an animal. I say *took for* an animal, because it was crouching down, its snout reddened with blood and it had something in its mouth – hair, bone, the remains of some creature it had hunted down and killed – but I couldn't have said what kind of animal it was. Certainly, it resembled nothing I had seen in the meadows before. Yet it was an animal, nevertheless: of that there could be no doubt. It wasn't a person, it was an animal, and when it saw me, or maybe when it caught my scent, it looked up, its eyes dark and bright, the piece of carcass still clenched between its teeth. It looked at me – and, for a moment, it was as if it *knew* me. The thing looked up and made a soft, hoarse sound, and though I didn't know what kind of animal it was, I could see its face – or, no, it wasn't a face I saw, it was an *expression*. An expression of – what? Triumph? I think it was that. Triumph. It looked at me, and it made that soft, hoarse sound – and then it turned and hurried away through the long grass, moving so quickly that I could make nothing out, other than a few fleeting and possibly inaccurate details. I thought it was black, or dark brown; I think it was about the size of a large dog – though it wasn't a dog, of that I am sure, and I am almost certain that it wasn't native to the island, but had strayed in from elsewhere. Maybe it was an illegal pet that had escaped from one of the houses further along the coast, maybe it was something that had strayed here from the high tundra – whatever it was, all I could have said for sure was that it wasn't a person. I walked over to where it had been when I saw it first, and it's strange, I wasn't really afraid, I felt numb – maybe I was in shock – and when I reached the spot I found nothing. No bones, no matted hair, no dead creature with its throat torn open or its eyes picked out. There was nothing – not even a spot of blood. Whatever it had killed, it had carried the thing away with it – and though, at that moment, it seemed that this vision was nothing more than a coincidence, even though it didn't even occur to me that there was any connection between this animal and what I had witnessed earlier, I felt sick with fear, all of a sudden, because I knew that something terrible had happened. I didn't know what it was, or who it had happened to, but I suddenly became aware of myself, alone in the woods, and I felt something was watching me still: the animal, or something else, I couldn't have said what. Something was watching me, with my scent in its nose and mouth, and at any moment, it would attack.

316

I wasn't conscious, then, of how I came to be running. I don't recall making the decision – if I had thought about it, I would have known it was the wrong thing to do because, as I crashed away through the trees like a startled deer, I felt something ebb from my mind, and then everything was dark, not black, but dim, as if seen through smoked glass, and then I was running blind, in utter panic, unable to think, and unable to stop myself. I ran through the trees and back along the path towards the house and, all the way, I was terrified something would appear at the gate, or halfway up the garden path, and swallow me up, in one bright, triumphant movement. In fact, I was convinced that it would come, and I knew I was running straight into its arms, and still I couldn't stop running. I didn't see anything until I reached the gate, and then I saw the door – it was open, and that shocked me, because I had no memory of that, and I thought that whatever was pursuing me was waiting there, inside the house now, the stink of it in the hallway, or on the stairs, but even then I didn't stop running. I didn't stop, in fact, until I was inside and, clawing desperately at the latch, managed to push the door shut behind me – and then I collapsed on the floor, everything going white, and then dark, and then, as I understood finally that I was safe, as I realised that I had escaped, there was nothing.

It's nine o'clock. I have been working since early this morning, drawing a new map of the path that runs from our house to Kyrre's, a map that is almost infinitely detailed: every tree, every rock, every patch of wildflowers marked out, the way the objects are marked out at a crime scene, everything doused in possibility, every shadow, every scuff in the grass, every fallen twig laden with a significance that has yet to be seen. It's ten years, now, since that day, and I am still trying to find some factual basis for what I saw, because, when I look back, I don't believe that what I am telling is completely true. How could it be? What happened that day was impossible. It doesn't matter that I remember it all just as clearly – just as *factually* – as I remember everything else: what happened out there, on the empty path, remains an impossibility and there is nothing I can tell myself that will change that.

I was ill for a long time after my vision of that day. Mother found me in the hallway, right at the foot of the stairs, and she saw that something was terribly wrong. I wasn't unconscious, but I didn't respond when she asked me what had happened, so she didn't know that Kyrre and the girl were gone. All she knew was that I was very ill, so she got me out of my wet clothes and half carried me upstairs to bed. I don't remember any of this – I don't remember anything that happened for a long time after that morning – but this is what she told me when I was well, and I have no reason to doubt her. She told me that I ran a high fever that night, and she couldn't get me to eat. I was shivering, and I couldn't talk for a long time, but I did drink, when she brought me water, which she took as a good sign. I also slept off and on, and that was better still. Mother has always believed in the healing power of sleep. There have been times when she's slept for twenty-four hours, thirty-six hours, or even longer. Dreams mend us, she says. Without dreams, we would all be insane. At the high point, when things were at their worst, she said, she sat with me while I slept and she noticed that my eyes were moving, which meant that I was dreaming, and though I struggled in my sleep and sometimes cried out, she let me sleep on. Dreams are the stories we tell ourselves to make sense of the world, she says. The only difference between the mad and the sane is that the mad do not dream well enough.

318

No doubt she is right and, whatever else is true, she brought me through the madness of the next several days alone and unassisted – but, to this day, there *is* no story I can tell myself that will make sense of what I saw. I can tell myself other things about what happened that summer; I can make certain statements about what I know to be true, in the ordinary way of things, but these are mere facts, and though any story conveys, or claims to convey, a factual history, what I can tell myself, what I can say is factually true, is really neither here nor there. I can say that Martin Crosbie's body was never found; I can say that, when his car disappeared, everyone assumed he had left the island – everyone, that is, who had any interest in the matter. I can say that Ryvold never returned to Kvaløya, though he did write and, later, sometime during the following spring, as I recall, he sent Mother the manuscript of a book he had written, a book that was later published, not only in Norway, but in several other territories. It was a book about the old stories, of course, though it was also a series of personal memories and reflections, and I read it carefully for what it might reveal about his mind but, though he touched upon art and the Narcissus story, and though he included a long section about his time in the north, he didn't mention Mother once. I was surprised, at the time, but I was glad he left her out of his story. There were too many stories about Mother and not one of them – not even Frank Verne's – was true.

After Ryvold left, the suitors gradually fell away – and Mother finally became the recluse that those stories had always described her as being. She is still painting, and the man from Fløgstad's travels up and down the country with her pictures, stopping off on the way at his sister's house in Mo I Rana, and even though the work has grown darker – as some critics see it, though what I see is quite the opposite of darkness – it continues to sell. Meanwhile, I decided what to *do* with myself. It took some time, but I knew, after that summer of drowning, that I belonged to this place, and I have no intention of leaving, or of ever becoming distracted from the work I have chosen. I can happily say that I never received any more gifts from Kate Thompson, though I also have to confess that I find myself thinking about her from time to time. It struck me as odd, to begin with, that it was Kate I thought about, not Arild Frederiksen, but then, I never met Arild Frederiksen and, other than a character in a book, he has never existed for me.

It was some time before Mother accepted that Kyrre Opdahl had just disappeared off the face of the earth. To begin with, when I was still ill, she had wondered why he didn't answer the phone, and I think she even walked down to his cottage on the shore to see if he was there. Then, when it was obvious that he was missing, she seems to have told herself that he'd gone off to visit a friend. Maybe he'd gone to Narvik again, or up north somewhere. It wasn't a very likely explanation, but she was preoccupied with me and I think she didn't want anything else on her plate. As far as I know, she didn't even register that Maia had also disappeared. She probably just assumed that the strange girl had gone away – she had been something of a vagrant, after all – and she was probably glad of it for, though she never did understand why, she quickly came to understand that Maia's presence in our house had been one of the main causes of what she later referred to as my *crisis*. She didn't say breakdown, though that would have been the conclusion anyone else would have come to, had they been present to observe my condition over the next several weeks. But there *was* nobody else. At no point during my illness, even on that first day, when she found me, mute and helpless with panic at the foot of our stairs – at no point whatsoever did Mother think of calling a doctor. Instead, she nursed me herself, day by day, till I was well enough to speak. And even then, when the slow process of recovery began, she didn't ask me about what had happened. She didn't want to know what I had seen – or, if she did, she didn't allow herself to ask the questions that must have been in her mind. Later, when I was able to get up and go about my normal business, I remember being shocked by that. How could she stop herself from asking those questions? Was it because she was afraid to reawaken the terror she had seen in my face? Or was it just her usual discretion? I couldn't say. All I know is that I wouldn't have been able to tell her anything, if she had given in to her curiosity. There was no story, no explanation that I could offer, whether to her or to myself – or none, at least, that made any sense in the plain light of day. Still, I was always aware of a gap – a dark, clean tear – in the fabric of the world, which I expected first Mother and then everyone else to notice at any moment. And maybe that was why I said nothing, because that gap seemed so obvious. I didn't say anything about what I had seen – or rather, what I hadn't seen at all, but surmised from events and clues that were lost in the rain or too preposterous to repeat. Besides, even before the rain, what evidence of actual mischief had there been? A few spots of dust or grease, a cry that could have been an animal or a bird, and a solitary teenager's sense that something was wrong. I don't remember making a conscious decision to keep back what I knew – though, in retrospect, it isn't so surprising. In fact, I don't think I decided anything at all. I was waiting, I suppose, for that tear in the universe to become visible enough to betray itself and maybe part of me was waiting for someone to find real proof – a body, say, or some sign of violence out in the woods – but at the back of my mind, even then, I knew there would never be conclusive proof of anything. What had happened belonged to Kyrre's world, the world of stories and fatal magic, and any attempt to tell what had happened in that world would only convince people that the old man had turned my head with his nonsense. I would be an object of scorn or pity, a hysterical girl who'd come upon a kill-site in the birch woods and panicked. Sometimes, I even told myself that I was exactly that – because what had happened, what I had almost but not quite witnessed, was impossible, and there had to be some other explanation that I was unaware of, something that would reconcile the world I knew with the world that Kyrre had always believed was out there, and that I had always believed was nothing more than a story.

It's nine o'clock, and I have been at work for several hours – which is how the days usually unfold, now. I get up early and I have a cup of coffee, then I go upstairs to what used to be the spare room and is now my workroom. I don't call it a studio, because that isn't what I do. I'm not an artist, like Mother: I'm a map-maker. I don't deny that my maps are shown in galleries, or that people buy them, but I never think of them as art. I consider them to be functional, though not in the usual way: they are maps, but you can't use them to drive from one end of the island to another – not unless you go *very* slowly – and their scale is such that you are more likely to get lost in the detail than to use them to find your way home. They also differ from other maps in the way they accommodate time. Every map has a limited lifespan, of course: roads are replaced and buildings are demolished, what was once woodland or meadow is now a supermarket or a car park. Maps provide snapshots of places, pictures that can last for weeks, or centuries, depending on how detailed they are, but nothing about them is truly permanent and there are times when what they leave out is crucial. My maps leave nothing out, though: they are so detailed that they are immediately obsolete, at least as navigational tools and, in that respect, I like to think of them as a commentary on how carelessly we look at the world. I've been making them for eight years now, in various forms: I began with this island, working outwards, one metre at a time, from Kyrre's *hytte*, in an infinitesimal charting of every object I found, every rock and pebble and bird's nest, searching – square by square, coordinate by coordinate – for the unseen, adjacent space that the stories unfold in. It sounds odd, no doubt, to suggest that the unseen could be mapped, but that is what I am attempting to do, not as fantasy, but as invention – invention, in the old sense, which is to say: revealing what there is, seen and unseen, positive and negative, shape and shadow, the veiling and the veiled. Some things can only be seen in negative, some bodies only become perceptible in the interference they create. About some – Kyrre Opdahl, say, or the *huldra* – the only location I can propose is what is not present in the map of where they do not occur. No one else knows this, but that doesn't matter. People buy the maps to hang on a wall, as if they were pictures, but they also suspect, even when they don't know why, that they are buying something that could be used. And that is what my maps intend – they try to give a sense of the world beyond our illusory homelands. Not for navigation, but for seeing. Because there are two ways of looking at the world and two kinds of seeing. The first is the way we learn from infancy onwards, the way of seeing what we are supposed to see, building the consensus of a world by looking out for, and finding, what we have always been told is there. But there's another way – and that is what I am after. It's the way we see when we go out alone in the world, like a boy going out into the fields, or along the shore, in some old story. When he's at home, he sees what he is supposed to see, but as soon as he leaves the safety of the farmhouse, or the village school-room, everything is different. He tries to go on seeing what he expects to see, but something creeps in at the edge of his vision – and he begins to realise that, out here, *anything* can be the *huldra*. Every thing he knows, every illusory detail of home, melts away, leaving him alone with a world too strange to witness. The *huldra*'s world – the real world – that the farmhouse and the village schoolroom try so hard to conceal.

I have never discussed this with Mother – or rather, I have never told her what it is I am attempting to do – but even if she doesn't know what I am trying to create, she seems happy for me. I am her equal now, not so much in her eyes, but in what she thinks is my own estimation, and that has made a big difference in how we live together. I am her equal, not because I have found something to do with my life, but because I have been permitted a terrible privilege. I have been allowed to witness something that could never have happened, and this event is always with me, like an invisible companion or a scar. I am her equal, in a way that doesn't matter in the least, because I have seen through the fabric of the world that everyone else agrees upon, and I have been obliged to start again, with measurements and pencil marks and blocks of colour on the finest paper that money can buy – and that simple, absorbing work has given Mother permission to stop worrying about me, once and for all. It wasn't something I would have thought of before, but now I can see that she *was* very worried about me, when she didn't know what I was going to do with my life – not because it mattered to her, but because she knew it mattered to me. Now she feels she can relax – maybe we both do – because she knew, all along, that I *needed* something, so I wouldn't just be her daughter.

I'm not making some grand claim to happiness or fulfilment here, though. I'm not saying I have a happy life, in the way someone else might understand it. I don't have *any* other life, in fact, outside my work. I don't need what other people seem to need, and I never miss what I have never wanted, but once a week, I take the track through the birch woods where Kyrre and Maia vanished, then I follow the Brensholmen road to the point where Kyrre's track veers off, on the shore side. The house was never locked when Kyrre was here – he didn't have anything anyone would want to steal, he'd say, though that wasn't strictly true – and I keep it just the way he left it. If he ever comes back, it will be as it always was: the cluttered kitchen, the old pots and pans, the spare room full of engine parts and old clocks, the wide alcove off the hall that was nothing but shelves, like some troll-child's secret library. I go once a week, and I keep the place clean, but I don't tidy up, and I only move what I have to move, when I'm dusting or using the vacuum and, afterwards, I put it all back exactly as it was.

Usually, I go on a Wednesday, first thing after breakfast. I let myself in and I make coffee – strong, the way he used to make it – then I give the place a bit of a clean, and make sure it's all sound. I work for a couple of hours – it doesn't take much – and I keep it brisk. Sometimes, there are small repairs to attend to, and occasionally, when I'm in a sentimental mood, I bring out Kyrre's old books and albums and flick through the pages, trying to make out who is who, or who *might* be who, in the photographs and clippings. Mostly, they show local events and family gatherings, but sometimes there are old stories out of the newspapers – local mysteries that kept people guessing for a while, thirty or fifty years ago, then got forgotten at summer's end. I sit for a while and look at the photographs, trying to make out which of the young men might be Kyrre, and who, among the people standing round, could be relatives of his, or maybe a sweetheart. I'm sorry, now, that I didn't ask him more about those pictures. Who was who, when and where they were taken, what the occasion was. I suppose I just took him for granted – though when I look back, I see that I was longing for answers to all those questions; it was just that I didn't know how to ask.

I miss him, of course, even though I don't wholly think of him as gone. Every now and then I turn round, or I look up from one of those picture books, and I half expect to see him coming through the door, or sitting in his big, creaky chair, surrounded by cogs and flywheels. There will be times when a thought passes through my head and I almost hear him listening in. '*Akkurat,*' he will say, in that way he has. Or that way he had when he was living. I don't think of him as gone, but I don't think of him as living any more, and I know, if I ever do see him, it will be something other than a man that I will see – which is odd, because I don't really believe in ghosts. I know he is dead, I am quite certain of it, and I don't believe that the dead come back to haunt us, yet I still expect to see him, one day, back home and safe in his own house. It's a kind notion, for me at least. I like to think there is something that he was working on, something he needs to come back and finish, and I like to think that I'll be there when he returns, drawn home by the smell of coffee and a last promise to keep. I always think I'll see him here, in the house – and I suppose, if the dead ever did return, then this would be the place they'd choose: low and set back from the road among its own stand of trees, Kyrre's house is almost invisible, and though I have spent my entire life going back and forth between this house and my own, I never noticed, before, how isolated Kyrre was. Isolated – and safe.

I go to the *hytte* too, and I do my best to maintain it. I don't like being down there for too long, though. I don't really understand why, but I feel uneasy. It's ridiculous, I know, but I can't help thinking that I am being watched. Like you do in the woods sometimes, or when you're walking out on the beach in the middle of the day, and you can't see anybody, but you can't quite shake off the notion that someone is watching, either. Of course, that's natural – it's far more exposed there and, sitting out front, on the lawn by the shore, I know I am visible to every single passenger on the big boats that chug up and down the Sound, just as I know all too well that I can be seen from the landing outside my room. Though I also know that there is no one there to spy any more. As always, Mother is hidden away in her studio and, without me, the house might as well be empty. Sometimes, sitting there on the old elmwood chair looking out across the water, or away along the shore, it feels as if the whole world is empty. All except for me, and whatever ghosts I choose to entertain – and I don't entertain ghosts very often. Yes, there are times when I half expect Kyrre to come driving down the track in his old van; if I'm not careful, I can even imagine that Maia is about to return, walking across the meadows, looking for another boy to drown – but, mostly, I stay away from those thoughts because, to be perfectly honest, I am not sure which of them I think I will see. Or which of them I *hope* to see. In the summertime, when the nights are white and long, I might go down and read for a while, the way the visitors always loved to do, sitting in a deckchair at three in the morning with a book and a cup of coffee under the midnight sun. When I do, I read old myths and legends, fairy stories and cautionary tales, to keep the ghosts at bay. They need somewhere to be, though, and if you don't find a home for them out in the wind somewhere, if you don't bed them down safely at the edge of the sea or the once upon a time, they spill back into this world and turn into ghosts and monsters, resentful and neglected and intent on doing harm. I am no more of a believer now than I ever was, or not, at least, in the way people usually imagine. I just need to know where everything is, and then, when I am sure, to make a little space for the mystery. I have no better word for it than that, but it's not a bad word, when all is said and done. I'm not crazy – I know enough, after all, not to talk about these things to the living – and I'm not an old-time believer, like Kyrre, but I am getting used to the fact that, in my house, there are shadows in the folds of every blanket and imperceptible tremors in every glass of water or bowl of cream set out on a table – and, some days, there are tiny, almost infinitesimal loopholes of havoc in the fabric of the given world that could spill loose and catch me out wherever I am. I know this – and I spend the best part of my time making such maps as I can, maps of the world as it is between one moment and the next, charging myself with the impossible task of finding, among the pencil marks and shading, some cold angle of meadow or fjord where old Bieggaålmaj, or some other restless and hungry god, gathers them all in, one after another, Mats and Harald, Martin Crosbie and Kyrre Opdahl, the girl Maia and the *huldra* she became, hidden away in the folds of the wind, where only the most careful of storytellers could find them.

NOTES AND ACKNOWLEDGEMENTS

I would like to thank the Scottish Arts Council and the Creative Scotland Awards for their invaluable support at the research stage of this novel.

Acknowledgements are due to Dag Andersson and Harald Gaski, in particular, for their advice, stories and suggestions, much of which informed the writing of this book, and to all my friends in the north, for their profound generosity of spirit, immense hospitality and quiet encouragement.

Tusen takk!